NO QUESTIONS ASKED

■ ■ ■ ■ ■ ■

THE DEFENSE DOES NOT REST

■ ■ ■ ■ ■ ■

Edna Sherry

Introduction by Curtis Evans

Stark House Press • Eureka California

NO QUESTIONS ASKED / THE DEFENSE DOES NOT REST

Published by Stark House Press
1315 H Street
Eureka, CA 95501, USA
griffinskye3@sbcglobal.net
www.starkhousepress.com

NO QUESTIONS ASKED
Originally published by Dodd, Mead & Company, New York, and copyright © 1949 by Edna Sherry.

THE DEFENSE DOES NOT REST
Originally published by Dodd, Mead & Company, New York, and copyright © 1959 by Edna Sherry. Reprinted in paperback by Pocket Books, Inc., New York, 1960.

Reprinted by arrangement with agent. All rights reserved under International and Pan-American Copyright Conventions.

"Edna Sherry's Apprehension of Murder" © 2022 by Curtis Evans

ISBN: 978-1-951473-87-7

Text design by Mark Shepard, shepgraphics.com
Cover design by Jeff Vorzimmer, ¡caliente!design, Austin, Texas
Cover art by Robert Maguire
Proofreading by Bill Kelly

PUBLISHER'S NOTE:
This is a work of fiction. Names, characters, places and incidents are either the products of the author's imagination or used fictionally, and any resemblance to actual persons, living or dead, events or locales, is entirely coincidental.

Without limiting the rights under copyright reserved above, no part of this publication may be reproduced, stored, or introduced into a retrieval system or transmitted in any form or by any means (electronic, mechanical, photocopying, recording or otherwise) without the prior written permission of both the copyright owner and the above publisher of the book.

First Stark House Press Edition: October 2022

NO QUESTIONS ASKED

Steve Lake is the homicide captain, but that doesn't mean Lieutenant Rand has to like it. That job should have been his. Then there is another murder to solve, and it looks like the victim could be a spy, selling out his country's secrets. It's up to Steve's team to find out who killed the traitor. That same day Steve stumbles on a situation that seems to suggest that his wife is having an affair. She lies about where she was all day. She's a lot younger than he is, and he just knows that she's seeing someone. So he starts to follow her. And Rand, looking to find the chink in the armor of his stalwart captain, starts to follow Steve. How could either of them know that the two trails would eventually meet?

THE DEFENSE DOES NOT REST

When his best friend, Max Gray, is accused of murder, Stephen Hargrave knows that his father will be the lawyer who represents him. He also knows that even though Max isn't capable of murder, the evidence is stacked against him. So, dispensing with his own scruples, he pushes for the whole story from Max—the story of his rescue in Korea by the charming and brilliant Larry Bellair; his marriage to the cold, calculating Carol; his new-found love with Larry's sister Avery. It doesn't look good for Max. He had every reason in the world to commit murder. He is the first to admit it. But somewhere in his story there must be a clue to the real killer. No one else had a motive, so who could it be?

Edna Sherry Bibliography
(1885-1967)

Novels:

Is No One Innocent? (1930; with Milton Herbert Gropper,
  based on their play, *Inspector Kennedy*)
Grounds for Indecency (1931; with Milton Herbert Gropper)
Sudden Fear (1948)
No Questions Asked (1949)
Backfire (1956; reprinted in paperback as *Murder at Nightfall*)
Tears for Jessie Hewitt (1958; reprinted in paperback
  as *She Asked for Murder*)
The Defense Does Not Rest (1959)
The Survival of the Fittest (1960)
Call the Witness (1961)
Girl Missing (1962)
Strictly a Loser (1965)

Short Stories:

The Crimson Girl (with Charles K. Harris;
  Munsey's Magazine, March 1927)
Strange Cargo (with Charles K. Harris; *Sweetheart Stories*, Jan 24 1928)

Plays:

Guilty? (1923)
Inspector Kennedy (aka *Homicide*, 1929; with Milton Hernert Gropper)
We Are as We Are (1934; with Emma Mandel)

Film Scripts:

Through Different Eyes (1929; with Milton Herbery Gropper)

7
Edna Sherry's Apprehension of Murder
by Curtis Evans

19
No Questions Asked
by Edna Sherry

163
The Defense Does Not Rest
by Edna Sherry

Edna Sherry's Apprehension of Murder

By Curtis Evans

For decades American novelist and playwright Edna Sherry, author between 1948 and 1965 of nine crime novels, has essentially been viewed as a one-work writer, based on the terrific success of her nail-biting 1948 crime novel *Sudden Fear*, or more truly its hair-raising 1952 film adaptation, which starred Joan Crawford, Jack Palance and Gloria Grahame. Unusual for a crime drama, it netted four Oscar nominations, including in the leading and supporting acting categories, respectively, for Crawford and Palance. (Grahame that year was nominated—and won—in the supporting actress category for the satirical drama *The Bad and the Beautiful*.) Happily today Edna Sherry's full and ample crime fiction legacy is being recovered, cut by cut.

Edna Sherry was born Edna Solomon in Cincinnati, Ohio on November 28, 1885, one of four children of Michael and Sally Solomon, native Prussian Jews. After the Civil War Michael Solomon had moved to Cincinnati, Ohio from New York City, where his father had been a tailor, and there had set himself up as a dealer in gentlemen's neckwear. Having married Louisville, Kentucky native Sally Levy and prospered substantially in the Cincy haberdashery trade during the last quarter of the nineteenth century, Michael Solomon at the century's turn moved with his family to Manhattan, where he lucratively took up real estate brokerage.

Edna attended Hunter College (then a women's college) in Manhattan and was awarded a degree in English from that institution in 1906. For several years after her graduation she was employed as an English teacher, but she left the teaching profession in 1910 after wedding Ernest Thomas Sherry, a dentist a decade older than she who came originally from Eydtkuhnen, East Prussia (today Chernyshevskoye, Kaliningrad Oblast, Russia). Ernest Sherry— a German native and presumably an ethnic Jew like Edna—was stated in newspapers to have been an elder brother of famed restauranteur, hotelier, caterer and confectioner Louis Sherry (whose renowned luxury chocolates still are sold today), although ostensibly the latter Sherry was not of German but rather French-Canadian descent. Had Louis Sherry, who grew rich from literally catering to the pleasures of New York's Gilded Age millionaires, attempted to obscure German-Jewish origins? The surname Sherry belongs to multiple nationalities and ethnicities, including the Hebraic. For example, the late 1959 baseball World Series MVP Larry Sherry, a pitcher for the LA Dodgers, was a Jew. Whether or not Ernest and Louis Sherry indeed were Jewish, that they were siblings was an accepted fact in the press.

After their marriage Ernest and Edna took up residence in Manhattan at a swanky apartment building on 54 Riverside Drive. The couple had two children, Ernest and Phyllis, and, completing the composition of the household, there was as well a live-in, native Hungarian cook. After more than a decade of marriage and motherhood, Edna, doubtlessly inspired by the massive stage success of *The Bat* (1920) and *The Cat and the Canary* (1922), made a stab at literary fame with her own mystery play, which she entitled *Guilty?* The play was purchased in 1923 by prominent Jewish native Hungarian theatrical producer Albert Herman Woods (formerly Aladore Herman), who had recently produced the hit sex farces *Ladies' Night* (1920) and *The Demi-Virgin* (1921); and would go on to produce the hit courtroom mysteries *The Trial of Mary Dugan* (1927) and *Night of January 16th* (1935), the latter of which was written by mystery devouring philosopher Ayn Rand. Edna seemingly was in good hands with A. H. Woods.

Guilty? was tried out on March 5, 1923 at Baltimore's Lyceum Theater by the George Marshall Players in a production starring lovely silent film actress Hazel Dawn and dashing English actor Henry Daniell, the latter of whom went on to a distinguished film career of over three decades' duration, which for mystery fans included a definitive turn as wicked Professor Moriarty in the Basil Rathbone Sherlock Holmes film *The Woman in Green* (1945). A review of *Guilty?* in the *Baltimore Sun* deemed the play's dialogue "stilted and unconvincing" but pronounced Sherry's plot "remarkably good" and concluded that the play held considerable promise if revisions were made. (Although Hazel Dawn was panned, Henry Daniel drolly was singled out for praise for acting his part of the "neurotic artist" with "grace and finesse" despite "being killed three times during the performance.") Sadly for Edna Sherry, however, the production's electrician turned the play into something of a comedy by repeatedly turning on the lights while the hands were still on stage shifting scenes, inducing from the audience "roars of laughter" as startled men rushed "for elusive exits." The play died a quick death in Baltimore.

Undaunted, Edna Sherry scored her first literary successes a few years later in collaboration with Milton Herbert Gropper, a once-noted, playwright and screenwriter of Rumanian Jewish derivation who, though a decade younger than Edna, had already had a half-dozen plays performed on Broadway, including the provocatively-titled hit *Ladies of the Evening* (1924), which was adapted by director Frank Capra as the hit 1930 film *Ladies of Leisure*, starring a youthful Barbara Stanwyck. The first of Milton's and Edna's collaborative successes—Milton is credited with dialogue and Edna with the story— was *Through Different Eyes*, a courtroom murder melodrama innovatively told in a series of flashbacks from multiple perspectives, in anticipation of the great 1951 Japanese film *Rashomon*. Milton's and Edna's *Eyes*, which was originally available in both silent and newfangled talking versions (regrettably the "talkie" version since has been lost) and marked the first significant film appearance of actress Sylvia Sidney, was well-received by critics. In a long, laudatory notice in the *New York Times*, film critic Mordaunt Hall praised *Eyes* as an "ingeniously conceived murder trial story, one that lends itself to three different shadings of the leading characters."

Later that year Milton's and Edna's locked room mystery play *Inspector Kennedy* (also known as *Homicide*) premiered on Broadway at the Bijou Theater. The play, which was packed to its melodramatic rafters with "a police inspector and a number of detectives, a leader of a dope ring, secret panels, a couple of mysterious murders and [several] men and women with motives that might have prompted them to commit the crimes," ran at the Bijou for only forty-three performances between December 20, 1929 and January 25, 1930. It was then successfully taken on the road, with productions staged in Chicago, Detroit, Pittsburgh, Wilmington, Boston, and Windsor, Ontario, among other locales. The title role of Inspector Kennedy was played, in his penultimate performance before his retirement, by hugely popular "road" actor William Hodge, who also directed the play. Of Hodge the *New York Times* noted, at his death in 1932: "'The William Hodge public' was a Broadway phrase meaning that whether or not the Hodge plays were successful in New York...he could be sure of a keen response almost anywhere in the country." Striking while the bloody poker was hot, Milton and Edna novelized the play in 1930 under the catchy title *Is No One Innocent?*

Oddly, eighteen years elapsed before Edna Sherry, who was now sixty-three years old, published her first solo crime novel, *Sudden Fear*, to near universal acclaim. "I unhesitatingly pronounce *Sudden Fear*...the best mystery novel which has come forth from a publishing house in the past year or more," gushed E. D. Lambright, editor of the *Tampa Tribune*, adding that the novel was "a one-sitting book—one that you will not put down until you have finished the last chapter, the last paragraph." Dorothy B. Hughes, herself a crime writer of great critical repute, affirmed (in the *Albuquerque Tribune*), "You'll race through the pages [of *Sudden Fear*], the suspense is that terrific," as did the *Boston Globe*'s Avis De Voto, who avowed: "[*Sudden Fear*] packs a wallop that will haunt you."

One of the entranced readers of *Sudden Fear*, so the story goes (this came straight from the horse's mouth, as it were: entertainment columnist Louella Parsons), was Oscar-winning actress Joan Crawford, who upon reading Edna Sherry's debut solo novel in 1950 saw in the story of an accomplished middle-aged woman playwright who rashly marries a much younger—and much scheming—actor, a fine vehicle for her histrionic talents, which had been honed since the silent film era. Crawford also served as the film's executive producer, and the result was a creative triumph both for the actress and the novelist.

The well-acted, smartly scripted, beautifully shot, evocatively scored and superbly suspenseful film was directed by David Miller, who would later helm another popular woman-in-peril thriller, *Midnight Lace* (1960), starring Doris Day and Rex Harrison; photographed by Oscar-winning cinematographer Charles Lang, who shot such thriller classics as *The Cat and the Canary* (1939), *The Ghost Breakers* (1940), *The Uninvited* (1944), *Charade* (1963) and *Wait Until Dark* (1967); and co-scripted by Oscar-nominated screenwriter Lenore Coffee, who back in 1929 had written the talking film adaptation of S. S. Van Dine's bestselling Philo Vance mystery *The Bishop Murder Case*, starring Basil Rathbone; and scored, in just his third filmic outing, by a young Elmer Bernstein, himself a future Oscar winner.

Rarely has a mystery writer enjoyed such a felicitous translation of her work onto film as did Edna Sherry with *Sudden Fear*— though it was not in fact the author's first time at the cinematic rodeo, recalling *Through Different Eyes* from nearly a quarter-century earlier. Perhaps as a result of her financial independence (her husband was very well off and she had inherited $10,000, or $200,000 in modern worth, from her late father in 1934), Edna was slow to follow up on the film's success. In 1949, she had published another crime novel, *No Questions Asked*, but it was not until 1956, four years after *Sudden Fear*'s cinematic debut, that she produced a third crime novel, *Backfire*.

Afterward, however, her crime novels (all of which were published, like her other solo novels, by Dodd, Mead in the United States and Hodder & Stoughton in the United Kingdom) came at a rapid clip: *Tears for Jessie Hewitt* (1958), *The Defense Does Not Rest!* (1959), *The Survival of the Fittest* (1960), *Call the Witness* (1961), *Girl Missing* (1962) and, lastly, *Strictly a Loser* (1965). This final novel appeared a year after the death of Edna's husband Ernest at the age of ninety and less than two years before her own death in New York City on February 4, 1967, as the age of eighty-one. While she never replicated the success of *Sudden Fear*, Edna Sherry produced a worthy body of crime fiction, largely in the "inverted" mystery form, that now is being belatedly rediscovered.

No less a judge—and a cranky, hanging one at that— than British crime writer Francis Iles (aka Anthony Berkeley Cox), author of the classic inverted mystery *Malice Aforethought* (1931), praised Edna Sherry's valedictory essay in the form, *Strictly a Loser*, as something that was rather the opposite of its title. Although a product of the United States, the intensely nationalistic Iles noted, Edna's novel was composed "in blessedly straight-forward English" and was "a good, uncomplicated story about a ruthless young woman who does not shrink from murder to further her own interests." At the end of his review Iles fearfully wondered: "Are there any real Susan Caldwells in this world? One hopes not. But Miss Sherry makes us feel there could be." Ultimately it is this frisson of fear which Edna Sherry induces in the reader—this apprehension of murder—that is the signal quality of her crime fiction, from *Sudden Fear* through the rest of its killing company.

□ □ □

Given her success in the field of a crime fiction, Edna Sherry seems to have been remarkably publicity-averse. It is as if having gotten away with her fictional crimes, as it were, she did not want to risk any personal exposure. In the course of my researches on the author, I have discovered not one single photo of her or any newspaper interview. Why this vanishing act, this deafening silence? Let me offer a notion.

However much Edna Sherry led a hole and corner existence in the heart of Manhattan, her only son, Ernest Thomas Sherry, Jr., managed once, to the great regret of his family, to make the national news in a big way. This was in 1930, not long before Edna's fellow New York crime writer Cornell Woolrich was similarly embroiled, like young Ernest, in a marriage annulment scandal; and perhaps this affair contributed to Edna's pronounced case of wallflowerism. During the summer of 1930 the story spread around the country like a rumor of war, via salacious newspaper daily headlines and Sunday pictorial supplements: eighteen-year-old Ernest Sherry, Jr., the "playboy" nephew of the late millionaire Louis Sherry and son of a wealthy dental surgeon on Riverside Drive, had gotten himself embroiled in a novel matrimonial pickle, one that was unique even in a sexually jaded metropolis that had been routinely diverted by the madcap social tumults of the Roaring Twenties.

There were, you see, these two pretty young sisters, Audrey and Nedra Baker, aged respectively twenty and nineteen in January 1930, when they made the acquaintance of Ernie Sherry, as he was familiarly known. Like characters in a Cornell Woolrich story, the Baker sisters had come to New York from the small city of New Castle Pennsylvania, the so-called tin plate capital of the world, hopefully seeking their fame and fortunes, despite their modest circumstances. (Their father, Harry Baker, was employed as a roller in New Castle's tin mill.)

In New York Nedra became an industrious mannequin, or model, at a dress factory, while her more voluptuous, butterfly elder sister Audrey, after graduating from the dancing school of Ned Wayburn, choreographer of the Ziegfeld Follies, was hired as one of the "little girls" (i.e., a chorine) at one of the speakeasies of the notorious Mary Louise "Texas" Guinan, the Prohibition Era's so-called "Queen of the Nightclubs." Audrey's classmates at New Castle High School had known that the girl had "it" (whatever "it" was), rhymingly declaring of her, next to her glamorous photo (complete with corsage and spit curl) in the senior annual:

She never misplaces her lipstick;
Her eyes often work overtime.
As a dancer and leader of fashion,
This maiden is simply sublime.

At Texas Guinan's place Audrey was a bright flapper flame who attracted many a persistent male moth, including young Ernie Sherry. Soon tiring of his attentions, as she later told the newspapers, she palmed Ernie off on her shyer sibling Nedra, with whom she shared an apartment, poor, overworked Nedra, having had "little opportunity to meet gentlemen" since moving to the city. Impressionable Ernie quickly proposed marriage to Nedra and she accepted.

Yet when the day arrived on January 22 for the couple to pay a visit to the city clerk's office and be lawfully wed, Nedra found that her heartless employers would not grant her time off to do the deed. Happily, or so it seemed at the time, Audrey obligingly offered to act as a stand-in for her sister at the city clerk's office, giving her name as Nedra, saving her younger sister the trouble of actually appearing herself as Ernie's chosen bride. Ernie deemed this a topping idea and together he and Audrey persuaded the more skeptical Nedra to go along with the scheme. The ceremony thereupon took place as planned and afterward Audrey delivered the marriage certificate and Nedra's new "husband" to her. Ernie and Nedra honeymooned in Montreal, Canada and lived together for several months as man and wife before the bloom came off the matrimonial rose and the disenchanted young couple decided to sever their union.

Ernie went home to his parents, incidentally explaining the actual circumstances of his "marriage" to his dismayed parents. His father promptly consulted a lawyer and after said consultation placed a phone call to Audrey explaining that she, not Nedra, was his son's legal wife. Now the fat was in the fire and sizzle it did, to the anticipatory salivations of the New York press corps, to whom Audrey, evidently loathe to miss a good piece of publicity when she saw it, gave extensive interviews, accompanied by numerous glamor photographs of herself.

Questions rattled in the newspapers like skeletons in gusty closets. Would young Ernest, who though the scion of a wealthy father who himself was employed in a twenty dollar a week clerking job (in today's dollars about $16,000 a year), owe alimony to Audrey, who had no intention of staying married to him? Could Nedra actually now be deemed the common law wife of Ernest? Had Ernest in fact committed bigamy? Would he owe *both* sisters alimony? The demoralized Ernie exasperatedly confided to the press his blunt view of the perplexing affair, avowing: "The quicker this thing is finished, the better. I'm sick and tired of the pair of them. I guess I was a fool, all right."

As would happen in the case of Cornell Woolwich, Ernie's official wife Audrey brought a successful annulment suit against her legal husband, asserting that the union had never actually been consummated. What further arrangements, if any, were made among the parties was not divulged in the newspapers. The sparks of the story, which had exploded in newspapers like a firecracker on the Fourth of July, faded fast with the summer season, although the next year a newspaper dramatically reported that "[b]lackmailers are trying to make things real mean for young Ernest T. Sherry, scion of the wealthy Sherry family of New York City, the man who married Audrey Baker...when he had every intention of marrying her sister, Nedra." It seems that $10,000—the same amount as Edna's future inheritance from her father—was being demanded from the impetuous youth if he desired to avoid further embarrassing "love publicity." However, Ernie—or, presumably, his parents—decided that, rather than fork over the dough, he would put a team of private detectives on his would-be extortionists' trails. Apparently this action frightened away future predators.

Audrey had another publicized encounter of an amatory kind, admittedly an occupational hazard of an attractive Thirties chorus girl. In September 1930, just after the dust had settled in the Sherry affair, Audrey was back in the news, having accused thirty-year-old "Broadway playboy" Rudolph Carl Bergstrom, a native Swedish Long Island real estate broker and president of Queens Garden Homes, Inc., of blacking her eye when she resisted the passionate advances he made upon person in an automobile. Recalling the Sherry imbroglio, two other unnamed women came forth soon afterward with similar claims against Bergstrom, who had also recently figured as the co-respondent in a husband's divorce suit. The outraged broker decried the assault accusations as "shakedown attempts" on the part of a trio of designing women.

The outcome of all this back and forth recrimination went unreported, but the *New York Daily News* left its readers with a memorable newspaper headline: *Police Quiz Guinan Girl in Whoopee*

Ride Attack Charges. (This is something that you do not read every day.) Five years later, Bergstrom committed suicide by shotgun blast in a locked room at a cheap hotel, inadvertently nearly slaying a workman in the hallway in the process and leaving a much depleted "fortune" of $150 in bills which he had sealed in an envelope cryptically addressed to an "Anna Smith." Fittingly, two different women came forward to claim the money. Nedra Baker died in 1988, apparently never having married (legitimately), while Audrey survived until 1999, expiring a day after her ninetieth birthday, by which time her surname had become Insley.

Unlike Rudolph Bergstrom, Ernest Thomas Sherry, Jr. managed, with the exception of his affair with the fabulous Baker girls, to stay out of the newspapers, but doubtlessly the embarrassment, while admittedly not nearly as mortifying as that which afflicted Cornell Woolrich (his wife had accused him of being a pallid, wan aesthete incapable of consummating their marriage) was enough to last a lifetime. Ernest II married unsuccessfully a second time, in Broward County, Florida in 1939, to a Louise Stanford Hensley, the union lasting less than a year. The third time proved the charm for earnest Ernie, however. He died in Seminole, Florida in 1979 at the age of sixty-eight, his third wife Elsa having predeceased him by eight years. Ernie's son from his third marriage, Ernest Thomas Sherry III, who was born in Manhattan in 1942, died just two years ago in Sarasota, Florida at the seventy-seven, unmarried and unattached, leaving no known family member to make the final disposition of his mortal remains. It is surprising that the family of someone as wealthy and successful as Edna Sherry faded so fully in this fashion, but it is in keeping with what seems to have been Edna's secretive nature. The author remained a mystery woman to the end.

◻ ◻ ◻

Dangerously unstable human relationships figure at the heart of the crime fiction of Edna Sherry, most famously in her debut solo crime novel *Sudden Fear*, but additionally throughout her crime fiction corpus. In *No Questions Asked*, stern, straight-arrow, ruggedly handsome cop Captain Steve Lake, while investigating the murder of a filing clerk at a scientific laboratory which seems to have major national security implications, comes to suspect his new young wife, the former Vicki Braun, the lovely daughter of a native Viennese music professor, of infidelity. Vicki clearly is telling him lies about her activities, but rather that straightforwardly ask her just what she has been up to on her mysterious assignations, Steve, in an act of potentially fatal folly, starts snooping around behind her back, becoming more paranoid with each step. Will Vicki, along with Steve's all-American young protégé, a winning young police sergeant named, seemingly inevitably, Johnny, be able to smooth over matrimonial matters before it is too late? And how much of a menace does glum and bitter Lieutenant Jeff Rand, who was passed over for promotion in favor of Steve and most definitely holds him a grudge, pose to the couple?

No Questions Asked is an effective crime thriller that one could easily see as a police film of the period, perhaps starring Dana Andrews of *Laura* fame in the role of the suspicious Steve. Edna Sherry tells the story largely through the perspective of her male cops, so that the novel seems to anticipate the Fifties police procedurals of Hillary Waugh and Ed McBain, rather than the gynocentric mid-century "domestic suspense" tales that her own *Sudden Fear* presaged. On a personal level, when Steve urges Vicki's music student brother Paul, after Paul has touched him for money, to get a job and learn the thrill of "taking in the first dollar earned by your own efforts," one might be reminded of Edna's playboy son Ernest, who was prompted by his parents to take a modest clerking position with the Interborough Rapid Transit Company, which operated New York City's subway system—though this action failed to hinder Ernie's playboy antics.

The Defense Does Not Rest!, which followed *No Questions Asked* into print a decade later, also looks at the mayhem which comes from a mésalliance. The novel has an interesting structure, being divided into two parts, a prologue and an epilogue. In the first chapter we learn that father and son criminal attorneys Edward and Stephen Hargrave have been tasked with defending a man who has been arrested and jailed for the crime of murder in the first degree. What follows over the rest of the prologue is a look at the recent life of wealthy Maxwell Gray: his war service in Korea with his friend Larry Bellair, who valiantly rescues him from certain death; Max's rehabilitation in Florida and his marriage while convalescing there to Carol Tyson, a pretty young secretary; and Mac and Carol's life afterward, both together and apart, in New York. We know that someone is murdered and that someone is arrested for the murder, but we do not know who is the murderee is, nor the identity of the accused murderer, until near the end of the prologue. In the epilogue we follow the dogged and resourceful efforts of the Hargraves, father and son, to save their client from seemingly certain death by judicial degree. The defense indeed does not rest—and neither should readers of this classic essay in criminal suspense, until they have reached its final, literally shattering, sentence.

—July 2022
Germantown, TN

Curtis Evans received a PhD in American history in 1998. He is the author of *Masters of the "Humdrum" Mystery: Cecil John Charles Street, Freeman Wills Crofts, Alfred Walter Stewart and British Detective Fiction, 1920-1961* (2012) and most recently the editor of the Edgar nominated *Murder in the Closet: Essays on Queer Clues in Crime Fiction Before Stonewall* (2017) and, with Douglas G. Greene, the Richard Webb and Hugh Wheeler short crime fiction collection, *The Cases of Lieutenant Timothy Trant* (2019). He blogs on vintage crime fiction at The Passing Tramp.

NO QUESTIONS ASKED
Edna Sherry

To Ernest
A small down-payment
on a very large debt

I

At 2 p.m. on that rainy Monday in June, things were quiet at Homicide. Captain Steve Lake was dictating a routine report to a police stenographer for his commanding officer. Sergeant Johnny Clark and Detective Bill Schneer were playing a hot game of gin rummy. Johnny was losing but you never would have known it from the grin on his good-looking face. At the window, Lieutenant Jeff Rand was staring down glumly into 20th Street at the rain rippling, wind-driven, along the gutters. The third-floor headquarters of the West Side Homicide Bureau could have been the offices of any business firm in the slack season.

The phone rang.

Johnny and Schneer each cocked an ear, Rand turned his head without moving his body, while Steve picked up the receiver. A phone call might mean anything. But it was only an inquiry from an insurance company which Steve disposed of in a single sentence. The gin players went back to their game and Rand turned again to the window. Steve went on dictating.

He was a man to attract eyes, handsome in a granite way, tall, lean, moving with an economy of effort. He had sharp-cut features with a salient jaw, thick brown hair with a deep wave in it which he loathed, frigid blue eyes which gave nothing away. He was thirty-eight years old and looked as if he had never been younger and would never be older.

He was a man who was hard on himself and, therefore, hard on others, a glutton for work, and, equally, an exacting boss. He had a strict sense of justice and no man under him ever complained of not getting a fair hearing. But Steve had come up the hard way, and his uphill climb and the very nature of his work had left him few illusions. In ninety-nine cases out of a hundred, he had discovered that human motives were shabby and selfish. He respected his wire-haired terrier, Nick, a good deal more than he respected most men. While the dog knew that a chewed slipper or a mess on the floor meant a sound beating, Nick also knew that when he was sick or hurt, he could count on the big man with the easy hands to sit up all night with him.

As Steve went on with his report, footsteps hesitated on the iron stairs and came on into the next room. A small woman in raincoat and galoshes stood staring uncertainly about her.

"Take that, will you, Rand?" said Steve, nodding towards her.

Rand, a sour-faced man of forty, with an afternoon blue chin, complied without answering. Without overt insolence, he did what he could to register his resentment of Steve as his superior officer. The tight line of his mouth and the set of his shoulders said plainly that if ability counted, *he* should have been Captain and Steve still Lieutenant and taking orders from him. Of course, he sneered mentally, he only broke cases in short order and saved the city's money. He didn't pull the noble stuff, busting in single-handed on a hood with a heater, because his pet, Johnny the candy-kid, was in trouble. Only a guy with Steve's luck could get a commendation from the Honor Committee out of it, instead of a dose of lead poisoning. If it had been Rand, the hood's gun wouldn't have jammed.

The small woman turned out to be a mystery story writer with a long list of questions as to police procedure. Rand heard her through without changing a muscle of his face. His stony eyes finally flustered her, her apologetic phrases about wasting the Department's time ran down like a spent record. Rand said:

"We are not allowed to answer questions, madame, without an order from the Commissioner."

The small woman's mouth rounded with surprise.

"But I don't want to know any *secrets*—just plain facts, such as how long your hours are and your salaries and who supplies your guns—"

Rand gazed over her head impassively. She gave up.

"How can I get an order?" she asked.

"You write a letter, madame. The address is 240 Center Street."

With birdlike twitterings, the small woman removed herself from Homicide. Rand came back into the inner room.

"Dames!" he snorted. "Mystery writers. 'How long are our hours?' That's a laugh. I shoulda answered her: 'Madame, there ain't any hours in Homicide. Nor yet days. We just work till we drop.'"

Steve looked up and grinned.

"Don't give me that," he said. "When you're on a case, I can't pry you off."

"No joke," Schneer put in. "Rand's second in command don't have a thing to do. He's gotta run down every lead himself."

"Then I know it's done," Rand retorted. "You saps look at everything and see nothing. I think on my feet."

"Rand, the one-man Department," Schneer gibed.

"Maybe you could learn something from him at that, Schneer," Steve said.

Rand's face darkened.

"Thanks for the plug," he said sardonically. "What does it get me?"

Johnny Clark, riffling the deck, laughed.

"Keep 'em crossed and wait for a break, Rand," he said.

"Ha! Little Lord Fauntleroy. The gentleman-cop." Rand's voice was oily with malice. "And maybe I could learn something from you. Suck up to the Big Shot, develop a taste for shoe polish, and who knows how quick your name's up for promotion?"

Johnny would not be drawn.

"How's about learning this?" he said good-naturedly. "A better man won out, so take it like a man even if you feel it like a bear."

"That'll be all, Johnny," Steve said sharply. "Rand, we don't punch time clocks here. Your case wrapped up?" Rand was carrying a gangster homicide independently.

"Just waiting for Red Varney to show. I need his testimony to cinch it," Rand replied sullenly. He resented Steve's partisanship even more than he resented criticism.

"Then call it a day. Anything comes in on Varney, I'll give you a ring."

"And if another call comes in?" Rand countered.

"Johnny and I'll handle it."

"And who'll take the desk in that case?"

Schneer said:

"You know something, Rand? I been practicing. I can answer a phone all by myself now."

Rand ignored him. Instead, he threw himself heavily into a chair.

"What a life! Either you don't know what a bed looks like or you sit and wait. Wait. Wait for somebody to get himself killed."

Steve smiled.

"You bellyache like a kid full of green apples, Rand. But you wouldn't change your job, if they offered you a bank presidency."

Rand deliberately yawned, without answering.

Steve went back to his report with a shrug. There was no pleasing Rand—short of resigning in his favor. Steve knew the score, realized to the full how and why Rand hated his guts. Since his own promotion four months ago, Steve had considered getting Rand transferred. He liked harmony on his team. But Rand was capable and Steve could understand his grievance. From childhood on, he himself had been passed over often enough to appreciate the feeling. He'd let things ride for a while. He had won over tougher men than Rand in the past. If he could once get under that rhinoceros hide, he was sure he'd find a right guy.

Harry O'Neil dragged in through the open door, his hat on the back of his head, his shoulders sagging, the picture of discouraged failure. Rand glanced up and did not trouble to suppress a derisive snicker at the forlorn figure.

"So you lost your man, young Harry," he jeered.

Steve rose and went into his own office. Over his shoulder he called: "I'll take your report in here, Harry."

O'Neil followed him in.

"Close the door," Steve said shortly. Rand's heckling of the younger men got his goat. He was damned if he'd let him gloat over the kid's misery. He had seen promising material ruined by just that kind of needling. Not that he himself coddled men who muffed their chores, but everybody was entitled to a hearing. "Let's have it," he said.

"I swear, Captain," Harry began in the middle excitedly. "He was there one second, not twenty feet away—"

"Begin at the beginning."

Harry pulled himself together.

"Yes, sir. Well, I took over from Lamb at eight this morning and from then on till one o'clock I had Pinelli under my eye every second. He had breakfast at Child's, he went to see his father, then he hung around that cigar store on Sixth Avenue for a couple of hours, and then he went to this bar and grill on 14th Street for lunch. I figured it was better I didn't go in, so I watched from outside. I could see every move he made through the glass front. Then, three men at the table in front of him got up to leave and for a second they hid him. When they moved, he was gone. He never showed at the entrance, so I knew it was the men's room. I went in there fast. The window was open and he was gone. I sprinted around the block but nothing doing. I lost him."

"That trick's so old, even a beginner ought to know it."

"I guess you're right, sir," he replied heavily. "I did know it at that. Only I figured if I showed in the grill I wouldn't be much good as a tail once he saw my face."

"Something to that."

"Gosh, Chief, you must think I'm a sap! This is the second boner I've pulled in a month," he said miserably.

"Nobody bats a thousand, Harry," Steve smiled.

The boy's eyelids flashed up hopefully.

"Then I don't go back in uniform, sir?" he breathed.

"Not today. But I'm taking you off tailing. You're not quick enough on your feet, it seems. Maybe I hustled you along too fast. You're not ready to handle a slick article like Pinelli yet. How are you with gals?"

"Pretty good, sir."

"Think you could get chummy with one of the taxi dancers at Tulipland?"

"You bet!"

"Her name's Lola and she's Pinelli's sister. Go there late and maybe you can date her after her job. You know what I'm after?"

"Yes, sir. And I'll bust a lung getting it."

"Good. And for God's sake take that hangdog look off your face." He rose. "Switch to night duty. Tulip-land doesn't operate by sunlight. Keep at her till you get something. I want Pinelli's connection with Joe Frost."

Steve went back to the other office.

The phone rang. This time it was business.

Steve hung up and turned to Rand.

"Well, Lieutenant," he said quizzically, "the waiting's over for the day. Will you take it or shall I?"

"Anything's better than sitting around this dump," Rand said ungraciously. "I guess Varney'll keep."

"Good. Johnny, get a squad car. Schneer, phone the M.O. and the morgue. Rustle up a photographer. No need for a print man in this rain. Body's in the open. Riverside Drive at 87th Street, couple of blocks below the Soldiers' Monument. In the bushes, under the wall on the park side."

"What's it look like?" asked Rand.

"Maybe suicide. Maybe murder. Gunshot, the cruise car said."

"Oh, the place is already cluttered up," Rand complained. "Time I get there, it'll look like a herd of elephants been stampeding."

"Keep your shirt on. They're waiting for us."

"Cruise car spot him?"

"No. A passer-by. He phoned the 100th Street Precinct. They called the Telegraph Bureau and the Bureau called us and also alerted the nearest prowl car. Good hunting."

Rand shrugged into his raincoat.

"Put on your rubbers, Rollo," he said to Johnny. "You're gonna investigate a homicide."

"Aw, gee, Loot," Schneer protested. "Just when I'm having a run of luck. That makes a dollar seventy you owe me," he added to Johnny. "Here you are. Ready, Lieutenant."

As the police chauffeur drove Rand and Johnny up Eleventh Avenue, Rand looked out sourly at the driving rain.

"'Will you take it, Lieutenant, or shall I?'" he mimicked Steve's question sardonically. "Polite like a fox. You bet he'd make damn sure nothing'd crab his day off tomorrow."

"You didn't have to volunteer," Johnny pointed out.

"No? And get a 'non-co-operative' on my tab? Nothing the Big Shot'd like better than to pile the dirt on me."

"Hooey. He bends over backward, giving every last one of us credit when we pull something off."

"No use talking to a dewy-eyed Boy Scout," Rand jeered. "Bet you send him flowers regular, too."

Even Johnny, conspicuously good natured, flushed at the gibe. For deeply hidden under his debonair surface lay a devotion to Steve Lake, close to hero worship, although Johnny would have died smiling before putting it into words. It was not merely because Steve had once saved Johnny's life at the risk of his own—any one of the Squad would have gone to bat for any of the others without counting the danger. It was because Steve represented his idea of what a police officer should be. For Johnny's underlying spring of action was a crusader's love for his work. After college, he had passed up the more lucrative opportunities open to a smart young man of good birth and well-to-do background because his heart was in detective work. This background had proved to be more an obstacle than a help in his chosen field. But hard work and unflagging good humor had overcome the handicap. Only Jeff Rand, invincibly soured, still mocked at Little Lord Fauntleroy.

A parked radio car, two precinct detectives and a knot of onlookers, in spite of the rain, marked their destination.

The dead man was lying, unnaturally crumpled, in the bushes, down the slope below the park wall. A hideous hole gaped behind his right ear. Even before the Medical Officer arrived, Rand knew that he had been dead for hours. He was stiff from rigor mortis. The blood around the gunshot was clotted and black, but the grass directly below the wound was an unstained green.

The dead man was in his mid-twenties, decently but not well dressed, and with unremarkable features. He looked like any one of a million white-collar workers. Rand, angling into the dead man's pocket without disturbing his position, found his wallet, a cheap, imitation-alligator affair. It contained his social security card and four hundred and eleven dollars. The name on the social security card was Leon Ferman. The four hundred dollars in fives and tens was separated from the eleven dollars by an elastic band around the larger roll.

Rand, businesslike and professional, dropping his derisive attitude towards Johnny, said:

"Not robbery, that's sure."

"But how come a wage-slave was toting four hundred bucks at all? That's a lot of potatoes."

"Could be there's a gun under the body and it's suicide. The moola's to pay for a classy funeral."

"You think a suicide would get himself all scratched up like that in these bushes or would he just lie down comfortably in the grass?"

"Something to that," Rand nodded. "And, from the look of his arms and legs, my guess is he was tossed over the wall. Well, we'll know in a minute. Here's the M.O."

Dr. Blum hurried down the slope, hunched inside his raincoat.

"Lieutenant," he grumbled. "Never saw it to fail. Minute it rains, somebody starts bumping people off in the open."

He stooped over the body and went to work. He whipped out a thermometer and thrust it inside the dead man's shirt and into the armpit. He pulled down the eyelids, looking for signs of drugging, tested the crumpled arms for rigor mortis and went perfunctorily through the other routine tests.

"Dead a good twelve hours, I judge," he said, recapping his thermometer. He waited while the police photographer, who had already arrived, took half a dozen flashbulb shots. Then he turned the body over but found little more of note. He summed up for Rand: "No gun. Homicide. No blood. Toted to the spot. Could be a .38 or a .45. Send him down. Tell you more when I get him under cover. Tomorrow okay for the post?"

"Sure, sure. No rush," Rand agreed.

Dr. Blum scuttled back to the shelter of his car.

Rand went methodically through the dead man's pockets, handing their contents to Johnny. There was the usual miscellany of knife, pencils, library card, handkerchief, cigarettes, matches and a metal button with the initials A.C.R.L. on it. Rand eyed it frowning and passed it to Johnny.

"Know what it means?" he asked.

"I don't. Some association, looks like."

"Yeah. Auxiliary of Chinese Riveters' League or something. Some of these guys are great joiners." There was a loud whine down the street. "Here's the wagon."

The body was loaded into the basket and the morgue wagon clanged away down the Drive. Rand and Johnny combed the spot for a considerable area. They scanned the curb for signs of the car which might have brought Ferman there. They found nothing.

"Okay, Sergeant," Rand said. "Nothing else here. The guy's home address on his social security card is 920 Bank Street. Might as well go down there now and get a line on him. Tonight, after six, I'll want you to go through that apartment building across the street and check every tenant whose windows look out on the Drive. If he was brought here in a car and dumped, somebody may have seen something."

"Right, You wouldn't want me to start on it now?"

"No. More people home after six. Doc says he's been dead at least twelve hours. Try to locate somebody over there who saw a car stop somewhere between one and four this morning."

"Yes, sir."

They returned to the squad car and drove off. They were in the 30s when Rand leaned forward and spoke to the chauffeur:

"Stop by 20th Street," he ordered. To Johnny, he added:

"Better park that stuff out of the guy's pockets before you rub all the prints off." He grinned cynically. "Give Schneer a little errand in the rain, too, shooting it over to the M.E.'s lab. Fresh air'll do him good. And I can make my prelim report at the same time."

The two men climbed the stairs to the Bureau where Rand gave Steve his findings. Johnny deposited the meagre array of articles from Leon Ferman's pockets on the desk.

"We're on our way now to Bank Street," Rand finished. "Probably find this bird annexed some hot-headed guy's gal and got cancelled in the process."

"That or blackmail," Steve said, eyeing the little pile of articles on the desk. "This four hundred bucks looks like he'd been collecting—Hey, wait a minute, Rand!" Steve was staring at the little metal badge. "A.C.R.L. Say, this could be something."

"That button, you mean? Sarge and I couldn't figure it."

"Yeah. The guy worked for the Government. Atcheson Chemical Research Laboratory uptown. They're doing some mighty hush-hush jobs. And their employees are screened with a fine comb. Can't get within a block of the place without identification—this badge thing. Hold everything, Rand, till I call and check on him."

The Atcheson Laboratory informed Steve that Leon Ferman was a filing clerk in the Government employ. He had been in his job for eight months, was satisfactory in his work and had never caused trouble or criticism. Today was his first absence, and a phone message at 9 a.m. had informed the switchboard operator that he was ill and would not report for work.

"Ill," Steve reflected as he hung up. "The world's prize understatement. And what a nice, considerate killer we're dealing with. Johnny, call the M.O. and ask him to do the post tonight instead of tomorrow. This may be a job for the Feds."

"In that case, Captain," Rand said. "Maybe you better take over. Rough stuff's my speed. I can spot a hood a mile off, but this scientific patter's way over my head."

"Okay, Lieutenant, although I'm no Einstein myself. What's that address—920 Bank Street?"

"No news of Varney while I was out?"

"Not a thing," Steve replied, getting into his raincoat. "Schneer, get this stuff from Ferman's pockets over to the 28th Street Lab. Rand, take over till Lamb gets in. He ought to be here between four and five. Come on, Johnny."

As Steve and Johnny drove down to Bank Street, Johnny said:

"Well, there goes your day off tomorrow."

"Yeah," said Steve resignedly.

"Bet you had a nice day all taped out, too."

"When you're in this as long as I am, you don't do any taping ahead. Seems to me," he added glumly, "killers have been running to Mondays and Tuesdays lately."

"You ought to switch your day."

"And wish it on some other poor sucker? What's the difference? This rain keeps up, the ball game and the races are out, anyway."

"Mrs. Lake still picking long shots?"

"Never saw anything to beat it. Never looks at a sheet, can't tell one jock from another, but she keeps on cashing 'em in at telephone numbers."

"I knew a kid like that at Dartmouth. Football, not horses. He'd settle on some goofy team without a Chinaman's chance and they'd win 53-0."

"Beginner's luck. Never lasts. Vicki won't like it so well when she begins tearing up tickets," said Steve.

"She'll take it. She's a swell little sport."

"She's all right." Johnny knew just how great an understatement of his feelings Steve's three words were.

As their talk gave way to a comfortable silence, Steve went on thinking about Vicki. Even after a year, he still pinched himself mentally to make sure his home life wasn't just wishful thinking. How come, he wondered for the hundredth time, that he rated such a gay, beautiful kid for a wife—a crotchety old stick-in-the-mud like himself? She was so full of fun, she made a Staten Island Ferry ride a treat, and her try at making a dancer out of his stiff old bachelor pins had them both shouting like two-year-olds. But there was more to Vicki than high spirits. She had a level head and ideas of her own. She had everything. Sometimes it gave him a helpless feeling, he had so little to offer on his side. If she had chosen someone like Johnny now—Johnny, blond as a Swede, still in his twenties, with his likeable grin and his easy air of know-how.

Steve's thoughts went back eighteen months, to the queer, crazy way he had met her in the first place, the grisly circumstances which had allowed their paths to cross at all.

He had been on duty the night the call came in, a homicide in the Chelsea district, not far from the office. Johnny had driven him to the place, the second floor of a private house, remodeled into small apartments, two to a floor; one a shambles; the other, across the hall, with a card on the door:

MAX BRAUN
PROFESSOR OF MUSIC

Steve's business was with the shambles. It proved to be the ordinary, pitiful story, so frequent since VE and VJ Day: an unadjusted, returned soldier at odds with his world, seeking the easy, bloody way out. He had shot at his wife and then himself. The soldier, who had survived Iwo Jima, was past help. But he had only wounded the frantic young wife. Her screams had brought a neighbor from across the hall—Vicki Braun.

In spite of her youth, Vicki had taken charge with astounding efficiency. She had made a tourniquet for the shattered thigh; she had given the hysterical girl two barbiturates which were beginning to take effect by the time Steve and Johnny arrived. Then, having done first things first, she had called Homicide. When the morgue wagon had taken the soldier away, and the ambulance had sped the wife to the hospital, Steve turned to Vicki for a detailed account.

"I'll tell you all I can," she said evenly. "But could you ask me just as well across the hall? The blood—there's so much of it—"

She sagged into his arms. Johnny's eyes met his above the inert little figure. That night, he thought the thing had hit Johnny the way it had him, but later events proved that Johnny's interest was just friendly. Steve had little time, however, for thought of anything but the terrific internal earthquake which was taking place in himself—the all-out dependence of her body in his arms, his own sudden hungry necessity to shield her, to serve her, to own her.

She recovered by the time they were in her own apartment, apologizing for making a fool of herself.

"So now I know how to faint," she grinned gamely, pushing back the horror of the past hour. She insisted on making coffee for them all—"If you don't need it, I do."

He sent Johnny into the kitchen to help her, and then cursed himself for doing it when he heard the steady, ready flow of their talk. He ached to follow them and join in. It wasn't his official position which kept him from it. It was an awkward stiffness stemming from their difference in years. Those two kids in the kitchen spoke the same language; he, waiting alone in the quaint bit of Vienna which was the living room, was centuries obsolete.

After a questionnaire in which she told him all she knew of the pitiful tragedy—the many quarrels, the soldier's escape into alcohol, the wife's despair, the climax of shots and screams—the two detectives lingered unaccountably, keeping enough coffee still in their cups to act as an excuse for sitting on and on.

They turned to other subjects. Vicki had a devouring interest in their adventurous profession, and Johnny, who rated Steve as a cross between the Almighty and Eisenhower, joined forces with her.

"Chief, tell her about the Burden case—when you walked along the cornice of the Wheat Building, thirty-three floors up, to get the killer—"

And again:

"Remember, Steve, when Smike Lonergan had me at the wrong end of a gun and you horned in—" He turned to Vicki. "His own hands and feet were tied, but he rolled himself over the floor and bit Smike's ankle so ferociously, the guy thought it was a rattlesnake." Johnny chuckled. "It saved my skin and we got Smike, but it cost Steve two pearly-white incisors when Smike kicked back on the reflex. At that, we'd have been goners, only Smike's gun jammed."

Steve could have throttled Johnny for that one—it wasn't bad enough that he was so much older, the chump had to spill that his even front teeth were due to the dentist's art. Next thing, Vicki would be calling him "uncle."

But Vicki's eyes were shining with thrilled admiration. Steve made an honest attempt to show off Johnny in return. There were plenty of tales to the boy's credit—he was short neither on brains nor on physical courage. But Johnny overrode him—and Steve let him. For the first time in his life he found limelight a very pleasant element indeed.

They were still sitting over the red-checked tablecloth when Vicki's father and brother returned from a Carnegie concert. Max Braun, the gentle, impractical little Viennese, was a surprising parent for the completely American Vicki. Paul Braun was a halfway link between them. From the first, Steve viewed him with a cool criticism. His hair was a little too long, his lips a little too mobile, his hands a little too expressive. Besides, it riled him to see Vicki fall all over herself to serve Paul, to relegate her vivid personality to the role of handmaiden.

There was a quality of unaccented hospitality in the little apartment which enfolded the guests without words. When the two officers did finally make a move to leave, the parting was not final. Max Braun, in his quaint, letter-perfect English (learned from his American wife), invited them for coffee the following Sunday.

Johnny made his excuses—rather lame ones at that, Steve thought—and through the ensuing months rarely joined the newfound relationship. Steve did not look too deeply below the surface. He was too delighted at being alone in the field to analyze his luck.

More coffee parties, and quiet *gemütlich* evenings at the Brauns' followed. Steve received a confused and unassimilated course in classical music; he heard, unappreciatively, golden notes issuing from under Paul's gifted young fingers, and listened to endless monologues on the glories and perfections of Janno Slevna, the world-famous pianist, whom neither Max nor Vicki actually knew, but whom Paul brought right into the little living room with his vivid raptures. Paul's teacher had managed an audition for the boy, before the great man, and even then the boy's future association with him was a burning question.

But music was not Vicki's whole existence. Of the three, she was the only one in touch with the American milieu. Steve took her to ball games, hockey matches, plays, where she was as much a part of the picture as he was. He discovered that, for a girl of her means, she had had an unusual training.

Max Braun was Professor of Music at the Lacey Academy, one of the most exclusive girls' schools in the country. One of the terms of his contract stipulated Vicki's attendance at the school. She had received the education of a society debutante without the background to follow it up. Her point of view and manners were Sutton Place, healthily reinforced by common sense and the brush with reality which a meagre purse brings. She had been popular with her classmates, but after graduation their paths diverged. While they were planning their coming-out parties, Vicki took a job as secretary. The give-and-take of office life had given her poise and self-reliance. Added to that, her mother's death, four years ago, had placed further responsibilities on her shoulders. She held down her job efficiently—in a year she had risen to be secretary to the president of the firm—and had also run the house for those two impractical dreamers, Max and Paul Braun. All this had given her an unusual personality, but at the same time it had left her little leisure for the making of friends.

To Steve, that was all to the good, and he made swift use of the situation. There was an odd note during the period of their courtship: Steve, up in arms at the burden she shouldered, tried to shield and serve her, handling her with the rather amusing delicacy usually reserved for bisque. Vicki, on her side, tried to include the hard-bitten cop in the category of Max and Paul—children completely dependent on her judgment and ministrations.

The evening Steve diffidently offered his savings to finance Paul's lessons under Janno Slevna, Vicki's liking and gratitude merged into acceptance of Steve as a husband. There were tears in her eyes, but they were happy ones.

After their marriage, a year ago, they saw more of Johnny. Steve urged him to come to dinner nearly every week, and Vicki backed him up cordially. He was always Johnny to her, but from first to last, Johnny called her Mrs. Lake.

Steve had watched the two of them together in the early days, not because he suspected either of them in the usual sense, but because he was dead sensitive of their youth as opposed to his years. Thirty-eight was still young, vigorous, even romantic, but set against twenty-two and twenty-seven, it creaked. But they never made him feel a thing. It was all his imagination, his own touchiness, he was sure. If anything, they stuck him on a pedestal, blithely unaware that that was the last place he wanted to be.

As the car rolled to a stop before 920 Bank Street, Steve shook off his personal thoughts and turned to the business at hand. But he did say:

"Johnny, mind running across to that drugstore and giving Vicki a ring while I go in? Tell her to expect me when she sees me."

"Sure thing, Steve."

II

Nine Twenty Bank Street was a pleasant old house with window boxes dressing the red brick with their green contrast. Mrs. Whiting, the owner, proved to be a lady of refinement fallen on hard times. The widow of a doctor who had practiced in the old house, she was keeping off the wolf by renting her rooms.

She was genuinely shocked at Steve's news.

"He's the last person in the world—" she exclaimed. "Now why on earth would anyone want to shoot that poor boy?"

"Will you tell me everything you know about him, please?"

"Gladly. But I'm afraid it isn't much. He was decent, respectable, paid promptly, kept good hours; he was an ideal tenant."

"How long had he been with you?"

"Nearly two years. And never a bit of trouble."

"How did he happen to come to you?"

"One of my lodgers, Mr. Ritchie, worked in the same place and told him there was a vacancy. My former tenant moved to California."

"That was at the Government Laboratory?"

"Oh, no. A business firm—I've forgotten the name, but Mr. Ritchie can tell you when he comes in. He's still there. He was the one who recommended the boy to me."

"Were he and this Ritchie friends?"

"Friendly, yes. But if you mean did they go around together, no. Mr. Ritchie is more of a social type. Mr. Ferman spent most of his evenings at home."

"Do you know why he changed his job?"

"I believe it was better pay. I know his new employers were very particular. He had to get three letters of recommendation. For good character and so on. He asked me to write one."

"And did you?"

"Certainly. Everything I knew about him was good."

"Did you have opportunities to judge what he was like—I mean his tastes, his hobbies, his education and so on?"

Mrs. Whiting paused in thought.

"Do you know, now you mention it, I don't actually know very much definite about him." She smiled a little. "I guess I'm rather a great talker myself—and he was a good listener."

"Did he have any visitors?"

"I never saw any. He could have had, I suppose. I'm often out."

"Was he fond of mechanical or scientific work?"

"I don't know. I do know he was a great reader. I think most of his money went for books."

"Did he ever speak of any relations, where he was born, such things?"

"He never talked about himself at all."

"How about mail?"

"Once in a great while a letter from Europe—Prague, I think it was."

"Didn't you ever think it odd for a man to have no ties, no local friends, no roots or connections here?"

"There are a great many unfortunates, Captain, who find themselves in that unhappy state through no fault of their own."

"Yes, you're right enough there. Well, suppose we have a look at his room. That may tell us something."

Johnny came in.

"No answer from your home, Steve," he reported quietly.

"Okay. Guess Vicki's over at her dad's."

Mrs. Whiting led them up to a third-floor back room, light, quiet, decently furnished and clean.

"I'll leave you, Captain. I'm sure you'd prefer to work alone."

"Thank you. And please tell Mr. Ritchie to stay in tonight. I'll be back to see him in a couple of hours."

"I'll do that," she said and left them.

The room told them no more than Mrs. Whiting had. There were no papers, none of the foreign mail Mrs. Whiting had mentioned, no signs of outside activities. There was a three-shelf open bookcase, well stocked with fat, dry-looking books. There was no fiction. Every book bore in some way on the subject of government, politics or economics.

"Commie, by gosh!" Johnny exclaimed, thrusting out a copy of Marx's *Das Kapital*.

"Maybe. Maybe not. Look at some of these." There was on old copy of *Mein Kampf*, all the writings of Masaryk and Benes, books by Harold Laski, the English Socialist, and by Winston Churchill, the English Conservative; American material by Sumner Welles, by Huey Long, by Franklin Roosevelt and by John L. Lewis. "I can't make out whether the guy was just a glutton for information or if this stuff is all camouflage, hiding an enemy agent."

"You've hit it, Steve. Nobody's quite that colorless and alone in the world just by accident. It's deliberate."

"Johnny, seal up this place. Then go on up and question those people in the apartment house on the Drive. I'm going to the lab to check. That'd be a hell of a note these days. A spy in government work. I'll be back here by seven or seven-thirty. Meet me here and we'll finecomb this room. Better phone Schneer to come and take over here while you're gone. Tell him to bring along a print man to go over the place. Don't leave till he gets here. And I want him to hold this Ritchie. He may know more than his prayers."

"Right."

Steve sped up to Gunhill Road through the still driving rain and asked for the Supervisor. His worst fears were realized. The office was already in an uproar. The intelligent switchboard operator had reported Steve's phone call and the Supervisor's first move was to check the files in Ferman's care. A single sheet was missing from one of the newest folders. The sheet contained a top-secret chemical formula on germ warfare and had been filed by Ferman the previous Friday.

As Steve arrived, the Supervisor, beside himself with worry, was shouting at the official searcher of the building. The latter's sole duty was to search every employee on his way in and on his way out, every day. The searcher, a man of nearly sixty, named Drain, was wilting under the Supervisor's fire. There were actual tears in his pale blue eyes, and his nervousness drove him almost to palsy as he continually wiped his sweating forehead.

"On my oath, sir, I searched Ferman exactly as usual," he was saying. "There was nothing. Absolutely nothing."

"Exactly as usual! What does *that* mean?" the Supervisor snapped.

"The regular routine, sir. An all-over frisk for weapons. Then all pockets turned out, shoes and socks off, then a tactual examination of all clothing for the crackle of paper. I swear to you, there was nothing."

"Did you see his naked back or stomach or legs or groin?"

"I don't *strip* them, no sir. But I would have *felt* anything."

"Not if it was pasted flat, you wouldn't." His voice rose to a roar. "Did you think this Ferman was going to put it in his pants pocket just to make things easy for you, you dolt?"

"He'd been here a long time, sir, and there's never been any reason to suspect him."

"Oh, as long as an employee doesn't send you a wire that he's a spy or a thief, you sit back on your fat behind and trust to luck? Drain, you're lazy, incompetent, guilty of the most monstrous criminal carelessness. You're fired without recommendation. Go back to your office and hold yourself in readiness to answer to the F.B.I."

"Just a minute," Steve cut in. The searcher stopped. Steve's cold blue eyes bored into the old man's. "Drain, why'd you do it?" His tone was quiet, but as gritty as sand.

"Sir?" Drain quavered, bewildered.

"What was your cut? How much did you get to pass Ferman without searching?"

"Never, never, sir!" he exclaimed. "I wouldn't do such a thing!"

"Don't give me that. Who was behind you? Who'd you sell out to?"

"I'm an honest man. A good American citizen. You can't say such things about me." Drain's manner stiffened with indignation.

"No? We'll say worse. And *do* worse. The only way you can help yourself now is to come clean, to give us a line on Ferman's murderer."

"Murderer?" The man staggered with shock.

"Yeah, murderer. Ferman served his purpose. But he might talk so they shut him up. You've served yours. So you're next on their list. Your only hope is to help us nab them before they get you, too. Who bribed you?"

Drain burst into tears.

"I swear to you, sir," he sobbed, "there was *nobody*. Maybe I was careless, because Ferman seemed so honest and trustworthy, but, on my life, I had nothing to do with any plot. I'm innocent!" He buried his face in his shaking hands.

Steve went to the phone.

"Send Larkin up to bring a man downtown.... The Atcheson Laboratory, off Gunhill Road. Hold him in the basement till I get down. No, no charge. Just hold him." He hung up and turned again to Drain: "Your last chance. You got something to say?"

"I don't know anything, I tell you."

"Okay!" Steve's voice and eyes were granite. "We'll see if a little solitude won't improve your memory." He added to the Supervisor: "Lock him up till my man gets here."

A guard led Drain out, completely demoralized.

"Captain, I think you're mistaken about Drain. He's trustworthy, I'm sure. Incompetent, but thoroughly honest," said the Supervisor.

"Maybe. I'm taking no chances," returned Steve shortly. "Now I want a description of the missing document. Kind of paper—size—written, typed or what? Better yet, show me one like it. And I'll look at the filing cabinet where it came from. See that nobody touches it until our men test it for prints. Meanwhile, how did you come to take Ferman on for the job?"

"He came well recommended by his last employers—the Stevens Cable Company. I have Ferman's card right here. His record was good. He had the necessary letters of recommendation. His personality was straightforward— After all, Captain, the position was just a routine file-clerkship. He never went near the actual laboratories."

"Sure," Steve commented dryly. "But he had the results of the lab research right where he could hand 'em out to any enemy of the U.S. Now, I'd like to see your switchboard operator."

But the only thing the switchboard operator could tell was that the message saying Ferman was ill was in a man's voice, an ordinary, polite voice without accent or distinguishing quality. She doubted if she would recognize it if she heard it again.

"Would you say it was a gentleman's voice or a working man's?"

"Well a—businessman's. He sounded kind of cool and deliberate. That's about the best I can do, Captain."

Steve left the laboratory and drove downtown. It was just six o'clock.

"Drive through West 81st Street," he told the chauffeur. Near Broadway, he got out at his apartment house. Before the door he noticed Vicki's parked Chevy, in the same spot where it had stood that morning. His trained eye noted automatically the dry oblong of asphalt beneath it. It had not been moved since the rain started last night.

He went up in the self-operating elevator and let himself into his apartment. Nick, the wire-hair, city-bred and apartment-trained, greeted him with a violent wagging of his tail but no barking. Vicki, in the kitchen, slammed the oven door, drowning out the sound of Steve's entry. For a moment or two he stood in the little foyer, undiscovered, watching her with something like hunger in the eyes which told nothing when there was anyone there to read them. This was a different man from the cold and calculating Captain of Homicide. This man was as vulnerable as an opened oyster.

Vicki was humming softly to herself as she stirred a steaming soup pot. In her dark blue dress, with its round white collar and cuffs, she looked like a schoolgirl, certainly not even her twenty-two years. Her incongruous youth struck him afresh.

He devoured her irregular profile with his eyes: the impertinent nose, the almost-too-wide mouth, the lovely young cheek-line melting into the little throat, the curve of the ridiculously long eyelashes. She turned from the stove and began to arrange a salad in small wooden bowls. There was no lost motion. She was efficient, deft, quick.

She continued her humming, a nostalgic Viennese waltz. Steve grinned a little to himself. She might rave over all that classical stuff with her father and brother, but he noticed when she was alone, she sang something with a tune to it. It was nice hearing her crooning, it meant she was contented. Unhappy people don't sing to themselves. And that was a constant silent question in Steve's mind. What did he have to offer against her sparkle, gaiety and color. Toughness, heaviness—half the time her joking with Johnny went right over his head.

He shrugged and threw off his wry thoughts. The fact remained, she was his, she'd married him of her own free will, she was affectionate, happy, waited on him hand and foot—what was he beefing about? That one about gift horses was good sense.

He reached back to the door and opened and closed it audibly. Vicki flew out to the foyer.

"Steve, honey! How grand! For once you're on time for a good hot dinner." She gave him a quick, light kiss on the cheek. "Go and wash up. Everything's ready."

"Can't be done. I just stopped by to say I'd be late."

"Oh, heck! Again! Cops' wives have some rights. I don't know what you look like anymore."

"I don't like it any better than you do."

"But you've got to eat somewhere. Take half an hour off and have your dinner. It's your favorite."

He would have loved to slip an arm around her little curving body and whisper: "You're my favorite, baby," but he was tongue-tied, inept. Maybe, someday, things like that would roll off his tongue at the right time, instead of later when he thought it over alone. Instead, he asked, as if food was important:

"My favorite? What's that?"

"Roast chicken. And enormous baked Idaho potatoes."

"I'd like to stay, but I've got to get downtown. I'll have a sandwich somewhere."

"Steve, you'll ruin your digestion, eating at all hours."

"I'm still pretty husky, after eighteen years of it." Then he could have kicked himself. Why did he always have to stress the enormous disparity in their ages? She was probably thinking: When Steve first became a cop, I was just four years old. Ass that he was! To take her mind off the idea, he changed the subject:

"What did you do all day? I tried to get you on the phone."

"Give you three guesses." Her grey-green eyes crinkled impishly.

"You went to see your father."

"Nope."

"Some concert with that brother of yours."

"On a Monday in June? Guess again."

"Give up."

"I made use of the badge."

"Badge? What badge?"

"For Belmont."

"You went to the races?"

"Sure. Why not? It's a shame to let it go to waste."

"But on such a day! The track must have been a lake."

"I'm good at mudders."

"What did you lose?" His attempt at lightness came out sour. He didn't want to bellyache, but he hated the idea of her out there alone in that mob.

"I won. Seventeen dollars," she crowed triumphantly.

"Hope you didn't drive in this weather?"

There was a moment's hesitation. She began to nod, stopped and then said:

"No. I took the train."

"Glad you showed some sense— Well, I've got to run. Don't know when I'll be back, if at all."

"Oh, Steve, no matter how late you are, come home. Those cots at the station house are terrible."

"I'll do my best. Has Nick been out?"

"Yes, I took him when I came in."

As he opened the door, she laid a hand on his arm.

"Steve, be careful, will you?"

"Nothing dangerous about this. Just routine."

"Swell!" She squeezed his arm and let him go. As he rode down in the elevator, his wrist-watch said six-twenty.

"Bank Street again," he told the chauffeur.

III

All the way downtown, Steve was frowning, as a man frowns when a hornet is buzzing, unseen but potentially invidious, about his head. Some fact, elusive and unclassified, was nagging him. He threw it off when he reached Ferman's house and plunged into an examination of the dead man's room. He sent Schneer home and began running through Ferman's clothes, the bureau drawers, he even pulled up the rug, looking for a cache for hidden papers. After a while Johnny came in and joined the search.

"Any luck uptown?" Steve asked.

"Nope. They all slept like tops."

"Hardly expected different."

"Hell, in books there's always a dame with a sick kid or a toothache, who sits for hours at the window in the dark and gives the cops a description of the death car, complete with license number. *We* should get breaks like that!"

"It's early days to sour on the case, Johnny."

"I'm not beefing. Only there's nothing to get hold of."

"The Feds may uncover a lead. I'm calling Rieger as soon as I finish here."

They went on searching. Steve discovered the only find that offered food for speculation. It was a small folder with a list of sailings of the Queen Steamship Line.

"Maybe he was just using this for a bookmark. Then, again, maybe he was planning to skip the country." He slipped it into an envelope, holding it by its edges. "We'll get Harris to test it for prints. If it was given to Ferman by one of their higher-ups—there's a pretty extensive line of enemy agent prints in Washington."

"Fair enough."

Ed Ritchie, the man who had recommended Ferman to Mrs. Whiting's, arrived, a toothpick poised jauntily in his mouth. He was about twenty-seven, thin, red-headed and cheery.

"You coulda knocked me over with a feather," he began. "A mild little runt like Ferman gettin' himself bumped. Who had it in for him?"

"We thought perhaps you could help us there."

But no amount of questioning elicited any facts or even suggestions. Ritchie and Ferman had worked side by side for a couple of years at the Stevens Cable Company. Ritchie had recommended Mrs. Whiting's room to him; the two men were friendly, but that was all.

"He was a nice little guy, Cap, but you just couldn't get chummy with him. It wasn't that he clammed up. He just didn't seem to have any ideas to talk about."

Steve could well imagine that nobody would be very successful at getting in a word edgewise with the chatty Ritchie. He did, however, give them the name of the restaurant where Ferman ate his dinners.

"The Central Europa, on 4th Street. A crummy joint, Cap. I went with him once, but never again. Blintzes, goulash, red cabbage, sour cream, meat cooked with prunes. The place stinks."

"Did he seem to know any of the other customers?"

"Not that I could see. Most of 'em were Russians and Rumanians and Czechs."

"And Ferman was American?"

"Oh, sure. At least Brooklyn." He chuckled at his own joke.

"Was he born in Brooklyn, do you know?"

"He never said. Had a room there before I got him in here."

"Do you know the address?"

"Me, I don't know Brooklyn from a hole in the ground."

"Did you hear anything here in the house last night?"

"I didn't get in until one."

"Hear anything after that?"

"Like what?"

"A shot, say?"

"Golly! You mean they killed him here?"

"Perhaps."

"If they did, I didn't hear 'em."

"Maybe you heard something else—shuffling, tramping, carrying a man down the stairs?"

"Not a thing."

"Did Ferman have a girl?"

"If he did, he kept her plenty dark. In all the time I knew him he never batted an eye at a dame. Didn't know they were on earth."

"Well, thanks, Mr. Ritchie. If I need you again, I'll let you know."

"Any time."

Steve sealed and locked up Ferman's room and left the house with Johnny. A uniformed man stayed, tilted in a chair, outside Ferman's door.

"Eaten yet?" Steve asked Johnny.

"No, I came straight down from the Drive."

"What say we try the blintzes Ritchie talked about?"

"Good idea, Steve. Waiters have eyes in their heads."

"Yeah. Trouble is, these Commies like to play cops-and-robbers. No chat over a table for them. Half their fun is meeting in some dark cellar with a password and false eyebrows. That is, if Ferman was a Commie. From the look of things, he could have been working for Franco or Tito or Peron."

The Central Europa was a good-sized, none-too-clean restaurant. Steve and Johnny took a table and scanned the purple ink menu. Steve ordered a Bohemian dish, but Johnny stuck to American spareribs and baked potatoes. A little adroit questioning of the waiter revealed nothing new. He identified Ferman from Steve's description, said he had been eating there steadily for months, but spoke to no one in the place and was always alone. He summoned the proprietor and the cashier at Steve's request. Neither of them could add a word, and it seemed to both detectives that they were speaking the truth.

While they waited for their food, Steve said:

"One thing about the case bothers me. These people don't throw cash around. Why didn't they snatch back that four hundred bucks after they killed him?"

"Maybe they had to get away fast."

"No. We agreed he wasn't shot where he was found. A .38 makes a hell of a noise. One of those tenants you talked to would have heard it. Besides, you say there was no blood on the grass."

"How do you tape it then?" asked Johnny.

"Well, if Ferman was a Commie—it should work out this way—there are two breeds of Reds—the have-nots who fill their empty stomachs on the Moscow tripe promising them the earth, come the revolution.

Then there's the parlor brand, the intelligentsia, the big shots who make so much money they take up Marx for a new thrill. The Hollywood breed the Senate investigated. They're as rabid as any May Day marcher. Well, if one of them was dickering for the formula for dear old Joe, the four hundred dollars wouldn't register with him. He wouldn't frisk a cadaver for such coffee money. God, no. He's above that. Too much sensibility. Outrage his artistic temperament."

"Think you've hit it. Specially as a private car has to figure in the setup, and the garden variety of Commie doesn't usually own one."

The food was set before them in thick white chinaware. As Johnny broke open his steaming potato, the buzzing hornet which had been nagging the bottom of Steve's consciousness suddenly rose to the surface and became a lucid, logical, startling sequence of facts. It had nothing to do with the Ferman case. Tabulated, it might have read like this:

(*a*) Vicki went to Belmont by train.

(*b*) The Belmont track was a spur-road terminal. All trains back to town started from there.

(*c*) The earliest train back to town left Belmont at ten minutes to five.

(*d*) From track to 81st Street by train and subway took at least a full hour, more likely an hour and a quarter.

(*e*) The earliest Vicki could have reached home by train was ten minutes to six.

(*f*) Enormous Idaho potatoes, which Vicki had announced for dinner, took a full hour to bake.

(*g*) At six o'clock, when he stopped at home, Vicki had said they were ready. How had she got back from Belmont by five, so that they could be ready?

The obvious answer was by car. Someone had driven her back to town before the races were over and she was keeping it dark. He knew she had not used her own car; the dry rectangle of asphalt under it was proof of that. She was lying to him, she was meeting some man out there. Cheating on him. A vein ticked in his temple, in time with the nausea of his heartbeat.

Sixteen years' difference. What did he expect? Twenty-two wants something that thirty-eight has forgotten how to give. It served him right. No, he was damned if it did. She hadn't had to say yes when he asked her to marry him. She must have cared for him. She left a home she was happy in, to come to him. She did it of her own free will, so he was entitled to a square deal

The vein ticked with a more sickening thud as he remembered how much more willing, even eager, she had been when he made that offer to finance her kid brother for a year's training under Slevna. All along, the knowledge had slept darkly at the bottom of his mind. Now, it rose to the top and showed itself as a bribe, pure and simple. She had let herself be bought, because she had the fool notion that the boy was a genius. And when the year was up, and he had suggested that Paul take a man's job and stop tinkering with the piano, this was her answer. The deal was off, so she thought she was free to run with anything she took a fancy to.

Immediately he took that back. She was too clean, too straight for that kind of filth. If she had picked someone up at the track, there wouldn't be any harm behind it. She was as friendly as a kitten, ready to play with anybody who put out a feeler. Whether the guy with the car was so innocent was something else again. The thing to do was to tackle him.

He'd find ways to learn who he was. He knew ways to make him lay off. Hell, it wasn't the worst crime in the world to accept a hitch home. What hurt was that she'd lied about it. Did she think he was some kind of a brute who'd beat her up if she told the truth? He squirmed away from that thought—she knew what he thought of most human beings, male and female. But, hell, when it came to her, she ought to know he'd bank on her to the last ditch. He switched to the other extreme. He was acting like a nut about the whole thing. Vicki was a good cook. Of course she knew ways of baking potatoes in the morning and just running 'em back in the oven for five minutes at six o'clock. She'd taken the train just as she said. With lucky connections, she could have made it. The thing to do was to ask her straight out — No, if he catechized her, she'd be on to it in a minute and sense he didn't trust her. He couldn't bear to upset the existing lovely relationship between them.

He saw Johnny's puzzled eyes on him and pulled himself together.

"This stuff's lousy," he said, pushing back his plate, hoping to pass off his tell-tale expression as distaste for the food. "While you finish up, I'll give Rieger a ring."

Rieger, of the F.B.I., listening intently.

"We had a similar case about a year ago," he told Steve, "at the Midwest lab in Toledo. Got all the earmarks—missing formula, innocent-looking file clerk, shot in a park, all inquiries about his connections a dead end.

"What was the formula?"

"Scorched earth stuff. Some chemical that renders farmland sterile from three to five years. We never did catch up with 'em. We think that one got out of the country. Not long after, Moscow bragged of having developed it."

"There was a folder in Ferman's room, sailing list of the Queen Line."

"My God! That's a help. We'll finecomb all outgoing passengers. What else?" exclaimed Rieger.

"That's all at the moment. I'll send you a DD-14 report in the morning."

"Too long. Can't I drop by 10th Street right now?"

"Okay. I'll be back there in fifteen minutes." He came back to Johnny.

"Nothing more we can do tonight," he told the Sergeant. "I'm having a powwow with Rieger. He's all hopped up about this. But no need for you to stick around. Go get yourself some sleep."

"Mind if I don't? I could take notes for Rieger. I'm still pretty fast with the pothooks."

"Sure, if you want."

It was nearly ten when Rieger, beaming with satisfaction, rose to leave.

"It's a regular pattern. We'll get 'em this time, sure as shooting. Thanks a lot. I'll take that sailing list along and test it tonight. Faster than sending it downtown. Seeing you."

As Johnny and Steve walked up to the subway, they passed a record shop blaring with both light and sound.

"Wait a second," Steve said. "I ordered a record here the other day. I'll see if it's in yet."

"Not going musical on me, Chief?" Johnny grinned.

"I've got a tin ear. You ought to know that by now. Drives Vicki nuts. This is for her."

"What is it?"

"Some Italian junk she goes for. *Toccata and Fugue*, whatever that means."

"Oh, Bach."

"Don't be so damned knowing, Johnny, or I'll have you back in uniform tomorrow."

It was nice to relax with Johnny, not to be a cop snooping for ugly motives, professionally or otherwise. For, excepting for Vicki, Johnny was the one human being on whom Steve banked and liked without qualification. Meanness and treachery were not in him. He had watched the boy ever since he had been transferred to Homicide and had yet to find a time when self-interest had come first with him. Johnny had made mistakes, of course, plenty of them. But they were all mistakes of zeal and fidelity. If he overstepped orders, it was because of a too-eager devotion to his work. And he never lied—the small, hard-to-nail lies to cover himself in a tight corner. He took punishment cheerfully and as a matter of course, simply recovering the ground he had lost as fast as he could.

Outside of work hours, Steve enjoyed the evenings when Johnny had dinner at the house. He had sound ideas and was often worth listening to about police theory. And it was refreshing to listen to his agile kidding with Vicki, even though Steve himself was too heavy-tongued to compete with the two of them.

They parted at Columbus Circle where Johnny got out. He lived with his parents at a very swanky 57th Street address indeed—for a police-sergeant. At 79th Street, Steve went slowly up the subway stairs. In spite of his love for Vicki—or just possibly because of it— there remained deep down in his policeman's soul the tiny abrading suspicion which he had tried so hard to throw off. Competent at his work, he would have seen instantly that the thing should be cleared up at once by plain-speaking. Professionally, he had no patience with misunderstandings which could be avoided by a simple question or two. But where it concerned his personal life, he couldn't do it. Suppose the worst was true, suppose she said she was sick of her bargain and wanted to leave him. In all his dingy, meagre, uphill life she was the one flashing, lovely thing he had ever called his own. He was a miser with a jewel. He couldn't face the risk of losing her.

He flung down the cigarette he had lighted and ground it furiously underfoot.

"You double-dyed, sneaking clue-sniffer!" he muttered with enormous self-disgust. "Making a mountain out of a—baked potato," and he made for home with a lighter step.

At the entrance to his apartment house a slim figure detached itself from the shadows.

"Steve—"

"Paul! What are you doing down here? Come on up."

"No— I can't— I just— Have you a minute, Steve?"

"Sure. What's on your mind?"

Paul Braun, so like Vicki, yet so different in his Byronic good looks, braced himself for the ordeal.

"I— I'm in a jam, Steve— I don't know what to do."

"Spill it, kid." Thoughts of women, of gambling, of bad company lit signals in Steve's mind. A boy of twenty could go down plenty of wrong turnings.

"Well, it's like this— You won't tell Dad or Vicki?"

"No. Strictly between us, boy."

"About two weeks ago, Dad gave me the money to pay the doctor's bill from the last attack of asthma he had."

"How much?"

"Thirty-two dollars."

"Go on."

"I was going to stop by and pay it after my lesson with Slevna. Well, while I was still there, Violet Claire came in—"

"The movie star?"

"Yes."

"Classy company you travel in."

"She's a friend of Slevna's. Anyway, he introduced me, and the three of us sat and talked. Slevna had a radio appearance and had to be at the studio at seven-thirty. So he suggested going out and having a bite to eat first. They asked me to go, too." There was a youthful pride in his voice which even his worry could not quench. "We went to a quiet little French place where they didn't even have prices on the menu. We only had a light supper—"

"Get to the catch, Paul."

"When the bill came, Slevna hunted all over in his pockets and found he'd forgotten his wallet."

"I see."

"He asked me if I had any money with me. Well, naturally, I gave him the thirty-two dollars."

"Naturally."

"It was only a loan, of course."

"Oh, sure. But it slipped Slevna's mind." Steve's tone was dry.

"That's it," Paul said seriously, not sensing the irony. "Slevna's too big, too wrapped up in his art to remember trifles like that."

"And you couldn't remind him?"

"Steve, I couldn't. I swear I tried. But I just couldn't get it out. He's been so wonderful to me—he's such a genius—"

Steve smiled and took out his wallet.

"Well, thirty-two dollars isn't all the money in the world," he said.

"It is, if you haven't got it," said the boy.

"Y'know, that's a big truth you just uttered. Look, Paul, independence is a grand thing—not relying on others for every dime you need."

"But what can I do about it?"

"Ever think about earning any?"

"How?"

"Well, in a small way you could give lessons. Pass on what Slevna's taught you."

"Oh, I'm not nearly ready for that. Besides, my day is full up with the work Slevna gives me to do."

"Evenings, too?"

"Evenings? No—I do have my evenings."

"It's just a thought, kid. I don't know any feeling finer than taking in the first dollar earned by your own efforts."

"I wouldn't know how to go about it—"

"Forget it. Here, take this and head for the doctor's pronto."

"Steve, I can't tell you—"

"Save the thanks. But why did you wait two weeks to tell me?"

"I—I thought Slevna might remember—but— And now Dad's showing symptoms of another attack—we may have to call the doctor again—"

"I get it. If he comes and mentions the bill—"

"That's it."

"Well, fix it up before Slevna puts the bee on you again," Steve grinned.

"Steve, you've got Slevna all wrong. He's so marvelous—"

"Okay, okay. I'm only a dumb cop. I don't understand genius."

"You're not dumb. You're swell. And I wish I had your common sense. But it's true, you don't understand Slevna."

"I'll struggle along not understanding him."

"If I could only make you see how far above most people he is—"

"Take your word for it. Run along now."

"You won't say anything to Vicki?"

"I said I wouldn't. But why not? Vicki's no schoolmarm."

"She'd be pretty shocked at what I did."

"You're nuts. What else could you have done?"

"Vicki would have said no when Slevna asked for the money. She'd have said it was Dad's money, not mine."

"You are making her out a George Washington. Well, don't think about it. As I said, it's strictly between us. Good night."

"Good night, Steve, and thanks again."

As he went up in the elevator, Steve's smile at Paul's small dilemma faded. If Paul was right about Vicki, how explain the discrepancies about the races? He frowned, deliberately crushing down his doubts. But the effort told. His mood changed. He was in a frame of mind to disparage and carp because of his inner disquiet. The nagging question at the bottom of his mind had turned into a rasp.

IV

He kissed her when he came in and held out the record he had bought.

"Here." He managed to keep the strain out of his voice. "This the highbrow noise you were talking about?"

"Steve! The Slevna recording! You swell person! Come on in and I'll play it."

"You'll play it when I'm out. I'm a starving man and I'll have some of that cold chicken."

She sat with him while he ate.

"Well, what gives at Homicide, buster?" she asked.

"The usual."

"Very chatty, aren't you?"

"What do you care about such lousy stuff?"

"It's fun knowing before I read it in the papers."

"Don't clutter up your head with it."

"Look, Steve, why do you always shut me out? Lousy or not, it's your work. That makes it my business, too."

"Your business is to let me forget it outside of hours."

"You trying to make a Nora in *A Doll's House* out of me, you lug?" she grinned.

"Over my head. I'm just a dumb cop," he said again as he had said to Paul.

"Dumb!" She wrinkled her nose at him. "I'd hate to kill a cockroach with you on the horizon. One look and I'd be booked for vermicide."

"Okay, okay, skip it. Change the subject. How come you got this lame idea about going to the track alone?"

"I told you. The Jockey Club's nice enough to send you a badge, so the least we can do is to use it."

"I'm not so sure I like you traipsing around race tracks alone."

She gave a little hoot of laughter.

"Well, listen to the he-man with a great big protective instinct for the little woman! Just a minute while I slip into my crinoline."

"Kid all you want. I still don't like it."

"Steve, honey, this is *nineteen* forty-nine. Didn't you know?" She patted his arm with the affection one gives a child. It riled him a little.

"The hell with dates. In my book, the guy who brings in the dough is still the head of the house."

She looked at him, a queer expression, part regret, part resentment, in her grey-green eyes. She said slowly:

"I realize that. And you know something? It's not too good."

"And what does that crack mean?"

"Those Victorian dames must have had to be awful liars, poor dears."

"Hey, stop jumping around like a grasshopper. What else do you know?"

She changed the subject, with something like relief.

"Oh, the grandest news! Slevna says Paul is too promising to drop. When he comes back from his European tour, he's going on with Paul's lessons."

"No matter how big they are, they still don't turn down thirty bucks a throw," he said dryly.

"That's ridiculous. Slevna could have hundreds of pupils if he raised a finger. Do you realize Paul's only the third one he's ever taught?"

"And what does that add up to?"

"Oh, Steve, you're impossible. Get it through your head that Slevna's the greatest pianist alive. It means that Paul is the real thing—that someday—"

"I still think you and your father are ruining the kid. What he needs is a job and a taste of responsibility. What is he—nineteen, twenty?"

"Age has nothing to do with it, if you've got a gift."

"Sure. Sure. I didn't have any gift. So I was bringing home dough when I was twelve. Just go dig yourself up a gift and you can let your father sweat, teaching eight hours a day, supporting you, and you can let your sister's husband stake you to piano lessons—"

"Steve!" she said in a strangled voice. "I didn't *dream* you felt like this."

"Never mind about me—"

"But I *do* mind about you—"

"We're talking about Paul, about a boy who passes the buck to everybody around him—"

"I *must* make you understand, dear. Paul—"

"I understand all right," he retorted bitterly. "Didn't I have a boy wonder in my own family? Come hell or high water, my mother was going to have a parson in the family. Joseph was elected. So what did that make me? The great big moneymaker. For Joseph's schooling, for Joseph's choir robes, for God knows what!"

She was around the table and beside his chair in a flash, pressing his head to her in a rush of sympathy.

"Steve, darling! Why didn't I ever know all this before? Oh, honey, you have no *right* to shut me out of the real parts of your life—"

"I told you I had a brother."

"Yes, you actually did break down and volunteer it once," she said indignantly. "But all this hidden inside stuff that you've kept bottled up—what's a wife for, if not to drag it out in the open?"

"Forget it," he said gruffly.

"I won't!" she returned. "Now I've got a wedge between the clamshells—"

"Okay. What d'you want to know?" he asked grimly.

"Everything. How you earned money, what happened to Joseph—everything." She perched on the hard arm of his dining-room chair.

"What *does* a school kid do? Sell papers, deliver groceries, shovel snow—"

"But how much could you earn at that?"

"Bigger cash came in while I put myself through High School. I got a night job at the phone company. For four years my only pillow was a telephone book. Some soft music, maestro, for the poor little wage slave—" His tone was sardonic, to the point of savagery.

"I'm beginning to understand a lot of things," she said half to herself. "What happened to Joseph?"

"Joseph, my dear girl," he said, with elaborate unction, "met up with a delightful blonde. So the hell with his 'call,' and with my mother's dream. He's raising chickens in a place called Selma, New York, and has four lovely kids. Now do you see why I take no stock in Paul?"

"The two cases aren't alike a bit. Joseph was probably shanghaied into it by your mother's will power and never really wanted to go into the Church at all. It's different with Paul. No matter what you say, Paul does have a real gift and a burning desire to be a pianist."

"At somebody else's expense."

"But, Steve, honey, what else can he do?"

"What I said—take a job over the summer and pay for his own lessons."

"First of all, he's got to be careful of his hands. There's practically no job he could take that wouldn't be a risk. Secondly, he's got to keep up with his practicing, hours and hours a day, until Slevna gets back."

"So I'm elected to go on footing the bill?"

"Certainly not!" she said quickly.

"Don't get me wrong. I didn't begrudge the boy a chance for a year. I was *glad* to do it—for you. But no cop's salary runs to financing a luxury article like a future pianist forever."

"Of course not. I'm not asking you to. You've done more than your share."

"Well, may I ask who takes over the cashier's desk if I stop?"

"Slevna told Paul not to worry about it. He said there were more important things than money in the world and more ways to repay him than in dollars. He must be a wonderful person!"

"Yeah," retorted Steve dryly. "I notice he *is* free with money—paying alimony to three ex-wives, to say nothing of the other dames he shacks up with—"

"Oh, columnists!" she came back, up in arms. "Famous people are just grist for their mills."

"Maybe. Ever hear the one about where there's smoke there's fire?"

"Steve, why do you always have your knife out for Slevna?"

"I don't like old goats. He must be pushing sixty."

"He's exactly fifty-two."

"Know all about him, don't you?"

"Well, naturally. He's practically all Paul talks about."

"You said something. And I'll tell you this: for my money, he stinks, and I'm a bit fed up with the subject if you're not—'Slevna this', 'Slevna that'—the walls at your father's just about papered with his pictures—Slevna with the crowned heads of Europe—*de*-crowned mostly, now—Slevna accepting the keys of the city, Slevna with his damn fool cigarette-holder a foot long— What the hell, let's drop it. Come to bed. I've got to get up in the morning."

Vicki began carrying dishes out to the kitchen, and Steve went on into the bedroom. The moment he was alone, he developed a half-ashamed disgust at his own boorishness. As he yanked off his tie, he muttered at himself in the mirror:

"What you need is a good swift kick. First you've got her all taped out as cheating on you, then you come home and level off on one subject after another—belly-aching about her going to the track, making a noise like a czar. Hell, you like to go, why shouldn't she? It's tough enough on the kid with a husband who's gone all day and half the nights. Then you start on the kid. Brother, maybe *you're* dumb and can't smell a genius a mile off. Then you crack down on the family hero. You're just one hell of a sweet-tempered rat."

Impatiently he jerked open the bureau drawer for his hair brushes to try to flatten out the deep wave he hated. The Clubhouse badge stared up at him, just where he always kept it; an oval bit of cardboard, with a tight-packed set of paper leaves clamped to it, one leaf for each day of the meeting, numbered in order. As one entered the track gate the attendant tore off the leaf for that day. The number 17 faced him. With a shock he remembered that the last time he and Vicki had gone to the races together had been the sixteenth day— nearly two weeks ago. The badge had not been used since.

His stomach turned over.

Carefully he dropped the badge back and closed the drawer. His breath came noisily through dilated nostrils. His jaws clamped together until the muscles bunched in his cheeks.

What did it mean? If she hadn't used the badge, hadn't gone to the track, why say so? To account for hours and hours of absence while she was—doing what? There had to be a showdown. He'd get the truth out of her, here and now.

He told himself to take it easy, not to go off half-cocked. All his life he had been self-sufficient when it came to a problem. He could handle this one. He forgot that in handling those other problems he had been objective; he had stood outside and had viewed them in their true perspective. Now, dealing with his own, his mind was muddy with a dozen personal elements:

First, an ingrained inferiority complex, with a two-pronged gad; the one prong, his boyhood, where his personality had played second fiddle to Joseph, and his only importance had been his earning capacity; the other prong, the contrast between Vicki's youth and his maturity.

(What could a guy offer a girl sixteen years younger?)

Next, his intolerant distrust where all human beings were concerned. This, too, had a double impetus, an impersonal one, arising from his work—

(Try being a cop for a lifetime and see 'em kill for a silver fox cape or

a pinch of snow!)

And a personal one, which dated back to the shy, formative age. He had been twenty-one at the time, and for all purposes alone in the world—his parents dead and his brother upstate. He met a girl, Rose Mulane, and fell reverently in love. She seemed so innocent and unworldly, that it was weeks before he dared ask to visit her. Even then he got a good deal of demure help from her before he brought out the formidable request. She began to color all his hopes and dreams. She pervaded but did not hinder his work at the Police Academy. He worked hard and did well, with the vision of a home, of Rose as his wife, always before his eyes.

He began to see a good deal of her, took her to pictures, on Hudson River boat rides, spent evenings at her home. He was diffident, tongue-tied, very nearly worshipful. Once, when she handed him a glass of lemonade, her hand brushed his. To Steve, the thunder of his heartbeats sounded like the roar of the sea.

There came an evening when her parents were out and they had the little parlor to themselves. There was a sweet intimacy in their aloneness, like a foretaste of the future. Rose's voice broke in on his thoughts, an unwonted petulance in her tone:

"Steve Lake, you can't possibly be such a stuffed shirt as you seem." He stared at her, at sea. She crossed to the couch where he sat and dropped down close to him. He could smell the freshness of her skin. She smiled at him, a new, queer smile that made him uncomfortable. "Steve, you're so swell—and so good-looking—" The smile faded, but her lips were still parted. Her voice dropped to a whisper: "Steve, Steve, can't you see how perfect it is? The folks won't be home for hours." She was all over him, her moist lips hunting his, her body close and demanding.

"Don't be such a stick. What's wrong about it? And, Steve, it's so wonderful!"

For a moment he stared, frozen and unbelieving. Then he was out of there, with the fragments of his dream clacking in time with his footsteps. Until he met Vicki, sixteen years later, he had never visited a "decent" girl again.

(Women are all rotten to the core. Remember Rose?)

And lastly, there was his jealous, possessive love for Vicki.

(She's mine. She's Mrs. Steve Lake. I'll hold her against all corners, damn it to hell!)

He was still standing transfixed at the bureau when Vicki came into the bedroom.

"Did you forget about Nick?" she asked. Her natural everyday tone brought him back to a sense of the present.

"By gosh, I did, at that," he said, with a tremendous effort which almost, but not quite, hid his inner turmoil. Vicki gave him a quick look.

"You're tired," she said. "I'll take him. I don't mind a sniff of fresh air."

"No, I'll go. It's still raining."

"Well, make it snappy, honey. Even great big cops get sniffles."

He didn't make it snappy. He allowed Nick to investigate curbstones, fire hydrants, even car fenders, in order to give Vicki time to get to sleep. He couldn't trust himself to talk—yet. His strategy worked. She was all but asleep when he came up, only rousing for a mumbled "G'night."

But there was no sleep in him. His mind shuttled back forth, now giving her the benefit of the doubt—

The gate attendant knows her from seeing her with me. Maybe he passed her in without tearing off the leaves of the badge, or maybe she forgot it and he let her through on sight— No, twice she had said, at six o'clock and just now, that she had used the badge. Well, he'd find out for himself—

He swung to the other extreme—

That's what comes of marrying a foreigner—okay, she's born here but her father's as European as the day he landed, I'll bet. What did it used to say in my school history book? "The French are a gay people, fond of women and light wines." All right, Viennese, then. Where's the difference? Probably worse and more of it with their voluptuous waltzes that'd heat up an Eskimo.

As the wakeful hours crept by, Steve's hurt began to harden into a grievance. Without actually believing Vicki guilty of anything worse than a petty lie (and a damned stupid one—look at her carelessness about the badge and the train times), she began to turn into an opponent, someone to catch out and show up, someone to use his superior cleverness to trip up. He would ask no questions; he would go about it his own way and bring her in and book her in his own good time. The fact that he was applying penal terms to a domestic crisis, escaped him completely.

More than that, the training of a lifetime—the primary principle of every peace officer's code, that a man is innocent until proved guilty—went down like a tenpin before the poison dart of suspicion.

V

In the morning, Steve bolted his breakfast, took the dog out and left the house with as little conversation as possible. He told himself to reserve judgment until he knew more, but last night's grievance was beginning to form a tight core of anger inside him, all the deadlier because his decent instincts fought against it.

At the door, Vicki asked him about his day off.

"Not a chance," he replied, "with this Lab killing in my lap."

"You boys ought to have a union," she railed. "Then they wouldn't dare snatch your day off away from you."

But as he rode down in the elevator, he asked himself if, under her apparent concern, there was not relief in her voice.

Once out of the house he threw off his private unease and lost himself in the welcome pressure of work. Before going to his own office, he rode down to Center Street. In a big bare basement room he found Drain with two policemen, one, a fat, jowly patrolman, the other a hard-mouthed plainclothes man. Evidently they had been giving the old laboratory searcher the "business," for they looked both weary and angry, while Drain himself looked shocking—dirty, tear-stained, exhausted.

"Hello, Cap," the patrolman said as Steve came in. "This dilly don't talk United States. Not a peep outa him. Maybe you can make him sing."

Drain shrank away with a terrified shriek:

"No! No! Please don't—"

Steve looked from Drain to the two men.

"Okay, boys," he said. "I'll take over." The two made for the door with alacrity. "And Hanson," Steve called after them. "Be a good guy and send in coffee for two, will you? I left without much breakfast."

The fat cop stared, then doused his surprise.

"Sure, Cap. Be comin' at you in a minute."

The door closed. Drain stood, scarcely breathing.

"Might wash your face over there, Drain," said Steve impartially. "You look kind of shot. Ought to be paper towels in that roller."

Drain's eyes widened. Then, on tiptoe, as if afraid to awaken the sleeping devil that might reside in this cop, too, he went and splashed cold water on his grimy, blotched face. From a pocket he pulled out a comb and ran it through his matted grey hair. By the time Hanson returned with two containers of sweetened and whitened coffee, Drain was almost presentable. He still looked fearful, but the hysteria was dying out of him.

"Sit down," Steve said negligently, leaning back in his own chair as if he had all day.

Drain slid into a hard chair.

"Better drink this stuff while it's hot," Steve went on. "Guess about all you can say for it *is* that it's hot."

Drain tried to sip the murky liquid, then gulped it in great restorative swallows. Steve watched him and smiled.

"Looks like you needed that," he remarked.

"I did, sir. And I thank you." There was an old-fashioned courtesy and dignity about him that struck a chord of sympathy in Steve. Drain reminded him a little of Vicki's gentle, unsuccessful father.

"Mustn't mind the boys," he said easily. "Sometimes they're a bit—impulsive—and work too hard at their jobs." Drain blinked nervously. "Now suppose you tell me a little about yourself."

"There's really nothing to tell, sir."

"How'd you get this job at the Lab? Pretty responsible post, I'd say."

"One of my old pupils recommended me."

"One of your—*pupils?*" Steve's eyebrows rose.

"You might not think it," said Drain in a low, shamed voice. "But I used to be professor of zoology at Clayton High School."

"That right?" Steve said politely, hiding his surprise. "What happened?"

"Ill health, sir. An obscure spleen disorder. I'm not blaming the System. They were patient and considerate—but continuous absences—I was dropped at last."

"I see. And then?"

"Many things, Captain. Druggist's assistant. Christmas card salesman. Even elevator man. My last position was guard at the Museum. That was where young Ellis ran into me. A good boy. One of my star pupils." A little pride trembled in the old voice. "He's one of the chief chemists at Atcheson now. He arranged for me to get the job of searcher. And a blessed relief it is. Light work. Not on my feet too much."

"Yes. Well. Now about Ferman. Naturally, as searcher, you saw him twice a day—"

"Oh, more than that, sir. He was very frugal and brought his lunch every day instead of using the Laboratory restaurant. I do the same myself, and we got into the way of eating together. I would make coffee on my little electric plate. It was very pleasant having a companion to eat with."

"Good. Then you'll have plenty to tell me about him."

In his earnestness, Drain's nervousness dropped away.

"But only good. Captain, I *know* boys and young men. Thousands of them passed through my hands. And I would stake my life that young Ferman was decent, honest and loyal. He never stole the missing document."

"What would you say if I told you that the Medical Officer reported last night that there were traces of adhesive tape on Ferman's thighs, indicating the way he smuggled out the chemical formula?"

"I can't believe it!" he exclaimed. "It's against nature. Ferman was a good boy."

"Possibly he felt he was *being* good in helping Communism along."

"He hated Communism, Captain."

"At least he told you so," Steve said dryly. "That's an old Red trick. I believe they call it dialectics."

"No, he didn't tell me so. But it seeped out in the course of talk—a righteous indignation against men who bask in the protection of the American Government even while knifing it in the back."

"What *were* his politics, do you know?"

"I don't, specifically. He was a very reticent boy. Never personal. What I know about him I gathered from generalizations or tone of voice."

"What sort of things did he like—theatre, music, sports?"

"None, I think. He was what you might call a *sad* young man."

"Just lately or during all the time you knew him?"

"Always—" He stopped and considered. "Wait. Yes. Lately—the past week, I would say desperately troubled."

"And he gave you no clue to the reason?"

"I never asked," said Drain simply. "A man is entitled to his privacy."

"But as searcher, guardian of the Laboratory secrets, wasn't it your solemn duty to be extra vigilant with a man showing such nervous tension?"

"I trusted him as fully as I ever trusted anyone. Even now I cannot believe he was guilty of theft and treason."

"Yet he was killed immediately after stealing the formula. Undoubtedly to shut him up, in case he got a change of heart and went to the authorities."

"It is a puzzle I cannot solve. The facts just don't fit."

"Do you know if he was contemplating a trip abroad?"

"I am sure he wasn't. He hated the thought of Europe. He once called it a cesspool infested by human maggots." Drain frowned in thought. "There *was* something, not long ago— Yes. He spoke of Alaska—and again of Tahiti—places with few people—with a kind of longing—" He stopped, his hand went to his mouth and his eyes widened. After a considerable pause he went on slowly, reluctantly: "Mind you, I still have complete faith in his integrity, but—"

"Yes?" Steve said very softly.

"Just last week he asked me—oh, very casually—but there was a certain stillness about him, if you know what I mean—"

"As if it was important," Steve amended.

"Exactly. He asked how one went about changing one's name legally."

"I see." Steve's eyes narrowed in thought, but he made no comment. "Now perhaps you can tell me something about his people?"

"He lived alone."

"I mean abroad. He received European mail. His parents or other possible relations?"

"He never mentioned anyone at all. But his dossier would show that. The Laboratory has complete files on all its employees. There is a day card with each worker's last place of employment and his references, and a more detailed record of his history in the extension files."

"Thanks. I'll look into that. Anything else you can tell me at all—any friend, any place he sometimes went to, anything that would make him less of a mystery figure?"

"Nothing I can think of now—"

"Well, if something does occur to you, tell Hanson you want to see me."

"You mean, sir, I am to be held here?" he asked in dismay.

"Not for long, I think. But it is not in my hands. It rests with the F.B.I."

Drain did not argue. He accepted the ruling with a pathetic docility.

"However," Steve added as he looked away from the old man's hopeless expression, "you won't be subjected to any more—er—questioning down here—I'll leave orders."

Drain achieved a watery smile.

"Thank you, Captain. I appreciate that."

Steve left Center Street and dropped into the F.B.I. office in Foley

Square, where he related what Drain had told him to Special Agent Rieger. The F.B.I. had been busy on its own. They had already investigated the extension files at Atcheson which Drain had mentioned. They had dug up a few meagre facts about Ferman. The dead man was American-born of Czech parents who had returned to Prague shortly after VE Day to visit a married daughter there. Leon Ferman had graduated from Erasmus Hall High School in Brooklyn, had gone to work for the Stevens Cable Company thereafter and was, by all visible standards, as unremarkable as a bowl of oatmeal.

The F.B.I. had practically taken over the case, with its involvement in espionage, enemy agent activity and subversive conduct angles. The murder was, of course, still in the hands of the Homicide Bureau, but it looked as if they were stymied until the Federal men turned up a lead to a definite spy ring.

Back in his own office, Steve sent Johnny to the Stevens Cable Company to gather any crumbs of information available. The Medical Examiner's laboratory on 28th Street was testing Ferman's garments, fingernails and the contents of his pockets for clues. Ballistics had identified the bullet which proved to be of foreign make from the Skoda Works.

On the Pinelli case, which Steve was also carrying, there were reports from Harry O'Neil and Detective Lamb, who were working on it, but nothing that required immediate action from Steve. With a wry expression he realized that there was nothing to keep him from his day off.

He was just leaving when Lieutenant Rand came in. With a meagre nod to Steve, just this side of disrespect, Rand went to the phone and ordered a Department car.

"How you doing, Rand? Any headway on your case?"

"Could be," he returned reticently. "I'll know more later."

Rand, carrying a gangster homicide independently, was not obliged to confide in Steve until he got up his official report, but it was usual for his men to discuss developments informally with Steve, getting the benefit of the Captain's experience and suggestions. Rand's answer was a slap in the face. Again, it crossed Steve's mind what a disruptive element Rand was in the office, but he had too many immediate pressures on his mind to do anything about it. He left the office and from a pay station called Vicki.

"Steve! You're getting your day off after all?" she exclaimed. Under her forced interest, he thought he read dismay.

"No such luck," he lied deliberately. "I just called to say that I don't know when I'll be through."

"Oh, try to be home by seven, Steve. It's Johnny's night for dinner."

"I'll do my best. You got any plans for the day?"

She gave a little trill of apologetic laughter.

"We—ell," she said, "I've got a last race ticket to cash from yesterday. I thought I'd go out and collect it."

"No hurry about your ticket. It's raining like the devil again."

"I told you I was good with mudders."

"Suit yourself. You going to drive?"

"No." She laughed again airily. "The train's good enough for us regulars."

"Okay. See you when I can."

He waited until one, to be sure the coast was clear. Then he went up to 81st Street and got into the parked Chevrolet. He tried to drive slowly through the splashing streets, but the gnawing devil in his heart pushed the little car to its limits. He reached Belmont Park at two o'clock. He went to the grandstand because he knew Vicki would go to the Clubhouse and he did not want her to see him. But he raked the Clubhouse with an eagle eye. It was an off day, due to the rain, the muddy track and the number of scratches, so that the crowd was comparatively small. If Vicki had been there, he should have been able to spot her easily. She was nowhere.

Finally he decided to go into the Clubhouse. On such a day she might be inside, either in the restaurant or the lounge. He could always make an excuse, say that he had salvaged a couple of hours of his day off, and had come out to join her. But if he could avoid a face-to-face meeting, it was much better. All he wanted was a glimpse of the unknown man whose attraction was so great that she had braved hell and high water to join him.

He scoured the Clubhouse. Vicki was not there.

By four-thirty he was back in his office, bewildered, baffled, in a black mood. The whole thing nagged him like a hangnail. He attacked some dull routine reports to keep his mind off the question. But the typing on the forms blurred before his eyes as he weighed what to do. Should he force a showdown, jockey her into a spot where she had to tell the truth? He ground his teeth. He was a brave man, he had risked his life numberless times, but he was deathly afraid of the truth Vicki might tell him.

At five, Jeff Rand strolled in and stopped at Steve's desk.

"How'd you make out?" he grinned.

Steve raised puzzled eyebrows without speaking.

"Don't give me that," Rand chuckled sardonically. "Hell, there ain't any rules against a man seeing a horse race on his day off."

"Oh!" Steve collected, his surprised wits. "For a minute I didn't get you. I didn't do any betting. I was just following up a thin lead."

"Why didn't you use a squad car?" The innocent friendliness on Rand's usually cynical face was maddening. It was as if the Lieutenant knew the whole nasty story and was needling him with relish. Of course, that was impossible. Nobody could know. Nevertheless, he would see about transferring Rand to East 67th Street. He didn't like him. But he said easily enough:

"What were you doing out there?"

"Same as yourself. Got a tip I might run into Red Varney at the track."

"Any luck?"

"Nope. Seems like Varney's still on the lam." He paused and then went on with what seemed to Steve to be slow, deliberate malice. "Trip wasn't wasted, though. Saw a couple of other people I didn't expect to run into."

A corded vein beat in Steve's temple. What was Rand driving at? Had he seen Vicki—and her companion? Where could she have been where he himself had missed her?

He dropped his eyes to his reports and Rand ambled on to his own desk. Fuming inwardly, Steve asked himself how Rand knew he was not using a squad car. Had he deliberately trailed him to the parking lot and watched him get into the Chevrolet? With a muffled curse he threw down his pencil, stuffed away his papers and left for the day.

He was not a drinking man, but he stopped in at the corner bar and had a double rye. It had about as much effect as a glass of water. As he got into the Chevrolet again he suddenly laughed out aloud. What a damned fool he was! Rand had seen the Chevy parked out front on 20th Street. All the boys knew the little coupe. Rand hadn't meant an earthly thing, except what he said. It was his own crazy suspicion, reading hidden meanings into simple statements. Rand couldn't help his dour face and glum manner. It was even understandable if he did have a sore feeling about the promotion four months ago. He was a good man, he had as much right to the Captaincy as Steve himself. If things had been reversed, maybe he'd be just as sore as Rand.

When he reached home, Vicki gave him the same pleased,

affectionate greeting as last night. She darted out of the kitchen, whence appetizing odors were drifting, to press her cool, soft lips to his and give him a quick little hug.

"Honey, you're lovely and early. Would you take Nick down? I can't leave this sauce or it'll stick."

Evenly, giving nothing away by his voice, he replied:

"Okay. Smells mighty good. Come here, hound. You're going to need your slicker."

Nick's tail went from violent wagging to a disconsolate droop. He hated the little raincoat. But he stood like a soldier while Steve buckled it on.

"There you are, young Nick. You're a gentleman and a scholar. Shouldn't be surprised if there was a dog biscuit going, when we get back upstairs."

While Nick enjoyed an unprecedented spell of delightful sniffing, Steve's mind was elsewhere. He asked himself if the thing was a mare's nest, if he was building up a structure that would fall at a touch—or a question. He could be wrong about the baked potatoes. Same thing with the badge. And he could have missed her in the Clubhouse. Why should he doubt her on such crazy, flimsy evidence? At least let him ask her point-blank and give her a chance to explain. All his training and professional career was founded on the principle of asking questions to get at the truth. This dodging away from a showdown was shadowboxing and bad medicine. He'd go right upstairs and have it out.

But instantly a new fact crossed his mind to deepen his suspicion and increase his resentment against her. Last night he had dropped into the apartment at six o'clock. Today, she had said she was going to the track to cash a last race ticket. If she had stayed long enough yesterday even to *buy* a ticket on the last race, she could never have made a train that would bring her home at six o'clock—to say nothing of having taken Nick for an airing as she had claimed. No two ways about it, she was lying, tangling herself in an ugly mesh of lies, until the moment came when she would convict herself by her own contradictions. In dozens of his cases he had trapped criminals by keeping them talking until they incriminated themselves out of their own mouths, just as Vicki was doing. Only in Vicki's case he didn't *want* her trapped, he shrank from finding her guilty.

But the cloud of small doubts was thickening into a miasma of malice. His inferiority complex, his insecurity as husband to so young and lovely a girl as Vicki, his panic jealousy that she was deceiving him, all pushed him towards a policy foreign and detestable to his intrinsic decency. When he came back upstairs, it drove him like some relentless force towards welding another link in the strangling chain.

He strolled into the kitchen, sniffed appreciatively at a pot, stole a radish camouflaged as a rose, and said casually:

"Say, what happened in the third race? The boys downtown had a bet on Seatag and they were all hopped up when it won. Then the foul claim came in over the radio. What did he do?"

She was half-turned away from him, but he saw the quickly controlled agitation of her rapid breath in the rise and fall of her breast and the squaring of her shoulders. But her voice was steady and assured: "He crossed the field and interfered with the favorite. I wish you'd taste this dressing and see if it's too lemony."

He felt sick. He *had* watched the race and nothing untoward had taken place. The name Seatag was a figment of his imagination. The fool! The stupid, lying little fool hadn't even covered herself by checking on the day's entries or results!

Deadpan, he tasted the salad dressing, said smiling:

"Tastes fine to me— Well, I'll go and wash up," and he left the kitchen. He walked blindly through the little apartment, and yet each room, each detail, registered with him. Everywhere there was evidence of Vicki's loving care and diligence. The simple mahogany furniture glowed like satin, mirrors sparkled, ash-trays were immaculate. The dining room table was set festively with gleaming glass and silver, with two tall candlesticks waiting to be lit. A curious duality took place in him: his spirit was nauseous with misery and shock, while his mind was commenting trivially that Vicki was a born housekeeper; funny, too, considering that she'd been a business girl; she really was one in a million— He sagged against the bathtub and hung on to the washstand. Vicki. *Vicki.* The only human being he had ever prized and loved. Lying, cheating—what was he going to do?

He hit the porcelain washstand a bruising blow with his fist. He was not going to give her up! But he'd tackle the man, by God!

He pulled himself together when Johnny arrived and played the host well enough to deceive the others. He mixed highballs for them all, and swallowed his own in two gulps. It helped fill the awful hollow in the pit of his stomach and loosened his tongue enough to mask his savage bitterness. He praised Vicki's shrimp Newburgh, bragged uxoriously at her talents as a home-maker, emphasized his luck at having such a wife, and then pulled up short, realizing he was making a chump of himself. The other two were eyeing him curiously.

"No fool like an old fool," he rapped out suddenly.

Vicki laughed and patted his hand.

"Steve, you got a head start on your way home," she accused, with a laugh. "One highball never made you all that proud of me."

"This show's for Johnny's benefit," he clowned. "I like married men on my team. If he sees what a happy couple we are—"

He didn't hear Johnny's light reply. The poison began to spread. *Had Johnny really been at the Stevens Company all afternoon?* He shot a glance at them; both young, handsome, pulsing with vitality. An ideal couple. Made for love. Johnny had always loved Vicki. Steve could swear to that. But the crazy kid had stepped aside when he saw that his hero, his idol, had fallen for the girl, too. Honest-to-God chivalry and self-sacrifice. But was it? Johnny was no hick. He was educated, sophisticated, he knew the score. *(Marry the old man, Vicki, you and I can take our fun on the side, it's got a marvelous kick when it's forbidden—)*

No, try as he would, he could not fit Johnny into that picture. Thievery, dishonesty, betrayal simply were not in the boy.

Who, then? he asked himself again.

VI

While Vicki cleared up, Steve suggested a game of checkers. It was better than talking. You could move stones from square to square and still go on batting your brain for the truth, for a hint of the unknown man. Johnny had won two games by the time Vicki came in and settled to her knitting.

Johnny leaned back in his chair, as if he had had enough checkers. "You know something, Steve?" he said. "We could be all wrong about Ferman."

"How do you mean?"

"Rieger's combing the Moscow outfit here. I don't think they figure."

"No? Why not?"

"Well, what have we got? This Ferman, a nobody, is picked for a tool. He's bribed to steal this top-secret formula. He does. He passes it on. Then he's killed to shut him up. Now, if he were a Commie in good standing, they wouldn't have to kill him, it would even be a waste of good material. They could use him again."

"Okay. So he isn't a Commie. Let's say he's working for Fascists. Why should *they* kill their own man?"

"That's just my point! The Commies may be behind this—probably are—but my idea is that Ferman wasn't one of them. He was coerced into stealing the stuff. Drafted by threats."

"He came and went as he pleased. One word to the head of the laboratory— And how do you fit in that four hundred dollars if he was threatened?" questioned Steve.

"Maybe it was passage money. Ferman was going to take the formula out, only for some reason they got leery of him and killed him instead. But forget that for a minute. Let's see what we've got on Ferman. Born of Czech parents in America. Killed by a Czech bullet from the Skoda Works. His parents returned since to Czechoslovakia. He was getting mail from there, his landlady said. Get it, Steve?"

"Sure. He's here, they're there. The old gag—do what we tell you or we liquidate your folks."

"That's it. Look at Czechoslovakia today. Torn in two with law-abiding Czechs overridden by a horde of Red vandals. Look what they did to Masaryk—and Benes, too, if you ask me—and how they bored into the police force and snatched the government. What chance would a decent Czech have to buck them if they held his family as hostages?"

"Could be, Johnny. And it ties in with Drain's story. That four hundred bucks could be Ferman's own money, drawn out to buy passage for his folks *to* America. And that talk of his about Alaska and Tahiti and changing his name—once he stole the formula and got his folks here safe, he was lighting out where they couldn't put the bee on him again."

Vicki had stopped knitting and was leaning forward in her chair, listening with interest.

"It all fits," Johnny nodded. "The Nazis were whizzes at that hostage stuff and the Reds learned fast. They did it in Canada, we know. They use non-Commies for two good reasons. First, because they're above suspicion and not so carefully watched; second, why risk the life of a nice fellow traveler when you can use a stinking Capitalist?"

"It may hang together, but it sure makes it tough for us. It knocks out tracing Ferman to a subversive group here. Whoever gave him his orders and later killed him, after collecting the formula, probably contacted him only once, maybe even by phone. Those rats are leery of showing their faces. So where do we go from here?"

"I don't know, Steve. But it clears the underbrush away. If we're right, we know *how* it was worked, even if we're in the dark about who worked it."

"Wait—maybe we *can* go a step further. That formula has to get out of the country. If Ferman wasn't taking it, they have to get somebody else to do it. Ferman's not the only poor sucker on their list, you can bet. They forced somebody to smuggle out that Toledo laboratory formula a year ago."

"What does that get us?"

"Leave it to Rieger. He'll finecomb outgoing boats and laboratory personnel, he can even check on Czechs here with connections over there—"

His eyes fell on Vicki. She was no longer listening. Her brows were drawn together in a puzzled frown. Steve went on:

"Come out of the brown study, Vicki. How's for a cold bottle of beer?"

She started, came back to her surroundings and rose.

"No wonder you're thirsty," she said. "Don't you boys ever stop talking shop?"

"Last night you were hell-bent it was your right to know about my cases. Now you get a taste, you gripe."

She laughed.

"You wouldn't expect me to be logical, too, Steve? Along with all those wonderful things you said I was at dinner. Give me credit for one or two little failings! Johnny, beer for you, too?"

"Yes, thanks."

When she came back with the beer, Steve had the radio on. He had struck a station where a book critic forum was discussing a recent best seller.

"I maintain," the radio was saying, "that Mr. Cosgrove's premise is wrong. And, therefore, his whole book is fallacious. Show me a man in real life who forgives a wife's infidelity, and you show me—not a hero, not the salt of the earth as Mr. Cosgrove insists—but a poor fish or, as in this case, a cardboard saint constructed at a typewriter."

"Just a minute," came a second voice. "Aren't you ignoring the possible nobility of a man who places his wife's happiness before his own?"

"Mr. Ross, may I compliment you on your high estimate of human nature?" said the first voice ironically.

"Piffle," said Steve and clicked off the radio.

"Oh, Steve, leave it on," said Vicki. "It sounds interesting."

"What's interesting about it?" he grated. The subject flicked him on the raw.

"Well, where would the Book-of-the-Month be without it?" Johnny laughed. "Nothing like a lovely little erring wife to increase sales."

"Just another way of saying how rotten human nature is," Steve rasped.

"Not necessarily rotten, honey," Vicki said judiciously. "People sometimes change and develop—what suited them five years ago fails to suit them now."

"So, in that case, let 'em foul their nest and shack up with anybody that takes their eye," Steve sneered.

"No, of course not, silly. All I'm saying is it's an interesting question. And, at that, there might be cases where infidelity isn't the worst thing in the world—"

"Mrs. Lake, don't tell me you've gone freedom-of-the-libido!" Johnny kidded.

"Stop it, Johnny! I mean it's a serious social problem and it ought to be *dealt* with as a problem—not as a crime."

"You won't find many husbands to agree," Johnny grinned.

"Then it's time a few husbands changed," she came back. "I can imagine situations—"

"So can I!" Steve snapped. "And there's just one way to deal with 'em."

"Well, really, Oliver Cromwell," Vicki laughed. "What's your one way?"

"Extermination."

"He *is* a Pilgrim Father, at that," Johnny chuckled. "What would extermination get you?"

"The satisfaction of knowing there's one less skunk in the world."

"*One* less? Do me a favor, go the whole hog and knock 'em both off."

"The woman might pay heavier by being kept alive."

"Steve Lake, if I thought you actually meant such rot—" began Vicki. Steve caught himself up and managed a wide, mechanical grin.

"Yeah, you're right," he said. "I shoot off my mouth but what does it add up to? No woman alive's worth sticking your neck in a noose. How's for a little three-handed gin rummy?"

After Johnny left, Vicki, clearing away beer bottles and glasses, paused, set the tray down and said:

"Steve, sit down a minute. I want to talk to you."

Automatically, defensively, he shied away from it. "It's late. Save it."

"No. It's important."

He stared at her in a blue funk. She was on to it, that he was wise to her. Trust a guilty woman to sense it, pick it right out of the air. That spiel of his about extermination threw a scare into her. God forbid that her rotten, stinking lover might get hurt! He was a fool to have tipped his hand like that. What was happening to him, anyway, to spill his guts like a jealous teenager? She was quick as a whip, she had caught it and was trying to beat him to the draw. He was damned if he was going to listen to a line about finding her soul mate and appealing to his chivalry. He could name the fancy words she would work off on him—generosity, magnanimity, et cetera, et cetera. He wasn't having any.

"It'll keep," he said with an ostentatious yawn.

"Steve, please. It's not easy but it's something I've got to tell you—"

"The dog's sniffing at the door." He walked out of the room.

When he came back upstairs, she was already in bed with the light out. He threw off his clothes in the bathroom and felt his way to his own bed. He lay, tense as a watch spring, silent, and poisoned by bitterness. After a long time, Vicki said:

"Steve?"

He did not stir.

"Steve, you know you're not asleep. You've got to listen to me."

He threw his answer at her savagely:

"Will you shut your trap and *let* me sleep? I'm a working man. Remember?"

"But this is—"

"Important. Sure. Sure. I know all about it. And I don't want to hear it. What d'you think of that?"

He turned his back with finality.

But the hours crawled by without a hint of sleep.

Savage, sore, vindictive and uncertain, he lay, his mind a treadmill, his thoughts jaded nags, circling wearily. He would have staked his life on her honesty and she had betrayed him. Why? There was only one answer.

He turned on his side, and looked at her in the other bed. She was asleep now and there was enough light from the street to make out her relaxed, innocent pose. One arm was flung across the pillow, her fingers half-curled. Her dense, dark lashes lay like fans on the childish curve of her cheek. The soft, firm chin was outlined against the pillow. One small, impertinent breast had escaped the V of her nightdress. The sight of it complicated his misery with desire. He wanted to take her, suddenly, brutally, without the restraints he had always imposed upon himself. Maybe that was the trouble; his lovemaking had been too scrupulous, too considerate. He had always approached her diffidently. He had felt that she was so young, so artless, that he ought to go carefully. But he knew now that she was not artless, she had schemed and lied, slyly if not skillfully. Perhaps her demure acceptance of his curbed passion was a blind, hiding a desire for fulfilment which he had not given her. Perhaps she ached, as he ached now, for the wild measure of ecstasy that lay in complete abandon and union.

He found himself upright at the edge of his bed, impelled to wake and take her in the full flood of passion. But, in the very moment of action, the echo of her words, spoken earlier, stopped him:

"There are worse things than infidelity."

His desire died. What did he want with an unwilling woman—a woman with her thoughts on another man? The hard core of anger in him petrified still further. This Steve Lake, tense and unreasoning, at the edge of his bed, was poles apart from the Steve Lake of yesterday.

VII

In the morning, this new Steve Lake persisted. But he was no longer bedeviled and racked. A cool, nerveless patience pervaded him. He had a job to do and he would go about it with the impersonal competence he gave to all his cases. He would not be precipitous, he would collect his evidence and build his case before taking action against his suspect. He gave Vicki no chance to reopen the subject of the "important" thing she wanted to tell him. He got out of the house fast.

This false calm endured at the Bureau. He accomplished a mountain of detail work, quickly and efficiently.

But Jeff Rand eyed the deep parentheses that ran from Steve's nostrils to the corners of his mouth with speculative eyes. In the back room, he whispered to Schneer:

"What's eating the Big Shot?"

"Whadda y'mean? I didn't notice anything."

Rand grinned sardonically.

"You wouldn't. But then you haven't made a study of him like me. You know something? The guy interests me."

When Steve went out at lunch hour, Rand waited a minute and then lounged out, too.

Steve ate no lunch. He took the subway uptown and got out at 79th Street. He walked warily up to his own block, ready to dodge into a doorway at an instant's notice. The Chevrolet was still parked near his entrance where he had left it last night. He started it up, backed it down the block about sixty yards and squeezed into a forbidden space in front of a fire hydrant. He was well screened by the cars in front and behind him. He turned off the motor. He pulled his hat low over his eyes and waited. It was twelve-forty.

The street was full of children, returning after the noon recess to P.S. 9 on 82nd Street. The door of Steve's building opened incessantly, and each time he held his breath in unwilling suspense. His eyes bored into the entrance to spot her instantly, but his mind and hopes were pushing her back with figurative muscles. He was avid to see her and burning not to.

At twelve-fifty, Vicki came out. Not hurriedly, but with the purposefulness of a known destination. She wore the same little blue dress with the white collar and cuffs and carried a white plastic handbag. No binoculars, although Steve had an excellent pair upstairs. As she turned unhesitatingly towards Broadway, Steve started up his motor. He let her cross the street before he pulled out of the parking place. He did not wish to overshoot the mark and get ahead of her. He saw her turn south on Broadway. It looked as if she were heading for the subway. Was she going to the track after all, to cross the trail with a red herring? That stuff at bedtime last night, something "important" to tell him. Sure, she knew he was wise to her. She figured he'd tail her today, so, like a shifty little fox, she was leading him straight out to Belmont to watch her make innocent two-dollar bets. There had probably been a long telephone confab this morning between her and her boyfriend, and they'd decided to lay low for a while. In that case, he was wasting his time, and he might just as well go back to 20th Street and earn his salary.

The traffic light turned green for east and west. Steve drove across Broadway and turned south. Vicki was standing at the corner of 80th Street at the bus stop. He pulled over to the right and waited, double parked, his motor idling. The Broadway bus which turns east at 42nd Street, didn't go within nine blocks of Penn Station where the race trains started. Wherever she was going, it was not to the track.

A southbound bus came along and Vicki boarded it. Steve swung in behind and trailed it. Acridly, he told himself that the chase would probably end at a department store, with Vicki innocuously buying kitchen towels, leaving him to stew in his own juice. But she wouldn't get away with it, he decided stonily. If it took all year, if he lost his job for unexplained time off to tail her day after day, he'd catch her with the goods. Vicki was his. And what he owned, nobody was going to take away from him. Not without paying. Paying in full.

At Columbus Circle she alighted and made her way east on 59th Street. Steve, taken by surprise, swung left after her, suspicious and grim. Horns sounded in protest behind him as he crept along, taking care not to catch up with her. He didn't even hear them, as he drove automatically, his eyes hardly leaving the slim blue figure ahead.

With the sureness of habit, Vicki turned into one of the lofty, palatial buildings which line Central Park South. Cornwall House. The place had a famous, much-advertised cocktail lounge. No doubt she and her unknown lover used it as a tryst, had a drink or two to promote the right mood, before— He could not bring himself to finish that thought. Instead, with an utter disregard of traffic regulations he made a U-turn and swung the car into the only free space on the Park side of the street—before another fire hydrant. One of the compensations of being a cop, he thought cynically; shadowing made easy. Three days ago he would not have dreamed of taking advantage of his position in even so small an infraction of the law.

He crossed the street to Cornwall House. Beside the main entrance, a smaller door led into the cocktail lounge. He took that, pausing in the tiny foyer. Above all things, he must not show himself, but equally, above all things, he must see the man she was meeting. If he stood in the little foyer, to one side of the arch that opened into the bar, he could not miss them as they came in at the opposite side from the lobby of the hotel.

The bar was noisy with the pre-lunch crowd, a well-dressed, smart company, full of chat and laughter. But Vicki was not yet among them. Either her man was late or they were wasting a minute or two in greeting and talk before making for the bar.

Directly opposite the arch where Steve stood, was another one, leading into the lobby of Cornwall House. He raised his eyes to that, to await her appearance.

His heart jolted. Vicki, her back to him, was framed in its borders. She was one of a group, standing before the bank of elevators which served the tenants. Even as he watched, an elevator came down, debauched its passengers and took on a new load. His jaw dropping, he saw Vicki step in with the rest of the waiting group and vanish, as the elevator slid shut and rose.

The thing took the wind out of him. He discovered suddenly that up to this moment he had not fully believed in Vicki's treachery. His own passionate desire to retain the status quo and his subconscious faith in Vicki's integrity had combined to give unreality to his suspicion and his pursuit. He knew now that he had been trailing her, *not* to find her guilty, but to uncover an innocent explanation for her dubious actions. Last night he had persuaded himself that his grimness, his resolve, his expressed view, "extermination," had been sincere, but, until this moment, the thing had been artificial, a game, a bad dream.

He found himself back in the Chevrolet, clutching the wheel with a grip that whitened his knuckles. He didn't remember how he got there. With gritted teeth, he told himself he had to be calm, he had to relax, reason the thing out and lay his plans.

The night before, his thoughts of an affair between Vicki and some man had been shadowy, vague, theoretical. But the sight of her in an actual hotel, going up in an elevator to a definite apartment with furniture, with a view of the Park, with a specific bedroom, gave a concreteness to the situation which brooked no more delay.

He forced himself to examine the circumstances as impersonally as he had handled any of his cases. The first fact to be considered was Cornwall House itself. It was a twenty-two-story building, a hostelry of first-class reputation and service. While transients could, on rare occasions, stop there for a night, it catered almost entirely to a rich and prominent clientele of permanent guests who rented suites, not rooms. Hollywood stars, directors and executives, on from the Coast for a few weeks, used Cornwall House as often as they used the Waldorf. Some of them kept apartments there all year round, even though they might not spend one week in fifty-two in it. In such cases, the suites were often occupied for months at a time by relations or friends of the moguls, who lent them living quarters instead of coin of the realm. The most famous song writer in America lived there; the heir to a fabulous fortune had closed his Fifth Avenue mansion, one of the last relics of the Astor-Vanderbilt-Gould era, and occupied half a floor at Cornwall House. Wall Street magnates, presidents of leading industries, Metropolitan Opera stars lived there, with or without their families, some relying on the hostelry's famous cuisine, some keeping house with their own staff of domestic servants.

Who, in that fabulous setup, could have met Vicki, could have reached such terms of equality with her, that she stepped into the building with the easy assurance of one of themselves? He thought instantly of her peculiar schooling. At the Lacey Academy, where Max Braun taught and where Vicki had been educated, she had known dozens of top-drawer socialites and called them by their first names. Steve and Vicki had occasionally run into one of them, on the street, at the races, at the ball game. They were too established at the top of the ladder to be snobs. They greeted Vicki cordially and naturally. Well, those dames had brothers, Steve reasoned. A young pup who had met Vicki when she was sixteen or so might have made it his business to keep up with her. Or, if he had happened to run into her after a lapse of years, might have made time with her to good effect. Who?

Cornwall House, he estimated, might house two hundred or more tenants. How in God's name was he going to locate the particular suite where Vicki was visiting and, far more important, the occupant of the suite?

It was an insuperable problem, for one cogent reason: Steve Lake, Captain of Homicide could stride up to the august desk clerk and demand a list of tenants, could even canvass the suites themselves and on some trumped-up excuse search every room in the building. Or he could confer with the house detective and request that a small, pretty girl in a blue dress with white collar and cuffs be shadowed to her destination and the information be transmitted to 20th Street. It was child's play. There was practically no fact that Steve could not run down in the name of the law.

But here he was not acting in the name of the law. For the first time in his life he had jumped the fence separating the guardians of peace from the violators of law and order. He wanted the name of Vicki's host with a voracity that consumed him, but a cloud of private motives gave him craft. When he discovered who his enemy was he intended to deal with him as he saw fit. But this was a personal affair. Pride, ego, hurt vanity demanded that the world should catch no glimpse of dirty linen.

He could ask no questions. He could not detail any man under him to investigate for him. He had no stomach for either ridicule or sympathy. The thing had to be done by him alone, and with the utmost secrecy.

There were one or two feeble, approximate checks he could make on Cornwall House. At Headquarters, he could go into the Record Room where a list of the city's voters was filed, building by building. But that was far from satisfactory. There was such a large floating population of non-voters in Cornwall House, from the Coast, from the motor industry in Detroit, and so on, that his list would be fragmentary. And even if it were fairly complete, what would it be? Just a list of names. How would he know which name was to be ringed with red and marked for punishment?

Another device would be to take up his stand, day after day, in the tiny foyer of the bar, which commanded the bank of elevators. Someday, by the law of averages or a lucky coincidence, Vicki would be the only passenger in the ascending elevator. When it made its one stop to let her out, Steve could note the floor on the mechanical contrivance above the ground floor elevator door. That would narrow down the field of operations, he could secrete himself on that particular floor and check which suite she entered.

He threw that out immediately. It entailed showing his face in the bar foyer to in- and outgoing customers, to the bartender, to the elevator man, if he rode up, or the house dick, if he made for the stairs. Steve knew in what suspicion stair-climbers were held in the minds of hotel detectives. Besides, the strategy was too damnably slow. In his mood of devouring jealousy he wanted to tear the huge building apart, he wanted to lay bare those two in their shameless treachery. And he wanted to do it now. He could not brook days of patient watching such as he employed on cases he carried.

The demoralized state of his mind was evident from the expedients that occurred to him: he played with the idea of disguise, overalls, make-up, a dirty face and down-brushed hair. While Vicki was still in the building, he could gain entry to door after door, in the guise of electrician or telephone lineman. His professional training and private common sense discarded it almost instantly. Even if he could slip by the watchful eyes in the lobby or the service entrance, dozens of tenants would be out and, therefore, would not answer his ring. And if he knew anything at all, he told himself with a violent curse, Vicki and her lover would answer no doorbell if the skies fell. A canvass of the building would leave him just where he was.

At long last he reverted to the method that had proved successful many times in his work. He would stick to his post, wait until Vicki came out of the building and then, catching her dead to rights, take her home and sweat the truth out of her. In his tortured savagery he hoped she would hold out against him for a little while. The new-born sadism which her betrayal had aroused in him itched to bruise the soft apricot bloom of her flesh.

He settled down for a long, grueling wait.

Jeff Rand, over the wall on a park bench, yawned and lit another cigarette.

VIII

For hours Steve sat at the wheel of his car, inattentive to the passage of time. He did no conscious, organized thinking, but occasionally small, clear-cut pictures, vignettes of his arid life, rose unbidden to his sore mind. He saw again the West Bronx flat of his boyhood. It was clean and decent. But when you said that, you said all. There was not one vestige of the small, gracious, unnecessary touches which turn a house into a home. There was no money for it. His father's wages as subway motorman constituted a bare living. What painful pennies could be scraped together over and above the cost of food and shelter had been earmarked for Steve's brother Joseph. To Steve's mother, the dream of having a son in holy orders took the place of clothes, diversion, rest and even love. She sacrificed herself joyfully, but she sacrificed Steve, too. She lost sight of his necessities and rights as a normal, pleasure-loving child. To her, he was a weapon in the forging, to storm the gates of her dream. Steve could hardly go back to a time when the chance of earning a nickel, at his mother's instigation, had not clashed with some game in the corner lot—and won out. He was an obedient boy and never complained aloud, but a small core of bitterness and jealousy grew up in him, against his brother, against favoritism, against life.

His case was curiously parallel to Vicki's and Paul Braun's, but where Vicki *gave* with open hands, Steve had *paid* with an inward grudge. This early memory colored Steve's attitude towards the setup in the Braun household. Paul irritated him as his brother Joseph had irritated him for accepting all sacrifices with a kind of greedy serenity.

Steve's mother might have cleared up the situation if she had been more perceptive; she might, with a few words, have won Steve to a willing cooperation in her zeal, but Bessie Lake was no psychiatrist, no student of fixations. She was a hard-worked, uncomplaining plodder, with her eyes on a star. The result for Steve was two-fold: a complex of inferiority with an inevitable jealousy; and a ready-made creed that not only did you have to rely on your own unaided efforts to get anything you wanted, but you had to fight tooth and nail to hold it.

The afternoon shadows lengthened. The buses that lunged by were beginning to be overcrowded with homecoming workers. The monument at Columbus Circle was bathed in a soft, pre-sunset haze. Steve sat on, as immovable as a part of the car. He did not even glance at his watch. His eyes never swerved from the wide, handsome entrance to Cornwall House. He thought that to the end of his days, the memory of that twenty-foot area would be clear in his mind to the last detail: the impressive doorman, grey-headed and grey-uniformed, with his ceremonious air as he wafted outgoing guests into taxis; the line of taxis themselves, new and shiny (no creaking, disreputable vehicles for Cornwallers); the occasional super-smart luggage brought out by bell-boys; the guests themselves, not so different in clothing or looks from the rest of humanity, but yet with their peculiar aura of being something special in a special world.

Vicki appeared in the doorway. Steve half rose to dash out of the car, then fell back, frozen with shock. She was not alone. A tall man, with a hand on her elbow, was guiding her across the sidewalk. He was well-dressed to the point of dandyism, yet his clothes bore individual touches that set them apart from the standard of mere fashion. His lapels were a bit wider, his coat a bit longer, his pockets a bit larger. He wore no hat and his longish, grizzled hair swept back from bow to nape in artfully careless ripples. In his left hand he carried a cigarette fixed into an absurd twelve-inch-long holder.

The man was Janno Slevna. Steve recognized him instantly from the pictures he had seen in Max Braun's home. Slevna's well-cut features, dissipated and slightly raddled, were as familiar to Steve as if he knew the man personally. The down-slant of the tired eyes, the massaged puffs below them, the full, mobile lips, were unmistakable. His handsome head was bent towards Vicki, and she was looking up at him, her grave face a mixture of admiration and anxiety.

Steve sat paralyzed, as from concussion. Slevna! A man years older than himself, a worn-out, dirty lecher! And Vicki! In all his mental writhings and imaginings, the idea of Slevna had not once crossed his mind. Dozens of times, Vicki had expressed a worshipful longing to meet the great man, but (according to her) she never had. Only Paul, it seemed, had ever penetrated the sacred circle. Max and Vicki had had to be content with the crumbs of manna which Paul brought home from the august presence.

And now—this.

At a beck from the doorman, a taxi slid smoothly forward and half hid the two on the sidewalk. A car door slammed. As Steve sat, numb, nailed to his seat, the two got in; the taxi pulled away and disappeared.

Steve never knew if it was five minutes or two hours that he sat on in the Chevrolet, stupefied, insensible to the life around him, as motionless as the steering post. He was as completely knocked out as if he had sustained a deadly uppercut. As a matter of fact it was close to an hour during which he sat, his eyes out of focus, his ears deaf, his mind eclipsed.

Habit brought him out of it. His hands, acting without apparent bidding from his brain, fumbled in his pocket and brought out a cigarette. They engineered the lighting of it and directed it to his mouth. After a drag down to his toes, Steve exhaled, shook his head like a dog after a ducking, and then came back to realities.

He had a dull, heavy pain in his chest, as if he had been hit over the heart with a hammer—as indeed he had been. The whole abominable truth swept over him like a suddenly flashed motion picture. Terrible images etched themselves on his mind. He saw Slevna's hands, those beautiful, trained wizards that produced ineffable melody, slipping experimentally inside Vicki's blue dress, closing round her little breast, that impertinent little breast which had excited him last night almost to ravishing her. Almost! Like a damned fool he had controlled himself, had respected her youth and innocence. Innocence! She was about as innocent as Rose, who had thrown herself at him, drooling and ruttish. He saw Vicki, standing before Slevna, while he inspected her firm flesh in the hope of getting an impetus from its fresh youngness. He saw Slevna's full lips travelling over that lovely, blooming body, the body of Vicki—Vicki, who was his, Steve Lake's and nobody else's, by God!

With a violent effort he crushed down his mounting rage and summoned back the nerveless, practical manhunter with a job to do. As if Vicki were an utter stranger to him, he asked himself coldly, callously:

"What have I got?"

He enumerated, much as if he were making a report to his superior officer:

(1) The first faint doubt on Monday as to how she could get a train home from Belmont early enough for baked potatoes to be ready by 6 p.m.

(2) The unused badge in the bureau drawer.

(3) The mention of the "last-race ticket" which clinched it that she couldn't have taken the train and been home at six.

(4) The fact that she wasn't at the track on Tuesday when he looked for her.

(5) The downright lie about the imaginary horse "Seatag" and the foul claim which never happened.

(6) Her remark last night that there are worse things than infidelity.

(7) Her panicky attempt Tuesday night to confess as soon as she realized he was on to her.

(8) Her practiced entry into Cornwall House, where she remained from one to five.

(9) And to top it all, her brazen exit from the place in Slevna's company, her worshipful attitude towards him and her going off in a taxi with him.

What more did he want? He didn't have to see them in bed to know what it added up to. It was open and shut.

There were other things, too—not facts, but indications that bolstered the facts as firmly as sandbags. For instance, on Monday night when he asked her if she had driven to the track, he remembered now that she had begun to nod, then thought better of it and said she had used the train. Again, her concern as to whether he was getting his day off yesterday and her relief when he said he wasn't: relief that she wouldn't have to spend the afternoon with him and was free to meet Slevna. That stuff Monday night about Slevna keeping up Paul's lessons. How did she put it?— "Slevna says there are more ways of repaying him than in dollars." Damn right there were, he thought savagely, grinding his teeth.

He relaxed his iron grip on his passions and allowed them full play. His rage mounted to an animal ferocity, more terrible because it was cold as a glacier; his brain froze to a useless patch of hate. He lost all reason in an icebound obsession for revenge. There was no agitation in him. He was a tiger, stalking prey, still as death until the final ravening pounce.

A good cop is, before all things, law-abiding himself. Steve was a superlatively good cop. It was second nature to him to obey orders, observe rules and respect the rights of others. And though he dealt exclusively with violent death, and had occasionally had to kill a criminal in the line of duty, the idea of murder had always been utterly foreign and abhorrent to him. His hatred of killers had made him their relentless pursuer, because he believed no man had the right to take another's life. If he did so, it was just and necessary for him to pay with his own. Neither in premeditated cold blood nor in emotional frenzy was there any excuse for a man who killed. The stuff last night about extermination had been just words, a safety valve blowing off angry steam.

Now, his values, his beliefs, his basic nature suffered an explosive upheaval. It was as if a subaqueous bulldozer had churned the bed of a mountain lake. Where before had been a smooth, blue, lovely surface was now a filthy, stinking quagmire of slime and sewage. His mind was closed to morals, to reason, to decency. The only thing that figured with him was to kill Slevna and get away with a whole skin.

Johnny and Vicki would not have recognized this new Steve who let himself into his apartment at seven o'clock.

IX

The apartment was empty except for Nick. On the foyer table lay a hastily scrawled note:

> Steve, honey, for once I hope you're late. I had to go over to Dad's. There's plenty of stuff in the icebox just in case. I took Nick for a minute, but no luck. So if you get home before I do, give him a run. Be seeing you.—V.

A bitter grin curled his mouth. She had to go over to Dad's! The rotten little tramp. Hadn't he seen her drive off with Slevna, probably to some night spot for dinner? They'd be hungry after their bedroom orgy.

He took the dog down, walked him scrupulously, without seeing or knowing what he did. He re-entered the self-service elevator, pressed the correct button, used his key on his front door, released Nick from the leash, all mere reflexes of his lower nerve centers.

Upstairs, he began pacing the living room, unaware of the movement, of his surroundings, of the dog's troubled eyes on him. His whole being flung itself forward towards Cornwall House to the project which was the only thing that existed, which excluded everything else in his consciousness.

The glacier chill which had enveloped him earlier persisted. There was no excitement in him. All his mental processes, his reasoning, his actions, were cool, cautious, logical. He developed an inventiveness beyond his natural temperament and let it guide him.

His first action was to call the Cornwall House on the phone. When he was connected, he said in a businesslike tone:

"This is the Manhattan Delivery Service. We have a package for Mr. J. Slevna at your address. Our driver reports that he tried twice to deliver it this afternoon, but was unable to do so. Does Mr. Slevna live there?"

"Why yes," the operator replied. "I can't understand—you could have left it with the package room clerk."

"I believe this was marked to be delivered personally and required Mr. Slevna's signature. Perhaps the driver had the wrong apartment. Our slip says 731."

"Just a minute and I'll check." After a short pause, the operator continued: "That was the trouble. Mr. Slevna's apartment is 512."

"I see. Thank you. We'll get it up there in the morning." He hung up.

Apartment 512. His lips twitched triumphantly. So it was as easy as that to locate his quarry. Now, the next step. Captain Lake of Homicide, possibly known to the house detective or other personnel of Cornwall House, had to reach apartment 512 without being observed. Even if he were not personally known, he could not afford to show himself. His appearance was distinctive enough to be remembered, his stony features, his bright cold blue stare, his lean greyhound carriage. The lobby of the hotel was definitely out.

There remained the service entrance. Some time during the long vigil on 59th Street that afternoon, there had impressed itself on his mind the narrow ramp and passageway beside the building marked "Delivery Entrance." Steve, in his well-cut business suit, would be instantly noted and remembered if he attempted admittance there, even if he carried a package and made a plausible explanation. That, too, was out.

Unless—

Again he submitted himself to the faculty which had led him to phone Cornwall House. The faculty—as effective as an inspired general—laid a plan before him, simple, complete and workable.

All members of the Force buy their own uniforms and keep them, even after they are transferred to the plainclothes branches of the service. On occasion, as for instance, at the time of a big parade, when a reserve force is required to handle the crowds, the plainclothes men don their discarded outfits and join the uniformed members of the Force. Again, a plainclothes man never knows whether he will be reduced to ordinary service and be back in uniform tomorrow.

Steve's guiding spirit nudged him slyly:

"Remember that murder yarn where a dozen people swore nobody entered the house? They all forgot the postman. He was so usual, not one of 'em actually 'saw' him. Get into your uniform."

He did—with many crafty refinements. He wound a folded sheet round and round his lean belly and fastened it to his shirt. Under his tunic it gave him a burly girth. He tore the sweatband out of his visored patrolman's cap, so that it was large enough to sink down, hiding his thick waving hair and forcing his ears away from his head, making a surprising, almost comic change in his appearance. Lastly he removed the denture bearing the two artificial front teeth which replaced those sacrificed in his engagement with Smike Lonergan. His upper lip sank in, further altering his expression and added a lisp to his enunciation when he spoke. He pocketed a bunch of keys, a tiny flashlight and his gun. He was ready.

He used the stairs instead of the elevator, so that he could wait in the protective darkness of the last landing until the coast was clear. He met nobody either in the front hall or on the way to the Chevrolet. He drove over to Fifth Avenue and parked the car near 61st Street and sauntered to Cornwall House.

He still strolled as he went down the ramp beside the building, but once out of sight of the street, he broke into a deliberate run, with the appearance of a man in hot pursuit of another. He dashed through a door into a dimly lit basement and nearly bowled over a man in the act of rolling out a tall can of ashes.

"See a man run in here?" Steve panted. "Little guy with black hair?"

The man straightened up with slow reflexes.

"I see nobody at all," he said with Norwegian stolidity.

"You been here all the time?"

"In and out. Bane getting out the ashes."

"Could you have missed him?"

"Maybe, if he come yust while I am in furnace room."

Steve brushed him aside and dashed up the flight of steep stairs. Just so, in a real crime hunt, he would have taken it as his right to go where he pleased without question. As he ran, he called back:

"Keep your eyes open. Grab him if he comes down again."

He found himself on the fire stairs, closed off from the front of Cornwall House by a heavy steel door. Very faintly strains of music from the famous Titian Room orchestra seeped through. He was on the ground-floor level. He began to count as he mounted the flights of stairs. He stepped quietly but he could have made all the noise he wanted. When he reached the fifth door, he paused and with infinite care opened the fire door an inch. He was right at the back of the building, facing a long, wide corridor which bisected the floor, with two rows of white doors stretching away towards a cross-corridor at the other end. It was well lighted. He could see on the nearest door a silver number: 563. He had to traverse that endless expanse to reach 512. Trust Slevna, he sneered, to be right at the front with a view of the Park. His high-minded, spiritual temperament couldn't stomach the sight of shabby roofs. He had to have inspiration, a beautiful panorama for his noble thoughts and acts.

He broke off, warned by the guiding force which had directed him so far to keep the thing impersonal, a chore to be done, without rancor or bias.

A couple rounded the corner of the cross-corridor, and came halfway down the hall where they paused at the elevators; an exquisitely dressed woman with her neutral escort. The elevator came up and they vanished into it. Nobody got out. The coast was temporarily clear.

Steve slipped through the fire door and covered the ground at a swift pace, eyeing the door numbers as he went. The long corridor ended with 534. He peered around the corner before he turned right. The cross-corridor was empty, too, but the first door he struck read 532. He sprinted across to the left of the main hall—526. He kept moving left to the very end of the cross-corridor. At the corner, 512 stared down at him, white and blank.

He wasted no time. He whisked out his bunch of keys and, with delicate, precise care, tried one skeleton key after another in the lock. He worked silently and fast, but the time seemed endless as he stood, his back to the corridor, vulnerable to any passing inmate or visitor. The sweat was pouring down from under the visor of his cap, but his hands were as steady as rocks.

The fourth key caught, held and turned smoothly. With infinite caution, he opened the door a few inches and peered in. The small foyer was dark. Noiselessly he slipped inside, closed the door behind him and stood, silent as a wraith, sizing up the situation.

Even when his eyes adjusted themselves from the well-lit outside corridor to the dimness of the apartment, the whole place seemed dark. Apparently it was empty. But he dared not accept any such easy premise without careful investigation. Perhaps, behind a closed door, there were lights and human occupants to constitute a danger. A man of Slevna's importance would live on a nearly regal scale, there would be servants—a valet, a secretary, a butler to complicate the situation. Slevna himself might have returned by now and be installed in some room. The slightest noise or warning would give him the opportunity to snatch up the phone and call the downstairs desk, unless Steve took him unawares.

For what seemed a lifetime he stood in the dark foyer, his ears stretched for the smallest telltale sound. Faintly, the murmur of traffic on 59th Street reached him, broken now and then by a motor horn. But inside there was not a sound. It still was too dangerous to assume that the apartment was empty. The hypothetical servant might be asleep, but ready to wake and jeopardize Steve's plans at the first alarm. He would have to search the whole premises before showing himself.

This was no new thing for Captain Lake of Homicide. He had the technique of silent, thorough reconnoitering at his finger-tips. But always he had been backed by the law, and nearly always by assistants, alert to come to his rescue in case he encountered trouble. Now for the first time he was aligned on the other side, he was the intruder, the quarry, the criminal who could afford to make no mistake.

Silently he moved forward through the foyer towards the room into which it opened. The room was unlit, but a good deal of light came in from outside. The large windows facing him were pearly from the high sky over Central Park. Right and left the firefly lights of Fifth Avenue and Central Park West buildings glowed with a beauty which all lights in the night possess. The room was a living room, imposing in size and splendid in proportion. In one corner the dark bulk of a concert grand piano was nearly lost. There were doors right and left, open and leading to other rooms. Steve tiptoed through the left door and found himself in a bedroom, also facing the Park and nearly as spacious as the living room. It was empty, but with swift malignance Steve peopled it as it must have been peopled that afternoon. So here at last he stood in the spot that marked Vicki's treachery and Slevna's infamy. His jaws bunched with the grinding rage of his thoughts. But again he caught himself up. This was not the time for the luxury of anger. He noted, with professional coolness, that there were windows facing both north and west. The bedroom was a corner room and marked the left end of the apartment. The bathroom, practically a part of the room, was likewise dark and empty.

He moved back, silently, through the living room to the right-hand door, and found himself in another room facing the Park. This room was much smaller and, as Steve cautiously flicked his flashlight over it, he saw that it was a sort of combined den and office. There was a small, flat-topped desk, on which stood two telephones; a smaller table bearing a typewriter, and two or three large, comfortable easy chairs. There was one door at the extreme right. Steve turned the knob with extreme caution, but it only led into a giant-sized closet—practically a storeroom. It even had a small window facing the street. It was fitted with shelves on which stood row upon row of music, some bound into volumes and some mere piles of loose sheets. The room had no other exit. Steve realized that he had traversed the whole apartment. There was no kitchen, no servants' quarters. The layout was like a distorted T, the foyer being the squat stem, and the three rooms forming the wide cross-piece.

With a breath of relief he congratulated himself on his luck. He had the place to himself. All he had to do was to wait until Slevna came in. If anyone came in with him, Steve would simply outwait him. When Slevna was finally alone and at his mercy, Steve would deal out his jungle justice.

X

Steve's immediate problem was to seek cover until such time as he chose to show himself. The apartment was curiously exposed, with practically no ambush, no niches, no draperies behind which to conceal himself. The only logical hiding-place was the music closet. Its main drawback was that if Slevna—or another—opened the door, Steve would be trapped with no exit for escape, while his opponent could dash out and give the alarm if he was quick enough.

A key in the lock of the closet door obviated this danger somewhat. Steve transferred the key to the inside of the little room and locked himself in. He hung his cap over the doorknob and switched on his flashlight to investigate his refuge thoroughly. On the floor in front of the shelves stood three handsome suitcases. Two of them were locked, with bright stickers on them, marked with an "S" which Steve read to mean "Stateroom." Evidently Slevna's European tour was imminent, and he was nearly packed and ready. Steve hefted one of them and confirmed this by its weight.

The third suitcase lay open and only half-packed. It contained no clothes, being apparently used solely for the pianist's professional needs and papers. A bed of sheet music covered the bottom of the suitcase to a thickness of four or five inches. On top of this lay two envelopes which Steve investigated. The first contained Slevna's passport with visas for Great Britain, France, Belgium, Holland and Czechoslovakia. The second held a steamship ticket for the luxury liner, *Azores Queen*, sailing Friday, June 23rd. That was the day after tomorrow. A small, Morocco-leather address book lay beside them. Steve picked it up and riffled through it to the letter L. It was a case of turning the knife in the wound—he was looking for Vicki's name and phone number in this intimate record book.

As the pencil of light from his flashlight whitened the page, he stiffened. There was, indeed, an address under the name "Lake" but it was his own. In Slevna's even European hand, there stared up at him the notation:

> Lake, Stefan, Captain of Homicide. 230 West 20th Street, New York City, U.S.A.

There was no sense to it. By no stretch of the imagination could Steve guess why his name and address were entered here among the list of notables from all parts of the globe. His eye caught princely titles and the names of world figures, financial, social and artistic. He turned to the letter "B" but found no Braun recorded, neither Paul nor Vicki. What was "Stefan" Lake doing in this galère?

He dropped the book back into the open suitcase. A thin fingernail of doubt began to scratch at his closed, implacable mind. Some of the ice which encased him began to thaw and flow in the mild temperature of reason. Stephen Lake, severe and uncompromisingly just, began to take over from the befuddled killer who had been in command for the past three hours. There was still not a trace of doubt in his mind that Slevna and Vicki were guilty of shameless outrage against him, but Steve, the good cop, who hated murder, was once more in the ascendant. He began to weigh the long-range effects of his plan.

He asked himself in precisely the words Johnny had used last night:

"What would extermination get you?"

Slevna would, indeed, be "one less skunk in the world," as he had told Johnny. But now the light of reason lit the question with a ray as bright as his flashlight. The point was, what would murdering Slevna do to *Steve Lake*? After he had advanced on a defenseless man, no matter how base, and had potted him like a clay pigeon, what manner of man would Steve Lake turn into? Granted that he got away with murder, successfully and completely, granted that he would not have to pay with his life for his crime, what way of life was left to a decent, self-respecting human being after committing cold-blooded murder?

His first reaction was almost farcical: he reached into his pocket for his denture and slipped it back into his mouth. But the mechanical action had sound reflexes in his consciousness: the gaudy masquerade was over. Steve Lake, now with no intent to kill, needed no absurd, toothless disguise to avoid detection.

His second act reflected his doubt of his own self-control. Slowly he took out his Police Positive, broke it and shook the bullets out into his palm. Subconsciously he feared that, face to face with this rip who had despoiled his marriage bed, passion, primitive and ungovernable, might pull the trigger against his own volition. He dropped the bullets into a pocket and stuck his now useless gun back in its holster.

Having reached so far on his return journey to sanity, he asked himself why he should remain at all. God knows he did not want to meet Slevna or talk to him—not even to revile or threaten him. The damage was done, he thought heavily, and words were as futile as bullets. Nothing he could do could change facts. People behaved according to their desires. If Vicki loved this worn-out Lothario, Steve was powerless to bring back the *status quo ante* by force.

Another subtle split in his casing of ice began to widen. The good cop began more and more to make himself felt. When had he ever arrested a suspect and turned him over to the Grand Jury without questioning? Even if the criminal convicted himself out of his own mouth, defense was still his inalienable right. Appearances were notoriously deceptive. A reasonable police officer jumped to no conclusions without all the facts. His mind leaped to the other extreme now. Suppose Slevna and Vicki had an innocent explanation of seemingly damning actions. Suppose Paul Braun had been with them, that Vicki had only been present in some minor role as listener-in to a pupil audition. That solution would hardly explain Vicki's presence at Cornwall House on three successive days—for Steve was morally certain that she had been at the Slevna apartment on Monday and Tuesday as well as today, and had covered the fact by pretending to go to the races.

Whatever the truth, one thing was certain: it had to be brought to light. If Steve had been distorting a harmless situation into guilt, open speech would clear it up. If the worst were true and an ugly intrigue was in progress, Steve had to know it in order to deal with the future and Vicki.

He put on his cap with an air of finality. He would skulk no longer in cubbyholes. He would go out and await Slevna openly and demand the truth.

As he laid his hand on the doorknob, he heard the sound of a door slamming. Footsteps, growing steadily louder and nearer, came to him. There was the click of a switch and a line of light appeared under the closet door. Steve realized he was too late to effect an appearance of openness.

Before he had time to make any move, he heard another click: the telephone receiver in the little room next door had been lifted from its cradle. A voice, with practically no accent, unless it was one of Oxford purity, spoke:

"Desk? This is Mr. Slevna. I do not wish to be disturbed. If there are any callers, please say that I am out." The receiver dropped into its place.

Steve hesitated no longer. He opened the door. Slevna was standing at the desk, his hand still on the phone, his back to Steve.

"Slevna."

Slevna spun around, startled. Then, as his eyes travelled with lightning speed up and down Steve's tall figure, his whole person changed into an image of abject terror. There was about eight feet of space between the two men, but Slevna began backing away, his hands pushing against the air in ungovernable panic.

"No! No! No!" he screamed. "You can't do this!"

"Do what?" The two words, dropped against Slevna's frantic accents, were icicles.

"It wasn't my fault!" Slevna shrieked. "You've got to listen!"

"I'm listening." A nerve began to tick in Steve's still face.

"What would any man do?" Slevna chattered. So this was the yellow skunk that Vicki loved. "I'm only flesh and blood."

"Let's have it all." The nerve was throbbing now with a life of its own.

"You would have done the same. On my oath, it was only the one time," he babbled. "I swear to God I wasn't going to do it ever again. I can explain. I couldn't help it. I only did it for her sake!"

All the pressures of the past three days converged into the muscles of Steve's right arm. Cold reason, even cold anger were gone. In a blood-haze of brute force he hit out. His fist caught Slevna on the point of the chin. Bone on bone cracked like a pistol shot. Slevna went down like a felled ox.

XI

Panting like a runner, Steve stood for a few minutes, unconsciously kneading his bruised knuckles. His brain was reeling with the horrible pictures Slevna's hysterical confession had evoked. He had wanted the truth. Well, he had it now, with a vengeance, he thought savagely. The hero of three divorce suits, the headliner of columnist tittle-tattle, had proved more noisome and viler than any smear campaign could have painted him. The lowest thug, stealing a pal's gun moll, would not stoop to hide behind a woman's skirts "I only did it for her sake!" Steve's skin crawled with loathing for having touched him.

He prepared to leave. He was finished here. Let Slevna and Vicki go their way. The comedy was ended. A pang of nearly unbearable pain went through him as the phrase crossed his mind. Vicki had quoted it from some Italian opera, pointing out the power of the simple, tragic words. The thought of Vicki, gay, serene, fastidious, wrenched him. His blood, his instinct interpreted for him. Never in the world was Vicki the instigator, the wanton, the nymphomaniac that Slevna had adduced. He would rouse the unconscious man from his stupor and make him eat his filthy words.

He knelt beside Slevna, pulled him up by his arms and shook him. Slevna's head bobbled on his shoulders like a loose doorknob. Steve's grip tightened and he jerked him to a half-sitting posture. Slevna's head rolled slowly on his neck and settled to rest at an unnatural, horrifying angle, his open eyes facing the floor.

For a few age-long seconds Steve knelt, turned to stone, with Slevna still in his grasp. Then he lowered him slowly, nervelessly, to the floor again. The truth hit him with the dull impact of a sandbag. Slevna was dead. Steve had seen too many dead men in his time to have any doubts. The single blow, delivered in wild rage, had struck the exactly scientific spot where it would be fatal. Slevna's neck had snapped like a celery stalk.

Nevertheless, in the prosaic routine of long habit, Steve felt for his pulse, leaned his ear to Slevna's chest, lit a match and passed it close before his eyes. There was no doubt. Slevna was dead. Even though Steve had abandoned his homicidal purpose, one instant's automatic explosion had nullified the counsels of conscience. He had murdered Slevna as certainly as if premeditation had still actuated him.

Steve rose from his knees. He drew a long breath. Slevna was dead. Nothing could undo that violent, fatal blow. What was the next step? Should he give himself up, brand himself as a killer, draw his wife, his friends into the terrifying maelstrom of a murder trial? Should he scrap long, future years of useful service to the dogmatic Biblical axiom of an eye for an eye, a life for a life? In theory that was exactly what he would have advocated. But when it came to the act, when he, the center of his individual cosmos, was the figure involved, when *his* life, *his* career, *his* associates were concerned, he did what practically every human being on earth would do—he turned sophist. He assured himself that he was not really a murderer, that a man should not have to pay with a lifetime for one second's aberration, especially when the provocation was so extreme. It would do Slevna no good now if Steve confessed and paid, and it would blacken and ruin many lives. He told himself he was being realistic, that he was making the best of a bad situation, that he was justified in protecting his marital honor, that it was not the business of the courts, but a private matter between Slevna and himself and God.

The inner voice which clamored for a hearing, he silenced ruthlessly. In short, he was in the grip of the strongest force on earth—the instinct for self-preservation.

He squared his shoulders and made his decision. He would do everything in his power to avoid detection. It should not be too difficult. Slevna's phone call to the hotel desk assured him that he had plenty of time. No one would be allowed to disturb the distinguished guest when he had specified that he wished to be alone.

Steve returned to the music closet. Methodically he set to work wiping off every surface he had touched—doorknobs, inside and out, the suitcase he had hefted, the envelopes, passport and steamship ticket. The address book he pocketed; in riffling through it his fingers might have touched dozens of pages, and he did not wish to spare the time to wipe them all. Besides which his own name appeared in it; a fact for which he had no relish. Too well he knew with what patient tenacity every name in that book would be followed up and investigated, if he left it in the apartment. He removed the closet door key from the inside of the lock, wiped it carefully and inserted it again in the outside as he had found it.

He stood for a moment in thought, reliving his silent entry half an hour ago into the apartment. He had touched nothing in any other room, except the front doorknob, which he would wipe clean on his way out. If he could get to the fire stairs and out the service entrance unobserved, he had nothing to fear. He paused, wondering whether to leave the light on in the room. He decided to put it out. At three, four or five in the morning that single light might be noticed from the street and wondered about. Alert taxi drivers, parked along the opposite side of 59th Street, might comment; might even notify the imposing doorman whom Steve had watched for so many hours that afternoon. He told himself that once he was clear of the building it hardly mattered when Slevna's body was discovered, but nevertheless he moved towards the wall to snap off the switch.

Suddenly the doorbell shrilled through the apartment. Steve stood frozen, his hand in mid-air. Then, with infinite caution he tiptoed noiselessly through the living room to the foyer. It might be any hotel attendant going through the motion of ringing Slevna's bell before entering with fresh towels, mail or to turn down his bed. He stood at the ready, set to deal a knockout blow to whoever should enter. It was the only way he could make good his escape without being seen.

But nobody fitted a key into the lock. Instead, the doorknob rattled and a girl's voice, with a charming foreign accent, pouted through the closed door:

"Janno! Jannocito! Let me in! I know you are there. For minutes I have been watching in the Playa. I have seen you enter. You are there, I know it well. I have seen the light in your window. Let me in, Janno mio!"

She waited. Steve scarcely breathed. Then came the pounding of small, soft fists on the door. The cooing voice changed to peppery anger:

"You think to throw away your Lolita now you weary of her? No, no, *amigo mio*, that will not be. Let me in, I say, or I will scream down the hotel!"

The sweat began pouring down Steve's forehead. He considered opening the door, dealing his knockout blow and making a dash for it. But the risk was terrific. The temperamental young lady had raised her voice, and it was reasonable to suppose that the tenants adjoining 512 had heard and were possibly peering out to see the fun. If he shut the girl up with a quick blow and then rushed out of Slevna's apartment, he would more than likely be seen. He could hardly deal out knockout blows wholesale.

The girl's voice came again, this time with a viperish menace, but mercifully in the low, level tones of hate:

"I know you are there. I give you one minute—sixty little seconds—to open the door. If you do not then open, I go. But *if* I go, it is not I who suffer, but *you*. Do you still close your door against me, Janno?"

Another pause. Then—and Steve could picture the expressive shrug which accompanied the words:

"*Buena. Mañana, por Dio*, you will learn to your sorrow. *Adios,* Janno *mio!*"

Steve thought he detected the diminishing swish of silk. There was no sound of footsteps. The thick pile of the carpet deadened the click of heels. He wiped his streaming forehead. This was a devil of a mess. The tempestuous little Spanish girl might or might not keep her word and go. It was just on the cards that she would take up her stand around the corner of the corridor, hoping to waylay Slevna if he went out.

At all events he would be wise to wait a while before daring to leave the apartment. He went back to the small office to turn off the lights. If Lolita had really left, it was as well that she saw no lights from the street. He wondered how she had managed to get by the desk, when Slevna had said so specifically that he was not to be disturbed. The only explanation that occurred to him was that she, too, lived at Cornwall House and had free access to the elevators. It would be simple for her to get off at her own floor and then find her way to Slevna's apartment.

The telephone rang.

The blood pounded in Steve's throat until he thought he would suffocate. His eyes turned into his numbed head to look at the desk where the piercing bell crashed danger to all his senses. But Slevna had said he was not to be disturbed, he repeated to himself, with an irritability, almost comic under the circumstances. First this girl and now the phone. His eyes snapped to comprehension. There were two phones on the desk, one marked with a celluloid insert "Extension 512," the house phone, the other with a different number in the base of its cradle, Slevna's private phone. Someone of Slevna's wide acquaintances was calling him up—it was too soon for Lolita to have reached a phone—perhaps even one of his professional retinue, his manager, his secretary, someone who knew he was at home and who might grow suspicious if he did not answer. Or it might be Vicki. Like a man rubbing salt into his wound, Steve wanted to hear the exact timbre of her tone in addressing her lover.

He whipped out a handkerchief and, protecting the receiver from his prints, picked up the private phone.

"Yes?" His instinct for self-preservation persisted. Without conscious thought he imitated as closely as he could Slevna's tone and accent.

"Slevna?" a man's voice asked softly.

"Yes."

"You obey orders, I see. It is exactly nine."

"Yes."

"You are alone?"

"Yes."

"When I say alone I do not mean merely that there is no one present in the room with you. I mean that if you have made any treacherous move, if this wire is tapped or if anyone is alerted to trace this call—" The voice paused, but menace hung in the air. Steve, his features sharpening with suspicion and incredulity, replied carefully:

"I have made no such move."

"You are wise." The voice breathed satisfaction without losing one degree of its cold warning. "You are aware of the consequences of any such act?"

"Yes."

There was a short, mirthless twang of laughter.

"Most men do, where their own hides are concerned," he sneered. Steve waited. The other went on, with a note of briskness: "You realize this is your last call?"

"Yes."

"Excellent." The voice was suave, but with an overtone of steel. "You have evidently reconsidered. Very wise of you, indeed." He paused, and Steve felt the need of a reply, but he was so at sea that he hardly dared commit himself until he heard more. He said inadequately:

"We are agreed there." Apparently it sufficed, for the voice went on:

"It is unprecedented for me to communicate with any of my instruments, but my colleague reports that you were somewhat rebellious when he spoke to you on Sunday."

"No. It was just that—" Steve broke off for lack of material.

"Just that you fancied yourself as a martyr?" There was another low laugh with no amusement in it. "A martyr and a patriot? Well, my dear Slevna, it is the easiest thing in the world for you to attain martyrdom. You have only to continue your defiant attitude and refuse to obey instructions." The voice drawled, as if savoring the words which rolled so blandly over the invisible wire. "As to posing as a patriot, I fear your past performances might interfere sadly."

"I realize that." Steve stiffened at the other man's implications. What had he stumbled on? Was this what the girl Lolita had referred to in her vague threat?

"Good. You are prepared to give complete cooperation?"

"Yes."

"My colleague informs me that on Sunday you made some rash but puny threats." The voice was cold.

"I—I was a bit distracted."

"You must have been, to lose sight of the situation."

"One says things in excitement—"

"There is no room for excitement in our plans. Either you carry out orders as before or—the situation remains. It is for you to decide."

"I will carry out orders."

"You have given up your hysterical idea of communicating with the American police?"

"I never really intended to."

"Again, you are wise. You realize what it would mean? Not only your own liquidation but— Well, enough. Understand, I do not trust you. I am aware that at the faintest opportunity you would turn like a cornered rat and betray us. You do our bidding only to save your skin. I regret having to use such base material, but your position makes you an ideal agent. The authorities treat you with almost the same immunity accorded ambassadors. I am explaining this fully to you so that you will get no foolish notions to try any tricks after you leave

America. You will be under observation every second of the day and night."

"You can trust me."

"For your own safety, I hope so. Now to business." There was no longer any drawl in the voice. It was crisp, direct, an executive issuing orders to his staff. "Listen carefully. I am giving you your instructions now. There will be no personal contact except for the instant of the actual delivery of the object to be conveyed abroad—by you."

"I understand."

"This is Wednesday night. Your boat sails Friday at 10 a.m."

"Yes."

"This object is of incalculable value. We do not wish it to be out of our hands until the last possible moment. On Friday morning you will undoubtedly be surrounded by your entourage and your friends. Besides, daylight is no ally of ours. Therefore at midnight on Thursday you will prepare to meet the bearer of this important document and dispose of it among your effects as you did last time. Is that clear?"

"Quite."

"At midnight exactly tomorrow night—not earlier and not later—you will leave your hotel. You will walk to Columbus Circle and enter the Park at the most southerly path. This leads to a dense copse of trees, bordering the wall. There is a single stone bench under the trees. You will sit down and await our man. There will be no words spoken. He will pass your bench and toss a rumpled tabloid on to the grass. You will instantly recover it. Inside, attached to the pages, will be the paper you are to convey. Repeat the instructions thus far."

Steve repeated them. As he spoke, his glance fell on Slevna's dead, staring eyes. It crossed his mind that he had built better than he knew in killing this traitor.

"Excellent," said the voice at the end of Steve's recital. "To continue. You will take the tabloid to your rooms. You will abstract the paper, a single sheet of typewriter size, which will fit easily inside a piece of sheet music. You will fold the paper twice lengthwise. This will result in a strip eleven inches long but only about two inches wide. You will insert this strip far back between the pages of the sheet music and fasten it securely to the pages with scotch tape. The idea of the folding is this: if by some extreme chance your effects *are* searched and your music inspected, this strip near the binding of the music will very likely be overlooked in the slovenly carelessness with which American and British officials carry out their duties." There was infinite scorn in his tone. "Again repeat."

Steve went through his summary.

"Correct," said the telephone. "Assuming all goes well, you—and the document—will arrive unmolested in London on Thursday, June 29th. You are stopping at the Savoy. You will immediately remove the document from the sheet music and transfer it to the inside pocket of your dinner-coat. At 9 p.m. a hotel valet will knock and ask if you have any clothes to be pressed. His exact words will be, 'If monsieur's clothes have suffered from the salt water.' You will take that for a password and hand him your dinner clothes with the document still concealed in the coat pocket. Repeat."

Steve repeated, verbatim.

"Very good. With the removal of your suit your mission is ended. You will forget you ever received, carried or delivered anything at all. Understand?"

"Yes."

"The thing is simplicity itself, as you can see. A slip-up can only occur through deliberate malice and treachery on your part."

"There will be no treachery."

"For your own sake, I hope not." The cold voice conveyed neither hope nor any other feeling except a deadly menace. "It depends solely on you as to whether we will negotiate an exit pass for a certain person or simply—an exit."

There was a click and the line went dead. At his end Steve hung up slowly, like a man in a dream. He lowered himself mechanically into a chair, almost overcome by the implications of the whole episode.

The first thing that captured his mind was the enormous coincidence. It was the sort of thing that simply did not happen. And yet, on close analysis, it was less incredible than at first appeared.

The "document," of course, was the formula dealing with germ warfare, stolen by Ferman. And if it seemed like a dream come true, that just when Steve was at work on the Ferman case this plum should fall into his lap, the fact was that no matter who handled the case—if Ferman had been murdered on the East Side, in Brooklyn or Queens—knowledge of it would still have come to Steve, due to the smooth interlocking system of precinct-to-precinct reports which welded the homicide branch of the service into one efficient unit.

The unheard-of coincidence lay in the fact that one of the spy ring was a man whom Steve knew and was trailing on a private and personal matter. And yet he wondered if the public realized how great a part coincidence and luck do actually play in police cases, and how often, when hard, plodding perseverance and the assistance of informers has proved futile, random chance has brought a case to a successful solution.

He recalled a nearly preposterous case of his own, some years ago. At the time he was living in a small apartment, kept in order by a visiting maid. He was working on a homicide, tailing a young garage worker, not because Steve believed him to be guilty, but because he was known to be a pal of the actual suspect who had gone into hiding. On the fifth day of Steve's unsuccessful pursuit, his partner had just relieved him and taken over the job when Steve remembered that his poker crowd was due at his apartment that evening. He found himself in the neighborhood of his visiting maid and wondered if he could arrange for her to come and serve for him. He rang her bell. She came to the door and asked him in. As Steve entered, a figure darted out of the hall into a back room, but not before Steve had caught a glimpse—of his suspect!

Steve always felt that the promotion he got out of that capture was unearned. Pure chance and senseless coincidence deserved the credit.

In the present case there was even a touch of logic to bolster the coincidence. Granting the staggering luck of Steve's presence at Slevna's at the crucial time, the pianist's connection with the case was reasonable enough. For the whole affair—espionage, theft and murder—had its rise in one locality. They knew little enough about Ferman, but all that they did know led to Czechoslovakia. Ferman's people were Czechs, they were back there now. Johnny's theory of coercing anti-Communists to do the bidding of those in power, under threat of liquidating their unfortunate families, might well be true. Well, Slevna was a Czech, too, the foremost unofficial representative of the nation. He meant Czechoslovakia in the world's eyes, as Paderewski had once meant Poland. What was more likely than for the Czech Reds to enlist this famous Czech to do their dirty work under pain of his own death or the death of his relatives in Prague? As a concert pianist he travelled abroad regularly and would excite no suspicion. The thing was a natural.

Steve took stock. He had killed Slevna in a fury of personal rage. The crumpled body, the staring eyes, the twisted neck filled the little room with a noxious horror. Ten minutes before, Steve's whole being had concentrated on getting away from this spot without leaving a trace of his presence behind him.

Now the picture had changed immeasurably. He had stumbled on this enormous outrage. He had learned exactly how the top-secret discoveries of America were being transmitted to potential enemies. He had actually spoken to the head of one of their spy rings—the authority of the telephone voice was unmistakable. And tomorrow at midnight one of their henchmen would stroll past a bench in Central Park, toss a tabloid newspaper on the grass and disappear from view—unless Steve Lake did something about it.

He sat in Slevna's armchair, deliberately pushing away the fact of hate, of revenge, of murder, of personal safety. A much bigger consideration loomed. He had a grip on one end of a thread as fragile as a spider's web. Somehow he must follow that thread until it led him to the spider at the center. Steve was a good American. He had thrown three years of advancement over his shoulder in order to do Army Intelligence work during the war. Nothing mattered except to break the back of this spy ring and to recover the formula before it reached its intended destination.

Poignantly he regretted Slevna's death—but only because he was no longer available to act as bait to catch the enemy. But the enemy must be caught. What was the best way to do it? The obvious move was to get in touch with Rieger of the F.B.I. without an instant's delay. Steve half-rose from the chair to pick up the phone. But he paused and sank back again.

The thing was like a portent to him. He saw suddenly how he had been throwing dust in his own eyes, how barren and futile his arguments had been. No amount of rationalization and evasion could hide for long from his own conscience the fact that Steve Lake was now a creature apart from other human beings, that from this night on he walked alone in a dreary place, bearing the intolerable burden of guilt on his back, like an old man of the sea.

Here was his chance to square accounts, to put his earmarked life to good use. If he told Rieger, and the machinery of the F.B.I. was set in motion, some ripple of activity might reach the vigilant eyes or ears of the enemy. The cold voice on the telephone had impressed Steve with its efficiency and craft. Every day the papers and radio carried scareheads about Communist agents—in the Army, the Navy, the Government agencies. The President himself was accused of blocking the exposure of Red espionage. Who knew, nowadays, in what high and inner circles their spies were not ensconced?

Whereas if Steve told nobody, and took upon himself the ticklish, delicate job of meeting and outwitting them, there was no way in which they could be forewarned. He realized fully the danger of his plan—and welcomed it. In the worst case he would have made payment in full. In the event of success, he would have secured the invaluable formula, laid the spy ring by the heels and, in a measure, evened the score by risking, if not sacrificing, his life.

The dead weight of guilt lightened, once he made his decision. With the resilience of human nature—and Steve was as human as the next man—he began to see the enormous advantage of his program. If he called in Rieger what could he have told him? How account for Slevna slugged to death? He could never have rigged up a story that would pass muster in Rieger's shrewd eyes. And for the life of him he could not have told the whole shabby, ugly tale of sneaking into Slevna's apartment in order to kill his wife's lover, of revolting against cold-blooded murder and still later of killing him in fury at Slevna's filthy slurs against Vicki. His pride, his vanity, his sense of decency rebelled against laying all this bare to any man. He grew hot with shame at the idea of telling Rieger that Vicki had fallen so low as to give herself to a creature like Slevna, a man who had betrayed both his own and his adopted country to save his skin.

Rieger would do what he could, but the law was impersonal and ground out its judgments on a Captain of Homicide as surely as upon a gangster. Steve could, of course, buy his liberty by pleading the unwritten law, but bitter and destroyed though he was, it was not in him to throw Vicki to the wolves, whatever she had done. She was only twenty-two years old. He wouldn't let a dog spend a lifetime under a blot like that. This was a far cry from the man who, last night, had said to Johnny:

"The woman might suffer more alive."

That man had been in the intolerable position of an impotent dupe. Tonight he had exacted payment—if unintentionally—and was no longer a victim. He would hide behind no woman's skirts- he cast a look of loathing at the dreadful figure on the floor who had met his death by that very act.

No. From all angles, silence was the thing. If he played a lone hand and had the luck to nab the spies, he could keep the whole dirty, personal story out of it. In the acclaim with which the exposure of the spy ring would be hailed, he could gloss over what details he chose. Success was the only cloak under which he could hide the truth.

He had plenty of confidence in his ability to carry out his program.

His opponents were tricky and efficient, and he did not underestimate his danger. But he felt he was a match for them and that it was well worth a try.

He did not lose sight of the immense importance of the situation. Even if the messenger in Central Park got away from him, there was no irreparable risk. The spy ring could be laid bare through another approach. All he had to do was to tell Rieger to cable British Intelligence immediately, and all the valets of the Savoy in London would be screened so effectively that the planted spy among them would be revealed. The English were just as adroit as the Americans when it came to eliciting confessions.

His mind was made up. He would act alone.

XII

The decision quickened all Steve's faculties. He was cool, proficient, alive to all details and contingencies. The first problem which faced him was to keep Slevna's death secret until after midnight tomorrow. If the enemy knew that their quarry was dead, they would fly to cover, there would be no messenger, no tabloid, no document. Concealment of Slevna's body was simple enough. The difficulty was to keep Slevna's friends and followers from asking questions and raising a hue and cry which might reach the ears of the enemy. Steve gave the point thought and believed that he could encompass this.

He went into action. His first move was to take hold of Slevna's inert body and maneuver it into the music closet. The dead man was big and heavy, but Steve managed it with the knack he had learned at the Police Academy at the beginning of his career. Then he went through the apartment looking for Slevna's outdoor wraps. On the living room couch he found Slevna's topcoat and cane. He remembered that the pianist had worn no hat this afternoon. He tossed the topcoat and cane into the music closet, locked the door upon the dead man and pocketed the key.

He stood in thought for a moment in the small room, ready to leave, but hesitant, as if there was still something to be done here. His eye fell on the ashtray beside the telephones. He snapped his fingers as the idea clicked into place. He went again through the apartment until he found what he was looking for—one of Slevna's twelve-inch cigarette holders. He slipped it into his holster, turned off all lights, taking care to leave no fingerprints. He went to the door, opened it a crack and peered out. The cross-hall was empty. There was no sign of Lolita. He let himself out of the apartment, walked down the cross-hall to the long corridor which ran at right angles to it. Again he peered cautiously before leaving cover. The long corridor, too, was empty, and he sprinted for the fire door.

Once behind it on the stairs he breathed a trifle easier. There was now only one more obstacle to overcome—the Norwegian handyman—and he would be safely away. He tiptoed down the five flights of stairs with barely a sound. When he reached the last flight to the basement he paused, listening intently. He could hear no sound of activity, either of ashcans being rolled out or chores of any other kind. But the man might well be still there, quietly reading his comics or on watch for the mythical quarry whom Steve had pretended to be chasing. He regretted now that he had told him to look out for him and grab him. He had no relish for a second meeting with the stolid Norwegian. He had not seemed overly bright, but he had eyes, and two looks were better—or, from Steve's angle, worse—than one.

He turned the corner of the last half of the flight and heaved a sigh of relief. The basement at the foot of the stairs was in total darkness. With the utmost care he felt his way towards the outer door. His progress through the musty, invisible passage seemed endless. Then his groping hands touched the metal service door. It was closed and bolted. Steve drew back the bolts with a handkerchief around his fingers, opened the door the fewest possible inches and slipped through. He hated leaving the drawn bolts behind him—in the morning someone might notice and remark it. When Slevna's body was finally discovered, and the murder of so famous a person was investigated, those bolts would lend truth to the handyman's fanciful story of a cop who had rushed up the stairs around the time of the murder. Wryly Steve wished he were one of the resourceful sleuths of fiction who would instantly pull a small magnetic gadget out of his sleeve, and applying it to the outside of the door, draw the bolts again to their locked position with the ease of a magician pulling a rabbit and all the United Nations flags out of a top hat. But he was neither a super sleuth nor a magician. With a shrug he negotiated the ramp leading up to the sidewalk, turned into 59th Street and walked at a normal pace over to Fifth Avenue where he retrieved his car.

At 81st Street he parked the Chevrolet and watched his chance to enter his apartment unobserved. He blessed the self-operating elevator which obviated doormen and elevator boys. Upstairs, outside his own door, he paused for a moment to think up a plausible explanation for being in uniform. Not even to Vicki—in fact to Vicki above all people—could he afford the smallest suspicious circumstance which might connect him with Cornwall House and Slevna on this critical night.

But his luck held. Vicki was not yet at home. Steve glanced at his wristwatch and saw to his surprise that it was only nine-thirty. He had been gone just an hour and a half in all, although it seemed centuries since he had walked Nick and then set out to kill a man.

Quickly he took off his uniform, unwound the disfiguring sheet from about his middle and got into his own clothes. While his hands were mechanically doing this, his mind was vaguely bothered by the fact of Vicki's absence. Slevna had arrived at home nearly an hour ago. In that case why was Vicki still away? If the two had separated around eight-thirty, where was she now? Had she gone to her father's to substantiate the lie she had written in her note? He hardly thought so. Such caution did not hang together with her extreme carelessness where the races and the badge were concerned. Then where was she? He could, of course, phone the Braun apartment if he chose. But he shrank from it. It would be an unusual thing for him to do, for he was not given to the small amenities, he was too inarticulate to show solicitude, no matter how deep his feelings. Vicki would wonder why, on this particular night, he was moved to this special attention when he had never done so before.

Suddenly the thought of awaiting Vicki and facing her as if nothing had happened became impossible to him. Her small-talk, light-hearted, facile and false, would be more than his taut nerves could bear, when he remembered that she had just come from Slevna's arms and that, in consequence, he had committed the sin of sins. He decided to spend the night at the Homicide Bureau, where he would plan out his procedure for tomorrow at midnight. He left the apartment fast.

On the street he found he was suddenly ravenous. He had had no food since breakfast. At noon he had followed Vicki to her rendezvous; at dinner hour he had donned his uniform and set forth to Cornwall House without eating. He turned into the first restaurant he came to and devoured a double portion of ham and eggs and two cups of coffee. Replenished, he went on to 20th Street. The place was deserted except for Johnny who was on the desk.

A measure of Steve's self-repugnance was reflected in the way he shied away from the younger man. He could hardly answer Johnny's blithe: "Hi, Chief. Quiet as a church social. Ten-thirty and not a soul dead."

Steve gulped, took a grip on himself and answered:

"I guess you could sleep if you tried. Go home and I'll take over."

"But why? What did you come back for anyway?"

"Got some paper work to catch up on." It sounded so glaringly weak that he added: "I have to wait for a call. The Ferman thing seems to be opening up a bit."

"So that's where you were at all afternoon. Why didn't you take me along?"

"Glutton for work, ain't you?" Steve grunted.

"Well, we're carrying the case together, aren't we? What's this new angle?"

Steve yawned elaborately.

"Tell you in the morning. Go on home."

"Okay." Johnny rose. But he made no move to leave. Instead he lit a cigarette and began to pace up and down. "Y'know, Steve, the more I think about Ferman the more likely it seems—what we talked about last night, I mean. If Rieger dug into local Czechs, with an eye to any who plan to leave the country—"

Steve's skin pricked. Johnny's theories were too apt for comfort.

"I guess Rieger can manage without hints from a cub detective," he said sarcastically.

"Oh, sure," Johnny nodded good naturedly. "I just meant together with that Queen Steamship schedule, it looked like a good bet."

"Did anyone ever tell you there are about thirty thousand Czechs in this district?"

"Yeah, I guess. It was just a thought."

"Rieger thinks on occasion. Suppose we leave that angle to him. Our job is homicide, remember?"

"Right. Forget I ever spoke."

"I'll do that. Now scram."

"I could take a little loose change off you at gin. Make the time pass." Johnny still lingered. Steve's patience cracked.

"Get out, will you? I thought I told you I had work to do," he barked.

Johnny looked at him, speculative and puzzled. Steve squirmed under the look. It crossed his mind that it was a mistake to be so friendly with a subordinate—especially as shrewd a one as Johnny. He all but read Steve's mind, and at the present moment that was something that Steve couldn't afford. But Johnny picked up his hat and moved to the door with a cheerful:

"So long. See you in the morning."

Alone, Steve began pacing the considerable space of the three connecting rooms. He waited until his ruffled temper had calmed down. He needed a clear mind. But he was not destined to do his secret planning for a while. There were footsteps on the stairs and Jeff came in, with a smug, complacent air.

"For God's sake don't you ever call it a day?" Rand commented pleasantly.

Steve's irritation returned ten-fold. Was he ever going to be alone to map out tomorrow night's program? He turned on Rand with less than his usual control.

"I never did work by the clock," he snapped.

"You and me both," Rand said sunnily. "I dropped by to tie up the loose ends of my case."

"Oh? You brought your man in?"

"Wrapped up like a candy box. I didn't close on him until I pumped Red Varney dry. Now the D.A. can go to the Grand Jury with an airtight case."

"Good work." Steve tried to be fair, but the words sounded grudging.

"Evidently your case ain't going so smooth," Rand said slyly.

"Where d'you get that idea?"

"Well, would you be here at this hour if it was in the bag?" asked Rand innocently.

"Maybe. I could be here just *because* it was getting hot." Steve could have kicked himself for letting Rand put him on the defensive, but he did not seem able to help himself. What was the matter, he asked himself savagely? Was his nerve slipping? Between Johnny and Rand was he going to cave in like a hysterical woman? But Rand was going on talking, and as Steve caught the drift of his words, his hackles rose.

"—not having been told the details, I wouldn't know what you're looking for, but maybe you're not looking in the right places."

"Now that your case is over," Steve threw at him evenly, "perhaps you'd like to take over mine."

"No, no. Not a bit of it," Rand said with an expansive gesture. "Not my kind of stuff at all. When it comes to *tailing* anybody, man or woman, there's nobody to hold a candle to you."

"Thanks." The tone and Steve's elaborate bow were an insult. Again he tried to pull himself together and stop making a show of himself before Rand. But he couldn't stop. That phrase "man or woman" had a double-tongued ring to it. What did Rand know and what was he up to? Did the whole world know that Vicki had been cheating on him? Had the look in Johnny's eyes been sympathy? And was Rand gloating over the fact that Steve couldn't hold his lovely young wife? His fists balled at his sides, and it was all he could do to control himself from smashing one of them into Rand's smiling face.

But Rand saved the situation by yawning and saying:

"Well, it's been a pretty full day. I guess I can leave my paper report till the morning. Okay, Captain?"

Steve nodded, and Rand strolled out without saying good night.

But Rand had done his dirty work, consciously or unconsciously. Steve's seething thoughts centered, not on tomorrow's problem, but on what Rand knew about Vicki and Slevna, how he came to know it, and to what use he would put the knowledge. When after tomorrow night the murder was discovered, Steve realized that anything Rand knew which pointed to him would come out in as damning a fashion as possible. Rand would relish throwing him to the dogs. Steve's ruin would feed Rand's hatred and make the Lieutenant a Captain. That it would put a noose around Steve's neck would be a side issue to Rand.

XIII

Steve saw Wednesday wane and Thursday wax. He spent most of the night on his feet, walking miles up and down the three rooms. Once in a while he cast himself into the chair at his desk, trying to clarify his thoughts by tabulating alternate procedures for his meeting in the Park. He had two vital things to do; first to recover the chemical formula which would be attached to the pages of the tabloid; second to capture the agent who brought it. The latter would not be easy. It might, in fact, be both dangerous and nearly hopeless. Steve did not underestimate the organization he was pitted against. He knew this enemy was wily and would walk into no naive trap. The bench in the Park might well be surrounded by other men in ambush to obviate the messenger's getaway. He knew, too, that dealing out death to accomplish their purpose was the first principle of their late revered leader, Lenin. Steve might be walking into a trap himself, as ruthless as the one which had caught Ferman. The one advantage which he had was that, with Slevna's death still unknown, the enemy might feel too safe to take extraordinary precautions. They thought they were dealing with a cowed victim, too afraid for his skin to raise an outcry. Moreover, Slevna was their intended overseas messenger. They would plan to keep him alive until after he had delivered the formula to their agent in London.

At seven o'clock, Steve rumpled the unslept-in cot, shaved and awaited the day's routine. At eight, Rieger of the F.B.I. came in to discuss developments in the case.

"We've got a full report from Prague," he told Steve. "Ferman's parents are decent, law-abiding conservatives, with no Red connections whatever. If they're anything in this game, they're mere pawns."

"That's how my Sergeant figured it," Steve replied. "Hostages to force the son over here to do their dirty work."

"I liked that Sergeant of yours. Head's in the right place." Rieger nodded. "Well, granted. We're still not much forrader. Ferman never in this world confided in his parents, you may bet. He did his chore for 'em and was killed to shut him up. But the formula has to get out of the country. They don't dare risk it in the mails, so they've got to have a bearer. It's a question of who, how and when."

"The Queen Line schedule help you any?"

"Yes and no. Nothing will slip by us, of course. But there are a dozen other steamship lines. My idea is that at one stage of the game Ferman thought *he* was to be the bearer and procured the Queen Line sailing list for himself. Only his prints are on it. But the actual man who will carry it may sail on any other line, he may fly, or he may take it to some other agent in the United States or Canada who will be the real messenger. Very simple," he ended with a snort.

"Needle in a haystack," Steve commented. His mind was churning with a storm of thoughts. He knew well that here and now he should open up and tell Rieger everything; that he was taking an enormous risk to national safety by acting alone against this formidable enemy who stopped at nothing. He weighed what would happen if he said coolly to Rieger:

"The real messenger was supposed to be Janno Slevna, the pianist. But he's dead. I killed him because he seduced my wife. No. I killed him because, after doing it, he hid behind her skirts like a cornered yellow dog. He didn't deserve to live." But that's neither here nor there, Steve thought. If I speak, a useful, hard-working man like myself will be snuffed out or buried in a jail. And the tabloids will gloat over Vicki as a slut and a tramp. Whatever she did, she's my wife. It isn't as if I'm letting the country down. I can get that paper back and I can nail that lousy Red in the Park. Damn it, a man's got some pride where his life and his wife's concerned. He said nothing aloud.

"We've let Drain go," Rieger went on. "He's just a bone-lazy hack, but honest. Of course we're keeping a tail on him, but I don't expect anything. Ritchie never had a thought of his own, Red, white or blue. Mrs. Whiting is exactly what she appears to be. And there Ferman's associates end. In my opinion, unless we nab this particular Commie ring, you're going to have an unsolved homicide on your hands."

"Could be."

"Still, you never know. We may get a break when we least expect it."

"From your angle, it had better be soon."

"You said it. Some of my men are going over that old case again—the Toledo lab murder and loss of the scorched earth formula last year. They're going over the sailing lists around that date, but this time with an eye out for Czech passengers rather than Russians. They may turn up a name that appears again on this year's sailing list."

"Well, good hunting."

After Rieger left, Steve forced himself to phone Vicki. He knew he should have done it last night, but he had been afraid that her quick ear would detect from his tone that something was wrong. Today he had recovered a measure of control and could trust himself to pass muster. But the shoe was on the other foot. Vicki was not listening for fine distinctions of tone, she hardly paid attention to his elaborate explanation for staying away from home all night. She was too busy trying to hide her own agitation.

"Look, Steve," she interrupted him. "Could you stop by here this morning?" she asked anxiously.

"Not possibly." His tone was clipped and acrid.

"I could come down there."

"I won't be here."

"But I must see you for a few minutes, it's important."

"What's on your mind?"

"I can't tell you over the phone."

"This wire's not tapped."

"No, it's too long and mixed up."

"I guess it'll keep."

"Steve, what were you working on last night?"

"My reports go to the Head of the Detective Division," he said dryly.

Her strained nerves burst into anger.

"I wish you'd stop being a stuffed shirt for once and behave like a human being! I'm not a complete idiot. When I say I've got something important to discuss with you—"

"Maybe you'd like me to send one of my men up to take a statement?" he said with heavy sarcasm.

There was a pause. Then she said thoughtfully:

"It's an idea," and hung up quietly.

He banged down the receiver. His nerves were ready to snap like stretched elastics. In three nights he had had practically no sleep. On Monday evening his first suspicion of Vicki had gnawed like a rat at his brain. On Tuesday the suspicion had grown to a probability as he spotted the amateurish lies with which she tried to cover her infidelity. On Wednesday his distrust had been shocked into certainty by the tremendous jolt of actually seeing her emerging from Cornwall House with Slevna. The look in her eyes, the mixture of adoration and fear, had been the final hammer blow to his passionate desire to believe the whole thing was some chimera of his own imagination. And as a crown to the deadly chain of events was the hideous fact that he had killed a man. He was close to the end of his rope.

He pulled himself together and picked up the phone again. He must not let the personal nightmare get between him and the job before him.

He called Cornwall House.

"Give me the desk," he said. When he was connected he went on: "Speaking for Mr. Slevna. He is obliged to attend an important personal matter and will not be in until late this afternoon or evening. If anyone calls, please explain."

"Yes, sir. Certainly."

The obsequious voice was entirely unsuspicious. Steve had a little longer breathing spell before Slevna's friends and professional family busied themselves over his invisibility.

One by one the day men straggled in. Harry O'Neil reported that he was making progress with the Pinelli girl and hoped to have the data Steve wanted soon. Jeff Rand ambled in as self-satisfied as a well-fed cat. With his case clinched, he was supposed to write up a complete report, but he pulled out a deck of cards and began an elaborate game of solitaire at his desk. Steve didn't even glance his way, let alone comment. Harry Schneer arrived and busied himself filling his lighter with fluid and flint. Johnny Clark was the last to put in an appearance. It was nearly noon when he reported. He told Steve he had spent the morning leafing through Ferman's books in the vague hope of getting some sort of lead, possibly from an underlined passage or a marginal note. The only thing he had found was a sentence from a book on espionage, which was heavily bracketed by pencil marks. It read:

> These men rarely show their faces. They communicate with their victims from untraceable pay stations or send messages composed of letters cut from magazines and newspapers.

Johnny had copied out the sentence and showed it to Steve.

"It's not much," he said. "But it shows the trend of Ferman's thoughts. He probably never even saw the guy who ordered him to steal the formula."

Steve nodded. Johnny did not know how close to the mark the sentence came. Steve could have told him that on Sunday one member of the ring had phoned Slevna to tell him he had been elected to do their bidding. Slevna had rebelled, and his protest had been reported to the head of the group. A second phone message, "your last call," had been received by Steve on Wednesday evening while Slevna lay dead at his feet. Slevna's threat to communicate with the "American police" had not brought an envoy to reason in *person* with the rebellious but desperate man. It had merely caused a more important conspirator to send his threat over the telephone wires. But Steve said nothing. Much as he liked and trusted Johnny, he could afford to confide in no one.

The phone rang. Schneer answered it and turned to Johnny. "For you," he said with a friendly snicker. "One of your dames. Not a bad voice, either. How do you hook 'em, Clark?"

Johnny came back to Steve and said in a rather strained tone:

"If you don't need me, I'll take my lunch hour now."

"Go to it."

"And there's another little lead I want to follow up. Okay if I take a bit longer than usual? "

In spite of his tense nerves, Steve had to smile a little. After the phone call it was obvious that the "little lead" wore skirts. Johnny wasn't usually so naïve, but Steve let it pass. He was a conscientious worker, he was entitled to a breather with a pretty girl now and then. Besides, Steve was glad to have him out of the office. He did not relish Johnny's shrewd scrutiny this day.

After Johnny left, Steve went into the lavatory, slipped a hand under his shirt and felt in his holster for the long cigarette holder he had taken from Slevna's apartment. He wanted to practice with it a bit; in the dark of Central Park it was going to be a valuable stage prop in his impersonation of the pianist.

The cigarette holder was gone.

XIV

Johnny ate no lunch, either alone or with a pretty girl. His phone call had been from Vicki, and there was such urgency in her tone that he hailed a taxi and was at 81st Street in fifteen minutes. In spite of his speed, he was reluctant to arrive. All his instincts were against it. But he had had no choice. Vicki had not asked; she had demanded.

She greeted him soberly.

"That was quick, Johnny. Thanks," and led him into the living room. Neither of them sat down. Johnny stood before the small electric fireplace, busying himself with a cigarette. He was very uncomfortable. There was something wrong about the whole thing, he felt. He had no business here in the capacity of confidant, helper and partisan. Whatever was bothering Vicki, it was Steve's place to be here. He hated the air of clandestine treachery that hung over the situation, caused by Vicki's final word over the phone: "Don't tell Steve. Just come."

Vicki moved restlessly about the room, handling objects aimlessly, picking them up and laying them down again without seeing them. Finally Johnny broke the silence:

"You wanted to see me, Mrs. Lake?"

Vicki gave her head a quick, impatient shake.

"Oh, for heaven's sake, Johnny! You and your 'Mrs. Lake!'"

He laughed deliberately. He said lightly:

"So you sent out a hurry call to discuss Christian names."

Vicki's nervousness dropped away. She said with dignity:

"It's all right, Johnny. You needn't be so scrupulous. I've known for ages that you love me."

He managed with a tremendous effort to continue his smile. But he could not control his blood vessels. Slowly every bit of color drained out of his face. His freckles stood out against his white skin like small tan flowers. Vicki went on gravely:

"I'm not playing the siren, Johnny. You needn't commit yourself. I *know*. A girl does. But it's important whether you love me enough to put me before your devotion to duty."

Stubbornly he clung to his airy manner as to a life raft.

"Well, now, that's an interesting point. Passion versus police work. Dalliance against detection. Love—"

"Johnny, I'm in trouble. Bad trouble."

Johnny gave in to the poignancy of her tone.

"All right, Vicki. Let's have it." It was the first time in his life he had ever called her "Vicki."

Mechanically they both dropped into chairs.

"I'll have to explain how things are first," she began. "I don't like sending for you behind Steve's back any better than you do."

"I know how things are, I think."

"Do you? *Do you?* You modest, loyal, blind fool, Johnny!" she said softly.

Their eyes locked. Johnny's heart pumped until it nearly suffocated him. Vicki went on, almost sorrowfully:

"It's a thing that can't be helped, isn't it? In the blood, or the nerve centers or whatever. It's not the point, just now. The point is—Steve. I care for him, Johnny, tremendously. He's so straight, so decent, so swell. I thought it was love. I was wrong. But that's all the more reason why I've got to help him now."

"Help *him?*" echoed Johnny, astounded.

"Yes. I think he's in a jam."

"Steve is?" There was a sharp edge of anxiety in his tone.

Vicki smiled.

"I needn't ask how you feel about *him*, need I? You'd die for him, wouldn't you, Johnny?"

"I wish you'd go on," he said urgently.

"I will. But be a little patient. It's a long story and rather involved. To begin with, you know about my brother Paul and Slevna."

"Yes, sure. But where does Slevna—"

"Monday morning my phone rang. It was Slevna himself.

Remember, I had never met him, never even seen him except on a concert stage. He introduced himself and was very particular about identifying me. He said: 'You are Paul Braun's sister, I know. But you are also the wife of Stephen Lake, Captain of Homicide?' I told him I was, and he said he wanted to see me. We made the appointment for that afternoon at one at his hotel, and he asked me to keep it to myself."

"Not so good."

"Oh, Johnny, you're as bad as Steve. A girl's as safe as houses, if she wants to be."

"Yes, that's true enough."

"Besides, remember it was Slevna who asked it. He's a kind of household god to us all—Dad and Paul and me. I'd do pretty much anything for him. But my honor," she interpolated quizzically, "wasn't involved. There was nothing personal in it at all. He merely wanted a—you'll never guess—a secretary!"

"But for the love of Pete—a man like Slevna! He must have barrels of 'em—social, financial, musical—what did he need you for?"

"I'm coming to it. He explained it very elaborately. So much so I should have been wise right away. I wasn't, though. I swallowed it all, hook, line and sinker—"

"Swallowed what?"

"He told me he wanted to write a short story. He said most artists have a hankering towards something outside their own line. He gave examples—Da Vinci and his flying-machines, Winston Churchill painting pictures."

"Something to that."

"I thought so, too. But he said he didn't want his own secretary—or any of his entourage—to know about it, in case it was a frost. With all his genius, he's as vain as a peacock. So it was to be a dark secret until it appeared in print. I wasn't to tell a soul, even my husband. I wasn't even to say I was at Cornwall House. I was to give him my solemn promise. It seemed a bit exaggerated and silly, but—it was Slevna. So I promised. When Steve asked me where I was Monday, I said I was at the races."

"I remember."

"Well, Slevna began dictating. My shorthand's a little rusty, so it was all I could do to keep up with him without listening to the sense of what I was taking down. It wasn't until I transcribed my notes that I began to take notice."

"It was something unusual?"

"It was the story of a musician—"

"Natural enough. An egotist would be autobiographical even in fiction."

"Perhaps. Here's the story in a nutshell. This musician—the 'I' of the story, it's all in the first person—is a much-married, much-injured, sensitive soul, disappointed in every human relationship except one—his daughter. She's a girl of eighteen, lovely, sweet, talented and utterly devoted to him, as he is to her. His whole life is centered in her. They have been inseparable—until a year before the story starts. At that time, when he was ready to leave for his concert tour, the government refused to give her an exit pass."

"Oh, it's European?"

"Yes. Prague. Slevna's own town."

"Go on."

"The musician storms at the authorities but gets no satisfaction. They are polite and bland, but unmoved. They explain courteously but firmly that there is a law: it is desirable to keep the youth of the country in the country. Even while I was taking this all down, it occurred to me that the stage had lost a good actor in Slevna. He acted it all out as he dictated, tearing up and down the room, gesticulating, there were almost tears in his voice."

"In other words it's Slevna's own story, thinly disguised."

"I thought so. And I began to understand why he didn't want his own secretary to take it down. It was pretty personal—he undressed himself down to the skin, emotionally. Well, that was as far as we got Monday. I made the date to go again Tuesday and came away."

"And told your little white lie about the races."

"Yes. Even if I hadn't promised so solemnly, it wouldn't have been easy to tell Steve I'd spent the afternoon alone with Slevna, at his apartment. He would have jumped to wrong conclusions."

"You've got something there."

"Don't blame him," she said defensively. "He can't help his disposition. It's not his fault if he's naturally jealous and suspicious. And his work hasn't made him less so."

"Detectives don't see the best side of people, you're right."

"That's it. Besides, he's always had this ridiculous inferiority complex—as if it mattered to me whether he was a few years younger or older!"

"Look, you don't have to make excuses for Steve to me."

"That's true. I'll go on. I went to Slevna's again on Tuesday. If anything, he was more excitable and nervous than the day before. My shorthand was getting smoother, I could listen while I took dictation. What I heard sounded like E. Phillips Oppenheim."

"It ought to sell. The magazines go for that stuff today."

"The point is, it began to dawn on me that the story *wasn't* for the magazines."

"I don't get you. I thought you said—"

"I got the impression that Slevna's hero was actually Slevna, the girl was actually his daughter, and the story was a sort of formal statement."

"Statement? For whom?"

"For Steve."

"Steve! Well, why didn't he make it direct to Steve?"

"You'll see in a minute."

"But why Steve at all?"

"He knew Steve was a police officer. I suppose Paul told him. Remember he's a foreigner, he wouldn't realize that a Homicide man wouldn't be the one to get in touch with."

"Get in touch for what? What's all this about, anyway?"

"You'll soon see. Slevna's 'hero' arrives in America, has his concert tour and is ready to go back to Prague and his daughter. Two days before he sails, he receives a mysterious phone call. He is ordered to be at a certain spot at a certain time to receive an important document. He is to transport this out of the country among his things and deliver it to someone abroad. Or else."

"The hostage! Good Lord!" Johnny stiffened in rapt attention.

"Exactly. At first he rebels. He's a good Czech and loves both his country and America, and he realizes that the voice on the phone is that of an enemy of both governments."

"All this is a year ago, you say?" asked Johnny sharply.

"Yes. The voice on the phone explains calmly what will happen to his daughter if he refuses to cooperate. Johnny, no fiction writer, let alone an amateur like Slevna, could make up such details."

"Such as?"

"Horrible things. The daughter will be taken into secret custody. Every day a strip of her skin will be flayed off and sent to her father— Oh, I can't go into it—" She shivered.

"Never mind. Go on with this 'story.'" Johnny's tone was grim.

"Twice during the afternoon Slevna gave himself away. Once he asked me if a repentant traitor who gave this government valuable information would still be put to death. He covered up immediately by explaining that a writer must have all his facts straight. The second slip he made—or rather the thing that made me wonder—was that he asked for Steve's full name and the address of Homicide. He put it down in a little book."

"Go on."

"Slevna's 'hero' finally gives in. He carries out their orders and delivers the document. His daughter is safe. He tries desperately to get her out of Czechoslovakia, but they still refuse her an exit pass. When he makes his next American tour he has to leave her behind again. That's as far as the dictation went Tuesday."

"And Wednesday?"

"Just a minute. On Tuesday night you were here. You and Steve discussed the Ferman case. You spoke about a document from the Toledo laboratory which was carried out of the country a year ago. Things began to fall into place. I was morally certain Slevna had done it."

"Tuesday night. This is Thursday," Johnny said sternly. "Why didn't you tell Steve at once?"

"I tried, Johnny, after you left."

"Tried! What stopped you?" Johnny asked.

"Steve himself. Do you remember the mood he was in? His talk about 'extermination' and infidelity?"

"Words!"

"No. That's a side of Steve you don't know."

"You mean you kept still about a plot against your government to save Slevna's skin?"

"I tell you I tried to tell Steve. He shut me up—"

"Bunk! Nobody could shut you up if you wanted to talk."

"All right. Perhaps I did temporize. I had good reason to. First, I was only *morally* sure about Slevna. I thought on Wednesday I'd get real proof. Second, I wanted to wait until Steve was in a better mood. In the savage temper he was in Tuesday night I would never have got to the story. The minute I said I had been alone for hours with Slevna for two afternoons, the dam would have burst. Steve would have been so wild with jealousy he'd have been deaf to everything else."

"Pretty weak, Vicki."

"Finally there was Slevna to consider."

"A traitor!"

"Against his will," Vicki continued warmly. "I'd like to know what *you'd* do if they threatened to flay your mother alive! Remember the old saying—if you hold a nickel close enough to your eye it will hide the moon? I wonder if you or anybody would deliberately throw someone dear to you to the wolves."

"Is Slevna's daughter so much to you?"

"No. But Slevna is. I told you he's been a sort of idol to my family for years. And now, just when he's giving Paul this tremendous chance—Johnny, believe me, I wouldn't let my country down; I knew I had to tell, but I did want to give Slevna the best break I could. I thought if I waited until Wednesday I might persuade him to go to the F.B.I. with the formula. Or, if he was afraid of arrest I was going to suggest that he give it to me. I'd hold it until he got out of the country."

"Well, what did happen Wednesday?"

"Slevna was in a pitiable condition. Nervous as a cat, never still for two minutes together. Jumped like a fool whenever the phone rang. He would burst out with short, broken sentences—"

"Such as?"

"Once he said: 'I did it once for her sake' and then 'I'm only flesh and blood, I can't hold out!' When I started to take it down he stopped me. Said he was only trying out lines of dialogue. I thought the time was ripe to show him I understood the situation and to advise him to go to the F.B.I. I did."

"How did he take it?"

"He nearly jumped out of his skin at the word 'police.' He was frantic. He said: 'If *they* find out I spoke to a soul, much less the police—Rosalie! What would they do to Rosalie?' He broke down and sobbed until I was nearly as unnerved as he was."

"And you still kept all this from Steve last night?" Johnny's face set into hard lines.

"You'd better hear all of it before you do any judging, Johnny," she said quietly.

"Let's have it."

"I managed to calm Slevna down a little and then begged him to put the whole thing to the authorities. There was no longer any pretense of a 'story.' He admitted the thing was for Steve, but only to be delivered to him after he'd written me that he had his daughter safely out of Czechoslovakia."

"Optimist, isn't he? Doesn't he realize it's like blackmail? The oftener he pays, the more they'll demand."

"Try and reason with a hysterical parent."

"Well, leave that. What happened next? This thing is vital. If he's carrying that formula out of the country, idol or no idol, Rieger's going to nab him."

"It gets a little—complicated from here on," she said in a queer tone.

"Well, finish it, please. I've got to act fast."

"Slevna agreed that I was right, but he said he wouldn't go to the F.B.I. until today. He was expecting a phone call last night from 'them.'"

Johnny groaned.

"Good God, Vicki! *That* was something to get our teeth into—and you still kept your mouth shut!"

"He told me to call for him this morning at eleven and take him to the proper authorities," Vicki went on, ignoring his charge. "It was five o'clock by that time and I had to leave. Slevna had an appointment somewhere uptown, so we came downstairs together. He was just asking me if he could drop me off when I saw my Chevrolet parked across the street from Cornwall House."

"You had driven to Slevna's?"

"No! That's the whole point! Steve had. He was sitting in it—or half out of it—Johnny, he looked—murderous."

"Oh, Lord!" Johnny groaned again.

"I didn't know what to do. I couldn't have a scene there. I was afraid of what Steve might do in the fury he was in. I was sure he would trail our taxi. I thought the best thing was to go home and wait for him."

"Well?"

"He never came at all. I waited an hour. I came to the conclusion that he had followed Slevna. I was worried sick. Finally I decided to tell the whole story to Dad. He might be able to explain to Steve better than I could. I rushed down to the apartment, but there was no chance to talk. The doctor was there, Dad was in the throes of a bad asthma attack, and for hours I was busy carrying out the doctor's orders. Finally the morphine worked and Dad fell asleep. I was back just where I started."

"Go on."

"I went home at eleven. By then I had decided how to handle it myself. I'd be gay and cocky, say I'd gone detective and had a spy to hand him on a platter." Her grey-green eyes swam with tears. "It was a beastly thought, offering up Slevna's little Rosalie. But I was seeing clearly now. Slevna was sailing Friday, and the formula was too important to risk. I had to do it."

"But you didn't," he accused.

"Steve never came home."

"He took over the desk from me. He spent the night at 10th Street."

"What time did he get there?"

"Somewhere about ten-thirty, I should say."

"Well, sometime during the evening he'd been home before I got there."

"How do you know that?"

"I went into the bedroom. Crossing the floor I stepped on something. It was Slevna's long, amber cigarette holder."

Johnny's jaw set stubbornly.

"Other people use long cigarette holders. Maybe Steve—"

"It had a gold band around it, with the initials 'J.S.' Here it is." She picked the slender little gadget from the table and held it out to him. Johnny took it. Without even looking at it he rubbed it from end to end with his handkerchief, casually but thoroughly.

Vicki smiled.

"Thanks, Johnny. It's not necessary. I've already wiped all prints off it."

He flushed.

"You're crazy," he denied. "There was no such thought in my mind."

"Then you're a mighty poor cop," she observed dryly.

"Don't let your imagination run away with you. You've got a melodrama all cooked up when the truth—"

"What *would* you say the truth is?"

"Why, something quite simple and homespun. Steve probably braced Slevna, got the whole story from him and had a drink with him after. Slevna lit a cigarette, cracked up long holders, said they keep the smoke out of your eyes and ended up by presenting one to Steve to try."

"Johnny, you're so swell!" she said softly. "I *wish* it was like that. But—it isn't."

"There's more?"

"I called for Slevna this morning at eleven as we had arranged."

"So?"

"He didn't answer the doorbell. I went out and phoned, and there was no answer to that, either. I didn't dare ask questions at the desk. I phoned his studio in the Carnegie Building. He wasn't there. I came home and phoned you. Johnny, I'm frightened."

"Rubbish! Steve probably has him under cover until time to meet the guy who slips him the formula. Don't you see? Slevna's the bait for the rattrap. When the rat shows, Steve cracks down."

"No. I wish that were the truth, but it isn't."

"Why isn't it?"

"Steve phoned me this morning before I left for Slevna's. If he'd known the whole story, he'd know there was no harm in my going to Cornwall House."

"Maybe he does."

"He doesn't."

"What makes you so sure?"

"His voice over the phone. He was bitter, cold, full of hate. And he was on edge, too. I know him so well. Something's wrong."

Johnny silently went over the short scene at the Bureau last night when Steve came in. He remembered how tense, how impatient, how sarcastic he had been; how he had made a weak excuse for coming and then bolstered it up by saying he was expecting a call about the Ferman case. When Johnny had asked for details, Steve had evaded him uncomfortably, and practically ordered him out of the office. Johnny had been puzzled then. Now he was a great deal more than puzzled. He was chill with fear. But aloud he scoffed:

"Got it all doped out, haven't you? Steve bumped him and took his cigarette holder as a souvenir. A real bright move—and exactly like Steve."

"Oh, Johnny, I hope you're right. Look, go back to the Bureau and tell Steve everything I've told you. I hate secrets from him. I hate any sort of secret. If we put it all out into the open, this nightmare will dissolve. I won't *have* Steve hurt and sore!"

"I'll do that." He rose and crossed the room. At the door he turned and added: "This is good-bye, Vicki. You won't be seeing me."

"Yes. Now we both know, it won't do," she replied steadily.

"I'll invent a girl or something for Steve's benefit."

"Yes—until someday there's a real girl."

"That's out." He achieved a smile. "Happy landing, Vicki."

"Happy landing, Johnny."

She smiled back with the tears running down her cheeks.

XV

When Johnny left Vicki it was raining again, a chill, steady, Novemberish rain. He hardly noticed it. He turned the collar of his raincoat up and began to walk unseeingly along the nearly empty streets. He had a problem to work out, but he lacked any rules to go by. He had promised Vicki to go back and tell Steve the whole story. That was simple enough. Once all the facts were out in the open, he and Steve could go on from there—provided all the facts *came* out in the open. But he was deadly afraid they would not.

For once in his life Johnny was close to panic. His blood ran cold at the implications of Vicki's story. He remembered Steve's ugly temper on Tuesday night, and read it now as the anguish of a man racked with jealousy. He analyzed Steve's mood last night at the Bureau, and had to admit it was the mood of a man who had something to hide. He reconstructed Vicki's story and viewed it from Steve's angle. The fact that she saw the Chevrolet across from Cornwall House told volumes. It connoted that Steve was tailing her, that he suspected a guilty relationship between her and Slevna. But he had asked Vicki no questions; instead, he had definitely avoided her and refused to listen to anything she had to say. Why?

Where had Steve been last night between five o'clock, when Slevna's taxi drove away, and ten-thirty, when he appeared at the Bureau, ravaged, hostile and tense? He had certainly made contact with Slevna. How else could the pianist's distinctive cigarette holder have come to be in Vicki's apartment? And if he had made contact with Slevna, what had he done?

All Johnny's loyalty and hero-worship of Steve revolted at putting into words the obvious answer. But he had to do it, he had to face and admit the worst, for Steve's own sake. Granted, then, that Steve had met Slevna. Probably he had refused to listen to Slevna as he had refused to listen to Vicki. Instead he had taken the law in his own hands. What was his word on Tuesday night—extermination? How, where and when this all took place Johnny could not guess. He did know that if Slevna were actually dead, he had been effectually hidden for the moment. No report of murder had reached Homicide as yet.

But Slevna was missing. He had answered neither door nor phone at eleven this morning, when he had a specific appointment with Vicki, nor was he at his studio. Johnny's comforting explanation to Vicki that Steve had put Slevna under cover was sheer bunk. If Steve had known the whole story of Slevna and the spy ring he would realize that the pianist would be under enemy observation day and night. He would not dare to be seen with him, much less smuggle Slevna away; it would defeat his own purpose, it would put the enemy wise, and all hope of nabbing them and the formula would be gone. Steve was too good a policeman to make such a *faux pas*. Johnny came to the reluctant conclusion that Steve had killed Slevna without learning any facts. It was a simple case of personal murder, temporarily undiscovered. But no murder remains undiscovered long. And a man as important as Slevna would be missed sooner than most. Any minute the hue and cry would be raised. What could Johnny do to help Steve at that crucial moment? How cover him, how be of use in steering suspicion away from him?

To be most serviceable and helpful, Johnny had to know the facts. How get them from Steve? The last thing he wanted to do was to go to Steve and say in effect:

"Look, such and such is really the case. You didn't know it and consequently killed Slevna in your ignorance. You're a murderer, but I'm here to see that they don't put the finger on you."

He knew Steve well enough to be sure that his stiff-necked pride, his difficult honor, would not let him involve Johnny as accessory after the fact. If he went to Steve and spilled Vicki's whole story, it would serve no useful end; indeed, it would actually prevent him from helping Steve. It was just in the cards that if Steve saw that he had made a frightful mistake he would deliberately give himself up and pay the full price for his passionate error. He knew Steve's dogged sense of justice too well to risk it.

How, then, was he to arm himself with the facts? How approach Steve and fish for information without showing his own hand? It was a ticklish question, and Johnny's footsteps slowed in his reluctance to reach the Bureau.

Then, with the optimism of youth, his mood changed. He told himself he was as melodramatic as Vicki; that Steve had his head in the right place and knew murder too well to indulge in it; that Slevna had reneged on his promise to go to the F.B.I. and had simply ignored Vicki's calls. Slevna was alive and well—and a traitor. He, Johnny, would go to Steve and together they would nab the pianist and sweat out of him information as to the spy ring.

He hailed a taxi and drove to the Bureau.

XVI

Johnny peeled off his dripping raincoat and hung it over a chair. In the middle room Jeff Rand was pounding a typewriter, with a sizeable number of sheets already executed. In the far room Harry O'Neil was asleep on one of the cots, and in Steve's own office, at the right, Steve appeared to be absorbed in a Police Manual. Johnny took the bull by the horns. He went into Steve's office and closed the door.

"I think I've struck oil, Steve."

Steve grunted without looking up.

"My 'little lead' paid off. I believe I know the guy who took out the scorched earth formula and who is slated to take out the germ warfare one."

Steve's whole body stiffened. The Police Manual slid to the desk. But his voice was under control. He said skeptically:

"Well, well. J. Edgar better look to his laurels."

Johnny flushed but went on steadily:

"I just got a lucky break, that's all."

"Go on. Who is this double-action Judas?"

"The pianist Slevna."

"I've heard of the gent."

"Then you know he's a Czech, too, like Ferman."

"He's also a few other things in my book. Patron of the Tarts mainly."

"I wouldn't know about that."

"What do you know?"

"The Commies have got him by the short hairs. He toes the mark or else."

"Quite a scenario." Steve looked amused. "Well. Don't die on third. Let's have it all."

"That's enough, isn't it?"

"It's plenty. Wish I could believe it."

"Look, Steve, I'm telling you straight —"

"Where'd you get this cloak-and-dagger romance?"

"From Slevna's secretary."

"That what they call 'em now?" A vicious note crept into Steve's voice. Johnny read it as a direct slur at Vicki.

"Yes," he said firmly. "When that's what they *are*."

"You're right, you don't know Slevna."

"That's neither here nor there. If Slevna's our guy—"

"Look, sonny," Steve said patronizingly. "You fell for a bill of goods. Slevna probably brushed off this secretary and she's putting the finger on him to get even."

"Maybe. But maybe not. Don't you think Rieger ought to know?"

"Okay, okay," Steve yawned. "I'll tell him."

"I'll give him a ring if you like."

"I could use a vacation," Steve said suavely. "Think you can run Homicide alone?"

Johnny stuck to his guns. Steve's whole attitude convinced him that his fears were well-founded, that Steve needed help but that he was playing a lone hand. Johnny couldn't leave it at that. He went on: "Don't be like that, Steve. I know it sounds fantastic. But fantastic things are sometimes true. If you don't want to leave yourself wide open with Rieger, why don't you and I go up and interview Slevna ourselves—"

The dam burst. Steve slammed a fist down on the desk with a crack like a pistol shot.

"Damn it, you green, nosy rookie! You belong back in uniform, and by the Lord that's where you'll be if you keep on trying to run this Bureau. This is Homicide, didn't you know? When a man gets killed, when we're called, we go. Not before. Now get, out! You hear? Get out!"

Johnny went without a word. As he opened the door he bumped bodily into Jeff Rand coming in. Rand had his report in his hand to deliver to Steve, but Johnny got the impression that the Lieutenant had been standing outside the door, and only made his move to enter when Johnny opened it.

Rand's feeling for Steve was well known to Johnny. It did not add to his peace of mind.

The afternoon crawled at a hearse's pace. Not an unnecessary word was spoken. Steve remained invisible behind his office door, Rand exchanged no acid badinage with Johnny, and Harry O'Neil snored gently in the far room.

At six Rand went out to eat and was back in half an hour. Johnny's throat was too dry to swallow food. He stuck to his desk, scared and miserable. At eight Steve appeared in his doorway. He had regained control of himself. He said pleasantly:

"Call it a day, you two. When I leave I'll wake Harry to take over."

"That punk?" Rand sneered. "Suppose a call comes in?"

"I'm on the phone. Remember?" Steve would not be drawn.

"Okay." Rand's lack of eagerness to leave looked studied to Johnny. Somehow, under his leisurely air, he seemed to be beating excited wings to go.

Rand strolled out without a good night. For all practical purposes Steve and Johnny were alone.

"Get going, son," Steve said nicely. "You were on last night till eleven. All work, y'know—" He completely ignored his earlier outburst.

Johnny took the high dive desperately.

"Steve, I didn't tell you everything before."

"Oh, more of the same?" Steve smiled good naturedly.

"Slevna's secretary's married."

"Really? Hope it doesn't cramp his style."

"Her husband's on the Force."

"Do tell! Anyone we know?" he drawled.

"She thought if she played cop herself and landed a spy it would be a great stunt. Silly, but just like an amateur. If she'd had sense and come right out with everything to her husband she could have saved a sea of trouble."

"Why didn't she?"

"She tried to."

"What 'sea of trouble' could she have saved?"

"I'm not—certain, Steve."

"It's an officer's job to *be* certain before he goes off half-cocked."

"I guess, at that, I *am* certain," Johnny said slowly. "Morally certain."

Steve yawned.

"You're a bit too literary to make a good cop," he scoffed. "You ought to be writing detective yarns instead of wasting my time."

"If you heard Slevna's secretary," Johnny persisted, "maybe you wouldn't think your time was being wasted. He's a traitor, but he isn't a bad guy—he did it because they threatened to rub out his daughter—and he only did it the one time."

Steve's mouth opened but no words came. His hand groped behind him for the edge of the desk and he leaned back heavily on his stiff arm. Then he found his voice.

"He only did it the one time," he echoed. With an effort he recaptured his derisive tone. "So that makes him a real good guy." His voice was a croak.

"I *said* he was a traitor," Johnny said steadily, sticking to his point. "But this time, when they braced him, he rebelled. He dictated the whole story to his secretary with a view to putting her husband, the police officer, wise. He did it once for the girl's sake, but he balked at doing it again—" Johnny broke off as Steve sank into the desk chair. His hands grasped a stout ruler on the desk and whitened with pressure. A deep rumble came from his throat, the words almost strangling him:

"He did it ... the one time ... then only ... for her sake...." The ruler snapped in two, the pale wood splinters quivering from the force of the break. He flung the two pieces of wood away and caved in on himself. The stresses of the last three days, the sleepless nights, the sudden realization of how he had twisted facts and actions to the point where he had committed murder, suddenly caught him like an engulfing tide. His face was grey, his eyes glazed, lines ran down his cheeks like rivers on a map. It was as if he were disintegrating before Johnny's eyes. Johnny couldn't stand the sight. He looked away. There was a long silence, so deep the ticking of the wall clock sounded deafening.

Suddenly Steve threw back his head and began to laugh, a loud, horrifying, raucous laugh.

"Of course he's a good guy!" he shouted between roars of bitter laughter. "But he's only 'flesh and blood!' 'What would any man do?' 'You'd have done the same.' It was 'just the one time,' as you say. And he did it—'for her sake!'"

Then he slumped over the desk, his head in his arms. Johnny crept silently out.

XVII

Johnny was still tiptoeing when he reached the ground floor. He was wet with sweat, and as he stepped out into the driving rain his stomach was fluttering with butterfly-tremors. The chill air struck him to gooseflesh. At the corner the neon light of the bar and grill gave him an idea. It crossed his mind that when Steve was over the worst of his emotional crisis he would need a drink badly. The whole Bureau used the corner bar. If Johnny waited for him there, perhaps Steve would be less intransigent and grim. He might still be able to help.

He turned into the warm, cozy bar and ordered a double rye. As it flooded his insides, he realized how badly he, too, had needed a drink. He sat staring into his empty glass, miserably turning over the whole ghastly situation in his mind. He was as sure as fate that Slevna was dead and that Steve had killed him. Where had it happened? What had Steve done with the body? Had he left any incriminating clues behind him? When the call finally came in, would Steve conduct the investigation himself? *Could* he and not give himself away? What could he, Johnny, do to steer suspicion away from Steve? Would Vicki gather the truth? And what effect would it have on their marriage? What on earth could Johnny do to help! A mocking voice broke in on him:

"If it isn't little Lord Fauntleroy! And drinking a real man-size shot of poison." Jeff Rand had moved to the stool beside him, nursing a mild highball. Johnny pulled himself together.

"Hiya, Rand. Thought you'd left long ago."

"Did it seem that long, sweetheart?" Rand grinned. "I've only been here five or ten minutes." It was true. But to Johnny, who had been through a cataclysm in those few minutes, it seemed hours since Rand, ambling out, had left him alone with Steve.

"Yeah, you're right, I guess," said Johnny vaguely. His brain was still pounding out questions. Rand's voice rambled on in his ears, but the sense of what he said did not penetrate. It was only when Rand took his arm and rose that he took in his words:

"—enough for mamma's boy on an empty stomach. Come on, I'll walk you to the subway."

"Thanks, I like it here," he returned. He had no intention of leaving.

"Waiting for the tin hero?"

"Meaning?"

"I'll draw it for you," Rand jibed. "Why don't you get wise to yourself, Elsie Dinsmore, sucking up to a stinker like—"

"Look," Johnny interrupted. "When I need advice I'll come running."

"Horatio at the bridge. Bounce back among the living, kid, before that bird takes you over the jumps."

Johnny yawned in Rand's face deliberately.

"How're your etchings these days?" he asked.

"Okay, okay," Rand shrugged. "Only don't say I didn't warn you."

"I won't say a thing," Johnny said solemnly.

"There's two dumb guys and you're both of 'em. So you won't come along to the subway?"

"I thought you lived in the Village?"

"That's right."

"Well, what's the idea of the subway for ten blocks?"

Rand's face took on a secretive grin.

"Got a little errand uptown first."

"That so?"

"Yeah. Y'see, I got a kind of tip-off if I moseyed around Cornwall House tonight I might jump the gun."

Johnny never turned a hair.

"Cornwall House? That's up near where I live." His veins were running ice. So Rand *had* listened at the door.

"Yeah, right in the income-tax zone."

"And what's with Cornwall House?"

"I won't know till I get there."

"You're sure a glutton for work, snooping in your off-time."

"I think maybe it'll pay off."

"Break it down into English. What gives at Cornwall House?"

"Ever hear of a guy named Slevna?"

"I've heard of Heifetz, too."

"Bright, ain't you? Well, I've got a pretty straight tip that somebody's gunning for Slevna—or maybe the gun's already gone off."

"Listens like double-talk to me." Johnny's heart sounded a rataplan. He wondered that Rand didn't hear it.

"Maybe so. What have I got to lose?"

"Not a thing." Johnny threw some change on the counter. He knew he couldn't wait for Steve now. He had to stick to Rand, either to dissuade him from going to Cornwall House or, if that were impossible, to be on the spot to take what steps he could to shield Steve.

"Be seeing you," said Rand, moving off.

"Wait. Might as well hit the sack myself as stay in this dump. I'll ride with you to Columbus Circle."

"That was a fast switch, sonny boy." Rand's dark face was full of malicious humor. "Maybe you'd like to join me. I always like travelling in twos on a case."

"Always supposing there *is* a case." They breasted the slanting rain on Seventh Avenue, heading for 23rd Street. "Personally I think it's about as cockeyed a trip as ever I heard of. Where'd you get this tip, anyway?"

"Oh. I have my little contacts," Rand said blandly.

"Bet you're wired for sound, too."

"Could be. Y'know, nobody's pushing you in the back to come."

They rode to 59th Street without a word. Johnny watched him covertly. Rand's face was a mixture of sly complacence and sullen resentment. Johnny realized how dangerous the mixture was. Rand knew that Johnny suspected him of eavesdropping. He had almost admitted it insolently. He must be very sure of himself, very certain that he had Steve in a tight corner to flaunt his contempt so openly. Johnny realized there was no chance of dissuading him from investigating. He also knew that Rand would watch him like a hawk. If there was any covering up to do, any tampering with clues, it would have to be done with consummate cunning.

As they climbed the subway stairs, Rand turned to him, a faint misgiving clouding his cocksureness for a moment.

"We're both off duty," he said. "If it's a flop, we don't spill, see?"

"Yes, Lieutenant," Johnny said gravely. "It'll be a secret just between the two of us."

Rand frowned but let it pass. He wanted Johnny along with him. If he found what he suspected he would find, the evidence would be all the more damning coming from Steve's best friend. Yesterday's vigil in Central Park had paid off, when Steve's wife had come out of the hotel with Slevna. Steve's face at that time, and the shocked paralysis which had assailed him, had been easy for Rand to read and interpret. Tonight, Steve's outburst to Johnny in the office had put the cap on the situation. Rand told himself that Captain Lake of Homicide was on the skids, and the thought was music to him.

He and Johnny turned into Cornwall House.

XVIII

Instantly Rand changed. His bearing became severe but dignified. He had a proper sense of his own position and a decent regard for others. Civilly he introduced himself to the night desk clerk. An expression akin to horror spread over the gentlemanly employee at the idea of the police in the sacred precincts of Cornwall House.

"We're looking," said Rand, "for a Mr. Slevna."

The desk clerk gaped.

"A Mr. Slevna! You mean *the* Mr. Slevna?"

"All right, *the* Mr. Slevna. What's his room number?"

"But—but—I don't understand—"

"It's not necessary for you to understand. Just let me have the number."

"But he's not in, Lieutenant."

"Oh? When did he go out?"

"He—well, last night, I think."

"You *think?*"

"It could have been this morning, sir."

"Don't you know which?"

"Not exactly, sir. You see—oh, dear—" He washed his manicured hands with invisible soap. "I hope he— What's the trouble, sir?"

"When was he in, to your actual knowledge?"

"Last night about this time. Wait, I can tell you exactly. It'll be on the phone slip."

"Phone slip?"

"Yes, sir. He called the desk—" The clerk fumbled with a small file of memoranda. "Here it is. At 8:53 p.m. Wednesday night he phoned down to say he was not to be disturbed."

"Go on."

"I spoke to him personally. That's how I'm sure he was in then."

"And what makes you so sure he's not in now?"

"This second slip. Here. At 9:10 a.m. this morning the day clerk left it for me, so that if anyone came or called I would know what to say."

"Let's have that slip," said Rand, reaching. He glanced through it. "Someone *calling for Slevna* at nine-ten this morning informed you that he would not be in until late this afternoon or tonight."

"Yes, Lieutenant. So of course I know he isn't in."

"When did you come on duty?"

"At seven."

"How do you know Slevna didn't get back before you came on?"

"He would have called the desk. He always does."

"He may have neglected it for once. We'll go up."

"Really, sir," the clerk was full of distress. "I couldn't—not without announcing you—"

"No announcing."

"But it's Mr. *Slevna,* sir. You realize who—"

"Where's the manager?"

The clerk's face cleared miraculously.

"In his office. I'll take you up, sir."

With relief he led the way up a small half-flight of stairs beside the desk, to a mezzanine gallery, and knocked on a door. Now that the responsibility of disturbing a star guest was shifted to other shoulders he was his suave, debonair self again. At a call from within he opened the door to the handsome office.

"Someone to see you, Mr. Galway," he said.

Rand introduced himself again and explained:

"We have reason to believe Mr. Slevna may be in danger of some sort. We are here to check up on him as a precautionary measure. Nothing to get excited about. Just take us up to his room."

Galway, a bald, capable-looking man, made no demur.

"Certainly, Lieutenant. You understand we like to protect our guests from annoyance, but if it is a matter of real trouble, I am sure Mr. Slevna will understand and excuse the intrusion."

"He may damn well welcome it," Rand observed.

"Indeed." Galway picked up an immense metal hoop with keys dangling from it. "But how anything could threaten him *here* under *our* eyes—"

"Probably a false alarm, but we have to look into these things."

Galway led the way to the elevator, where he made some esoteric signal, for they were joined by a beefy individual, unmistakably the house detective. The desk clerk scurried back to his duties and Rand, Johnny, Galway and McGuire, the detective, took the elevator to the fifth floor.

Galway rang the bell of 512 twice without results.

"Better open up," said Rand.

The manager used the master key, switched on the foyer light and stood back, letting Rand and Johnny go first. Johnny was tense with apprehension of what they might find. He half-expected a sprawled figure on the floor of the dark living room ahead of them. He set his jaw and schooled his features to a dead-pan blankness.

The manager snapped on the living room lights, then those in the bedroom. The whole place had the placid air of the usual. Rand looked everywhere, in the bathroom, in the clothes closet, under the bed.

"I think it *must* have been a false alarm," said Galway, faintly supercilious.

"This the whole apartment?" Rand asked.

"There is a small office—" He led the way. One glance was enough to prove it was empty. Rand gnawed his lip.

"Well, that's that," he said with something like chagrin. Johnny's heartbeats began to grow normal. Then, as if unwilling to give up,

Rand added: "Where's that door lead to?"

"A closet," said Galway.

Rand tried the door.

"Open it up," Rand ordered.

"Now really, Lieutenant, I've been very cooperative and forbearing. I did an unprecedented thing to bring you up here at all, but I have limits. When it comes to prying into Mr. Slevna's private concerns, when you see for yourself that there is nothing amiss—"

"Open it up," repeated Rand.

Galway shrugged.

"I refuse all responsibility, you understand. The thing is your baby from here on in. I'm doing it solely because I never resist an officer of the law."

"That's your angle. Here's mine: when I report to my superior that I investigated the Slevna rumor I have to be able to say that I searched the *whole* apartment, not everywhere except one closet. Get it?"

Galway nodded resignedly and selected a slim key from the ring. The lock turned back smoothly; the manager threw open the door.

"There you are, Lieutenant, now you'll be able to report—Great God in Heaven!" Galway fell back, gasping with shock. Rand stepped forward and stood for a second, looking down at the crumpled body with its head at a ghastly angle. His dark eyes were alight with something that filled Johnny with more horror than the body on the floor. Despair crept through him as he read relish and triumph in Rand's eyes.

But the Lieutenant wasted no more time on personal emotions. In clipped tones he asked Galway: "This is Slevna?"

Galway nodded, speechless. McGuire stooped and supplemented: "Sure is. The poor guy's neck's broken. Well, wadda ya know!" Rand glanced at the keyhole inside the closet door.

"No key. He was killed, stashed in here and locked up. Coat and cane shoved in after him, so it would look like he really *was* out. Our killer is a clever gent. Thinks of everything. Sergeant, call the M.O. Get me the whole outfit. Print and camera men. Morgue wagon. The works."

Johnny stepped towards the phone, but Rand was too quick for him.

"Hold it! Don't use that phone till it's dusted by the boys."

"Right, sir."

Before Rand could say more, Johnny was out of the room and on his way downstairs. Instead of using the booths in the hotel he strode through the lobby and out. On the street he began to run to the corner where a magnificent drugstore gleamed colorfully through the slanting rain. He fumbled for nickels as he ran.

His first call was to 20th Street. Steve answered.

"Look, Steve." Johnny stuttered in his haste. "I'm up at Cornwall House with Rand. Hell's loose."

There was a pause while Johnny waited for some comment. Finally he went on:

"You there, Steve?"

"Yeah." The voice was grim. "I'm here."

No questions as to what "Hell's loose" meant. That told Johnny volumes. Steve said:

"Pretty fast work of Rand's. How far is he?"

"Just started. I'm phoning the M.O. and technical men."

Another pause. Johnny could almost feel Steve weighing and considering silently.

"I'm in a pretty good spot to lend a hand, Steve," he ventured.

Steve spoke, decision firming his tone to crispness: "There's just one thing you can do—"

"Anything."

"Slow it up. Keep Rand there as long as you can. I need time."

"*Time?*" Johnny echoed stupidly. His jaw dropped. Steve was going to run!

"You heard me," Steve said evenly.

Johnny pulled himself together. If that's the way Steve wanted it—

"Look, Steve. On Second Avenue, near 51st Street, is the Angelus Garage. Dad's Cadillac is there. I'll give the night man a ring he should let you have it. If you're short of cash, stop by the house. Dad always has a few hundred in the safe—"

"Thanks," Steve cut in. "That won't be necessary."

"But your Chevy'll be spotted—"

"That's my angle. All I want of you is to keep Rand on the job up there until twelve. Can you do that?"

"I'll do my damnedest."

"Good."

"I'll work like a snail if that's what you want. But Steve—maybe if you sit tight—"

"One thing more. You never called here. Understand? If Homicide knows nothing, if it doesn't go on the blotter, the newspaper boys don't get tipped."

"Okay."

"And when you call the M.O. and so on, you keep names out of it. All you report is a *stiff*. Get me?"

"Yes."

The phone clicked as Steve hung up. Slowly, mechanically, Johnny hung up, too. He couldn't believe it. Steve—*Steve Lake*—taking it on the lam like any yellow punk—it couldn't be happening. But Steve had said practically—all Johnny could do was to delay the alarm—give him a head-start till twelve o'clock—he thought of Vicki—he had to warn her—the first place Rand would head for would be Steve's home—

He dialed Vicki's number. When he was connected he said guardedly: "Vicki? You were right."

"Slevna is—?"

"Yes."

"Who—how do you —?"

"Rand. He seems to be wise to the whole business. He was hell-bent to investigate. I came along to do what I could."

"Where's Steve?"

"At the Bureau—*now*—"

"*Now?* What does that mean?"

"He's running for it."

"Johnny, are you insane? *Steve* run for it!" She actually snorted.

"I know. It sounds crazy. I can hardly—but he *said*—"

"You misunderstood him—"

"He asked me to slow up Rand—to give him time—"

"I don't care what he *said*. I know Steve—"

"Vicki, what can we *do?*"

"Leave it to me," she said coolly. "Nothing'll happen to Steve while I have a tongue in my head. I'll swear Slevna tried to—"

"And *I* know Steve better than that. He'll move heaven and earth to keep your name out of it."

"I'll beat him to it," she retorted promptly.

"It'll be a dirty business."

"So what. Headlines for a few days. Maybe even a movie offer." She laughed, her voice trembling.

"Vicki, you've got what it takes. Only—Slevna was stashed away in a closet. That's not so good."

"I'll think up something," she said composedly. "Thanks for calling."

Johnny phoned the Medical Officer and technical men. Then he went back to Cornwall House where he found Rand busy gathering data from the manager as to Slevna's professional family. He glanced up as Johnny came in, his shoulders dark with rain, but he made no comment. Nevertheless, Johnny was sure that he knew Steve had been alerted. It was as if he did not object to that, as if it would suit his book perfectly for Steve to decamp guiltily. Rand wasn't bloodthirsty. He didn't necessarily want Steve to burn, he only wanted Steve's place. Rand went on to Galway:

"Miss Helen Cousins, the secretary. Mr. Felix Benjak, the manager. Mr. Harry Klemm, the press agent. Get 'em here. Fast. No family in America, you say? Now, about dames?"

Galway held out imploring hands.

"Please, Lieutenant, what earthly purpose could it serve to—"

"Somebody killed him—"

"But no woman could strike a blow sufficient to break his neck—"

"Maybe not. But dames have brothers and boyfriends. Give."

"This is intolerable. I am answerable to the Board of Directors for the impeccability of Cornwall House—"

McGuire cut in:

"It's murder, Mr. Galway. We got no choice."

Galway gave up with a hopeless gesture. McGuire said:

"I'll give you the dope, Loot. Slevna's a boy with the skirts, but he don't—didn't—play the field. One at a time. Very hot while it lasted. No eyes for has-beens or might-bes."

"Okay. Who's the current one?"

"Violet Claire, the movie star."

"How long has she been aces?"

"A good two months."

"And her predecessor?"

"Lolita Perez, the dancer."

"Mex, eh? Hot stuff, quick temper if she was brushed."

"Perez would use a knife," McGuire pointed out.

"Her boyfriend mightn't. Get her. Now, about these ex-wives of Slevna's. Locate 'em, bring 'em in. My Sergeant'll go with you and take charge."

Johnny knew this was all just window dressing. If Rand had believed any of these people had anything to do with Slevna's death he would not have allowed McGuire a finger in locating them. He would never have taken a chance that the guilty one among them would be forewarned by the hotel personnel. Rand's real concern came at the end, casually, as if it were a mere afterthought.

"I want the daytime desk clerk."

"He's asleep," said Galway.

"Wake him."

"But what could he tell you?"

Rand replied in measured, complacent tones:

"He can describe the murderer's voice for me. He talked to him over the phone this morning at nine-ten. He said Slevna wouldn't be in till late, when all the time—" he jerked a thumb towards the gruesome music closet.

During this questioning, Johnny had not been idle. He worked his way around behind Rand's back and stood at the desk, his hands behind him, a handkerchief concealed in one of them. Carefully he polished the two desk phones and the edge of the desk itself. He itched to get to the cane in the music closet, but for the moment it was out of the question.

While the manager went to arouse Pitkin, the day desk clerk who lived in a tiny aerie under the Cornwall House tiles, Rand put McGuire through a questionnaire about Slevna's appearances in the lobby on Wednesday.

"Sure I was around," the house detective said. "He came down about five with that little secretary of his—"

"Miss Cousins?"

"Nope, the special."

Rand's ears moved a trifle, like a bunny sensing danger.

"What's her name?"

"Search me. She's new. Been comin' afternoons all week. Slevna sent down word to let her up without announcing."

"Sure she was a—secretary?"

"Five'll bring you ten she was. Nice enough lookin' kid, but not Slevna's speed."

"You never can tell. Variety, y'know."

"I can tell. The kid wore the same togs four times in a row."

"*Four* times? She was here today, too?"

"Yep. Earlier today, though. Before lunch. Didn't stay, came down lookin' kind of puzzled and beat it."

"Describe her."

"I did."

"Be a little more concrete. Light or dark, plump or thin—"

"Medium. Little red in her hair, nice loose wave. Shape just right.

Very young and fresh-looking. Extra-long eyelashes."

"Congratulations, McGuire. You've got a photographic eye. But you mean to tell me she's got all that and Slevna took no notice?"

"That's right. They came down together and grabbed a cab. I've watched Slevna with dames for years. This girl was a secretary. Period."

"I want her found."

"You'll have to do that chore yourself, Loot. I got no notion where to look for her."

"I'll do that, I assure you. Go on with your story."

"Slevna came back in alone. About eight-thirty, judge. That's the last time I saw him."

"You didn't see him go through the lobby later last night or this morning?"

"Nope."

"Could he have got out of the hotel without you seeing him?"

"Easy. I eat and sleep, y'know, and go to the bathroom. Or he could of stepped out of the elevator and across into the bar without coming through the lobby at all. He could reach the street direct from the bar."

But the Medical Officer, who had arrived and got to work by now, knocked the props from under that supposition. Slevna, he announced, had been dead for fully twenty-four hours. Rigor had come and gone. The M.O. said he could be more definite when he did the post—an analysis of the stomach content would show exactly how far along digestion of Slevna's last dinner had progressed. No doubt whoever he had dined with would come forward and confirm the exact hour of the dinner. They would be able to place the time of death within an hour or so.

The print men began dusting with their insufflators while Johnny stood helpless in an agony of dread, with Rand's cold eye returning to him with a significant regularity. Flash lamps plopped as the cameramen shot the scene for the record.

Pitkin, hastily dressed and red-eyed from sleep, came in. The sight of the honored guest of Cornwall House with his neck twisted like a Thanksgiving turkey's, was nearly too much for him. He gulped frantically to keep his last meal down, and a fine dew of sweat appeared on his forehead and upper lip. He told his meagre story about the phone message at nine-ten that morning.

"Break it down," demanded Rand.

"Sir?"

"Describe the man who phoned."

"But—but—"

"Young or old?"

"Well—neither, noticeably. He did have a kind of authority—a sort of self-possession, if you know what I mean."

"I think I know," said Rand grimly. "Go on. Foreigner?"

"Oh, no. No accent at all."

"Educated?"

"Well, yes, sir. At least refined and grammatical."

"It could have belonged to a friend of Slevna's?"

"Oh, easily."

"Didn't sound flustered or panicky?"

"Not at all. Very composed."

"Cold proposition, eh?"

"Not exactly. My impression was more—he was impersonal and civil. That comes closest."

"It never struck you as—fishy, for another person to call instead of Slevna himself?"

"Very usual, Lieutenant. Mr. Slevna was a man who required a good bit of service. It would be natural for him to ask someone else to do his phoning for him. I never gave it a second thought."

Rand dismissed him with a nod and turned back to Galway and McGuire.

"Unquestionably Slevna was killed here in this room some time after eight-fifty-three last night. I'll want that desk clerk downstairs to come up—you can take his place, Mr. Pitkin—and among you all I want a complete picture of who came in and up here after eight-thirty last night. I'll want the doorman and the elevator boys. The killer got in, so somebody must have seen him."

Beginning with McGuire, Rand dredged the silt of their memories. One after another he quizzed and catechized the elevator men. With the aid of the night clerk he verified that every passenger in every elevator from 7 p.m. on had been announced from the desk, and was on legitimate business in Cornwall House and duly accounted for. The elevator men achieved astounding feats of memory. But no one of them had conveyed an unclassified visitor up to any floor at all, much less to the fifth, specifically. Again Rand turned to McGuire:

"What about the stairs? A well-dressed man could ease into the lobby from the bar and slip up the stairs, couldn't he?"

"He could, but he didn't," McGuire came back. "It so happens for once

I was on the job without a break until one in the morning."

"With one eye on the fire door?" Rand jibed.

"That's right," McGuire said imperturbably. "You'd be surprised, Loot, how important a part of my job those stairs are. Gentlemen sneak thieves don't use elevators. And when I say nobody slipped through the fire door and up the stairs from the lobby, you can take it as true, one hundred per cent."

"Up the stairs from the lobby," Rand echoed. "Any other way of getting up the stairs besides from the lobby?"

"Sure, the basement. But there's always a man on the job down there until the service door is locked for the night."

"Get me the man who was on the job last night."

Another tousled employee was routed from his slumbers, a phlegmatic Norwegian handyman named Anderson, who stunned them all with his first sentence:

"Sure, I know who did it."

"Who was it?" Rand rapped out, his nostrils flaring.

"Little feller with black hair," said Anderson.

"You saw him?"

"No."

"Then how do you know?"

"Cop said so."

"Cop? What cop?"

"He bane come running after little feller."

"Running where?"

"Up the stairs."

"The fire stairs?"

"Ya-as."

"Now let me get this straight. What time was all this?"

"Could be eight o'clock. I am just finishing taking out ashcans."

"All right. So what happened? A little fellow with black hair—"

"No. Cop."

"What cop?"

"Yust a cop. Come running after little feller with—"

"But you said there *was* no little fellow—"

"That's right. Yust cop, looking for him."

"Oh. The cop *said* there was a little fellow—"

"Ya-as."

"But *you* didn't see him?"

"I bane taking out ashes. Cop asked me to grab him."

"How could you grab him if you never saw him?"
"Cop says grab him if he comes down."
"And did he come down?"
"No."
"What did the cop do?"
"Went after little feller with black hair."
"Went where?"
"Up the stairs."
Rand let out his breath in an audible sigh.
"Now we're getting somewhere," he said. "This—*cop* went upstairs."
"That's right."
"Did he find the little fellow?"
"I don't know about that."
"Why not?"
"I don't see nobody again."
"What do you mean? The cop had to come down again."
"Nobody came down. No little feller. No cop."

The luminous spark of relish and triumph lit Rand's eyes again. Johnny knew exactly what thoughts were going on in Rand's mind: they were going on in his own. Both detectives saw how artistically simple Steve's entrance into Cornwall House had been.

"Now, Mr. Anderson," Rand said softly, "I want you to describe this cop to me."

Johnny held his breath.

XIX

Anderson appeared to enjoy the limelight. His ruddy moon face was split by a pleased grin. His Mediterranean-blue eyes shuttled from one to the other of his distinguished audience. It was a great moment in Nils Anderson's life when the august manager of Cornwall House hung on his words.

"Cop was a big feller," he began.
"My size?" asked Rand.
"Bigger. Big as him." He indicated Johnny. "Only fatter."
"How do you mean—fatter?" Rand frowned.
"Belly."
"Sure about that?" This was not so good.
"Sure. Uniform just about busting over belly."

Rand's eyes narrowed speculatively. They met Johnny's and moved away. But to both men the same thought occurred: all uniforms are supplied by the Department tailors, and all uniforms are built to *fit*, be the policeman ever so stout or ever so thin. There was no such thing as a cop on duty bursting out of his uniform. It would have been noticed at morning inspection and corrected without delay. Anderson's "cop" was marked as a phony and his belly tagged as a disguising pillow.

"All right," said Rand blandly to the handyman. "The cop was big and fat. What else?"

"Ears stuck out."

"Did, eh? Was he light or dark?"

"Don't know. Cap came down too far to see."

Another boner. Policemen's caps fit their heads. Rand smiled at Steve's stupidity, and it was all Johnny could do to keep from explaining:

"It *wasn't* stupid. Those tricks were only meant to fool the handyman—and they did. When it came to investigators seeing through the dodge they'd have a tough time running down the man who hid behind a uniform." Instead, he said aloud:

"Lieutenant, you want me to check on all costumers to find out who rented a policeman's uniform recently?"

"It's an idea," Rand drawled. Then to Anderson: "Anything else?"

"Ya-as. Cop had bad teeth."

"Well!" said Rand admiringly. "You're certainly a great observer. What about these bad teeth?"

"Big hole yust in front of mouth. No teeth."

Rand bit his lip to keep from grinning. It was child's play. The whole Bureau knew the story of Steve and Smike Lonergan, how Steve, tied like a bundle on the floor, had rolled over and bitten Smike's ankle; how in his anguish Smike had kicked back, knocking out two of Steve's teeth.

The thing was open and shut to anyone who had the key to the solution. Johnny knew that Rand did have the key. Somehow he had got wind of the personal angle in the Steve-Slevna setup, and for all practical purposes his case was wrapped up.

But Slevna's official family was beginning to arrive, and Rand had to go through the motions of questioning each one of them, demanding alibis and checking their answers. Miss Helen Cousins, the dead man's secretary, created a diversion and a delay by having hysterics.

To Johnny, anything that kept Rand on the job was all to the good. His efforts to calm Miss Cousins were inept in the extreme. He didn't even care if Rand noticed it. His one object was delay. Every five minutes he looked at his watch, almost unaware that he did so. But Rand was well aware of it. After half a dozen such glances, Rand said in an amused tone:

"You don't have a date, do you, Sergeant?"

"No. No. Not at all. I've got all night."

Rand's lips twitched.

"I believe you," he observed dryly. Then he looked at his own watch and added: "Ten-fifty-two. Two hours since we discovered the body. Guy can do a lot in two hours. Get a good piece on the way to Canada if you like that country. Or even a nice start on the road to Mexico if your tastes run that way."

"That's right," Johnny agreed non-committally. He felt like shooting Rand in his tracks.

The last witness to arrive was Señorita Lolita Perez, although from the standpoint of distance she should have been the first, since it developed that she lived in Cornwall House and was at home when McGuire tried to get in touch with her. But for Señorita Perez to make a public appearance without due preparation was unthinkable. Not that she showed signs of deliberate art. Her make-up was applied with so delicate a touch that she gave the impression of a flower-like girl, risen dewy-eyed from innocent sleep. Her appearance was a blend of lusciousness and piquancy which was quite unfair to the male sex. Even the hard-boiled Rand handled her with kid gloves.

"Now, Miss Perez, nothing to be frightened about—I understand you were quite friendly with the deceased."

"Long ago, señor."

"How long?"

"A year—seex months—four months—"

"That's not so long ago."

"Even yesterday ees sometimes long ago, señor."

"I see what you mean. Once you split up—"

"You say eet very well, señor." She turned the innocent battery of her brown velvet eyes on him. Rand cleared his throat.

"Now, Miss Perez," he asked self-consciously, "how well did you know him?"

"We were *simpatico—como se dice?*—devoted—"

"In other words pretty intimate."

"Yes. Eenteemate," she nodded like a pleased child.

"But not any longer. How is that?"

"You know, señor, how thees thing go," she said with a charming shrug. "First one ees warm, then the taste change, the heart lose eets heat—*quién sabe?*"

Rand reddened a little and looked as if he thought Slevna had all the luck but hadn't known when he was well off.

"While this—er—cooling off was going on, did you quarrel with him?"

"Quarrel? *Jamas*—but never, señor."

"Parted good friends, eh?"

"As you say," she agreed.

"When did you see him last?"

"Not since long—Febrero—Abril—many months."

"Now let me ask you, while you were—er—friendly, did you know if he had any enemies?"

"Yes," she replied readily.

Rand stared.

"He did! Who was that?"

"I do not know any names, *exactemente*. I know only that he fear greatly some person, some *enemigo*, who will put heem in prison."

"Prison? What for?"

"*Traicion, espia—como se dice?*—I have one leetle suspeecion Señor Slevna was spy."

A small dart of hope ran through Johnny. If this spy stuff was played up, it might help Steve and protect Vicki.

But Rand's reaction was much less pleased. His mouth opened in astonishment. He had missed overhearing the early part of Johnny's talk with Steve, and this angle was news to him—and unfavorable news at that. If Steve had been tailing Slevna yesterday afternoon on spy business, that let out the personal angle—Rand shook his head. No man's face froze to the rage Steve's had shown when Slevna came out of Cornwall House with Mrs. Lake. Where did Mrs. Lake figure in the thing altogether unless it was the way Rand had taped it? The Cap's little wife had been stepping out and he had caught her in the act. It explained everything. He wished Miss Perez hadn't brought up this cockeyed line, and he didn't attach any importance to it. Still, for Johnny's benefit and for the record, he couldn't ignore it.

"How do you know all this, Miss Perez?" he asked.

"Señor Slevna talk een hees sleep," she said placidly, batting her incredible eyelashes at him.

Rand grew red as fire as McGuire suppressed a snicker.

"I see. Well, Miss Perez, thanks for your help. You try and remember something more definite about this—er—enemy—and when you do, let me know."

"Yes, señor. *Con mucho gusto.*"

Lolita made a swanlike exit.

The morgue wagon had taken the body away, the print and cameramen were finished, the M.O. had done his job, there were no more witnesses to interview at the moment. It was just eleven. Rand arranged to leave a patrolman in the apartment and turned to Johnny:

"Well, nothing more here. Might as well go down and report to the Captain." There was real gusto in his voice.

Hopelessly Johnny agreed. How could he stall Rand for another hour? It would only take them ten or fifteen minutes to reach 20th Street from here. And Steve had said twelve o'clock.

The unseasonable chill rain was still lashing down as the doorman swung the revolving door and inquired: "Cab, sir?"

Johnny grasped at a straw.

"This place has a swell bar. I could do with a drink before we call it a night."

To his surprise, considering the relish Rand had shown to get back to the Bureau, the Lieutenant agreed. He sipped his Southern Comfort leisurely. He made only one remark:

"Yes, sir, a good car could be halfway to Albany by now in spite of the wet. Ready, Sergeant?"

It was eleven-twenty.

XX

Steve never knew how long it was after Johnny left that he sat bowed over his desk, his mind a chaos, his whole existence disrupted and demoralized. His very soul was sick with the realization of disaster. It was not alone the fact that he had killed a man. Indeed, in this particular case he had probably done Slevna a sort of backhanded favor. The egotistic pianist would undoubtedly have welcomed death in one swift, unexpected blow rather than the ignominy of trial as a traitor with a shameful death at the end of it. Possibly, too, his daughter's life was in less danger, now that she could not be used as a lever to force her father to more deeds of treachery. The Czech Communists would more than likely drop her from their reckonings as a handy tool.

What wrecked Steve was the knowledge of his own criminal folly. He had not sought the truth sincerely; he had only worked to build up a case, a watertight case against Vicki, regardless of the fact that the circumstantial evidence did not fit her character. For four days now he had been crushing down the certain knowledge he had of her decency and integrity. Occasionally doubts had assailed him when he made his mental accusations of deceit and infidelity against her. Never once had he raised a finger to clear the thing up by a straightforward question or two. Indeed, when Vicki, both on Tuesday night and this very morning, had made strenuous efforts to lay the whole story bare, he had repulsed her bitterly and harshly.

He saw at last, and far too late, the origin of that bitterness and harshness. They rose from his own ego. He had played the Captain of Homicide in a domestic crisis. He had taken command with a high hand, enforcing his own professional methods in a matter where understanding, tolerance and warmth were demanded. With cold, smug satisfaction he had pursued his project to trap her, to jockey her into a spot where *she* would be abased and *he* would be in a strong position to mete out punishment or forgiveness as he saw fit. He clutched his head in a frenzy of self-loathing as he remembered his dictum of Monday evening: "In my book, the guy who brings in the dough is the head of the house." He remembered, too, the regret in Vicki's tone when she answered him: "You know something? It's not too good." His own tyrannical, jealous arrogance had prevented her from telling him of the Slevna business right from the first. She had told her petty white lies about the races because she could not rely on her husband to understand and trust her. He had failed her. Was that failure what she meant when she said: "There are worse things than infidelity?" He dropped his hands in despair.

But in spite of the whole ghastly calamity Steve could not wallow for long in a sea of torment. He was essentially a man of action, and there was work to be done. He would face his emotional crisis when he had to, but first there was an enemy to be laid by the heels.

He saw suddenly that last night's decision to act alone was bombastic posturing, mere blatant strutting. He, Steve Lake, was going to play the hero, hog the limelight, make a grandstand play in the guise of reparation, atonement, self-sacrifice. What did his petty, personal dilemma matter compared to this grim game where the stakes were whole nations? Who was he, a mere Homicide detective, to think he could handle delicate espionage work like this?

He did what he should have done twenty-four hours ago—picked up the phone and called Rieger. He would tell him everything, asking only that Vicki be kept out of it, letting his own rage at the traitor be the ostensible excuse for the fatal blow.

Rieger was not in.

"What's Rieger's home phone?" Steve asked the clerk on duty in a kind of desperation.

"Won't do you any good. Rieger's in Delaware."

"Can he be reached?"

"No, he's moving around."

"When do you expect him back?"

"Hard to say. Tonight or tomorrow, depending on the breaks."

"If he gets in by eleven-thirty, tell him to ring me."

"Right. You'll be there up to eleven-thirty. That it?"

"Yes. Tell him to call the minute he gets in."

"I'll do that."

Steve hung up, inordinately disappointed.

The phone on his desk rang. He frowned, hoping ardently that it was no new case arising to complicate his plans. It was Johnny with his "Hell's loose." Steve thought fast. With Rieger unavailable, he now had no choice but to carry out the meeting in the Park himself. He might not handle it as well as Rieger, but there was no other way out. He considered calling back and asking for another of the F.B.I. men to take over. But Rieger was the espionage expert. The other men at Foley Square—counterfeiting agents, Customs specialists—what could they do that Steve himself couldn't do as well? It was Rieger or himself. But he needed time. Rand had to be stalled. Over the phone he let Johnny believe he was decamping. It served two purposes. Johnny would do everything humanly possible to delay Rand till twelve. And it kept Johnny from rushing down to mix in the Central Park adventure if he got so much as a hint of it. Steve felt that two men on the job would not so much double the danger as quadruple it.

Steve dropped the receiver back and considered this new development. He cursed Rand for his officiousness, his spying and his vindictiveness. This altered everything. Rand was out for his scalp. The very fact that he had gone to Cornwall House before any Homicide call had come in to the Bureau indicated that he knew plenty. How much? Steve began to tot up the significant things that pointed to knowledge on Rand's part. That business at the track, the remark about using a Department car, the sly comments about tailing anyone—"man or woman," he had said. Did that mean that while Steve was shadowing Vicki, Rand was shadowing *him?* If that were so, and Rand had seen Vicki and Slevna come out of Cornwall House— And today, just after Johnny had explained to him about Slevna's "secretary," and he had ordered him out of his office, Rand had come in with his report. He had been too disturbed to notice it then, but it came to him now how pat Rand's entrance was; as if Johnny's exit had caught him eavesdropping at the door and he had skillfully used his report as an excuse for coming in. It all added up to the certainty that Rand was sure of his facts and intended to use them to Steve's undoing and his own aggrandizement. There could be no appeal to Rand's decency or *esprit de corps*: Rand was that rare exception on the Force, a bad loser and a lone hand.

Rapidly Steve went over the stages of the investigation at Cornwall House as he himself would have conducted it, and as he knew Rand was now doing. It was only a question of minutes when, entry through the hotel lobby having been discounted, Rand would get around to the service entrance and the Norwegian handyman. He groaned as he remembered the amateurish devices he had used. Rand would instantly see through the unnatural bulk and the missing teeth. He knew that Johnny would do all he could to prolong the investigation, as Steve had requested, but Steve could picture Rand's eagerness to get back to the Bureau and put the finger on him. With all the odds on Rand's side, he would do it blandly; he would bring the handyman along on the pretext of having him view photographs of the whole force in order to identify the "policeman" who had run up the service stairs. He saw Rand's hollow surprise and shock when the handyman pointed at Steve as he unquestionably would. Rand would then proceed to work backward, bringing to light Vicki's visits to the dead man and drawing the inevitable filthy conclusion. Outwardly reluctant, Rand would take the regrettable but compulsory next step—putting Steve under arrest. Steve simply could not afford to be arrested before twelve o'clock. He would have to get out of the office. After twelve Rand could do as he pleased; he could handcuff him, throw him in a cell and book him for premeditated murder. But before disgrace, trial and prison caught up with him, he was going to get the enemy in Central Park.

He could not wait for Rieger's call, unless it came within the next half-hour. He knew a preliminary investigation took hours, with prints, pictures, medical examination and questioning, but this was a special case. It was just on the cards that Rand, overeager to nail his quarry, might leave Johnny in charge and come down himself much sooner and upset everything.

The phone rang again. That would be Rieger, he thought with relief.

It was Vicki.

"Steve, honey," she said. "Thank goodness you're there. Johnny called—with his cockeyed idea that you're running away—"

"I'm not running." The blood was pumping through him as if it were being forced by pistons. Vicki's light, cool, confident tone, taking it all in her stride, identifying herself with him, without a trace of resentment or disgust, acted on him like a shot of Benzedrine.

"Of course you're not!" Vicki went on. "Oh, Steve, I've been such a fool—"

"You! When it comes to fools, you're in the midget class compared to me." He found himself, of all things, laughing!

"Could be. Look, Buster, when they—take you, keep your mouth shut. Just don't talk. Will you do that?"

"What's in your mind?"

"I can't go into it. But do that and I'll cook corn beef and cabbage for you for Saturday."

"You're pretty darned confident."

"Leave it to Johnny and me. Promise?"

"After the mess I've made of things, I guess I'd better."

"Steve Lake, don't you go humble on me! I like you the way you are."

"Vicki—Vicki—" His voice was a croak.

"That's all for now, honey. Just don't worry. And you're my favorite person." She hung up.

The world changed. All the maudlin self-reproach, the shame, the doubts, the hopelessness dropped from him like a cloak. His nostrils flared with youth and vigor and self-confidence. To hell with Rieger! If he wasn't a match for a Commie single-handed, he didn't deserve the luck that had flooded to him over the telephone. He'd get out of there fast, before Rand messed things up with his damned meddling.

One lucky thing about it was that Johnny was second in command up at Cornwall House. He'd do all the phoning and keep the reporters out of it till the last possible moment. That way the enemy would not hear a radio report or an extra blaring Slevna's murder and run to cover.

Like a giant refreshed, he rose to wake Harry O'Neil who would have to take the desk. Then a saving shred of his usual caution gave him pause. Just in case things got tough in Central Park, it would be well to give Johnny an inkling of the situation and the time and place. If anything slipped up, if, by some chance, they got Steve before he got them, he would make sure that somebody else would carry on and nab the whole dirty gang. Then, too, there was Rand and the murder charge to straighten out. If he himself were not able to answer the arraignment, he would fix it so that no mud would cling to Vicki's skirts, whatever Rand did.

He sat down again at his desk. It was a ticklish note to compose. He must strike just the right note, he must tell just enough, he must rely on Johnny to read between the lines. After some thought, he wrote:

JOHNNY:
The pianist Slevna's been selling us out, taking valuable documents to the Commies. I caught him red-handed, and when he resisted I slugged him. The guy had a glass chin, or I hit harder than I meant to. Anyway, I did for him. I locked him up so his death wouldn't get out before his scheduled meeting with the enemy. They're meeting him at midnight (they *think*) in Central Park, just off Columbus Circle, to deliver the stuff to take out of the country. They're meeting *me*, only I'll be a little ahead of time. In case I'm not as smart as I think I am, get there fast. The paper will be stuck inside a tabloid. If I turn up smiling, tear this up. Otherwise you can show it to the Chief and to Rieger.
                STEVE.
PS. One of the valets in the Savoy Hotel in London is a Red agent. Tell Rieger that.

He sealed it into an envelope, addressed it and laid it on the desk in the middle of the office. Then he went into the far room and shook Harry O'Neil.

"Take over, Harry; I've got to leave."

Harry sat up, blinking.

"Sure thing, Chief. Gosh, I had some swell shut-eye. Still raining?"

"Yeah, I think so. Hold the fort till I get back."

"You're coming back? As late as this?"

"I'll be back by twelve-thirty—or not at all."

"Okay, Captain. In case anything comes in, I can get you at home."

"Rand and Johnny'll be in soon. One of them will relieve you."

"I don't mind taking the late trick. That nap fixed me up fine."

"Good. Seeing you."

It was just ten o'clock.

Once away from the office, he wondered what to do with the time on his hands. He would have loved to go home and spend an hour with Vicki, to savor the sweetness of her loyalty and absorb more of her cheery courage, but the apartment was the first place that Rand would go when he found Steve had gone from the Bureau. On a sudden whim he turned west, deciding on a quick visit to Max Braun. He had a real regard for the gentle little Austrian, and knew that he was on the sick list. On the way he stopped at a bakery and bought some of the cakes filled with whipped cream that reminded Braun of his beloved Vienna.

Late though it was, Steve found him huddled in his dressing-gown at the dining-room table, a cup of his eternal coffee clasped in his two hands. He looked thin and peaked after his attack of asthma, but was cheerful and uncomplaining. He hailed Steve and the cakes with equal pleasure.

"Stefan! This is splendid. To come out of your way on a night like this. And the cakes! *Zärtlich! Entzüchend!* Wait. I get you a cup."

"Sit still. I know my way around here. A cup of coffee just hits the spot. How you feeling?"

"Entirely well. Last night was another story. Vicki told you how I was a nuisance with my *verdammte* asthma?"

"You ought to be careful in this weather."

"Care does nothing. The attack comes, the attack goes and I am once more myself. Here is sugar and hot milk. How is it with you?"

"Can't complain—not with a wife like Vicki."

"She is a dear girl, my Vicki. So gay, so *frohgemut,* and yet with such good sense and judgment. I am lucky in my children."

"Maybe you deserve the luck," Steve smiled. All the tension and stress seeped out of him in the comforting presence of this winning little man who made so much of his good fortune and so little of his bad.

"You, too, my boy. How often I have thanked you in my heart for giving Paul his chance—"

"Forget that. Where *is* Paul?"

Braun's face took on the look of a plump, gratified seraph.

"You will never guess. Would you believe it, with all the practicing he must do by day, he has taken on an evening class at the Turner School. The pay is trifling, but he says every man should do work that brings a return. Man!" he laughed softly. "That *Bübchen!*"

"Swell!" said Steve with a warmth flooding through him. So his talk had penetrated. And he had been all wrong. There was good stuff in Paul, as in all the Brauns. His heart contracted suddenly as he thought of Paul's grief and horror when he heard about Slevna. How would he ever make him understand?

All at once he found he could not bear to face Paul with the guilt of Slevna's death on his hands. He put down his cup, looked at his watch and rose.

"I'd like to stay a while, but I didn't know it was so late. I've got a little job to do before I go home."

"At this hour? You work very hard, Stefan."

"This will only take a few minutes."

"Nothing—dangerous, I hope?" Braun said with a smile.

Suddenly, perhaps for the first time in his life, Steve ached to unburden himself, to lighten his load by sharing it.

"Yes," he said soberly. "It's damned dangerous. Would it be too much for you to listen to a pretty grisly story? You can help me a good bit by explaining to Paul—and Vicki."

"*Lieber* Stefan. What else is an old man good for but to help in time of trouble?"

The tale came flooding out. Braun sat, his head bent, his eyes staring at his empty coffee-cup. At last Steve finished, and Braun looked up. His eyes were full of tears.

"My poor Stefan, you have suffered. And you must suffer more. My heart goes out to you in pity."

"I'm not looking for pity. I've been a chump and I've got to pay for it. What hurts is that others must pay too—Vicki—Paul—even you."

"We take what life offers," he shrugged.

"I thought if you could explain to Paul—I don't want him to hate me for what I did."

"Paul is an American," Braun said quietly. "He will think you did well to exterminate a traitor. I will not tell him of the misunderstanding about Vicki. That he might find hard to forgive."

"Thanks. That's a load off my mind."

"But about this meeting in the Park. You are taking unnecessary risks by going alone. It is not right."

"It's the only way it can be done—and not scare them off. I'm not kidding myself. I know they've had watchers around there all evening to see that a troop of F.B.I. men don't surround the place. It's one man alone or we lose them."

"But when they find it is not Slevna who meets them?"

"Leave it to me. They won't ever get that far. The meeting's for twelve o'clock. I'm slipping into the Park from the east side, not the west. And I'm slipping in half an hour early. I'll catch 'em with their pants down."

"I hope you are right," Braun sighed. "I do know you are a brave man."

"All in the day's work. Look, if I do mess things up—I mean—"

"I know what you mean—"

"There's hardly a chance in a thousand—but if I do conk out—try to get Johnny Clark to stick around Vicki. He's good medicine."

"I will do that. You are also a *good* man."

Steve grinned.

"Getting real soppy, ain't we? Well, here we go."

Braun held out his hand.

"God be with you," he said simply.

XXI

The visit with Braun had done Steve good. He felt singularly at peace. He faced the slanting rain with his head up. The hardy exhilaration he had felt after Vicki's phone message had moderated to a quiet, steady confidence, tempered by a realization of the danger of his mission. Life was suddenly an excellent thing, something to hold on to and savor fully. Even the thought of Rand and the coming inquiry into Slevna's death did not trouble him. At the best he would be cleared entirely; at the worst he believed he would have to pay only lightly. And whatever the punishment, there was Vicki to come back to at the end of it.

His mood could not have been better for the job ahead of him. His mind was unclouded with doubts or fears. He had a clear estimate of the risks before him, together with a complete command of the professional skill to combat them. He was no longer over-confident; he was wary, competent and steady.

He looked at his watch. It was five minutes past eleven. He walked to the subway and rode to 59th Street. When he came upstairs into Columbus Circle, it was eleven-twenty-five. Across the street Rand and Johnny were just entering the downtown side of the subway. The sidewalks were nearly deserted in the pelting rain, but scores of taxis went swishing through the streets, their windshield wipers waging a losing fight against the streaming glass. Steve walked to Seventh Avenue, a block east of the designated meeting place.

He gave a quick glance around, looking for anyone following him or lurking near the entrance. There was no one. He slipped into the Park drive and made his way up its shining asphalt about fifty feet. The traffic noises fell away to a hum, the street lighting gave way to a dim flicker from the mist-shrouded park lights, there was neither a person nor a vehicle in sight.

He turned left, past a line of benches, on to the grass. Immediately he was swallowed up in a darkness as smothering as black velvet. He was at the eastern end of the copse of trees which the man had designated over the telephone. Steve crouched low to avoid silhouetting himself against the lighter background to the east. He trod with a noiseless Indian step that was part of his police training. Slowly, with infinite caution, he slipped from tree to tree, working his way west towards the specified single bench. At last, his eyes growing used to the dense gloom, he could make out a pale oblong about thirty feet ahead of him—without doubt a white stone bench. He stopped, flattened behind a sizeable tree. This was as good a vantage point as he could hope for. Carefully he raised his arm to his shoulder holster to transfer his gun to his coat pocket. It froze in midair.

A cold ring of metal pressed into the back of his neck. A voice, just as cold, said:

"Don't move." It was the voice of the man on the telephone.

XXII

Rand and Johnny came up the stairs into the Bureau, both wet, both in a hurry, but poles apart in frame of mind. Rand was whistling. His eyes were still alight with the relish and anticipation which the night's work had kindled in them. Johnny came in, heavy-footed and full of dread.

At sight of Harry O'Neil seated at the desk in the middle office, a trace of relief fluttered within him. In spite of Steve's definite intention to bolt, expressed over the phone, some part of Johnny's mind had refused to credit and accept it. Now that he saw that Steve was actually gone, he was curiously divided. There was the practical relief that Steve was on his way to physical safety and had outwitted Rand's cat-and-mouse designs. But there was, too, a blankness, a feeling of being heavily let down. Steve Lake on the run simply did not make sense.

Rand strode to the desk and said:

"Where's the Captain?"

"He left." Harry, who had been Rand's target for many a jeer, spoke sulkily.

"Left, eh? How long ago?"

"Ten."

"Ten." Rand flicked up his wrist and looked at his watch. "Eleven-forty. You on for the late trick?"

"I'm not sure. He may be back."

"Oh? He may be back," Rand echoed in amusement. "He tell you that?"

"He said he'd be back by twelve-thirty if he was coming."

"*If* he was coming. And if he wasn't?"

"He said you and the Sergeant'd be back. One of you would relieve me."

"Now I wonder," Rand grinned broadly. "How did Captain Lake know that Clark and I would be back?"

"I couldn't say. He didn't tell me."

"And of course he didn't tell you *why* we'd be back?"

"No."

"You're damn right he didn't. Nor yet where he was going. Right?"

"Home, I guess. I know I said I'd call him there if something special came in."

"*You* said. But what did the *Captain* say?"

"Hey, what's all this about? If you want to connect with him so bad call his house, why don't you?"

Rand ignored the veiled insolence. Blandly he said:

"I don't waste the city's money on unnecessary calls. If there's one place the Captain *ain't*, it's home. Well, Sergeant, shall we toss to see who takes over here?"

"No need. I don't mind staying," Johnny said. He was itching for Rand to leave so that he could call Steve's number.

"There's a note here on the desk addressed to you," Harry said to Johnny.

Johnny reached for it eagerly. No stamp. Steve's writing. He tore it open fast and devoured its contents. He nearly hit the ceiling.

"Eleven-forty!" he shouted. "Read that! Call out the riot squad. And get going, but fast! Those bastards are due up there at twelve!"

He was out of the office on a run and took the stairs four at a time. Downstairs he had supreme luck—a taxi was cruising past the station house just as Johnny hit the sidewalk. He was in the taxi before the driver could shift gears.

"Columbus Circle!" he yelled. "And move!" He flashed his badge at the man. "Drive like you never drove before! Through lights, against traffic, only get there in nothing flat. I'm responsible for any laws you break. It means a right guy's life."

The driver was young and quick in the uptake. In a matter of seconds he was slipping through the knot holes in the Eighth Avenue traffic.

Steve stood utterly still as the cold steel ring pressed into his neck. His stomach tightened like a fist as he realized that he had been outmaneuvered. He had counted on the enemy being too leery to arrive before twelve, and had thought himself so clever to think up this plan of getting the jump on them by covering the bench with his gun at the ready. He cursed himself silently.

"Both hands in the air, please," said the cold, polite voice.

Steve complied.

"What are you doing here?" the man went on.

A tiny spring of hope welled up in Steve's chill interior. The man had not shot him instantly, he had ordered his hands up, which meant he did not trust him but would still parley with him. The situation might be saved after all.

"I think you know why I'm here," he said calmly.

"Do not beg the question. I wish a definite answer."

"I came for the document in the tabloid."

A faint breath of relief came from the man behind him. Steve realized that, in spite of the man's cold, inhuman calm he was full of fear for his own safety. Steve might be anyone—a chance passer-by who could unwittingly upset the spy's plans and catapult him into limelight and danger; or an officer of the law, predicating others in the background, to catch him red-handed if he used his gun. That was all to the good. A frightened man made an easier opponent.

"You do not obey orders." The voice was as cold and hard as ever. "You were told to leave your hotel at twelve, neither earlier nor later."

"There were people at the house—I made my excuses earlier than I needed for fear I might be detained if I waited until the last minute."

"Orders are orders."

"Circumstances alter cases," Steve countered. His mind was divided into two distinct parts: one half was paying strict attention to every intonation and word which the man spoke, the other half was weighing the chances of getting at his gun and shooting over his shoulder. It was devilish dark, but the white of his hands must be outlined against the black tree trunk like a cut-out. It was wiser to wait. Later, if he allayed the man's suspicions and he was off guard for a split second—

His task was immediately complicated by the man's next move. There was a click and a pencil of light from a small flash played over Steve's head and shoulders. It was instantly extinguished. The man spoke in a slow, clay-cold tone:

"You are not Slevna."

"That's right."

"Explain!" The voice was deadly.

"Slevna's in a blue funk. Actually ill with the whole business. I believe he would have dropped dead if he'd come face to face with you. Y'know he's a magnificent artist, but a bit short on nerve. One of the failings of genius, I guess. So I volunteered to come for him." Steve spoke leisurely, with assurance and a nonchalance he was far from feeling.

"You volunteered. And how, may I ask, did you know about the 'whole business'?" The silk menace was as dangerous as a rapier.

"Oh, Lord, I've been in on it from the start."

"What start?"

"Last year, the first one. He never would have come for that one if I hadn't primed him with enough liquor to give him Dutch courage."

"And what, may I ask, is your interest in the matter?"

"Interest? I'm all for it. Naturally. I'm in love with Slevna's daughter."

There was a pause while the man digested this, and Steve held his breath.

"Who are you?" the man asked at last.

"Better if I'm anonymous, don't you think? I just receive the thing, take it to Slevna and bow out. Why not get on with it?"

"I am not entirely satisfied."

"I see what you mean. You're right to be careful. Anyway I can assure you I'll be glad to oblige."

"You will answer some questions."

"Anything you like. But look, it's damned uncomfortable with my hands up like this."

"You will stay exactly as you are."

"Oh, very well. But get on with it."

"Did Slevna tell you the procedure he was to follow?"

"Oh, sure. He spilled his guts. Don't blame the poor devil. He had to talk or bust. And he knew it was safe with me."

"Repeat what he told you."

"Well, he was to come here and collect the tabloid, take the paper out of it and slip it among his sheet music. As soon as he hits London he puts it in his dinner-coat pocket and gives the whole suit to the hotel valet. As soon as that's over, his daughter gets her exit pass."

"And did he also tell you how he threatened to go to the American police?"

"Did he! Who do you think persuaded him not to?"

"You seem to have considerable influence over our mutual acquaintance."

"That's right."

"Under the circumstances, it seems strange that my watchers never reported seeing you with him."

"I'm not a New Yorker. I hopped a plane when Slevna wired me. That was after his phone call from you on Sunday."

"You are glib, my friend. You have an answer for everything. But if Slevna had consulted the Secret Service and they sent a man in his place, that man would know all that you seem to know."

"Listen. Who's doing who a favor here? I'm putting myself in a damned dangerous position to help enemies of my country. If it wasn't for the girl I'd tell you to go to the devil. You and Slevna both. Now make up your mind. Either hand over the formula or go on your way and find another sucker."

The gun pressed even closer against Steve's neck as the man stiffened. And in that split second Steve knew he had made a ghastly and fatal blunder. The voice grated in his ear:

"*Formula?* Who but the laboratory or the F.B.I. could know it is a formula?"

Desperately Steve took the only chance left to him. His hands still high, he suddenly kicked the man in the groin with all the force he could muster. There was a shrill squeal of agony. The ring of steel no longer pressed into his neck. He turned like lightning to struggle for the gun. There was a roar and Steve rocked as if he had bumped hard into a stone wall. In the wet dark he steadied himself and clutched for the man's right arm. He found his wrist and twisted. There came a quick series of orange spurts, but they spent themselves harmlessly in the air. At last the gun clicked impotently. But a red haze hung before Steve's eyes, needles were digging into his vitals, his breath was shortening and the strength was oozing out of him as if a tap were turned on.

The man, still doubled over with pain, but beginning now to struggle to free himself from Steve's grasp, backed Steve against the tree. It was a blessed support. Braced upright he twisted the man's wrist mercilessly until the nerveless fingers loosened their hold. Steve caught the gun in his left hand by the barrel. It was hot and comforting in his shaking hand. With one supreme effort he brought it down on the man's head. As the man sank to the ground Steve crumpled slowly on top of him.

Johnny thrust a bill at the taxi driver and was out of the car before it rolled to a stop. He dashed into the nearest entrance to the Park. Gun in hand he hared over the invisible grass. The place seemed utterly deserted. He was well inside the Park when he slowed down. He looked at the luminous dial of his watch. Seven minutes to twelve. He was in time. Steve had said midnight. But he had also said that he would be there ahead of time. No doubt he was behind one of these confounded trees, at the ready for the approach of the enemy. Softly, just audibly, he gave the peculiar whistle which he and Steve both used in time of danger. He waited for an answering whistle from Steve. There was nothing.

And then, sharply, deep in the Park, the dark was stabbed by a fiery arrow. Johnny threw himself forward as more red spears flamed in the blackness. He threw caution to the winds and turned on his flashlight as he ran. It limelighted the two prone men, huddled together in a horrible travesty of an embrace.

An instant's examination told him that both men were breathing. But before he could make a move to render any aid, the Park was alive with people. Taxi drivers, parked on 59th Street, hurdled over the wall, a radio car pulled up with a whine of its siren, and Jeff Rand appeared from nowhere.

Together Johnny and Rand bent over Steve, turned him over with infinite caution, looking to see if he was wounded. Low down on his white shirt a dark patch was spreading from a tiny welling center. The man from the cruise car took one look and ran for a phone. Johnny tore off his shirt and made strips of it. Together he and Rand wound it about Steve's middle to stop the flow of blood.

"That little Mex at Cornwall House had the right dope," Rand muttered. "Honest-to-God spy stuff." He drew a loud, harsh breath through his nostrils. For Rand it was the equivalent of an intense emotional disturbance. He went on, in an unwilling, grudging tone: "Why the hell couldn't he *tell* somebody instead of bucking these rats alone?"

"Because it was a one-man job," Johnny answered, a curious jubilation in his voice. (Steve Lake run out? He might have known!)

"So he pulls a Dick Tracy," Rand grunted. And then, as if the words were dragged out of him: "But I'll give the Big Shot this—he sure as hell's got guts."

"You can say that again, brother," Johnny said gruffly. "Say—there's that paper to get—"

He ran to the unconscious stranger, located the tabloid and transferred it to his own pocket.

In a blessedly short time a Roosevelt Hospital ambulance from around the corner came clanging into the Park. Both men were loaded into it. Johnny swung aboard and went along with it. During the whole trip his lips were moving in a silent, unconscious colloquy, a queer colloquy for a seasoned Sergeant of Homicide:

"Make it a flesh wound. Just a scratch like they get in the movies. All right, even something kind of serious. But pull him out of it, won't You?"

XXIII

Vicki and Johnny sat in the visitors' room on the fourth floor of the hospital. They had been sitting for hours, it seemed to both of them, yet neither one of them indulged in the relief of pacing the room for fear the other would sense the harrowing worry that was eating into both of them.

"These things take time," Johnny said for the fourth time. "Even an ordinary operation where they know what they're looking for—"

"Yes, of course," Vicki returned through stiff lips. "And probably it isn't so long at that. Until they prepare him and then the anesthetic and the—"

"Exactly." There was a pause.

"What time is it?" She had asked that over and over. Each time Johnny had looked gravely at his watch and replied without comment.

"Ten minutes past two."

"This man McDonald—"

"Biggest surgeon in New York. We were lucky to locate him so quick."

"If anybody can do anything, he can," she whistled in the dark.

They were as artificial as two people at a tea party. Johnny lit two cigarettes and gave her one.

"Thanks. I seem to be smoking like a chimney," she said with a feeble attempt at a smile.

"That's natural. Eases things a bit. It's a strain, waiting—"

"Not being able to help!" she said, suddenly so tense that she was gasping. Johnny, too, came to life. He struck one fist into the other palm hard.

"That's the worst! If only it had been me!"

"If only you'd been together, as you always are on cases!"

"If I had dreamed he was meeting that devil! I never should have left him alone!" he groaned.

"How could you have known, Johnny?"

"I ought to have guessed something was in the wind."

"No. Steve would have sent you away. Don't you see? He went alone deliberately. He risked his life with his eyes open because of—of what he had done."

"You're right there. That's Steve all over."

"When I think—*I* could have saved him from all this misery and pain—"

"You? Where do you get that idea?"

"If I'd told him straight out about Slevna—"

"Look, Vicki. People act according to their nature—and the nature of the people they deal with. God knows, I wish it was me up there on the operating table. But no matter how tough it is for Steve, it's no use glossing over the truth. The thing was primarily his fault. Or the fault of his nature. I was inclined to blame you plenty this morning when you said you tried to tell him and couldn't. It sounded pretty weak to me."

"It *was* weak. I should have *made* him see—"

"You couldn't have. *I* tried to. He closed up like a clam. He wouldn't let anything penetrate. He had this notion you were—"

"Cheating—"

"Yes. And he was deaf to anything that contradicted it."

"But it's not his *fault*," she said. "You can't help being jealous. Oh, Johnny, if only I had the last few days to live over!"

"Vicki, I gave you credit for some brains. It's both ridiculous and—and—vicious to blame yourself. And Steve'll tell you the same. Things happen the way they do because people are the way they are. If you and Steve had behaved differently, you wouldn't be you and Steve."

"I know," she said wearily. "But he's paying so terribly dear for a—mistake."

Johnny groped for a change of subject.

"Did you let your father know?" he asked.

"I didn't. It was so late and he hasn't been well. Tomorrow is always soon enough for bad news."

"That's true. Only I thought—you'll be all alone tonight—"

"I won't go home," she said quickly. "I'm staying here till I can talk to him. I've got to let him know I'm with him a hundred per cent—"

"He knows that from your phone message."

"Yes. You know, he actually *laughed* over the phone. I could feel his relief—and—well, joy, really, while we were talking. Oh, Johnny, he's got so many swell things about him. He's so straight and decent—"

"Who are you telling?"

"You don't think he'll—they'll—arrest him for—"

"When he lands the head of a spy ring? And accidentally does for one of them in the line of duty? Don't be silly."

Their eyes met.

"Yes," she said steadily.

"They'll more than likely promote him."

Dr. McDonald, tall, distinguished, radiating efficiency, stood in the doorway. The two turned to him in breathless expectation.

"Mrs. Lake," he said gently. "You're going to have to be brave."

Vicki stared, her lips parted.

"Doctor—you —"

"I'm afraid the Captain won't do."

"Oh, *no!*" she breathed. Johnny moved towards her as she swayed, but she steadied herself. "Tell me."

"The bullet tore into the soft parts of his body with resultant internal hemorrhage. There is little we can do."

"Oh, surely—surely—there must be something—"

"I wish most deeply that there was. Your husband is a brave man. I have done everything I could. But it is not enough."

Vicki covered her face with her hands for a moment. Then she raised her head.

"Is he conscious?" she asked.

"Yes. And fairly comfortable."

"May I— I must go to him."

"I came for you. He wants to see you—and," turning to Johnny, "and you."

They followed him down the long, silent corridor to a door.

"We used local anesthesia so that there are no after-effects. Try not to tire him, but it matters little either way. Nothing can help or hurt him."

Steve was lying flat with no pillows, his eyes wide open. He was white under his tan, but otherwise looked as usual. When he saw them he said:

"Stand close where I can see you."

They came to the bed and stood side by side, looking down at him. A faint but genuine smile, without bitterness in it, quirked his lips.

"Johnny, if you messed up a case like I did this one, I'd have you back in uniform by morning."

"Messed, hell!" Johnny scoffed. "You put that Commie on ice, didn't you? He was out like a light for an hour from the wallop you gave him. First thing he said when he came to was 'I'll talk.' So we figure to land the whole ring. I should mess up cases like that!"

"I mean the private angle. If I had the sense God gave worms I'd have known Vicki was no tramp."

"But I *did* lie to you, Steve." She tried hard to be as natural as the others. "About the races, I mean."

"You sure did. Next time read the Belmont entries. Seatag's an oyster, not a racehorse."

"Steve—Steve—" Vicki's voice broke.

"And for the Lord's sake keep it light," Steve scolded. "Don't cry over me. I don't like you when your nose is red."

"Here's a laugh," Johnny cut in quickly, giving Vicki a chance to control herself. "Rand's downstairs waiting for news, chewing his cigarette to rags."

"Can't wait till I conk out for his promotion?"

"You've got him wrong for once. He did a spectacular flip-flop. Busted right down and said: 'I'll give the Big Shot one thing, he sure as hell's got guts.'"

"Rand, the hard-boiled? Is that something! Well, tell *Captain* Rand I thank him."

"Tell him yourself, Steve."

"Look son. This is it. Who're you kidding?"

"Cut it out," Johnny said gruffly. "*Show* the guts. Hang on and fight it."

"Damn it, Johnny," Steve snapped. "I'm tired and weak and full of pain, for all the dope they shot into me. Stop wasting my time and face facts. I hate it like the devil. But that's the way it is, so that's the way we take it."

"Steve, honey—" Vicki's cry was heart-stricken.

"That goes for you, too, Vicki. It wouldn't have been so hot—for you and me both—living with a guy who knocked off an old codger out of dumb jealousy. This way—" Again he grinned quizzically. "Bet you now they stake me to an Inspector's funeral." He yawned suddenly, and his words began to come in snatches. "… one swell year …what more do I want … getting sleepy … y'know something …. standing there … your nose *is* red … and Johnny with no shirt … even so … you two kids …"

THE END

THE DEFENSE DOES NOT REST
Edna Sherry

To Flora and David
with love

PROLOGUE

CHAPTER 1 . . .

Edward Hargrave, senior member of the law firm of Hargrave and Hargrave, stalked into his office, dropped his briefcase on his desk and slumped tiredly into his swivel chair. A dynamic man of fifty-eight, proud of his low-nineties golf score and usually looking ten years younger than his age, he showed today unaccustomed lines of worry and frustration in his face. He sat for a moment, frowning, then flipped the tab of his intercom box: "Please ask my son to come in, Miss Best."

A minute later, Stephen Hargrave hurried in, his decided limp in no way slowing him up. His angular face reflected his father's disquiet.

"Well?" he asked sharply.

"Not well at all, son," Hargrave answered grimly.

"But you saw him?"

"Oh, yes. I've just come from the jail."

"What does he say?"

"That he's innocent."

Steve made an impatient gesture and dropped into a chair.

"Well, of course he's innocent! I mean, how does he explain this idiotic arrest?"

"He doesn't. He says he knows no more about the whole ghastly affair than I do."

"But he must have an inkling. If he didn't do it—and I know damn well he didn't—somebody else did. He's the only one in a position to give us a lead."

"I pointed that out to him. He says he hasn't a clue."

"But for God's sake, Dad—!"

"I know," said Hargrave cheerlessly. "We're stumped for a defense."

"Did you tell him that?"

"I did indeed. He answered that innocent men aren't railroaded to the chair. That no jury would convict him on such flimsy evidence."

"Flimsy!"

"I tried to make him see that it was anything but flimsy, that motive, opportunity and lack of alibi constitute a powerful case against him. He insisted that, in the long run, truth has to prevail."

"As if that settled it! But he was always like that. Believes the best of everybody and thinks that everybody else does the same. What's more, if he had a line on the real culprit, wild horses wouldn't drag it out of him."

"You think he's shielding someone?" Hargrave asked, quick to grasp at the implication.

"I have no idea," Steve replied helplessly. "I only know he never committed a foul murder like that."

"I agree. But our moral convictions get us nowhere. There's a murderer here and a damned clever one. The whole thing looks like a colossal frame. If we don't smoke it out in a hurry, an innocent man is going to pay."

"You should have said that to him." Steve started up from his chair and began to limp up and down restively. Then he turned and faced his father almost accusingly.

"Look, Dad, you didn't go about this right. Your competent courtroom manner's no good here. You have to gain his confidence, get him to open up. This isn't just another case—"

"I know," Hargrave answered wryly. "This is my son's friend. The kid you grew up with and worshiped from the age of ten or thereabouts. I realize all that." He looked up at the worried face above him. "Steve, I tried every shot in my locker. I was his father's friend. I'm the father of his boyhood chum. I know him inside out and I know it's not in him to commit murder. But you yourself put your finger on the crux of the matter when you mention my 'courtroom manner.' It was no good. The trouble is I'm thirty years older than he is. I'm the older generation. There's a steel curtain that prevents any real communication of the kind we need."

"But if his own lawyer can't make him talk, who can?" Steve asked blankly.

"You."

"Hey, wait a minute—"

"Now, for God's sake, boy, don't give me any of your usual high-flown objections about betraying his confidence or rubbish like that. I've had enough quixotism this morning to last me a lifetime. Just get the facts lined up, will you please? Your best friend's charged with first-degree murder. Unless I can get my teeth into some sort of a defense, we're sunk. To us, it means the loss of a case. We can survive that. But to him, it's a little matter of the chair. Our only hope—his only hope—

is to dig into his daily life, root around in the mass of information which only he can hand us, for something to give us a start. You said yourself we have to make him open up. I tried and failed. So you've got to do it for his own good. What's wrong with that?"

"I'll tell you what's wrong. He always did spill everything to me because he knew for sure that it'd never go any further. Now you're asking me to go and worm things out of him in a spirit of friendship and then turn around and betray that friendship—"

Hargrave shot him a look of combined irritation and affection.

"Grow up, son, or else find another profession. Criminal law is no place for a man with scruples and ideals. We've got just one objective—to get our man off—"

"I know, I know. But how d'you think he's going to feel—"

"If you don't do it, he won't feel a thing. He'll be dead," said Hargrave shortly.

Steve sank into his chair, looking racked.

"For God's sake, Dad," he muttered again.

"Listen, son," Hargrave said more gently. "How's this? You go and talk to him. I promise you it'll be strictly off the record. I won't make use of a word without his okay. And I'm not asking him to point the finger at anyone. All I want is a complete picture of the scene and background in order to get some sort of perspective on the case. As it is, I'm hogtied. I haven't got a thing to go to court with." He pushed back his chair and now it was he who stood over Steve accusingly. "I'm as upright as the next man, I think. But when I hear you splitting hairs about 'betraying a confidence' when a useful, decent man's life's at stake, I'm close to vomiting. Is that clear?"

Steve gave a pale grin.

"Sure. You're right, of course. I have to save him in spite of himself. And you're not fooling me with your 'off the record' line either. If the poor guy lets one tiny clue drop, you'll latch onto it and play it for all it's worth in court. Well, okay. Even if he never talks to me again, I'm going to save his life. If I can." He paused, troubled. "But don't set too much store on my succeeding.

"If you can't, nobody can."

"Well, the thing is, we were very close up to about five years ago. We're not now. Oh, sure, we see each other, the underlying good feeling's there. But ever since he went to Korea and then afterwards—we sort of drifted. I don't know too much about his recent life. Just surface stuff."

"There's your job: to find out. If the underlying feeling's still there, it shouldn't be too hard. I'm not going to offer any suggestions as to how to go about it. You know that better than I do. But I want you to turn him inside out. No detail's too small to record and report. I want practically a diary—a day-to-day log. He probably knows things which have no significance to him but which may light up the sky for me. Talk to him hour after hour and work up your notes at night. I figure a week ought to see it through. That seem reasonable?"

"I guess so. Of course, it's going to take time to get back on our old basis. The way we were when we were kids."

"Well, if you need more than a week, take it. Just bear in mind that once I've got your report, it'll take me time to digest it and more time to follow up any promising leads. But don't feel pressed. Sit down with him and chin is all. I don't think it'll be too hard. He's been mulling alone in that dismal cell of his. It's my belief he'll welcome the chance to relive happier days. Good luck to you, son."

Ten days later, Steve walked into his father's office with a sizable manuscript in his hand, which he threw on the desk.

"Well, there's your 'day-to-day log,'" he said. "It's all there, down to how long he likes his eggs boiled. You were right. He was glad to talk without thinking about being cagey. He really opened up. But I'm damned if I can see one word in it to help the defense."

Hargrave lost no time. He began to read.

CHAPTER 2 ...

Lieutenant Maxwell Gray put the last touch to the map for tomorrow's reconnaissance, laid down his pen and decided to call it a day. The January night was bitter cold but the glowing fat-bellied stove made his tent snug and warm. He yawned, stretched and began to prepare for bed. He took off his wristwatch, wound it and laid it and his wallet on the chair next to his cot.

But the stove that warmed the tent also made it stuffy. The habit of years asserted itself. Max knew he wouldn't settle down to sleep unless he took his usual short walk and a ten-minute sniff of fresh air first. As long as he could remember, at home, at college and now in the army, it was a practice he followed, rain or shine. He was known for it and had stood a good bit of kidding on the subject. He threw a glance of wry longing at his cot, then, almost compulsively, reached for his heavy coat.

The icy Korean night was an electric shock. The wind that knifed down between the hills rocked him and it hurt to draw breath.

"This is crazy," he told himself after three minutes of it. He turned back to his quarters.

The sight that met his eyes in his tent stopped him cold. Standing by his cot, someone was going through his wallet. At the sound of his entrance, the figure whirled. Max expected fear or guilt but there was neither; just a sputtering reproach: "What the hell! You always stay out at least ten minutes!"

"Time enough for you to get clean away." Max's voice was colder than the night outside. He recognized the boy as one of his more promising privates—what was his name?—Baldwin—Berwyn—Bellair, that was it.

The boy advanced to Max's desk and threw down two ten-dollar bills.

"Okay," he shrilled. "So you caught me. Call the patrol. Put me in the brig. Get me court-martialed. Get me hanged. Shooting's too good."

"Been drinking?" asked Max sharply.

"I'm as sober as you are," he shot back.

He couldn't be more than twenty, Max thought, with his smooth fair cheeks that looked as if they'd never felt a razor, for all that he was tall and well-set-up.

"Then you're just a common thief?" said Max. He remembered now. This kid had done a terrific job on a patrol last month, when the SCR300 radio had been hit and had gone out of commission, so that they had lost contact with the command post. They couldn't report their new position and their own artillery threatened to wipe them out. Then, in the blinding snow, this kid Bellair, without a word, had jerked off his gloves and performed some kind of magic so that the radio had gone back into action.

"Sure I'm a thief," he said defiantly. "By inheritance, by choice, by necessity. Wanna make something of it?"

Max pulled off his coat and cap and sat down. In the face of the boy's near-hysteria, he clamped down on his own anger.

"Sit down," he said coldly.

Larry Bellair stared, his mouth half-open. Then slowly, he dropped into the chair opposite Max, the two ten-dollar bills lying on the desk between them like an indictment.

"Now then, what's this about 'inheritance'?"

"What's it to you?" Bellair muttered sullenly. "You got me. Turn me over to the M.P. It's their job to grill me."

"Watch your tongue, soldier!"

"Why should I? You can't do more than hang me."

"I'll only hang you if I have to," Max said evenly. "I remember that radio job you did last month. It showed your know-how and maybe saved a good few lives. You're a valuable piece of property belonging to the army. If I can salvage you, I will."

"Yeah, sure, a real asset," he jeered bitterly, "who stole twenty bucks from your wallet—"

"Why only twenty? There's nearly a hundred in it."

"I only needed twenty."

"Been shooting craps?"

"No."

"Cards?"

"No."

"Well, God knows it can't be girls in this neck of the woods. What did you need it for?"

"Having a good time?" Bellair said savagely. "You're not fooling me with your cat-and-mouse line."

"Answer the question!"

"What's the use? You won't believe me." In spite of himself, he was softening up.

"Maybe not."

"It sounds crazy."

"I'll be the judge of that."

"Okay. You asked for it. Sergeant Heinz has a Thurlow's *Aerodynamics*, latest edition—that's the last word on airplane motors—"

"I'm acquainted with Thurlow," Max said dryly.

"Yes. Well. Heinz wants twenty bucks for it."

"And that was such a necessity you were willing to steal for it?"

"Yes, it was."

"Why?"

"What's the use? You wouldn't understand."

"Try me."

Larry Bellair shrugged. All the fight had gone out of him. The sullenness, too. Only a dreary hopelessness was left.

"If you must know, I've got a new slant on a gadget for a plane engine. At least, I think it's new. Thurlow's book would tell me if someone else has hit on the idea and patented it. If so, I can't afford to waste any more time on it. That hog, Heinz, wouldn't even let me look at the index."

There was a long silence. Max's face was still stern but he had to control the lightning flicker of his lips. He said: "Maybe I can help you."

"I doubt it," said Larry unflatteringly.

"Do you know who I am—I mean to say, in private life?"

"No."

"Ever hear of Gray-Stevens?"

"Gray-Stevens Aircraft Motors?" Larry came to life.

"That's right."

"You!"

"Well, my dad. I'm just a green hand at the plant but I think I'd know that much."

"Christ! How unlucky can you get! If I'd known that—" He slumped in his chair.

"Yes? If you'd known that—?" Max prompted.

A glint of sour humor quirked Larry's mouth.

"I'd have sucked up to you in the hope I could land a job with you if they ever do something at Panmunjom."

"Why'd you pick on me to rob in the first place?"

"On account of you always take a stroll before bedtime. I've been watching you for days and you're always out ten minutes or more. I damn near froze timing you."

"Bellair, what did you mean by 'inheritance'?"

"Oh, what's it matter?" he said impatiently. "A crooked father never got a man a day off his sentence."

"Let's hear about your father."

"Look. That slipped out. I did what I did and I'm sunk. I'm scared as hell but I'll take what's coming to me without blatting about my father."

"All right. I believe you. But I want to know anyway."

"Okay. You're the doctor." Larry shrugged. "He was a genius. The plane companies bid for him like the ball teams do for a DiMaggio. He made big money because he was so good. But that didn't keep him from going crooked and selling out his company to competitors. It's my guess it wasn't the money as much as some kind of a kink. He liked to double-cross people. Made him feel smart. He did it once too often. He collected eighty thousand dollars from a rival company for a set of top-secret plans but he was careless and his own firm got wise. He lit out just in time to beat the sheriff. Never been heard of since. I was six months old at the time."

"How'd you find out all this?"

"My mother divorced him and married again and my stepfather adopted me. Then my mother died when my stepsister was born. I thought he was my real father until I was about thirteen." A dark flush crept over his fair skin. "He caught me rifling his pants pockets. So he sat me down and told me the whole story. Said we had a problem. 'We,' mind you. He was a swell guy. I thought I was cured. Tonight's the first time since then— Damn that louse Heinz—"

"I guess we've got a problem, Bellair," said Max.

Larry burst into tears. He dropped his head on the desk and cried with the uninhibited ease of a four-year-old.

Max stared at him, at the unruly yellow thatch of hair, the youthful curve of cheek visible against the splintery wood of the desk. He was only twenty-five years old himself and he was understandably frightened. It was his job to report Bellair, denounce him as a thief and make an example of him for the sake of morale. He knew the army *Manual* and he knew his duty. He wasn't gullible and he was up on all the tricks and dodges a cornered criminal resorted to. Bellair's story, along with his tears, might be as phony as a lead quarter. And there was also the natural resentment that his privacy, his tent, his wallet had been invaded. His mouth tightened. Do Bellair good to learn early that crime didn't pay. Might keep him straight afterwards. And he—Lieutenant Gray—wouldn't be sticking his neck out for going against the rules and laying himself open to disciplinary action from above.

Larry sat up, brushed his eyes and nose unselfconsciously on his sleeve.

"You better not waste any more time," he said, composedly. "You could get into trouble yourself." He might have been reading Max's mind.

"When I want advice, I'll ask for it," said Max acidly.

"Sorry, sir," he said quickly. For the first time Larry showed the customary respect due a superior officer. For no good reason, it made Max feel something between a worm and a tyrant. It drove him to go on questioning, putting off the moment of official action.

"How come you're so short of cash you couldn't raise twenty dollars?"

"I send my allotment home."

"Good God, you're not married!"

"No, sir. To my sister—my half-sister, that is."

"You've still got your pay, haven't you?"

"I send a good bit of that, too."

"Why?"

"My stepfather died two years ago. What he left us is just about enough for food and rent. I worked at Douglas, so we got by. But since the army got me—"

"Well, your allotment to your sister takes the place of your salary," Max probed. "Do you have to screw yourself down to your last dime?"

"She's got a thing about writing the way I have about machines. So she has to have an education. Costs dough." He leaned forward, his face animated. "This idea I've got. If it's new and any good, I'd sell it for a lump sum. It'd see Avery through college and if we ever get out of this hellhole alive, I can go for an engineering degree on the GI bill. That's why I have to know. I can't afford to waste time on it if somebody's ahead of me."

Max yelled at him: "You goddam crazy kid! Why in hell didn't you come to me and borrow it?" He picked up the two ten-dollar bills and shoved them into Larry's hand. "Go buy the Thurlow. And keep your hands in your own pockets from now on."

"You're—you're forgetting about this?" Larry stuttered.

"No. I'm not forgetting. As I said, we've got a problem. Let's lick it together." Larry stared at him, his mouth trembling. "And for God's sake, don't start thanking me! Maybe I've got a stake in this, too." He managed a sickly grin. "You say you inherited a touch of larceny from your father. Maybe you inherited something else, too. When this ratrace is over, Gray-Stevens can use an automotive wizard."

Larry's eyes dropped.

"You—you wouldn't shake hands with me, would you, Lieutenant?" he murmured to the floor.

"Why don't you shut up?" Max grunted and stuck out a hand.

But when he was alone again, his doubts came back. It was an open and shut case, evidence, confession and all. He was compounding a felony, arrogating to himself the role of judge and jury which wasn't his at all. Away from Larry's engaging naïveté and candor, his common sense and duty reasserted themselves. That kid, with his winning grin and his emotional tale, was probably snickering in his bunk right now at Lieutenant Maxwell Gray, prize sucker.

To hell with the little crook. It wasn't too late to put the thing on a legitimate basis. He could report to Captain Stagg in the morning.

Plenty of time. The captain wouldn't expect to be aroused at this hour of the night for a case of petty pilfering. Even if the kid's story was true, what kind of an army would they have if a man could commit a crime and get away with it by spinning a yard of sweet-talk? And it was a premeditated thing. Bellair said himself he had watched Max's habit of taking a walk before bedtime. That cold fact didn't jibe at all with the artless tears. The kid could probably turn them on and off any time it suited his purpose. There was only his word for it that this was the first time he'd stolen since he was thirteen. Didn't they say a criminal's best asset was an innocent look and a glib line? No two ways about it, he must speak to the captain in the morning.

But the morning came and went and Max said nothing and did nothing. He didn't even keep a weather eye on Bellair to check if he was going straight or not. He told himself the whole incident was just a big crap game: he was fading his own hide against the kid's future.

CHAPTER 3 . . .

February 25th was bitterly cold. The steep-sided Korean hills were blanketed in snow and ice, the white variegated only by a few blasted trees, rising black and bare in the howling wind. A U.N. patrol action was planned for that night, the objective an enemy ammunition dump on a finger ridge known as Anonymous Hill, a spot about a thousand yards before the enemy's main line. The patrol action was assigned to a reserve engineering unit in order not to weaken the main U.N. defenses by using a front-line company. The job fell to Lieutenant Maxwell Gray. He received the patrol plans the day before and selected twenty-nine men for the project.

Six of them would creep up the slope of Anonymous Hill, plant their dynamite and attach their wires and fuses. Eight men would comprise a protective fire-support squad twenty yards behind this first group. One man in each squad carried an SCR300 radio for direct communication with the command post, in case extra heavy supporting artillery should become necessary. Five other men were to approach the hill at a considerable distance from the first two squads, creating a diversionary action to draw attention away from the men who were mining the ammunition dump. The remaining men acted as fire support to the diversionary squad. The patrol was planned for 2100 hours, in order to coincide with the usual harassing missions fired by U.N. artillery every night at that hour. It was hoped that it would keep the enemy under cover while the patrol made its way to the objective.

Lieutenant Gray's preparation for the patrol was thorough. He briefed his men in detail, giving them all known characteristics of the terrain and the routes of advance and withdrawal. His final word was:

"After the mission is accomplished, you will meet at the specified rallying point before proceeding back to your base, where the sergeant will conduct a roll call. If any man is missing, either dead or wounded on the field, the whole unit will return to find him and bring him in."

The object of this directive was to raise the men's morale. It would weld them into a team. The certainty of help in case of misfortune was heartening. Lieutenant Gray added a final instruction:

"The only exception to this rule is myself. I shall remain at a safe distance to observe the exact results of our action for my report."

The lieutenant's careful planning and organization paid off. The six engineers in their snowsuits blended into the white scene and were unobserved. They laid their explosive and attached their fuses. As expected, the roar of their own artillery drove the North Koreans into the sandbagged bunker beside the dump and even the diversionary action went unchallenged. At 2330 hours, twenty-nine men, without a single casualty, met at the rallying point behind a clump of blackened trees, sixteen hundred yards from their own front line.

The men were jubilant but the cold was shattering. Sergeant Wilson took a quick count and said: "Okay, men. Back to the base."

Larry Bellair stepped forward.

"Sergeant, I ask permission to wait a few minutes."

"What for?"

"The lieutenant."

"You heard his orders. We were not to wait for him."

"I know. But— There's no danger this close to our lines. I can get back safely."

"Orders are orders."

A soldier cried: "For Gawd's sake, let's move before I freeze solid!" The sergeant gave the order to march and joined the men.

It was simple for Larry to drop out from the end of the line and slip back unobserved to the rendezvous. As he stamped up and down to keep warm, he called himself a fool to wait. He was asking for trouble. He was disobeying orders. The lieutenant knew his way around and needed no nurse. Not an enemy shot had been fired so the lieutenant had to be all right. And still, some queer obstinate hunch held him, stamping the brittle snow, the wind pulling water from his eyes that froze on his cheeks.

Suddenly, a saffron glare filled the sky, followed by a series of ear-splitting roars. Larry's stiff lips widened to a grin. Mission accomplished. Farewell to the dump. The lieutenant would be along any minute now. Larry decided to wait for him. As long as he'd made this big gesture, he might as well get credit for it. It couldn't hurt his chances any for the Loot to know. He would understand that Larry was trying to show his appreciation for that business last month. And Gray might even stick in a word to soften the Sarge's wrath.

An eternity passed: ten minutes. Larry stamped up and down, half-frozen. The lieutenant had to be back by now. But he wasn't. Larry's hunch hardened to a conviction. He ventured out from behind the protection of blackened tree trunks and began, unwillingly, to retrace the path they had traversed three hours earlier. It was open ground and he was horribly vulnerable in the added light of the dump flames. He was mentally frozen by fear as well as physically stiff with cold.

He had crossed half the level ground between the lines when he heard a groan. He scanned the white scene frantically, trying to locate the sound. A flash of light struck an answering gleam from some object, fifty feet away: the reflection of the glare above on the metal of a rifle. Larry forgot his fear and raced forward. Lieutenant Gray was lying in a queer white heap, looking for all the world like a bundle of dirty wash. His white snowsuit was flecked with spots which Larry guessed were blood. He dropped down beside the lieutenant, sick with fright.

"Did they get you, Lieutenant?" he quavered.

Max's voice was weak but it drew a sob of relief from Larry: "No. Tripped the wire of a goddam booby trap halfway down the hill. Fell the rest of the way."

"Anything broken?"

"My leg, I think. Started to crawl. Couldn't make it." His voice faded. "Sure ... took ... a beating ..."

"Which leg?"

"Right."

With something to do, Larry forgot his terror and became an efficient workman. His first move was to turn his back to the wind, pull off his coat and the layers of heavy clothing beneath it, and remove his shirt and undervest. For the seconds that he was exposed, the cold was agonizing. He got back into his clothes and tore the two shirts into strips. Then he laid his rifle under Max's right leg and began wrapping leg and rifle together with the strips until they formed a rough splint, immobilizing the broken leg. Max grunted and groaned during this and once lost consciousness. But as the bandage began to take the weight off the leg, the pain eased slightly and his head cleared.

"How come you found me?" he asked.

"Hunch. Reported for roll call and then ducked back."

"A break for me. Half-hour more, it'd be the deep freeze."

Larry split the end of the last strip in two and made a firm knot.

"Anything else hurt bad?"

"Something wrong with my shoulder."

"Can't do anything about that here. What else? There's some blood on you. Did the booby trap get you?"

"Just numbed my legs. I fell so fast, I escaped trouble. Blood's from the ice—scraped my face the whole way down the hill."

"Fine. Think you can sit up a second?"

With Larry's help, he managed. Then Larry faced him, kneeling astride his thighs, and pulled his body forward until Max hung like a bundle over his left shoulder.

"Hey—you can't lug me—" Max began. "I—weigh—"

The protest was lost in another blackout. Somehow, Larry got to his feet with his unwieldy burden. He staggered forward toward home. The going was rough. Ice and snow made every step a risk. He steadied his load with a raised left arm around Max's waist, so that he shouldn't roll off. After a century of struggle, they reached the group of blackened trees that was the rendezvous. Six hundred yards. Sixteen hundred to go. Close to a mile. Larry was breathing noisily by now. He was strong and fit but Max was no lightweight. Six feet of bone and muscle, even without a pound of fat, was taking its toll.

Max's voice came faintly to him: "Drop me here—go on for—stretcher—"

Every fiber in Larry's body ached to obey. He said angrily: "Don't be crazy. It's close to a mile. Fifteen minutes—another fifteen back—you'd freeze solid."

"Well—take a break—you—can't go on—" Larry knew if he once put Max down, he'd never get him back on his shoulder.

"Shut up, why don't you?" he panted.

He floundered on. With every step, the load got heavier. His muscles screamed with pain and the icy air burned his laboring lungs. He began to get lightheaded. Max became an enemy, a hateful millstone, an old man of the sea he had to lug around forever. He could have killed him gladly. And still, he put one foot before the other, blindly, doggedly, resentfully.

Now he was swimming with dizziness, reeling, rocking, stumbling. Then suddenly, he was down. On his hands and knees with Max, an inert bundle stretched beside him. Cursing and sobbing, unconscious of his own movements, he somehow maneuvered Max onto his back, the injured man's head hanging forward, touching his own. Bracing himself, he tried to get to his feet again.

He couldn't make it. He strained, he labored, he sweated, the sweat freezing even under his clothes. He couldn't get off his hands and knees. He sprawled like a St. Bernard bringing in a casualty. The change of position and the shifting of his burden brought some easement. Automatically, he crawled forward on his hands and knees. For a while it went well. Max's body, lying horizontally along his back, distributed the crushing weight almost comfortably. He made a hundred yards without trouble. Then the ice, the rocks, the iron earth began to bite through his gloves and trousers like needles. Every move was a quadruple agony. Pain darted up his arms and thighs. And Max's head kept bumping his own maddeningly at every step. Unaware of it, Larry was shedding a flood of tears. But still he kept on, inch by racking inch.

He never knew the moment when his Gehenna ended. A sentry heard his sobbing approach before he saw him, and investigated. Two stretchers with bearers appeared in quick time. Both men were borne back to the first aid station. Larry's clothes and gloves were in rags, his hands and knees flayed raw. Max was deeply unconscious.

The war was ended for both of them. Max was flown, first to Tokyo, then Stateside, with a shattered thigh and knee, a cracked collarbone and a delayed concussion. For months, he was shuttled from one hospital to another before his final discharge.

New skin formed quickly on Larry's hands and knees, but an inflamed pericardial condition, resulting from the excessive strain on his heart, kept him under treatment for weeks. He, too, was discharged at last as recovered but with a medical warning to avoid all strenuous exertion for a time.

CHAPTER 4 . . .

Max sat in a beach chair under a sun umbrella, writing a letter to his father. Curative sunshine fell on his outstretched legs while his head and shoulders were comfortably cool, both from the umbrella's shade and the fresh breeze that was blowing off the Gulf Stream.

He was at that promising stage of convalescence when the patient is restive for action and the return to normal life. He wrote:

> It was swell having you down here last week and I sure hated to see you go. But with the Korean War off and the Cold War on, I guess Gray-Stevens needs you more than I do. How'd you make out with the big brass in Washington? Did you land the contract or was it just Old Home Week for you and the Colonel? If it was a contract, I'm going to ask you to let me out of the fool promise I made you. Three weeks' more loafing around this dump is going to give me jitters if there's a chance of lending a hand at the plant, even if I only act as errand-boy and take a little legwork out of your schedule—

A sand fly buzzed noisily and he raised both hands to rout it. The breeze caught up his letter and sent it skidding over the sand. He was still awkward in his reflexes and somewhat slow in navigating. Before he could get out of the low beach chair, there was movement near him and a girl stood over him, holding out the retrieved letter.

"Please don't move. It flew right in my lap," she said rather breathlessly.

Max looked up. A slim figure in a yellow cotton dress stood over him. He had an impression of a childish heart-shaped face as he answered: "Oh! Thanks. Thanks very much. Stupid of me to—to—"

It wasn't like him to stammer over a trifling incident. Put it down to the fact that he had not spoken to a girl in more than a year and a half, unless you counted the fortyish nurses who had clanked endlessly around him in one hospital after another. Any girl would probably have tied his tongue; a pretty one stymied him. And this one was pretty, no question about it. She stood there, as timid as he, absurdly long lashes hiding her eyes.

"That's all right," she murmured with (he thought) brilliance. "I was glad to save you the trouble."

"Well, thanks," he repeated fatuously. "Thanks a lot."

His diffidence gave her nerve. The veiling lashes lifted a centimeter. She said with great daring: "You're not very well, are you? If there's anything I can do …"

A wave of terrific well-being swept over him. He laughed.

"I'm fine," he said. "Lick my weight in mice."

She didn't smile. She said gravely: "But you have been ill?"

"Ill? No. Just marking time till a few broken bones knit."

"Oh! You fell?"

"That's right. Me and Jack and Jill. Down a hill."

She still didn't smile. But her eyes went wide and he saw that they were the pure blue of a Siamese cat's. In fact, with her tawny hair and the odd shape of her face, she reminded Max of a lovely demure little kitten.

"Were you skiing?" she asked, trying to sound knowledgeable.

"No. Just tangling with some North Koreans."

"Oh!" She packed the syllable with more acclaim than the Medal of Honor.

He was encouraged. His glance past her located her beach chair thirty feet away, all but baking in the September sun. He got out of his own chair with creditable speed and said: "You're going to roast over there with no umbrella. I'll just pull your chair over into the shade."

She murmured solicitously but feminine instinct kept her from taking the small chore away from him. He established her chair beside his own under the umbrella and said with a grin: "Better, huh?"

"Yes, thank you. Only—" The lashes fluttered in embarrassment.

"Only what?"

"Do people just talk to each other down here without—"

"Certainly," he said vigorously. "This beach is a sort of club. We're all members."

At last, a tiny smile widened her mouth.

"Then it's all right?"

"Sure. Done all the time." She sat down. "You must be new here."

"I came Monday."

"Thought so. No suntan. Another week, you'll be a coffee bean like the rest of us."

"Oh, I won't be here for a week."

"Just touring through?"

The pure blue eyes were suddenly distressed. "Please—please don't ask me questions!"

To Max, she was like a kid with a skinned knee. He wanted to pull her onto his lap and comfort her. But you don't pull a strange girl of twenty-odd in a cotton dress that revealed lovely curves, onto your lap. You did what you could with lame words. He said gently: "Look. If you're in a fix— If I can help you—"

"But I don't know you," she said faintly.

"I'm all right," he said reassuringly. "Everybody tells me their troubles. I'm known for it. I could write a book. You just come right out with it and we'll stick pins in it together."

She took a long time to answer. But finally she got up courage to say hesitantly: "If I just knew what to do. Maybe you could advise me?"

"Certainly I could. Let's have it."

"Well, I'm a secretary. There's a convention of hotel men here this week and I came down with my boss. It was all right until yesterday. But then last night—" She broke off helplessly.

"Made passes, did he?" Max prompted. "Then what happened?"

"I—scratched him—"

"Good for you."

"He was furious—"

"Hope you disfigured him for life. Go on."

"Well, my room at the hotel is engaged for the rest of the week. So that's all right. But he's got my ticket back to New York and he won't give it to me."

"Stranded, eh? Well, that's no problem. I'll lend you the fare back."

"Oh!" she said, shocked. "You think I was hinting for that! I only meant—if you could talk to him—make him give you my ticket—his name is Hebert—"

"Sure. Glad to. What's your name?" As she shrank delicately back into her shell, he added hastily: "When I talk to him, I can't just demand a ticket—I have to say 'Miss So-and-so's' ticket—"

"Oh. Carol Tyson," she said as reluctantly as if she was parting with a valuable.

"Okay, Carol. When's a good time to find him?"

"I don't know exactly. What with the meetings and the cocktail parties—"

"How about the dinner hour?"

"I don't know where he'll be. We don't eat at the hotel. We just have rooms."

He looked at her sharply.

"Do, eh? Then since last night—what did you do today about breakfast and lunch?"

She flushed.

"I've got some money—only not enough for fare back to New York. I had a big late breakfast."

"And what were you planning to do about dinner, may I ask?"

"I—I hadn't thought."

"Well, I have. You're a growing girl, Carol. You need your food. You're going to have dinner with me and we'll lay out a plan of action for friend Hebert. Okay?" She was obviously troubled, so he added: "What's wrong with that?"

"The whole thing sounds so cheap!" she said, vehemently. "So sort of planned. Like one of those New York gold-diggers with a made-up story to get a free meal."

"I take it you're not a native New Yorker."

"I live there now."

"But originally?"

She hesitated again, as if this invasion of her privacy robbed her of something precious.

"A little town in Pennsylvania," she said finally.

"What little town?"

"Uh—Umatta. You won't know it."

"You're right. Never heard of it."

"Nobody has."

"Too small to hold you?"

"Well, it does have nine thousand inhabitants," she said, taking him literally. Then, suddenly, as if she at last accepted his trustworthiness, she dropped her reserve and for the first time, volunteered information. "After my father died and I was all alone, I thought I'd do better for myself—I mean get a bigger salary—in New York. There isn't a secretary in Umatta who gets over forty a week."

"How long have you been in New York?"

"Two months."

"Always with this Hebert?"

"Yes. Up to now, he was perfectly all right."

"Florida air went to his head, I guess. Of course, he's married—they always are."

"Yes. He's got a teen-age daughter."

"The old rip! Well, we'll have no trouble at all about the ticket. One word from me—"

"Oh!" She was shocked again. "But that's like blackmail. I couldn't let you threaten such a thing."

"Won't have to. When he sees you've got a champion, he'll hand over your ticket like a lamb. So it's okay about dinner. Eight o'clock?"

She agreed shyly.

At eight o'clock, she was still wearing the yellow cotton. Max deduced that she was living scrupulously within her salary and that she had no backlog justifying extra clothes for the Florida trip. The fact affected him in two ways: he respected her for it and he wished intensely that he could buy her a hundred little useless but satisfying luxuries.

The dinner was a success. He learned very little more about her but under gentle urging, found himself talking more expansively about himself than ever in his life. He told her how he and his father lived alone together in the house in the East Sixties where he had been born; about the plant on Long Island where he had worked after getting his engineering degree; about the rambling "cottage" at East Hampton where he had spent most of his summers; about his forty-foot boat, about his polo ponies which he had sold just before going to Korea.

Her delicate eyebrows knitted in a puzzled frown. She asked: "Don't such things cost a lot of money? Could you have all that on just a salary?"

He grinned to himself. In spite of her bashful, defenseless makeup, she had a level little head, he thought.

"I couldn't, of course," he said. "It happens that my mother was the last of the Douglas Maxwell branch and inherited the whole estate. When she died, fourteen years ago, half of it came to me."

"Then you wouldn't have to work at all?"

"I would, Carol," he told her definitely. "Without my work, I'm nothing."

She nodded quickly.

"Oh, of course, I see that. I mean, a man of your ability couldn't just fritter away his life."

"I don't know about the ability," he smiled at her. "Thing is, I love it. The boat, the fishing, the polo are just fringes. Nice but not necessary."

At ten o'clock, he said with a spark in his eye: "Shall we locate your boss? Time for his—lesson."

She sat, her eyes curtained, for a long minute. When she raised them, they were dark with concern. She said breathlessly: "Would you do me a favor?"

"Sure thing. Just name it."

"Well— Oh, I can see you're going to get into a fight with him—on my account— I can't let you—you're still an invalid—I couldn't bear it if you got hurt—"

"You're right, you know," he said wryly. "I'm not exactly an invalid but I'm not up to a fist fight either. Suppose we give Mister Hebert a miss. I'll buy you a brand-new ticket back to New York."

She was enormously relieved. She let out her breath in a long sigh and all her tension vanished. And this time there was no mention of cheapness and gold-diggers. Instead, she said with crystal practicality: "I'll pay you back five dollars a week. But there'll be a delay at the start until I find another job and begin drawing a salary. Is that all right?"

The poor, decent naive kid, he thought. Aloud, he said with dazzling inspiration: "I've got a better idea. I promised my dad to stay here three weeks longer. September's an off month. Not a soul here I know. I just can't stick it alone. Would you take a three weeks' job at say, a hundred a week and all found, as a sort of companion? I give you my word there'll be no Hebert maneuvers."

"I know that! I wouldn't be here now if I didn't trust you."

"Well then?"

"A hundred a week's too much."

"Name your own figure," he said amused.

"Seventy-five's plenty."

"Seventy-five it is—but I foot the bill for uniforms."

"Uniforms?"

"Well—outfits—sports clothes—a dance dress or two—I've got to get in some leg exercise—swimsuit— Okay?"

Her face lit up with rapture.

"I ought to refuse," she breathed, "but I just can't."

The whole setup was equivocal and slightly disreputable. Normally, the fact that the girl had accepted even a dinner invitation, let alone the ambiguous job he offered, would have struck him as the height of fishiness. But the situation was not normal. Conditioned by a tough year in Korea and months in hospital, Max was behaving like a starry-eyed teen-ager. He had some slight excuse: nobody could have linked the shy uncertain Carol with designs or ulterior motives. If anyone needed protection, it was Carol herself.

They spent all their waking hours together, they swam, they fished, went to dog races and bingo games. Carol combined two seemingly incongruous attitudes toward Max: she showed a lovely maternal solicitude for his health and comfort, but she deferred to his judgment in every move they made. She never offered a suggestion or made a decision. She would listen to him, her eyes wide and trustful, and agree with any plan he proposed. The effect on Max was a kind of divine confusion. He felt nine feet tall, he yearned over her protectively and his blood was in a ferment to possess her.

The rest was inevitable.

On the fourth of October, after a typical Florida idyll, they motored up to Miami in a Drive-Ur-Self and were married at the sleek City Hall. He wired the news to his father and then he and Carol shopped for an engagement ring. Carol chose the largest square diamond in the place. To Max, it looked absurd on her small hand but he understood her feeling clearly. She was just a kid at Macy's at Christmas time with *carte blanche*. She was drunk with the power of free choice and couldn't resist going the whole hog. When she drew his attention to a string of small milky pearls, it confirmed his belief.

"Do you suppose they're real?" she asked in an awed tone.

Of course, he bought them, too. Her ecstasy carried over into the night and Max's fears of her bridal shyness were groundless.

A week later, they presented themselves to Max's father in New York, the aura of happiness almost visible around them.

Spencer Gray was a shrewd business man and a capable engineer. But he was also the product of his ancestry. Without being a snob, he set tremendous store on tradition, background and blood. He was proud of the stock he stemmed from, and his deepest wish was that the Gray line should be carried on by Max's issue.

When he met Carol, he was appalled. Not that she was unpresentable in looks or speech. But he had the aristocrat's sixth sense (totally lacking in Max) of recognizing his own kind at a glance. And Carol was definitely not his kind.

But he loved Max and set himself deliberately to cast no shadow on the boy's evident happiness. He greeted Carol with all the warmth he could summon, while he secretly cursed himself for leaving Max alone those last three weeks. In Max's vulnerable condition, he had been ripe for any pair of pretty eyes. That Carol's eyes were exceptionally pretty, he did not deny. But his experience and acuteness penetrated the pure blue irises and found nothing behind them. Her artless glances and respectful attitude did not impress him. He looked for a trace of character, of mettle, of breeding in her and sensed only the trivial grace of the kitten she resembled. Here was no mate for Max, no fit mother of Gray sons.

They arrived about seven in the evening and had just time to wash up before dinner. As Max led her up the graceful oak stairs and into the large solidly furnished bedroom, overlooking a tiny but charming back garden, he drew her into his arms and kissed her.

"Well, this is your home, darling. I hope you're going to like it."

"It's lovely. Such enormous rooms."

"I like space. Don't you?"

"It must be awfully hard to keep clean."

He laughed at her quaint practicality.

"Don't let that worry you. Morgan's a tower of strength."

She gathered that Morgan was the butler and her eyes lighted with interest.

But when they were downstairs again in the comfortable living-room-cum-library, with Max's father drinking sherry, Max a Martini and Carol nothing at all, Morgan, announcing dinner, proved to be a stocky, strong-looking woman of fifty, her Welsh origin apparent in her coal-black hair and intensely blue eyes.

Max gave a whoop and kissed her soundly.

"Morgy! You old scout. Come and meet my wife."

Carol greeted her charmingly but evidently missed Morgan's outstretched hand. Max covered the stiff moment while Morgan withdrew her hand, with chatter: "Morgy's the babe who gave me all my spankings. Hairbrushes were a big item in the budget."

"Not as big as was warranted, Mr. Max. When I remember the tricks and pranks you and your friend Stevie played with me—"

"Oh, go on, Morgy. You loved it," Max laughed.

"If I loved it, 'twas only because I knew naughty boys were healthy boys," she returned coolly. But her eyes were not cool. As Carol expressed it later alone to Max: "She looked as if she wanted to eat you up."

"How's Cooky?" Max asked Morgan.

"Mrs. Whelk is no longer with us. Her legs gave her trouble last year and she had to retire."

Max turned a concerned look on his father who said: "It's all right, Max. She's turned out to clover in New Jersey."

"A pension, of course?"

"Of course, a pension," Spencer Gray nodded.

"A pension?" Carol echoed quickly. "I thought only English people—squires, sort of—did that."

Max just smiled at her.

"And who's in the kitchen now?" he asked.

"An extremely competent—ah—dietician—I believe they call them—who is paid by the hour. The present incumbent is a Mrs. Evergreen who gets along famously with Morgan. I hope she lives up to her name as she cooks very well indeed. To bring you completely up to date, Esther Hart married at the ripe age of forty-seven and has been displaced by a 'daily,' also by the hour."

"You never said a word about all this when you were down to see me."

"My dear boy, I thought you had quite enough on your plate, without bothering you with our domestic upheavals."

The dinner was evidence of Mrs. Evergreen's ability but it was quite simple: a clear soup, roast beef, *rissolé* potatoes, grass-green peas, deep-dish apple-pie and cheese. (No salad. Both men balked at what they called "rabbit-fodder.")

Spencer Gray evidently read the question in Carol's eyes.

"You'll have to get used to our all-male ménage, my dear," he told her nicely. "Or better, if your taste runs to daintier fare under glass or silver bells, I'm sure Mrs. Evergreen will oblige."

"Oh, everything's wonderful," Carol said, flushing at having her thoughts read so accurately. She did indeed believe that rich people ate pheasant and caviar daily.

Max began to question his father about the Long Island plant. His eagerness to get back into harness was evident and his father brought him up to date on personnel, orders in hand, work-progress and research. Courteously, the older man kept including Carol in the talk: "We still call ourselves 'Gray-Stevens,'" he explained. "But there hasn't been a Stevens in the firm since my father's day."

"It all belongs to you and Max?"

"Yes. A family affair. Not a very big one, though. Nothing like Douglas or Martin but important in its way because our research department has done some extraordinary work."

"You mean inventions?"

"Occasionally. More often, improvements, especially in the field of airplane motors."

"And you sell them to other factories?"

"Well, when it's a matter of patented ideas, it is generally on a royalty basis."

"That's smart. You get paid but they're still yours."

Max laughed.

"Carol, we'll have to put you on the Board. You've got a real business head."

Over coffee, which Carol refused, she pushed back her chair and said: "I know you'd like to talk with your father, Max. I'll just go up and unpack."

She had a satisfactory moment when Spencer stood and Max opened the door for her. This was like in books.

There was no port to linger over, at the old-fashioned round mahogany table, and the two men repaired to the library. Spencer lit a cigar and Max a cigarette.

"Well, Max, you gave us quite a surprise."

"I know," Max apologized. "I shouldn't have done it in this hole-and-corner way. I was in a kind of fog—"

"A pink-and-golden fog, I take it," Spencer said, trying to speak lightly.

"That's right. Nothing existed but Carol and me."

"I understand."

"And it wasn't only that. Carol's so timid and unsophisticated. A big New York wedding with hordes of strangers would have thrown the poor kid."

"But weren't her people rather distressed?"

"She hasn't any. Her mother died when she was small. Her father was a high school teacher in the little Pennsylvania town where she was born. He died last year. I gather he didn't leave much—"

"The teaching profession is notably underpaid," his father nodded.

"Carol had been trained as a secretary and she thought New York offered bigger chances."

He told his father the whole naive story of their meeting and courtship. Spencer Gray schooled his features to nothing but interest. Inwardly, he was heartsick. The last Gray married to an insipid little nobody, with nothing to offer but inch-long eyelashes and desirable little breasts. As he regarded the lengthening ash on his cigar, he suddenly hoped to God that he had envisioned the worst. But what if the guileless simplicity were a mask? Nothing about her rang true to him unless you excepted the few terse comments she made which involved money. He recalled the sharpness, even disapproval, in her tone about Mrs. Whelk's pension. And her astute, somewhat greedy comment on Gray-Stevens' royalties. His old dream of holding a grandson in his arms curdled.

Upstairs, at bedtime, when Carol gathered that Max expected to go to work next day, panic darkened her eyes.

"But—Max—I'll be all alone— The house is so big without you—" He kissed her.

"Now look, honey. My loafing's over. You knew you married a workingman."

"Yes—but—everything's so strange. I don't know anybody at all—"

"We'll soon fix that. Jerry Savile's a pal of mine and he's got a lovely wife. In a day or two, we'll have them over—then there's the Ryders—you'll soon have more friends than you can count. Tomorrow, you just make yourself at home—sort of shakedown—get acquainted with Morgan—"

"Morgan! You talk like she's one of the family."

"She's a lot more than that. Sometimes, you can't bear your own family. Morgan's a honey."

"Has she been here long?"

"Fourteen years. Actually, she was a nurse—took care of my mother in her last illness—then afterwards, when Dad and I were left alone, she gave up nursing to take over the house and me—"

"I see."

"You just put yourself in Morgy's hands—let her show you over the house—"

"That can't take very long—"

"Hey, here's an idea. Those rags we bought in Florida are nothing. How about getting yourself some real clothes? With your looks and a few stunning dresses, you'll knock everybody dead."

The demur was replaced by interest.

"But, Max, I don't know about such things. I never bought a dress in my life for more than twenty dollars." It sounded like a virtue. "I wouldn't even know where to go."

"Oh—Bergdorf—Hattie Carnegie—No, wait a minute. My mother used to get nearly everything at a place on Madison—Julienne Brak, the name was—I remember hordes of boxes being delivered—"

"But darling," she said shyly. "I haven't any money."

Max chuckled.

"You don't need a dime, honey. Charge everything. Just say you're

Mrs. Maxwell Gray. And if they don't believe I could have snared anyone as pretty as you, tell 'em to call Gray-Stevens for confirmation."

Max's first night at home with his bride was everything he could have asked for.

CHAPTER 5 . . .

In a month, some of Spencer Gray's misgivings died down. While he could summon no real fondness for Carol, he had to admit that her presence in no way disrupted the warm relationship between himself and Max. She made no attempt to monopolize Max and seemed quite content to let the *status quo ante* go on unchallenged. On many evenings, she withdrew tactfully, as she had on the first night, leaving them alone in the library while she went upstairs to try on the spoils of the day's raid on Julienne Brak. Her manner to Spencer Gray was resolutely deferential. But she seemed to resist any effort that tended to break down the formality between them. In his presence, she appeared to be little more than a permanent guest in the house.

But aside from this ceremonious attitude, she bloomed with well-being and drew real admiration from Max's friends. Jerry Savile, Tom Ryder and Steve Hargrave gave the equivalent of wolf whistles at the sight of her, and Nancy Savile pronounced the general sentiment: "Darling, Brak ought to pay you to wear her clothes. You're a better ad than a Bert Piel commercial."

They were all fond of Max and ready to welcome his wife into the fold. But they found her curiously impervious to intimacy. She was placid, she was amiable, she was obliging. But as Max once overheard Nancy say rather helplessly to Gigi Ryder: "She just won't take her hair down."

Gigi, the acid oracle of the group, replied: "There's no hair to take down. There's not a damn thing behind that Sweet Alice Ben Bolt puss. Men are such idiots!" (But then, it was common knowledge that Gigi had made a strong play for Max before she married Tom Ryder.) Max did a slow burn. Women! Even the nicest of them had claws.

But while Carol was not outgoing, she was as absorbent as a sponge. She sat and listened and hoarded what she heard. In a few weeks, she was indistinguishable from the others in manner, speech and habits. She no longer refused a drink before dinner, she made a point of never seeing a play except on first nights, and read, if not the books themselves, at least the reviews of the current best sellers. That first winter, she went obediently to opera, concerts and hockey games, and made the appropriate noises.

Nevertheless, she was an outsider in the group. And this was not snobbishness on their part. She was Max Gray's wife and therefore acceptable. In the circumstances, they tactfully ignored the usual stress on ancestry and the "right" schools. It was Carol's own lack of real interest and warmth that alienated them. She seemed to come alive only when the talk turned to things that money could buy. And when jewelry was the topic, she actually sparkled.

In November, Max received a letter from Larry Bellair. Max read it at the breakfast table while his father and Carol made polite and desultory talk. He was about to announce the fact but stopped himself as he read further. After reporting that he had entered M.I.T. on his G.I. bill and was getting along splendidly, Larry wrote:

> I've got this funny feeling about you. Actually, we've only talked to each other twice in our lives—the first time in your tent when you caught me red-handed, stealing, and the second, when I had a lucky hunch and hauled you in that night. But still I feel closer to you than to anyone in the world. Now don't get me wrong—there's no question of gratitude or repayment involved. If I saved your life, you did the same for me. If you had put me under arrest as you should have, I wouldn't be here now. I prefer coffins to jail any day. So that makes the score even between us. But I think of you as a sort of father-confessor. You know the worst of me and this lousy failing I've inherited. That's a big help. I don't have to put on with you. And when and if I get this damned irresistible itch toward larceny again, I'll yell for you and ask you to come running. Max, I know it's a part of me, as much as astigmatism or fallen arches are a part of some people. They go to doctors. I'll come to you. Is it a deal?

Max knew that his father would be tremendously interested in hearing from the boy who had saved his son's life. But that guileless moving paragraph was for his eyes only. Larry's lapse in Korea was strictly between the two of them. In fact, in view of Larry's ingenuous explanation of it that night, and his subsequent enormous service to

Max, Max had managed to bury it so deep in his subconscious, that it could almost be said to have ceased to exist, even to him.

As soon as breakfast was over, he tore up the letter and dropped it in the wastebasket. That way, he could save himself from lying to his father and yet respect Larry's confidence.

Driving out to the Long Island plant with his father that morning, Max mentioned that he had at last heard from Larry from M.I.T.

"There's a young man I've been wanting to meet," the older man said.

"I, too. In the hospital, as soon as I was past the hypo-and-bedpan stage, I bombarded Washington for his address. But he'd been discharged and I couldn't get a line on him. I had a vague idea he came from the West but I hadn't the faintest notion of the town or even the state. All these months, I've been racking my brains as to how to get in touch with him and pay back a little of what I owe him."

"Max, I have a suggestion. There may be the making of a fine sort of friendship between you and Larry. Don't spoil it by putting him under obligations to you."

"I'm under obligations to him. I'd just like to even the score a bit. I'm quite sure he could use a little financial aid."

"Nothing wrong with financial aid," said Spencer. "But it could come more gracefully from me, don't you think?"

"Well—"

"Suppose we run up to see him one of these days. You might wire him to meet us in Boston for dinner—better make it a Sunday so he's sure to be free."

Max did that and on the following Sunday flew up with his father. Carol did not go. She gave two reasons: first, she was afraid of flying, and second, she said sweetly that it seemed a stag sort of occasion. (Spencer was unaccountably relieved at her decision.)

They met Larry in the bar of the Copley. The situation had the makings of stiffness in it. The boy was nearly as much a stranger to Max as to his father. And neither Gray was the hail-fellow type to bridge an awkward moment. It was Larry who broke the ice with candid lightness.

"Hello, there," he said, coming into the bar a little late. "You're thinner. You must have lost ten pounds. Too bad you didn't do it before I toted you in that night." His engaging grin took the curse off the incident and made the "toting" a routine job with nothing heroic about it.

Equally, he took the introduction to Spencer Gray in stride. There was nothing flippant in his attitude but neither was there any truckling. Over dinner, Spencer asked him to relate the whole story of the rescue.

Without self-consciousness, Larry said soberly: "It was rugged. When I look back, I don't know how the hell I did it. Those last thousand yards on my hands and knees—I couldn't do it again in a million years. There was Max, piggyback on me, his doggone head bumping mine at every move." He laughed. "We must have been the funniest darn sight in Korea."

"And afterwards?" Spencer asked. "You got over it? No permanent damage?"

"Well, they tell me not permanently," said Larry unconcernedly.

"You mean there were aftereffects?"

"Well, my hands and knees healed fast. I'd have been back on duty in a week except for the—I don't know myself what it is—something to do with the pericardium—strain or whatever. They say it's only temporary but until it clears up, no strenuous exercise. Well, that's no problem. I'm so busy with my courses and tutoring kids for a little extra jack, I wouldn't have time for a run around the block, even if I was allowed."

Max and his father were shocked. Spencer was the first to recover.

"Look, my boy," he said with the warm intonation usually reserved for Max alone. "Max has told me a bit about your situation. How you and your sister are alone in the world. I should say, were alone. Will you accept the fact that you've inherited a family—Max and myself? That the unusual circumstances take the place of blood ties?"

Larry's grin widened.

"Will I! Mr. Gray, you couldn't give me anything I want more. To have somebody to go to for advice—"

"And more practical things, Larry," Spencer smiled. "Now be a good lad and let me help you a bit financially."

"Oh, money. I don't need a thing. With the tutoring and my room being so cheap, I'm sitting pretty."

"That may be. But Max says you've got a sister who needs help from you—"

"Not anymore. Avery struck oil. She won a scholarship at U.C.L.A. and she does babysitting at terrific rates. She loves it, too. Says it's wonderful to do her homework in a quiet house while the kid sleeps."

"But there surely must be something—?"

Larry opened his mouth, then closed it.

"Go on, Larry," Max prompted.

"Nothing."

"Come on. Give."

Reluctantly, it came out. Larry's rooming house was at a considerable distance from the campus. It was a matter of two buses and a few blocks' walk to and from classes. It did take quite a bit out of him each trip. There was a boy ("stinking rich") in his class who had smashed his Porsche speedster in an accident. He was asking three hundred for the remains—the engine was worth that alone—and Larry could fix it up himself for peanuts.

"Well, of course," said Spencer, delighted. "But wouldn't you rather have a new car than an undependable wreck?"

Larry's eyes sparkled.

"Oh, no, sir. Half the fun'll be fixing it up myself. And you don't get the speed out of a Chevy, say, that a Porsche gives you."

"No good," Max laughed. "We don't want you banging yourself up hot-rodding. Gray-Stevens is counting on you for its research department."

"Now I've got everything." Larry sighed with content like a six-year-old. Spencer took out his checkbook and wrote a check for a thousand dollars. Larry refused it.

"Five hundred's plenty. Three for the car and the rest for parts and straightening the chassis. I won't take more."

While Spencer wrote another check, Max asked: "Whatever happened about that idea you had in Korea—" He hesitated, not wanting to refer to their first meeting.

Larry had no such qualms. He said unabashed: "It's a good thing I got hold of that Thurlow. Saved myself a lot of time. The thing was patented three months ahead of me."

"Well, it's something to have dreamed up a gadget that was worth patenting even if they beat you to it. Gray-Stevens wants you more than ever."

The meeting was felicitous from start to finish. Max urged Larry to spend Christmas vacation in New York with them and Larry hailed the idea.

"Would you take me through the plant?" he asked eagerly.

"Sure thing. I'll even show you where your desk'll be the day after you graduate."

Larry chuckled.

"Max, don't be sore. But God bless the booby trap that got you."
They parted on terms of hearty goodwill and liking.

CHAPTER 6 . . .

The Christmas visit was a success, too. Larry drove down in the rehabilitated Porsche and demonstrated its soundness with elation. He took Carol in his stride, showing just the permissible amount of admiration.

All of Max's friends liked Larry and included him in the various holiday parties. Besides, Larry had several classmates in New York and had more dates than he could handle. When Spencer Gray gave him a latchkey for these late nights, Larry felt truly that he was a member of the family.

Carol was civil to him but cool to his charms. Once, she said to Max in their room: "He talks enough about that sister of his. If he's so crazy about her, you'd think he'd spend Christmas with her."

"California's three thousand miles away. Probably the fare was an item."

"With you and your father champing at the bit to spend money on him?" she asked satirically. By Christmas—now a three-months bride—she was far more outspoken than the timid girl of Key Largo. (But only with Max. To his father, she was unswervingly demure.)

"We are, at that," he laughed. "But I doubt if Larry'd have accepted it. We had the devil's own time getting him take the price of that jalopy he drives."

"But he did finally take it," she pointed out dryly.

Max sobered.

"Look, honey. Do you realize I wouldn't be here at all if wasn't for Larry?"

"I know," she said, with a dainty touch of mimicry. "'He saved my life.' So he figures he has a mortgage on you."

He frowned.

"You've got it all wrong. Larry figures nothing of the kind. But I feel a tremendous debt. There's nothing on earth I wouldn't do for him. Don't you understand that?"

"I can't say I do. After all, what did he do? His simple duty. If one soldier's in trouble, another one is bound to give him a hand. I think you're just a soft touch for any smart operator that comes along."

This was probably the first moment of Max's awakening from his "pink-and-golden fog." Her attitude jarred him. And he had a fleeting impression of suddenly peeping behind a curtain. Was this girl, talking about soft touches and smart operators, the shy kid of the Florida beach? He was very thoughtful that evening at the Ryders' dinner, in spite of the freely flowing liquor.

It could not be said that he fell out of love with her at once. He still found delight in her pretty ways and her pretty body, but a picture began to emerge—and not a pleasant one. It was the picture of a small-minded, grudging personality with a narrow, shabby point of view and a trick of assessing everything in dollars and cents. He tried to excuse it on the grounds of her meager, pinched childhood but it was the first split in the fabric of romance.

At first, it did not trouble him too much. He was satisfyingly busy at the plant, they had plenty of friends and entertainment to fill their leisure hours and Carol was consistently sunny while the novelty of unhampered spending kept her happy. And he was particularly grateful to her for her charming deference to his father.

But in March, Spencer Gray went the way of all flesh. One moment, he was walking up the stairs with Max after a nightcap in the library, the next, he collapsed with a gasp on the top step. Max caught him in his arms and shouted to Carol to phone Dr. Liggett.

In the agonizing minutes of waiting, Gray lay so still that Max had the dreadful feeling that his father was already dead. But suddenly, his eyes opened and he spoke faintly but distinctly: "Max—this house—always live here—don't like to think of it as abandoned— And that boy—Larry—never forget—he gave you your life—"

"Sure, Dad, I promise. But don't talk anymore just now."

Dr. Liggett, plump, bumbling, old friend as well as family physician, arrived and did what he could to ease the stricken man's condition. No younger, abler man could have done more. Spencer Gray was for it. He lingered for ten days, then drifted from sleep into death.

Max was hard hit. For days, he was numb with shock. External things did not register with him. He was hardly aware of Carol's comforting gestures and he had no clear memory of the funeral.

Then came the period when he began to miss his father at every turn: the chummy evening chats, the helpful suggestions of the older man in business problems. Spencer Gray's love had been a warm blanket and now the blanket had been yanked away, leaving Max cold and desolate.

But nothing lasts in its original intensity. Max would mourn his father all his life. But he was young, he was forward-looking, and tangible affairs filled his mind and his days. His father's will loaded him with responsibilities and work. He inherited the other half of the Maxwell fortune which his mother had left to her husband. And he was now sole head of Gray-Stevens.

His training at the plant had been wisely planned from the first. Spencer Gray had rotated him from department to department, a few weeks or months in each, so that he had had a fair grasp of operations, procedures and policy by the time he left for Korea. In the six months since his return, the emphasis had been on the executive side of the business. Max had been at his father's elbow during conferences, sessions with customers, board meetings and consultations with the head designer, the chief of research, the plant manager and the shop superintendent. These were all extremely competent and dedicated men. They eased Max's path through the first difficult months, tactfully steering him away from the mistakes of inexperience but never usurping the final power of decision which was Max's alone. He began to gain self-confidence and, having a clear logical brain, skill and efficiency. Gray-Stevens hardly hesitated in its smooth-running management through its change in leadership.

Max was less successful at home. After a few months to let him get over the pain of his loss, Carol began a rather crude campaign for changes. She hated the old house with its solid, handsome, outdated furniture, and envied the Saviles' and Ryders' smart Sutton Place apartments with their picture windows, their built-in kitchen appliances, their rose-tiled bathrooms and smart Swedish decor.

At the first sign of Max's returning awareness of her, she broached the subject.

In the dark of their bedroom, she could not see his face but his voice was a dash of cold water: "Move? Definitely no." He had a curious reluctance to mention his promise to his father.

"But darling, we can't live in this old barn all our lives."

"Why not?"

"Well, for one thing, the stairs."

"The stairs! A couple of kids like us?"

"Darling, you've had so much trouble, I hate to add to it," she said with pretty reluctance. "But they're bad for me. I get breathless—and dizzy— I don't believe it's good for me to climb stairs."

"You're going to see Dr. Liggett first thing tomorrow," he said, concerned. The suggestion shocked him since his mother and then his father had succumbed to heart failure.

Dr. Liggett might be rusty in the latest medical techniques but he had the experience of forty years' general practice behind him. And he knew human nature. He reassured them both and salved Carol's dignity by laying the "palpitation" to her nerves. He prescribed some milk-sugar pills to give her a sense of importance and told Max privately that her heart was as sound as a bell.

There was no more talk of moving but Carol planned some small retaliations. Max learned of the first of these almost at once. On the day of their visit to the doctor, they walked home. Passing Cartier's window, Carol admired a diamond clip. Max, feeling a little tender toward her (even "nerves" made her an object of compassion), steered her into the shop, bought and charged the clip.

Two weeks later, when Cartier's bill arrived, it not only listed the $3500 for the clip but $9000 for a bracelet. When he asked her about it, she said ingenuously: "Oh! I thought as long as we had a charge account ... And it was so cheap. Nancy's isn't a bit better and it cost a lot more—"

Max was anything but niggardly but it crossed his mind that the "cheap" bracelet cost more than Carol could have earned in two years.

"It's all right," he said. "But after this, suppose we shop for jewelry together."

Tears sprang into her eyes and her lips trembled. "I see," she said sorrowfully.

"See what?"

"I thought—after all, we're married. Isn't a wife a full partner?"

"Yes, of course. But so is a husband, Carol. I'm entitled to know beforehand when you spend a considerable sum of money."

"It's not spending, exactly. Diamonds are an investment."

He smiled, amused at her mixture of naïveté and business sense.

"Well, let's invest together, after this," he said and rumpled her hair.

She didn't defy him over this point: she got around it. On one occasion, when he was in San Diego, she bought a pair of costly earrings. ("I just had to have them for Marge Lansing's wedding and I knew if you'd been here, you'd have said yes.") On another occasion, she asked him to go with her to Parke-Bernet where a really elaborate necklace was to be offered at auction. She knew at the time that he would be tied up in an important meeting with certain top brass from the Pentagon.

Their first summer was dismal. Carol hated the East Hampton "cottage," a rambling structure of fourteen enormous rooms, even more than the town house. She didn't like surf-bathing, she didn't like fishing, she didn't play bridge. She met most of the cottagers but had nothing in common with them. Max drove to the plant every day (it took him hardly longer through the sparse traffic than from New York). She was left to her own devices and she had none. The Hargraves owned the cottage next to theirs and Steve was constantly enlisting Max as a fourth at bridge in the evenings. On Saturdays, Max's boat was her rival. She was afraid of the water and wouldn't set foot in it. Max gave up one or two weekends to keep her company, but as she seemed no more contented with him than without, he soon fell for the lure of the water and the weakfish.

The weakfish were responsible for the first overt step in the breakdown of their marriage. Max and Steve, and one or two other dyed-in-the-wool fishermen, got up at 5:00 or even 4:00 A.M. when the weakfish began running. Carol awoke the first time, complained bitterly and eventually moved to another bedroom so as not to be disturbed by Max's early rising.

When they returned to the town house after Labor Day, she continued this separation. She took possession of their old room and asked Max to move into his father's room at the front of the house. ("I find I sleep better alone in a room," she said apologetically.) The two rooms did not connect. The only way from the one to the other was out of the door and down a considerable stretch of hall. If Carol had ideas that this hard-to-get attitude made her more desirable, she was wrong. Max resented it at first and missed her. But to his own surprise, this phase passed and he discovered that privacy and the lack of nagging more than compensated for the loss of Carol's physical attractions.

And she did nag: about the house; about East Hampton; about Morgan, whom she disliked; about Larry, when Max sent him any trifling gift; even about Max's habit of walking round the block before bedtime.

They were not completely estranged. All through the second year of their marriage, Carol would periodically present herself, shy but ardent, and a sort of reunion would be accomplished. It took nearly the whole winter for Max to arrive at a reluctant cynical conclusion: when Carol wanted a piece of jewelry, a fur coat or an unusual sum of money, she used his bed as a springboard. Never once did she give herself without a price-tag tacked on to the gift.

There was one fault which he had never found with her—philandering with other men. The standards of their set were fairly flexible and there were the usual number of mildly illicit affairs which ran their lighthearted course and fizzled out like spent rockets. Several of the married and unmarried men of their crowd, attracted by Carol's looks, made a tentative play for her. Her response—disapproval tinged with a faint contempt—put them off permanently. Her attitude was, of course, a relief to Max, but slowly he began to realize that it was due less to morals than to temperament. She was basically cold. Money and valuables seemed the only things that could kindle real warmth in her.

His own feeling for her died a natural death, smothered by her apathy. Three years after their marriage, they were more like fellow-guests in a resort hotel than husband and wife. They did the same things, went together to parties and theater and occasionally entertained at home. Max's indifference was tempered by pity: Carol seemed to get so little out of living.

But even the pity vanished after an ugly little incident. At dinner, one evening, Carol was inordinately upset. One of her diamond earrings was missing. She had worn them the night before, had left them in her jewel case on her dresser, and when she returned in the morning from her bath, one of them was gone.

"You're sure you had them both when we got home?" Max asked.

"Positive."

"And your other jewelry?"

"I only wore the earrings and my bracelet. The rest is in my safe-deposit box."

"And the bracelet's still there?"

"Yes."

"Then it's certainly not theft or the bracelet'd be gone, too. You mislaid it or it slipped down somewhere."

"I searched. I tore the room apart looking. It's gone."

"Look again. Then if you don't find it, I'll notify the insurance people."

"Yes. But, Max—it isn't only the value of the earring—"

"What then?"

"It's a horrible feeling that someone in the house is dishonest."

"You mean Mrs. Evergreen or the daily cleaning woman?"

She spoke in low, pained tones: "They had neither of them arrived for the day when I missed it. The only one in the house besides us was—Morgan."

Max stared at her.

"Carol! Don't be ridiculous. I'd as soon accuse myself as Morgy."

"I'm not accusing her. But she was in my room while I was in my bath. When I came out, she'd brought up my breakfast tray."

"Suppose she had. The Crown jewels could've been sitting there and Morgy wouldn't touch them. Get that right out of your head. And give your room another going-over."

The next evening when Max came home from the plant, he found Carol on her bed, pale, shaking with nerves, almost hysterical. Through floods of tears, she explained brokenly, with defensive emphasis: "All I did was ask her if she'd seen it. I didn't say a word about taking it— Oh, Max, she flew into a dreadful rage—I was afraid she was going to hit me—"

"You're talking about Morgan?" he asked evenly.

"Yes—and then she flounced out—" Sobs choked off the words.

"Go on."

"I was trembling like a leaf—"

"What about Morgan?" he asked stonily.

"The next thing I knew, she marched in again and demanded that I go through her trunk—"

"Why her trunk?"

"Well, she was all packed—"

"Packed! Morgan?" The temperature of his tone dropped fifty degrees. "You're telling me that just because you asked Morgan if she'd seen your earring, she threatened to leave?"

"She ... did ... leave ..." said Carol in smothered tones.

Without a word, he went out of the room and the house. He knew that Morgan's only relative was a married brother living in Jamaica. He was sure she would go to him. He knew the address because he and Steve Hargrave had been there often in their childhood with her. He got out his car and headed there at once.

A tight-lipped Morgan had a different tale to tell: "She accused me outright, Mr. Max. Her very words were: 'You're the only one who had a chance to take it.'"

"She didn't mean it, Morgy. She didn't know what she was saying. She was excited. Now get your things together and I'll drive you home."

"It's no longer home to me, Mr. Max."

"Oh, nonsense. I tell you she was hysterical. And I promise you she'll apologize as soon as she calms down."

"I couldn't live in a house where I'm doubted. I made her go through my box before I left, so she'd see for herself I wasn't taking the thing with me."

"But, Morgy—after all these years— The house won't be home to me without you," he begged helplessly.

"It hasn't been home to me since she came into it," Morgan said bleakly.

"But why?"

"It's not for me to say."

"Say it anyway, Morgy. I'm in a fog about the whole thing."

"It's not my place to open your eyes, Mr. Max."

"Of course it is. You've always done it when I was mixed up. Don't stop now. That's an order."

Morgan took a deep breath. You could almost see her making up her mind. She spoke woodenly: "Then if you must have the truth, she wants no interference. She thinks she can handle you better alone. She was afraid of Mr. Gray, God rest him, and tried no tricks on him. But she wasn't afraid of me and it's my belief the earring isn't missing at all. It was just an excuse to push me out, so there'd be nobody you could turn to, while she milked you dry." Her brilliant blue eyes sparked with both recklessness and devotion. She was going against all her canons, she was violating her deepest principles by speaking her mind about one of her "betters" to another, but the occasion warranted it, even if it destroyed her pride in her own status. "She's a monster with ice in her veins, with appetite for nothing but money. Get rid of her, Mr. Max, before she destroys you entirely."

He tried to discount Morgan's Celtic intensity, but the nagging doubt was there: Carol hated Morgan and, against tremendous odds, had managed to get rid of her at last.

Morgan did not come back. Max arranged a generous pension for her as his father had done for Mrs. Whelk. A "daily," paid by the hour and neutral as a robot, took her place. But Morgan's influence became stronger than her actual presence when the facts bore out her prophetic words: Carol confessed with tearful humility that she had found the earring, hidden in a crack of her dresser drawer.

Her airs and graces, her attack of nerves in the face of his grim indifference, her emotional accusation that he no longer loved her, had, for her, the unexpected effect of a boomerang. He said coolly: "I believe you're right. There's no love at all between us anymore. We'd be far better apart." She was too stunned to answer. He went on: "Money seems to be the one thing that matters to you. Well, you needn't worry on that score. I'll provide ample alimony, once we're divorced."

A storm of frightened tears answered him. She seemed to be in an absolute panic. Stuttered screams came through the sobs: "Divorce!—Never—never—you can't—I won't—"

She became so hysterical that he called Dr. Liggett, who, this time, provided real sedation, instead of his usual milk-sugar pills. Alone with the doctor, Max explained elliptically that they didn't seem to hit it off and that his proposal of divorce had brought on her attack. Liggett smiled benignly.

"These things look so big, close to, my boy. Every couple goes through them. They mean nothing. Why don't you send her away on a little vacation? A week apart and you'll both be ready to laugh at yourselves and each other."

Max proposed it, and to his surprise, Carol was more than willing. She chose the last place in the world Max would have suggested for recuperation from an attack of nerves: Atlantic City.

Things were a little easier when she returned. She had made friends with a couple, stopping at the same hotel; Alec and Ilma Benger, both six or eight years older than Carol but full of a hilarious gusto for life, more understandable to her than Max's standards. The probable truth was that with Max's friends, she felt at a disadvantage and had developed a defense mechanism to offset her sense of social inferiority. The Bengers, once they knew she was "the" Mrs. Maxwell Gray of Gray-Stevens, gave her the incense due her position—a position as far above the Bengers as Max's friends were above the Carol Tyson of Umatta, Pennsylvania. Not that the Bengers were unpresentable; they were fairly well-educated, prosperous and self-respecting. Alec was a successful dress salesman and Ilma had been a well-paid corset buyer before her marriage. If they were slightly crude, it was a crudeness that did not jar on Carol.

They did get her into one questionable habit: they had implicit faith in liquor as part of a good time. They were never drunk but they were often "high." Carol, who had never cared for even a predinner cocktail, went along with them. Somehow, she found straight whisky easier to down than a Martini and discovered that after an evening of spaced drinks, she could forget Max's frightening suggestion of divorce and sleep soundly.

When she returned to New York, she kept up the friendship. Ilma Benger's homage, along with her genuinely amusing personality, provided many enjoyable afternoons for Carol. They went to lunch and the movies together, they had long "visits" on the phone and often played gin rummy together at Ilma's pleasant apartment on Riverside Drive. There was usually a highball at their elbows during these sessions.

The friendship was no secret from Max. He welcomed anything that gave Carol an interest in life and suggested inviting Ilma to the house. It was the one thing she never did. She took Ilma to the Colony and other swank places for lunch but never opened the doors of the old house to her. Max wondered why. It never occurred to him that in Carol's eyes, the ponderous 1900 furnishings were not impressive enough and that she preferred to let Ilma's imagination paint an exalted background for her new friend from the upper ether. Actually, he gave it little thought. The main thing was that Carol was a trifle more satisfied and consequently easier to live with.

CHAPTER 7 ...

All through this period, Larry Bellair flashed in and out of Max's life like a bright engaging Puck; but a Puck with a serious side as well. At the end of his second year at M.I.T., Max begged him to accept plane fare to California so as to spend the vacation with his sister. Larry countered: "It's grand of you to offer, Max. I'd love to see Avery but there's something else I want more."

"Lay it on the line, kid."

"I want to spend the summer at Gray-Stevens. No salary—or just enough to eat on."

"Can do. What department?"

"No particular one. Call me a sort of roving observer. I want to get the feel of the place. Remember, only two years more and I'll be a fixture there."

"You remember. I'm afraid by the time you graduate, the Dean'll offer you jobs at much more glamorous places than our little outfit."

"They can keep 'em. I'm a Gray-Stevens man from way back."

He lived with them at the East Hampton cottage that summer and while he boiled with enthusiasm about his days at the plant, his evenings and weekends were not so successful. Carol, without a single uncivil word, made him feel less than welcome. But he closed his eyes cheerfully to this and set himself to win into her good graces. He had plenty of opportunity. On the evenings when Steve snagged Max into a bridge game, Larry kept Carol company and drew her out on the principle that the most popular person in the world is a listener. Carol did talk, unable to resist any ear for her "grievances." But she, not he, guided their talk. When he asked her about her girlhood in Umatta, she dismissed it with a cool "Flat. I'm even bored thinking about it," and returned to complaints of the cottage, the dampness and the dullness of the life at East Hampton. She put up with his company and was never definitely rude, but there was an underlying contempt in her manner to him at all times that Max resented. It was too subtle to put a finger on or express in words but it was there and made one more point against her in Max's book.

Only on one evening, did she warm to him. They were all at a Country Club dance and Larry admired her earrings while they sat out a dance. (He was still being careful of physical exertion.) For the next ten minutes or so, until the others returned to their table, Carol, flushed and animated, described her growing collection of jewels. But it was Larry's idle comment that won him her solid approval: "Shouldn't think you'd have to buy stuff. Max's mother must've left him 'family jools' by the hatful."

It had simply never occurred to her. But she lost little time implementing the idea, even crediting Larry with the suggestion when she broached it to Max. During the following winter, half her "visits" to Max's room had, as their mainspring, one of the Maxwell show pieces.

At the end of his third year at M.I.T., Larry did go to California but again refused Max's offer of plane fare.

"I don't need a dime," he insisted. "I've got all last summer's salary salted away. If you'll remember, all I spent was gas for the Porsche to and from the plant. And half the time, not even that, when we crawled there in your sedate equipage."

"Don't you smear me as an old fogy," Max grinned. "Seventy miles an hour is plenty on these roads."

"If only I could keep the Porsche down to seventy!" Larry grinned back.

"We'll miss you at the plant."

"Not as much as I'll miss it. But I've got to see Avery graduate. I'm all the family she's got."

"Of course. I suppose she'll come on East after commencement?"

"You don't know Avery!" Larry's grin widened. "You know what that kid did? With all her classes and exams, she found time to write a thing called a pilot sketch for a TV series. You know—a sample sketch with the outline of several more to follow. All on her own, she bought herself an agent and hypnotized him into submitting it. The next thing she knew, she'd landed herself a contract to write the first thirteen sketches. How do you like that?"

"Real Cinderella stuff. Or do I mean the fairy princess who could spin gold?"

"We-ell, iron ore, to begin with. They don't pay too much to unknowns. But it's a start. If the show catches on, she can up her prices and really go to town."

"I'll bet on her. She must have plenty on the ball to strike with her first cast."

"You and your weakfish," Larry laughed. "When you meet her, she'll bawl you out if you mix your metaphors that way."

"I'm looking forward to it—meeting her, I mean."

"No chance. She's stuck on the Coast with this contract."

Larry drove to California in the Porsche and on his way back, stopped in East Hampton for the Labor Day weekend, with Max and Carol. His trip seemed to have had the effect of champagne on him. He sparkled with high spirits, he roared with laughter at the smallest joke and wouldn't be serious for a moment.

"You sound like you struck oil," Max observed, smiling, one evening.

"Oil? No. Who wants it? Aladdin's lamp's the ticket."

"Oh? Where'd you pick it up?" said Max, going along with the gag.

"On the road. There it was, big as life, right on the Turnpike."

"And of course it works?"

"That remains to be seen."

Max suddenly thought he understood.

"Larry! You little devil. You're on to another idea for a gadget."

"Could be."

"How about talking about it?"

"Not in the talking stage yet," he chuckled.

"Well, it can't be as funny as all that," Max grunted.

"It is to me."

And Max couldn't get another word out of him.

The weekend was satisfactory to Max in another way. Carol's

attitude to Larry underwent a change for the better. She made an effort to be more cordial to him and the vague contempt in her manner was gone. Max wondered a little at this reversal but he was too pleased to question her about it. Sufficient unto the gift horse, he told himself with a grin.

All that winter, Larry kept coming down to New York for weekends, sometimes in the Porsche, sometimes flying. Max noticed that his clothes improved in quality and cut. Now and then, when the three of them were going out together, Larry would present Carol with a sinfully expensive corsage. When Max protested, he said airily: "I'm rolling. I get top prices tutoring the rich boneheads." But Max wondered if he was as chary of accepting help from his sister as he was with him.

But he didn't give it—or Larry—much thought. He was much more troubled by Carol that winter. She still saw Jima Benger and a few of Ilma's friends, but began to withdraw more and more from Max's crowd. When Nancy Savile, almost certainly out of regard for Max, invited her for lunch or canasta, she always refused. She had a variety of excuses. She had a headache, a nervous chill, or most often, palpitation of the heart, she would claim. When it was a matter of evening invitations, she would tell Max to go without her. The thing that bothered him was that he had to believe her; she really did look ill. When he urged her to see Dr. Liggett, she snapped at him. In fact, she had only two moods these days. She was either in tears or she was waspish. And she still deviled—but now without blandishments—for pieces of his mother's jewelry.

She spent more and more time in her bedroom. She bought a huge television set and had it installed there. For hours on end, day and night, she would lie on a chaise longue, watching indiscriminately, not even bothering to rise and switch channels. And most of the time, Max noticed, there was a drink beside her. Not that she was ever drunk, but she did manage to get through a considerable amount of whisky. Once in a while, when she was sufficiently mellowed, she would explain almost amicably to him: "I hate the stuff. But Dr. Liggett says a heart patient needs it as a stimulant."

"But, Carol, he didn't say you need it," Max would say. "He's told you time and again your heart's okay."

"Well, of course, he says that. You don't tell a heart case the truth. It would only aggravate the condition."

He wasn't worried about her heart since Liggett's reassurance but he did worry about her ill appearance and general deterioration.

One evening when they were due at a big charity affair, Carol begged off as usual.

"I'm just not up to it. If you're so set on it, go without me."

"I'd rather you came, too."

"I can imagine!" she jeered. "So you can work up sympathy with your snooty friends. So they can say: 'Look what poor Max is stuck with.'"

Max turned off the TV set and pulled up a chair beside her. He laid his hand on hers and said in the friendliest tone he could muster: "Look, Carol. I'm damned sorry about all this. Suppose we both stay quietly home together and look it in the face."

"Look what in the face?"

"Ourselves. What's wrong? We started out so well together. Why did everything go to pot?" As her lips began to quiver, he added: "Now, for Heaven's sake, don't cry. I'm not blaming you. Maybe it's my fault but I don't know how or why. How did we get to this point where we're strangers—worse than strangers? You wouldn't bark at a stranger the way you do at me—"

"Oh, of course," she flared. "I'm the one. Everything's my fault—"

"I don't say that at all. But something's wrong and I don't know what. That's what I want you to tell me."

"Leave me alone!"

"No, Carol, I won't. I've left you alone too long. For a year I've been going around like a semi-detached bachelor—to dinners, parties, my bridge club, always with a silly excuse that you're too ill to come."

"It's true! I am!"

"If you're ill, why won't you see the doctor?"

"That fathead!"

"It needn't be Liggett although he's a pretty sound man. Dad swore by him—"

"Oh, sure," she said viciously. "If your father thought so, that makes it right. What I think doesn't count. My ancestors didn't come over on the *Mayflower*. So I'm nothing. He made that plenty plain!"

Max held onto his patience.

"We'll leave Dad out of it. He's been dead three years, you know. He couldn't have anything to do with this fix we're in."

"Oh, couldn't he! Not much! Try to tell me he didn't pass on his ideas to you that I'm dirt and you're the upper ten!"

"Carol, that's ridiculous and you know it. I fell in love with you. I thought you were the sweetest, loveliest thing in the world—"

"And look at me now! Is that what you're trying to say?"

"Carol," he said quietly. "Tell me one thing: were you ever even the least bit in love with me or was I just a handy meal ticket?"

"That's right! Insult me! Get out of here! This is my room!"

"You really hate me, don't you?" he said slowly.

"That's my business."

"It's mine, too. If you're unhappy, so am I."

"You? With all your lovely sympathetic friends who fall all over you because you've got such an impossible wife?"

He ignored this; it could only lead to more wrangling. He said: "We're unhappy together. We hardly exchange a civil word. We'd both be better off apart—"

"If you dare to bring up divorce, I'll scream the house down!"

"I intend to bring it up," he said firmly. "I've got some rights, too, you know. What have you got against divorce? I'll see that you're independent, either a whopping lump sum or plenty of alimony. Any way you want it. You can have a fine new life—"

She sat up in the chaise longue and threw her words at him: "Once and for all, Max Gray, I won't hear of divorce. Now let me alone, do you hear? I've got troubles enough." Her voice rose hysterically.

Max got out of the room.

In June, Larry graduated cum laude. Max flew up for commencement and the two drove down to New York in Larry's new car. This was nothing less than a small scarlet Jaguar that ate up the road like a tongue of flame. He explained it readily to Max: "Avery's graduation present. Of course, it cost practically nothing—for a Jag, that is. You should have seen it when I hauled it away."

"You seem to specialize in high-powered wrecks," Max said, amused.

"Well, naturally it's mostly fast cars that get into accidents," Larry told him reasonably. "If you put that much money in a car, you want your money's worth in speed. And if you're not a damned good driver, chances are the car ends up on the scrap heap and poor guys like me get a look-in."

"Well, slow down, will you please. I'm not at all interested in 100 mph or better."

Larry laughed but he did slow down.

He went to work at once at Gray-Stevens in the research department. But he didn't live out at East Hampton that summer. His sister's contract on the Coast was expiring, she had acquired something of a name as well as valuable contacts and she was coming East to freelance. Larry spent his spare time looking for an apartment for the two of them. Max begged him to let him help with both the rent and the furnishings but Larry refused.

"I'll do this much," he promised. "Any time I'm in a hole, I'll call on you. But for now, I can manage without a handout."

"Handout, hell!" Max said. "Call it a loan if you want. Pay me back when you're a Gray-Stevens vice-president."

Larry grinned.

"Shylock! Think of the interest!"

He was a likable boy and quite aside from the fact that he owed his life to Larry, Max felt very close to him, with something of the warmth he would have felt for a young brother. They were five years apart in age, but Max at thirty had the feeling that in many ways Larry was no older than when they first met. Larry grew older but he didn't grow up. To the rather serious-minded Max, this was an attractive and refreshing trait.

Moreover, he had never forgotten that revealing letter Larry had written him four years before. The straightforward plea for help against temptation, his looking upon Max as a "father-confessor," had touched the older man more than he could say. It engendered in him both deep affection and a sense of responsibility toward Larry. He held himself in readiness to be of service but was profoundly thankful that the service was not needed.

CHAPTER 8 . . .

In October, Avery Bellair came East. Larry asked for time off to meet her plane and Max suggested going along to the airport, too.

"Committee of welcome. Make the kid feel valuable," he said.

"Better not. It'll upset her plans."

"Plans?"

"Yup. She's got it all laid on. Told me to invite you and Carol for dinner tomorrow night."

"That's crazy. She'll have unpacking to do; she'll be in a strange town and a strange apartment. Much better if you both come to us for dinner."

"Sounds reasonable but orders are orders. I talked to her on the phone yesterday in L.A. and that's the way she wants it."

When Max told Carol, she refused flatly to go, not even troubling to give one of her usual excuses.

"Why should I put myself out for Larry Bellair and his sister?" she said sullenly. "You can treat him like God's grandson but I don't have to." Her voice rose to a jeer: "He didn't save my life."

Max didn't argue; he was, in fact, slightly relieved. Carol was less and less an asset these days in any gathering. He ordered a profusion of flowers to be sent to Larry's new apartment in the afternoon and went alone at eight that evening.

The apartment was in a reconstructed brownstone on East Forty-eighth Street. Larry's apartment was two flights up.

When Max reached the door marked "Bellair," there was a scrawled sign tacked to it: "Walk in. Mixing the dressing. Can't answer."

Max chuckled and turned the knob. He found himself in a big living room as wide as the house. He had an impression of blond wood, gray and coral decor with a brilliant splash or two of emerald green. The over-all effect was charming. It had a simplicity which even a man knew was expensive. Max guessed that Avery's TV earnings had helped pay the bill and wished for the hundredth time that Larry wasn't so infernally independent with him.

A voice from the end of the living room called: "If that's Larry, bring me the capers. If it's Max, come and be met." Max, still chuckling, walked back to the six-by-six kitchenette. He was all prepared to take Larry's kid sister to his heart but he was not prepared for what he saw. She was outstandingly beautiful. Even the straight-line, disfiguring coverall could not hide her slim grace. And nothing could take away from the loveliness of the vivid eyes (so different from Larry's light Scandinavian blue), from the rightness of her small resolute features or the glory of her hair which fell in rich loose waves, the warm shining red of an Irish setter's coat.

"Brothers!" he snorted. "He cracked up your brains, your enterprise, your babysitting prowess. But not one word about your looks."

"You mean it?" she asked delightedly. "I am considered pretty in L.A. but I wasn't sure about New York standards."

"You pass *cum laude* and I do mean *laude*. I was expecting a leggy kid, maybe even braces on your teeth."

"That's because Larry seems so young. Peter Pan in person. Will he ever grow up, do you think?"

"Don't change the subject. We're talking about you."

"Oh, fine. Keep it up." All this time, she was intent, pouring olive oil, a drop at a time, into a bowl while she stirred with her other hand.

"Don't you think you're in the wrong end of TV?" Max asked. "Oughtn't you be on the screen itself?"

"There's a thing called acting. You need it to get on any stage. I haven't got it."

"But you can write?"

"I don't know yet. The stuff I've been turning out on my tripewriter means nothing. It was awful."

"It seemed to catch on."

"I was lucky. I'd heard about Peggy Lister, this phenomenal child-actress. She was under contract to a big network and they couldn't find a vehicle for her. So I sat me down and ground out a sketch where she was the prime mover in bringing an estranged married couple together again. Also outlines of three or four others where this sickening little ray of sunshine saved everybody from crippled children to corporation presidents. High-grade garbage. And the more I poured the saccharine on, the more they ate it up. I couldn't take it anymore. When I sat down to write, I gagged. So I didn't sign on for the new series."

"And now?"

"I've saved enough to give myself a breathing spell. I'll write what I want to write and see if I've got stuff."

Larry came in with a jar of capers and an avocado. Avery said: "Now both of you get out of this little hole. Somebody mix a drink and by that time, I'll be ready."

Just as Larry poured the Martinis, she came in minus the coverall. In her low-cut lime-green dress, she was delightful.

The dinner was informal, consisting of a huge casserole piled high with spaghetti and meatballs, and an even bigger wooden bowl overflowing with green salad. Max, the notorious salad-hater, polished off both items.

Over coffee and a distinctly good brandy, they talked as if they had known each other all their lives. Avery cleared the table and stacked the dishes in the kitchenette while Larry chose records and set the hi-fi going. Max sat, happier and more at ease than he had felt for years. He did no thinking, just let himself ride on a wave of well-being. Only one fleeting idea crossed his mind: he must raise Larry's salary so as to conserve Avery's savings. She must be given every chance to do what she wanted.

Avery had lived in California all her life. She had never been East.

She was giving herself a week's holiday to get acquainted with New York, before buckling down to work. Without a definite word being said, Max and Larry constituted themselves a committee to show her the town.

Every evening and all day during the weekend, the three ranged over the city together. Max, as with most New Yorkers, saw things he had never seen before. He did take them to dinner at the stock smart places, but now and then, Avery (secretly primed by a volume called *The Little-Known Gotham*) suggested odd restaurants in off-trail neighborhoods and they visited those, too. Chinatown, Little Hungary, the Lower East Side, all came in for a play and they ate lobster Cantonese, stuffed cabbage rolls, and knishes indiscriminately. They saw Broadway hits and little-theater plays. They wandered through the gardens of The Cloisters and through the crooked streets of Greenwich Village. Avery's favorite excursion was a ride up Riverside Drive at night. They used Max's Cadillac so that they could all sit comfortably together in the front seat. Avery never got tired of the mystery and beauty of the Hudson, its dark surface spangled with long reflections of the jersey lights. They would park far up the Drive and sit for hours, talking without effort.

Out of the welter of talk, Avery's main characteristics emerged: she was utterly natural and she was level-headed. She said exactly what she meant but there was no acid in her. Her attitude toward Larry was full of affection but affection didn't keep her from a clear-sighted recognition of his faults. She treated Max as if he was without roots. She never referred to his wife, his affluence or his position as Larry's boss. They were simply three congenial equals.

When the week was over, the jaunts were over, too. Avery declared that after a long day at the typewriter she was only fit for a bathrobe and an easy chair. Besides, it was part of her job to watch television, good or bad. Company distracted her.

Larry went back to his pre-Avery schedule of social life with his growing crowd of friends, male and female. Max discovered that he had nothing to go back to. The week with Avery and Larry had unsettled him for any other sort of companionship. He was restless but not unhappy. He made no effort to go against Avery's edict but she was constantly in his thoughts. Now and then, he sent her a trifling gift but it was well into November before he saw her again.

Larry came over to his table in the plant commissary at lunchtime. "Quarantine's lifted. The opus is finished and off to the agent. Avery wants you for dinner tonight."

Max remembered that he had an appointment for that evening but he ditched it without a qualm.

"Swell," he said. "But tell her not to prepare. Let me take you both out."

"Will do."

Larry went back to his own table with the other research assistants. He never ate with Max but was careful to stick to his own level in the caste-system of the plant. He never presumed on their friendship and avoided any appearance of "teacher's pet." And he rarely mentioned his own work in the research department. Max had to go to his chief for a report on his progress. The report was considerably better than good. The head of Research was enthusiastic about his newest assistant and recommended giving Larry unusual latitude in developing a certain idea he had outlined. This had to do with a prop-jet engine, aimed to accomplish vertical takeoff, and Larry's ideas, the director reported, were brilliant.

"I've handled a lot of scientists in their swaddling clothes," the director said with a queer fire in his eyes. "I'm not one to call a goose a swan but it's my belief we've got hold of an honest-to-God genius in that boy."

"I think he'll go far myself," Max nodded, gratified.

"Far isn't the word, Mr. Gray," he said with something like reverence. "He's bound for the very top."

Max and Larry drove home together that day as Max's Cadillac was in the shop for some trifling repair, and Max wondered whether he should tell him what the director had said. He had no fears that it would turn Larry's head; the boy had a sober appreciation of his own ability but regarded it merely as an attribute he had been born with, along with his blue eyes and yellow hair. There wasn't an ounce of vanity in him. After a long, silent stretch along the parkway, Max did finally tell him. Larry laughed.

"Well, I ought to have inherited something decent from my old man along with his light-fingered tendencies."

"Oh, shut up," Max grunted at him. "You'd think you robbed a bank every weekend to hear you." It was the first mention of Larry's "inheritance" between them since Korea, and it embarrassed Max much more than it did Larry. He was glad of a diversion.

"Turn off here, will you," he said, as they neared Jamaica. "We've time to stop by and say hello to Morgan. The poor old girl's been ailing lately."

"Anything serious?"

"I'm afraid so," said Max gravely. "I've had her to Steinholz, the best man there is—"

"Good Heavens! Steinholz! Then it's—"

"So he says."

"Does she know?"

"I think so but you'd never guess it from her manner."

"She's a grand old sport, your Morgy. I like her."

"And she likes you. Come in with me and get her to laugh. She always says you're a sound for sore ears."

Morgan, her once-sturdy body shockingly diminished, refused to recognize the angel of death. She sat in an armchair, indomitably cheerful and as curious as a magpie about everything that concerned Max. Larry kidded her within an inch of her life, asked her to marry him and planned where to go on their honeymoon. She played up to him with gusto, reminding him they had a witness and if he reneged at the chapel, she'd have the law on him.

When they left, both men were sobered, as much by her gallantry as by her imminent death.

But even the thought of Morgan could not quench Max's urgency to see Avery again. He presented himself as early as was decent that evening at the Bellair apartment.

"Dr. Livingstone, I presume?" he grinned foolishly. "I was all set to sneak in and smash your typewriter."

"I like you, too," she said deadpan. "Larry, why don't we have a Martini before we leave? Drink to the big moment."

"Hail to the script?" Max asked.

"Well, that, too," she said with a flashing smile.

Larry was just pouring a dividend when the phone rang. Avery picked it up and then held it out to him: "It's Iris Dalton."

"The Hornet," Larry groaned. "I wish she'd start buzzing around somebody else." Into the phone, he said winningly: "Hello, honey, what's on your mind?"

There was an inarticulate clamor in the phone which did indeed sound like buzzing. Larry exclaimed: "What! Tonight? I thought it was next Friday." After more humming, he said: "Well, okay. I'll be right over.... Sure we will. The Jag'll get us up there in no time." He hung up and said to the others: "You kids'll have to get along without me. Seems I'm due at a dinner dance in Croton. That gal Iris'd make a wonderful secretary. Never lets you forget a date."

And he was gone. Avery and Max looked at each other and laughed.

"Do we still go—without our chaperon?" she asked lightly.

"That's up to you," he said, suddenly strained.

"As far as I'm concerned, we do. Your position's a little more delicate."

"Don't worry about me."

"I'm not the worrying kind. But you do have a wife and you're rather well-known on the local scene. A Winchell crack won't do you much good."

"I couldn't care less. Get your wrap," he said shortly.

"I've got a much better idea. I expected to have dinner for you two at home, so I marketed this morning. There's a terrific steak in the icebox. Also bisque of lobster and other frozen delicacies. I pay time and a half for kitchen boys."

They prepared the meal in a hilarious mood and ate it with sincere appetite. Over the strong, clear coffee, Max asked: "How is it you weren't asked to this Croton dance?"

"Oh, I was. Larry hauled his whole crew over here Sunday evening. I went over big. I could be dated from now till New Year if I liked."

"Why don't you like?"

"They're so raw. The girls are all about nineteen—"

"While you're a doddering twenty-three."

"And all that goes round in their minds is rock 'n' roll and speed and jam sessions. Maybe I'm an egghead but they bore me to death." She hesitated and then went on honestly: "There's another reason too. They're all so damn rich. Take this Iris Dalton—her father's the copper Dalton—she's got five fur coats and owns her own plane. I don't exactly envy her those things but it's still a disadvantage to travel with a crowd like that."

"It doesn't seem to bother Larry."

"Oh, Larry. He'd be at home with Princess Margaret. He could marry Iris tomorrow if he wanted. She absolutely stalks him."

"But, Avery, you can't fill your life with just work. You've got to have friends—"

"I've got you," she said simply.

He felt the warmth, the buoyancy go through him again. "An old stick like me," he jeered. "And damaged wood at that."

"Don't fight it, Max," she said firmly. "You loved me the minute you met me. And I loved you. What do we do?"

He let the waves of enchantment wash over him. He looked at her and words were unnecessary. But it wouldn't do. He pushed back his chair and reeled over to the fireplace, trying to grasp at sanity. But she followed him and stood close and suddenly, they were drowning in a dizzying kiss. Then he held her at arm's length.

"It's no good," he said harshly. "I won't have it this way. I love all of you."

She laughed softly.

"Stick-in-the-mud. Any way you want it. Come help me with the dishes."

CHAPTER 9 . . .

When Max got home, he was primed for a final settlement with Carol. This time he would not take "No" for an answer to his request for a divorce. But the light was out in her room and he could hardly rouse her from sleep to discuss it, without raising questions in her mind. He was taking no chances that, by instinct, she would connect Avery with his urgency. Twelve hours more or less didn't matter. He would talk to her first thing in the morning. He didn't sleep at all but the night was too short. The thought of Avery, her beauty, her wit, her charm, her sweet understanding lit up the dark.

Next day, a Saturday, he had the day free. He waited until ten to go into Carol's room. She was in bed, her breakfast tray across her knees and she was talking on the phone. As he came in, she was saying: "Alec going, too? Well, I'll think about it and call you later."

He closed the door, closing out the hum of the vacuum cleaner which the cleaning woman, Agnes, was using in the hall.

Carol cradled the phone and turned to look at him.

"If it's one of your social gatherings, count me out," she said with no other greeting. "I'm thinking of going to Atlantic City for a week."

She looked as if she needed it, he thought. Her face was thin and her eyes were tormented.

"That's all right," he said. "But I want to talk to you first."

"Make it short. I have to pack."

"That'll wait. This is more important."

"Well, well. I didn't think I rated being consulted in your important affairs."

"It's your affair, too," he said bluntly. He stood at the foot of her bed, staring down at her.

"Well, for goodness' sake, sit down then. I get a crick in my neck looking up at you."

He pulled a chair to her bed-side and sat down. "Carol," he said abruptly. "You're just as unhappy with me as I am with you. Let's end it, shall we?"

Her whole face tightened.

"So you're back on that tack," she said spitefully. "I told you a long time ago, divorce is out. I haven't changed my mind."

"I'm here to ask you to change it. Look. I don't know what you've got against divorce. It's no disgrace, it's done all the time. In fact, it's a blessing when two people have made a mistake—"

"I haven't made any mistake."

"What do you call it? You're miserable here. You hate this house, you hate my friends, you hate me. Apparently, the only thing about me that's bearable is my money. Well, you'd have the money. And your freedom, too. You can live in the newest apartment in town with every new-fangled gadget on the market. You can choose your own friends. You can even marry again. I won't tie any strings to your alimony."

"No."

"What in God's name have you got here?" he asked urgently. "You coop yourself up in this room all day long. You hardly see a soul. You haven't a single interest in life. When we do go out, once in a blue moon, you don't even wear your jewelry anymore—which was about the only thing on earth that used to gratify you—"

She stiffened.

"All through?" she said through her teeth.

"Not by a long shot."

"Save your breath. I will not divorce you."

"Then I'll divorce you," he said stonily.

"That's what you think," she jeered. "I'd like to see you try it. I'm not quite as dumb as you think, you know. When you first began this divorce talk, I looked into it. I even consulted Alec Benger's lawyer. So I know what I'm talking about. You've got to have grounds for divorce in this state. And I haven't given you any."

"There are other states."

"Oh, really?"

"Yes. I can go to Nevada and in six weeks, I'll be a free man." Her inexplicable mulishness made him harsher than was wise.

There was a long pause with only the whining of the vacuum cleaner outside, breaking the silence. Carol pushed her breakfast tray to the foot of the bed. She turned to her bed table, and as coolly as if she were alone in the room, picked up the flat silver flask of bourbon that stood on it. There was a shot glass beside it and with a steady hand, she poured a full drink. Max watched her as she drained the glass. Straight whisky at ten in the morning, he thought with a shudder. She set down the empty glass.

"A stimulant for my heart," she said blandly. Then she added in a level tone: "You'd better not. I'm warning you for your own good."

"Warning? Is this a threat?" he snapped.

"You could call it that," she said airily.

"A threat? To me?" he scoffed.

"And to your little pal Larry Bellair."

He stared at her blankly, chilled by her assurance. Her pure blue eyes swept his face and she smiled.

"Larry Bellair," she said softly. "The boy wonder. The little giant who's going places in Science with a big S. How far do you think he'll go when I spread it around in the right places that he's a thief? I understand the Government's pretty particular about the higher-ups in top-secret positions. All those loyalty tests and things—"

"Are you out of your mind?" he shouted at her.

"I never was saner." She batted her long eyelashes at him archly. "And he isn't going to like it that his 'father-confessor' gave him away, is he?"

In a lightning flash of horror, the past came back to him. Only once had the word "father-confessor" been used between Larry and him. He saw again the breakfast table, four years ago, when Larry's first letter had arrived. He had read it, torn it across and across and thrown it away, to conceal its contents from his father. Was it possible that even then, in the very first months of their marriage, Carol had been devious enough, conniving enough, vile enough to scrabble in a wastebasket, piece together the letter and hold it all these years, awaiting the moment when she could use it as a club against him? For it would be against him. He could no more ruin Larry's future than he could shoot him dead. Carol's threat, to a man of Max's caliber, was far more subtle and deadly than any threat to himself would have been.

Her soft feline murmur penetrated his befogged mind: "... won't dare to show his face again among decent people. And all that talent gone to waste. A pity. But do you know, I think I'll enjoy doing it."

He stood, his fingers flexing spasmodically. In all his life, he had never dreamed that he could want, could ache to commit murder.

"I ought to kill you!" He was still shouting.

Again came the long pause. But this time, the silence was absolute; the vacuum cleaner had stopped.

CHAPTER 10 ...

Max never knew where the next few hours went. He had rushed out of Carol's room, afraid to trust himself alone with her in his savage mood. He did know that he had shut himself into the library and had tramped endlessly up and down the long room, his mind in chaos, his rage still white-hot. At one period, he was conscious of movement on the stairs. He heard Carol's voice, evidently speaking to a taxi-driver: "Take these two and then come back for the large suitcase."

There was the final slam of the front door and he was vaguely aware that he was alone. He resumed his frantic plunging about the room, feeling like a mouse in a maze, trying to scrabble his way out of the hideous impasse. Whichever way he turned, he was up against a ghastly alternative: if he dropped the divorce suit, he would lose Avery; if he went ahead with it, he would destroy Larry.

Suddenly, he picked up the library phone and dialed. At the sound of Avery's voice, he said abruptly: "Is Larry there?"

"No, I'm sorry. He went to Philadelphia for the football game."

"Good. I'll be with you in five minutes," and hung up.

He wasn't very much longer. Avery met him at the door with a puzzled frown.

"Something's happened," she said. "You sounded frightful on the phone and you look a wreck. Come in."

"Yes. I've got to talk to you."

"Have you had any lunch?" she asked sharply.

"Lunch? I—no—that is—"

"I thought so. It's past three o'clock." She grinned comfortably. "Sit down while I fix you a sandwich and some coffee. Ply the man is my motto."

He dropped into a chair and discovered that he was dog tired. He didn't move a muscle until Avery came back with a tray.

"Don't talk till every crumb's gone," she ordered.

Obediently, he ate the sandwich and drank the coffee. She carried out the empty tray, came back and sat across from him before the fire.

"Now," she said.

"There's not much to say," he said bleakly. "Just that it's no good. You'd best forget me."

"Talk sense, Max."

"I'm trying to and it's damned hard. I spoke to Carol, offered her anything to divorce me. She refused."

Her mouth widened in a candid grin.

"Then I'm afraid, my darling," she said, "you'll have to take me without benefit of clergy."

"I told you last night I won't have it that way."

"Max, don't tell me I've got a prude on my hands!"

"You miss the point. I want you—any way I can get you. But that part's not half of it—not a quarter or a tenth. I want all of you—I want to see you with cold cream on your face and ink on your fingers—I want to be with you when you're tired and cross and have a stomach ache—not just when you're radiant in a low-cut dress—I want to tell you all about the everyday snags I strike at the plant—and brag to you when I do something smart—"

"A wife," she nodded. Her face sobered. "Max, you won't misunderstand when I say I think you should take things in your own hands? This isn't the time to play the little gentleman. It's a time for self-preservation. You and Carol are horribly mismated. You're living a half-life. Even if I weren't in the picture, you owe it to yourself to be free of her, to go to Reno yourself and make a clean break."

He stared at his hands without speaking. A slow frown gathered on her face. At last, she said: "Tell me all of it, Max."

"There's nothing more to tell," he said carefully.

"I'm entitled to the truth, I think. What are you hiding?"

"Hiding?"

"What's Carol got on you?"

"Got on me?"

"You sound like a talented parakeet. But I'm not fooled. A blind man could see she's using some sort of axe over you—what does she know that you're ashamed of?" She came over to him, sat on the floor at his feet, leaning her head against his knees. "Cheated on your income tax? In line for a paternity suit? Murder somebody? Darling, I couldn't care less." She broke off, watching his face sharply. Again, her tone sobered. "No. That's all out of line. None of it's like you. Max! Max! What is her hold over you?"

"I can't tell you, Avery," he said simply. "I'd go like a shot to Reno tomorrow if I could but—" His shoulders rose and fell wearily.

For a long time, they sat in silence, Max in a dull apathy, Avery, her agile mind darting back and forth like a busy squirrel. Finally, she said: "Max, I won't ask you to tell me if you can't. But if I should guess, you won't lie to me?"

"Don't guess, Avery."

"I must. I refuse to sit down under her 'No' without trying to overcome it."

"Avery, I ask you, please don't guess."

"All right, I won't guess. I'll tell you. It's Larry, isn't it?" When he did not answer, she went on: "Of course, it stands out a mile. Like the last three pieces of a jigsaw. She knows something bad about Larry and she's threatening to expose him if you leave her. What did he do? Help himself to one of her bracelets?"

"Nonsense! Stop it, Avery!"

"Max, I've known about Larry since just before my father died. Larry doesn't know that I know but Dad felt he had to tell me so that I could keep an eye on Larry—help him—hold him back if he gets that horrid urge—I was shocked at first—I was only a kid myself—and then—and then—" Her voice deepened. "It's so unfair—a taint like that, handed on from his father—as much a part of him as the color of his eyes—he's got so much else that's worthwhile—"

"That's the point, the whole point," he said, no longer quibbling. "Larry can't be judged by ordinary standards. My research director tells me he's a genius, that there are no limits to his future. Gray-Stevens can't keep him long, we can only give him time and scope and experience until he's ready for something much bigger. I can't jeopardize that future for a paltry little escapade that happened five years ago."

"If it's so paltry, it won't hurt him," she said sensibly.

"It will in this case. You've heard of the 'security angle' in Government work. You know how they crucified Robert Oppenheimer because a relative—or somebody—had been a fellow traveler. A word—a whisper of scandal—and a man's finished, no matter how hard and how loudly it's denied. And it can't be denied, here, because Carol's got the proof in Larry's own writing." He told her the story of the letter which he had torn up and thrown away. "When she told me," he finished, "I got out of there fast. I was afraid I might kill her."

"She needs killing," she said quietly. "People as venomous as that ought to be scotched like snakes."

"That's true. But it doesn't help us any. We know we're not going to kill her. Well, she's twenty-eight years old. Probably good for fifty years or more. What are we going to do about it?"

"Give me a little time to think about it."

"I've been thinking for hours. There's nothing."

"I think Larry ought to have a say in this."

"Absolutely not. You've got to promise not to give him the slightest hint."

"You're thinking he'll pull a Duke of Wellington—'Publish and be damned'?" she smiled.

"He might."

"I doubt it. He's got good qualities but he's not all that noble. Larry looks after Larry very competently."

"Well, I won't have him put to the test. This is my worry."

"And mine." Her eyes were very soft.

He made a hopeless gesture.

"Don't I know! I could shoot myself for letting you in for this—"

"Don't shoot." She managed a smile. "I like you alive." She sat up energetically. "Max, we're too close to this to see it properly tonight. Let's forget it for a few hours. I'll get my coat and we'll go to a movie. We'll sit in the balcony and hold hands and kiss each other in the dark parts—"

He caught her in his arms and kissed her then and there. She leaned back in the circle of his arms and laughed up at him.

"That's better. Now you're the Max I love."

"You're such a lovely lovely thing. But—"

"No buts."

"I can't help it. We're not kids—"

"We are for the next few hours. I think we'll buy popcorn. And after the show, around nine or ten, we'll go down to Luchow's and eat something uncomplicated like potato pancakes."

They followed her program to the letter and at eleven, when he brought her home, he was surprised to find how happy he felt. Nothing was solved, but her hearty naturalness gave a wholesome flavor to the evening that brought him to balance.

As the taxi drew up before her door, she glanced up. There was a light in her apartment.

"Larry's back," she said. "Better not come up."

"You think he'd mind—about us?"

"Hardly. Larry's a live-and-let-live type. But he's very quick on the uptake. And I'll bet it sticks out all over me. If you're there, I'm sure to give myself away. So if you're really set on keeping all this from him—"

"I am. All of it. Even about us."

"Then I'll say I went to a movie alone. By tomorrow, I'll have myself in hand."

"Tomorrow. Can we see each other?"

"Of course— Oh!" Even in the darkness of the doorway, he could see her dismay. "I completely forgot. I won't be here. I'm flying up to Boston. My best friend at U.C.L.A. is getting married and I'm maid of honor. Darling, can you manage without me till Tuesday?"

"It'll be tough," he said more lightly than he felt. "But I'm a big boy now."

"Fine. Go home and try to sleep. And don't worry. It'll come right."

Surprisingly, he did sleep soundly that night. His previous night's wakefulness may have had something to do with it but he did absorb something of Avery's invincible serenity.

When he awoke Sunday morning, he was much calmer. He no longer felt that murderous urge toward Carol. His thoughts were all on Avery and the simple happiness of the night before.

None of the "help" came in on Sunday and he went about getting his own breakfast cheerfully. The familiar house felt friendlier without Carol in it. He read the Sunday papers and spent an hour cleaning the high-powered microscope which was one of his hobbies. At lunchtime, he raided the icebox and finding a nearly untouched roast beef (probably intended for last night's dinner) made himself sandwiches which he ate with cold beer. After that, he went for a sizable walk, ending up at his club. The first person he saw was Steve Hargrave, who hailed him with delight.

"Willie Clay and Jim Lassiter are sitting in the library with their tongues hanging out. We've been looking for a decent fourth since two o'clock."

Max was only too glad to join them. They were all good bridge players and it was seven o'clock before the game broke up. Clay and Lassiter, both married men, were due at home. Steve, a bachelor, suggested dining at the club and Max welcomed this, too. He had known Steve all his life, had seen him ride through a devastating attack of polio and the subsequent lameness, with courage and humor. Max's companionship throughout those years had not been a matter of pity. He had admired and loved Steve for his own qualities.

But he was aware of Steve's passionate gratitude, even adoration, toward him for his gift of friendship at a time when too many boys found Steve's disability hampering.

As the two men strolled toward the club dining room, Steve limping cheerfully along, it occurred to Max how little he had seen of Steve in recent years. They fished and swam together at East Hampton, played cards, were often guests at the same dinner parties, but the old intimacy was in eclipse. It crossed his mind that Steve was an ideal person to tell his troubles to. Besides his sympathy and tolerance, Steve had a sharp mind. A lawyer couldn't be in criminal practice unless he had. And Hargrave and Hargrave were among the best-known criminal lawyers in the country.

After they had given their orders, Max was nerving himself to open the subject of Carol to him, without mentioning Larry's name, when a shadow fell over the table and Jerry Savile said: "Hi, kids. I'm a grass bachelor, too. Nancy's in White Sulphur. Can I eat with you?"

The opportunity passed.

CHAPTER 11 ...

After dinner, the three men separated. Jerry had an appointment, Steve went back to the cardroom in search of an evening game and Max felt an urgency to get away. All through Jerry's light dinner patter, a feeling had been growing in him: what was he thinking of, running to Avery, to Steve, spilling his troubles like a wrought-up schoolboy? This was his problem, for him to think out and resolve. He must deal with Carol himself. And before he dealt with her, he must understand her. What was the real Carol like?

As he walked up Madison Avenue, he thought back to his first meeting with her and the ensuing weeks before their marriage. She had been lovely to look at and as timid as an antelope. She had been considerate of his health and full of thoughtful little gestures for his comfort. Had that all been put on, a snare to catch a well-heeled husband? He couldn't be sure. He had been so girl-hungry at the time that all his judgment had been clouded by sex. At the moment, Carol had been just an utterly desirable prize.

When had he begun to see her in perspective? He thought of her eagerness to choose the largest diamond ring in Miami and her obvious hinting for the string of pearls. He went on to her steady appetite for jewelry and more jewelry; to her unforgivable treatment of Morgan; to her apparent ill-health for the past year; to her growing aversion to him, suppressed only when she wanted still another ring or bracelet. Was greediness the key? Was she lining her nest for the future? No. It didn't hang together. If she wanted security, money, independence, it was hers for the asking. And she had refused it, refused to divorce him at all costs or for any price. It didn't make sense.

He found himself at his door and a determination hardened in him. Face to face with her, any discussion developed into recriminations, sneers, hysteria and an attack of nerves. The very sight of him seemed to bring out the worst that was in her. Perhaps the written word would not aggravate her into malice. Pen and paper were neutral and tolerant. If he could put it to her reasonably and plainly in writing, ask her what she wanted, perhaps even quote actual sums (the dollar sign was potent) he might persuade her to accept an opulent freedom at the simple cost of divorce and forget the threat she had flung at him yesterday.

He threw off his hat and coat and went directly to the library. He sat down at the old-fashioned desk and pulled out paper. He wrote:

"November 16th. Dear Carol:" and sat wondering how to start. And then, suddenly, without effort, the pen was moving steadily across the paper:

"It's 8 o'clock and I'm alone in the house. If it takes all night, I'm going to analyze this wretched situation and try to make you see that divorce and only divorce is the only answer to our sorry excuse of a marriage...."

He covered three sheets of paper, front and back. He wrote straight from the shoulder, enumerating her faults and his own. He taxed her with disliking him and admitted that the feeling was reciprocal. He called it insanity for them to stay chained together and even suggested that there was dynamite in the situation. (He read over all this and cooled his pen to a suaver argument:)

"I refuse to believe that you would do what you threatened yesterday. It isn't like you. We may not be suited to each other, but that doesn't mean that either of us is necessarily base or evil. I am writing this to the Carol I knew five years ago, appealing to your sense of fairness and generosity...."

Again he read over what he had written. It struck him as feeble, stilted and indecisive. The letter whined. There was no firmness in it.

Perhaps harshness was the answer—an iron counter-threat. Quickly, he added a postscript:

"I advise you for your own good to give up your vicious tactics and not to fight a divorce. I can be as tough as you and I intend to be free, no matter what methods I may have to use."

Without further consideration, he sealed the letter and addressed it to the Traymore in Atlantic City. He went to the corner and dropped it in the mailbox. When he got back to the house, he was still restless and dissatisfied. Already, he regretted sending the letter. It was inept from start to finish, from the groveling wordiness of its beginning to the bravado of the postscript. He realized why it was so ineffective: he was deathly afraid of Carol's threat and he had written under the stress of that fear. He knew he was utterly helpless against her because he could not allow one whisper of her smear against Larry to get out—Larry, to whom he owed everything, Larry, of whom Spencer Gray's last conscious words were: "That boy—Larry—never forget—he gave you your life."

He realized that he had no choice. He was utterly in Carol's hands. He was chained to her for life if that was the way she wanted it. Avery was lost to him; the future stretched bleakly ahead....

The telephone beside him rang.

He lifted the receiver and stiffened at the sound of Larry's voice. Avery must have told him. He was calling to reassure Max, to take up his cudgels, to put Max still further in his debt, in spite of Avery's doubts on the subject.

But there was no such hint in Larry's light greeting: "Hi, Max. Busy?"

"No. What's on your mind?"

"How's Carol?"

"Away for a few days."

"You're home all alone?"

"That's right. Why? Something I can do?"

Larry laughed.

"There is at that," he said.

"I'm your boy."

"You could really help me out of a hole."

"Name it."

"Well," Larry laughed again. "I'm supposed to be somewhere tonight—and I ducked it—"

"I get it." Max smiled. Probably that girl Iris Dalton was in his hair again.

"If you'd just back me up in case— Say I was with you from along about eight o'clock till—let's see, it's nearly ten-thirty now—make it from eight to ten-fifteen—better make it a business conference if you're asked—"

"Who the hell would ask me?"

"Can't tell—if they check up—"

"Okay. You were here from eight to ten-fifteen. Say no more."

"Thanks, Max. You're a big help."

Max hung up, still smiling. Larry and his girls. Well, anyway, he knew nothing about this Carol mess. Avery had kept it to herself as he had asked her to do. Avery.... He sat, dreaming, steeping himself in the memory of her loveliness, her honesty, her sane humorous outlook, above all, her incomprehensible love for him. What the hell had she seen in him, a stodgy, dry-as-dust stick, when she could have had all the world to choose from?

He was roused from his dream by the front-door chimes. A little surprised—it was well past eleven—he went to the door. Two men stood there.

"Mr. Maxwell Gray?"

"Yes."

"Lieutenant Brown." He flashed a badge and indicated the other man. "Sergeant Rossi."

"Yes? What is it?"

"May we come in?"

"Certainly." He threw the door wide and led the way to the library. In the few seconds until all three were seated, Max's mind raced furiously. The meaning of the phone message was coming clear: Larry had succumbed again and was involved in some sort of theft. In his innocent-seeming request, he was setting Max up as an alibi.

Lieutenant Brown, a tall, thin man with a steady eye, asked: "Do you know a Mr. Laurence Bellair?"

"Yes, of course. He's a business associate."

"When did you last see him?"

Without an instant's hesitation, Max smiled and said: "Why, about an hour ago."

"He was here?"

"Yes. All evening."

"Can you be more specific?"

"Yes. Our appointment was for eight and he was on time. He left about ten-thirty, give or take a minute or two."

"You were together continuously from eight to ten-thirty?"

"Yes. We were working on a project—"

"Project? What kind of a project?"

"Research. Afraid I can't be more explicit. It's more or less hush-hush— Oh. Perhaps I should explain. I'm Gray of Gray-Stevens Aircraft Motors. Bellair is one of our experimental engineers. We were figuring the costs of this new project—" He smiled. "We're both pretty hot on it—couldn't stop worrying it even on a Sunday evening."

The lieutenant's granite face did not alter but the information created a subtle change in his tone. The head of Gray-Stevens was someone to be reckoned with. Perhaps, too, the solid, old-fashioned dignified room had its effect. At any rate, he was believing Max, though all he said was: "I see."

"If you want to get in touch with him, I can give you his address. He should be home by now."

"We have his address."

"Well, then—? Why the questions?"

"One more question, Mr. Gray. Did Bellair use his car?"

"You mean to come here?"

"Yes."

"I can't be sure. He didn't mention it but it's possible—I wish you'd tell me what this is all about."

"At nine thirty-five tonight, Bellair's car, a 1956 Jaguar, figured in a hit-and-run auto death. At ten-forty Bellair called Headquarters and reported his car stolen from East Sixty-third Street where he had parked it."

"That figures," said Max promptly. "He did use his car. Then he left here, couldn't find it and called you." He hoped the shock he felt did not reach his voice.

"It's not quite that simple, Mr. Gray. This stolen-car report gag is an old routine. A man commits a vehicular homicide, drops his car and scoots to a phone, reporting it stolen. I don't say that's the case here but we have to check. I ask you again: you and Bellair were continuously together from eight till ten-thirty?"

"That's right."

"In that case, he's clean."

"Who—was killed in the accident?" Max asked.

For the first time, the lieutenant's lips flickered with the shadow of a smile.

"Not a very useful citizen. In fact, the driver of the death car saved the city a good piece of change."

"How is that?"

"At nine-thirty tonight, a candy store on East One Hundred and Fourth Street was held up by three teenage boys. The owner's yells brought the officer on the beat. But by the time he got there, the leader had stabbed the owner to death and lit out. He dashed across the street in front of the Jaguar and was killed instantly. We've got the other two. As I say, hardly a desirable citizen, the dead boy. But that doesn't excuse the driver of the car."

"No, I see that."

"If he had stopped, he'd be in no trouble at all. Bystanders said it was entirely the boy's fault. But the fact that he hit and ran makes him guilty of a felony. It's a thing we've got to be strict about. Otherwise, every hot-rodder in the country would mow down citizens regardless."

"Yes, of course. Have you any clues to the driver?"

The flicker of smile widened.

"The street was fairly crowded—a mild Sunday night—We've got descriptions of the driver all the way from a white-haired albino to an African native. No two alike. But one man did have the sense to get the car's number. That's how we located it so fast."

"Oh. You've got the car?"

"Double-parked, twenty blocks away. Empty, of course. It's downtown now being processed."

"Processed?"

"Fingerprints. Between you and me, I don't expect too much from it. Contrary to public belief, the steering wheel of a car is a poor field for prints. All drivers slide their palms up and down the wheel, rubbing out any stray print that may be on it. If we're lucky, we may get one off the door. And if we're really shot with luck, it'll be on record." He rose. "Well, thanks, Mr. Gray. I guess that does it. Sorry to have bothered you but—"

"No bother. Only too glad to help. If you need a signed statement or anything—"

"If we do, I'll let you know. But I doubt it. Looks like a plain case—these young hoodlums can't resist a Jaguar, seems. Good night, Mr. Gray."

As soon as the door closed on the two men, Max poured himself a stiff drink. He needed it. For the first time in his life, he found himself on the wrong side of the law and it was an unpleasant sensation. But looming far larger, was his relief that his first suspicions of Larry were baseless. Both Avery and he were wrong: the taint was gone, Larry, at twenty-five, was no longer prey to the ugly impulse to steal. What he had done was regrettable but forgivable. The kid had panicked and run away. He would have to see Larry....

Larry. What must he be feeling right now? He was a sensitive, emotional boy and he had just killed a human being. He was probably close to hysteria. Max's hand went out to the phone, to talk to him, to reassure him, to calm him down. But before he could dial, the front-door chimes sounded once more. He thought it was Lieutenant Brown again with some tricky question which he might muff and bring down the whole house of cards. As he went to the door, he was sweating.

It was Larry. He looked at Max with a sheepish grin and said: "May I come in?"

Max threw the door wide and led the way back to the library.

"This is a damn silly thing to do. They might be watching you."

Larry's grin widened.

"No. I've been watching them. I just saw 'em leave. It's safe enough." He eyed Max's half-full glass. "I could use one of those."

Max poured him a drink and handed it to him. "Now, let's have it all from start to finish," he said.

"Yeah. But first I want to apologize, Max. Not giving you the lowdown on the phone. But I was afraid with all the extensions you have here—"

"I told you Carol was away."

"Well, the maids—"

"They're none of them here at night and on Sundays they don't come at all."

"I didn't know that. So I was—er—cagey on the phone. And one other thing I want to apologize for, Max—"

"Oh, for God's sake—"

"No. I have to say this. It was a foul thing to ask you to go to bat for me just because you think you're under obligations to me. If I know you, you'd rather take a beating than—"

"How would you like to shut up?" said Max gruffly. "Forget it, will you. What I want to know is why in hell you ran away like a panic-stricken idiot—"

"Panic-stricken is right. Try to get the setup, Max. This boy dashes out—oh, God, the feel when he hit! It was a—a foreign neighborhood—and crowded—I bet you now every man and boy on that block carries a switch-knife— I—I lost my head—all I could think of was to get clear— When I came to my senses, I was in the Eighties on a quiet cross street. Not a soul around. I began to realize—and— plan—so I ditched the car and took a bus back to my apartment. After I phoned you and knew I could count on you, I called the police and said my car was stolen from near your house. That's all of it."

"Just a minute. Haven't the police talked to you?"

"Oh, sure. This Brown. Same guy who was here. He showed up fast—as soon as they looked up the owner of the Jag. He asked a million questions and did a lot of sniffing—I think he wanted to smell if I'd been drinking."

"Well, had you?"

"No, thank the Lord. Not even a beer."

"Could he tell anything from your manner— I mean, you must have been pretty jittery."

"Nix. I put on a damn good act. The cop was eating out of my hand when he left. But I wanted to find out if he'd check with you so I took a taxi up here. Sure enough, the police car was before the house. So I stuck around till they left— That's it, I guess."

"Not quite, Larry."

"What! Didn't you—? Did you let Brown smell a rat?" Larry's whole face tightened.

"No. I lied like a trooper. He seemed satisfied. He believed me all right."

"That's the beauty of being Max Gray of Gray-Stevens. Your word goes a long way."

"Did Brown tell you about the boy?"

"Yeah. A goddam little murderer—"

"Did he say that if the driver had stopped, he wouldn't have been in trouble at all—that it was the boy's own fault?"

"Sure." Larry looked at him knowingly. "And did I use that! I said that naturally the driver of a stolen car didn't dare to stop even if he was in the right. That clinched it with Brown." He took a long swallow of his drink. "Boy, I needed that."

Max cleared his throat. Embarrassed, he said: "Larry, I couldn't persuade you to clear this up, could I?"

"Clear it—? What do you mean?"

"I mean, go to the police—tell 'em you lost your head—"

"And get you pulled in for perjury? You crazy or something?"

"If you'll risk it, I will."

"Well, I won't. For God's sake, Max! The kid's dead. And good riddance. The thing's over. What good would it do to stick our chins out? Can you imagine that Brown? He'd be so sore we put one over on him, he'd see we both got good stiff jail terms."

"Okay. I guess you're right."

It was late when Larry left. But Max, restless and unsettled, felt he could not sleep without his usual pre-bed walk. As he ranged almost unseeingly along the nearly deserted streets, he tried to argue himself into Larry's viewpoint. The boy was dead, and, as Larry said, probably good riddance. It was understandable that Larry had panicked among a group of aliens who might have spoken with switch-knives first and listened afterwards. They had both lied to Lieutenant Brown but their lies had hurt nobody. Brown was apparently satisfied and the whole incident was closed. For nearly five years, Max had tried his best to show his gratitude to Larry for the immense service he owed him and had never succeeded. Moreover, all his efforts had been merely financial; a few dollars which he never would have missed (and which Larry had consistently refused). Now, he thought disgustedly, when Larry did need a hand, here he was, balking at it because it dealt him a blow in his damned self-esteem. To hell with that, he told himself, go home and get some sleep.

CHAPTER 12 ...

On Monday, Max combed the *Times* for news of last night's happenings. On an inside page, there was a short account of the candy-store owner's murder by a trio of teen-agers, one of whom had found a swift Nemesis, being killed in flight by a hit-and-run driver in a stolen car. The car, belonging to Mr. Laurence Bellair, said the account, was later recovered, abandoned by the thief a mile away. No mention of Larry's alibi or of Max. The dead boy was Manuel Rivas, seventeen, recently released from a two-year hitch in a state reformatory.

On Tuesday, there was no mention of the incident at all.

On Wednesday, when Max returned from the plant, Carol was home. As he came into the hall, she appeared at the library door. He had a spurt of hope: she had had his letter and had come home to negotiate.

"Hello, there," he said, as pleasantly as he could manage. "You're back early. I thought you were staying a week." There was no use acting sore, in spite of the poisonous threat she had made last time he saw her. If she was willing to come to terms, he'd meet her halfway.

"There was something I had to attend to." She, too, was pleasant.

Max stared at her. She looked wonderful. The tormented look was gone from her eyes. She had natural color in her cheeks and her lips were dewy and fresh-looking. She was as pretty as when he had met her five years ago.

"Well, it seems to have done you some good," he said. "You look wonderful."

"I feel wonderful. I'd like to talk to you."

"Sure. I'll have a quick shower and be down in a jiff. Think you could have a Martini ready?"

"If you like," she agreed quietly.

If he didn't whistle in his shower, he felt like it. Things were going to be all right. His letter must have been more effective than he thought. Or, if not the letter, some sort of miracle had taken place. Carol acted like a new person. Perhaps, he thought with sudden hope, she had met someone, had fallen in love and had come back to arrange a quick divorce in order to be free herself.

When a few minutes later, he came clattering down the stairs and into the library, his Martini was waiting.

"Better close the door," Carol said, as he appeared. He closed both the door to the hall and the one leading into the dining room. She poured his drink and measured out a moderate bourbon for herself. They both sat down. She took a thoughtful sip and said: "I got your letter."

Now it was coming. He could scarcely breathe for his excitement.

"It wasn't a very smart letter," she said mildly.

"I realize that. I'm not too good with a pen."

She smiled, looking for all the world like a beautiful Siamese cat.

"It wasn't what you wrote. It was when you wrote it."

"When ...?"

"Don't you ever read the papers? Oh, of course, I know you swear by the *Times*. But it's not the only paper in the world."

"What are you getting at?" A faint chill went through him.

"Ilma reads the *New York Cry*," she said, naming a sensation-mongering tabloid. "She's crazy about it. She even buys it in Atlantic City. It goes all out for love-nests and crime and murders. Where the *Times* and *Tribune* give a bare outline, the *Cry* prints columns of details. You were one of the details yesterday. Ilma showed it to me. Would you like to see it? I've got a copy upstairs."

Max pulled himself together. He didn't quite see where all this was leading but he did know that Carol's soft, temperate tone was a distillation of pure malice. He said in as unconcerned a voice as he could muster: "May I ask what all this is in aid of?"

"You don't know?" she asked archly.

"I can't say I do."

"Then I'll quote the opening of your letter. It's dated November sixteenth—that's Sunday night—and it begins: It's eight o'clock and I'm alone in the house. If it takes all night, I'm going to analyze—' Do I have to go on?"

"You do indeed," he said coldly. He felt cold.

"The *Cry* says you told the police that at eight o'clock Larry Bellair was with you and that he stayed till ten-thirty. So of course he couldn't have killed that boy and run away afterwards." There was faint mockery in her tone.

"Well?"

"Which is the truth—what you told this Lieutenant Brown or what you wrote me?"

"They're both true. It didn't occur to you, I suppose, that I finished the letter later—"

"After ten-thirty? Is that what you did?"

"That's exactly what I did."

"Then how does it happen that the postmark on the envelope is November sixteenth, nine-thirty P.M.?"

"Rubbish. You made a mistake. I'd have to see that to believe it."

"I'm afraid I can't oblige. The letter's in a safe place—a very safe place. But if I ever hear another word from you about divorce, I'll take it to the police. Your dear friend Larry will go to prison for manslaughter and you'll go with him as accessory after the fact. It just so happened that Mr. Hagen, Alec's lawyer, was down for the weekend. I asked him what happens to people who hit and run and lie about alibis— Oh, don't worry. I didn't let Ilma hear me. No sense in letting her put two and two together. Not that she could, because of course she didn't see your letter. Or Mr. Hagen either. I believe a weapon is more valuable if only one person handles it."

He glared at her, the same murderous urge tensing every muscle. She dropped her eyes, the long curling lashes shadowing her cheeks demurely.

"So now we understand each other," she said serenely. "Remember: at the first word from you about divorce, I go to the police. At last, I can crack the whip."

He took her by the arms and shook her furiously. "I ought to kill you! The way one kills a venomous snake!" he shouted, unconsciously echoing Avery's words.

The door to the dining room opened and Cora, the "daily" who had taken Morgan's place, announced that dinner was served. Max turned on his heel, snatched up his hat and coat in the hall and dashed out of the house.

He walked blindly, battling with his own savage impulses. He racked his brains, trying to hit on some way out. He ground his teeth as he realized how untouchable she was. In the eyes of the law, she would appear a virtuous wife, deserving, not only of justice, but of sympathy for her deplorable ill-health of the past year. He wouldn't have a leg to stand on in any court, even if he dared to sue for divorce. And of course, he couldn't. He'd be a real heel to let Larry in for a prison term just to get himself off the hook.

Again he wondered what the real Carol was like. Piecing together Larry's letter and waiting all these years to use it. Poring over the tabloid like a ferret, sniffing out the deadly contradiction between Max's unfortunate words and the postmark. Why had she rushed home from Atlantic City to add this new threat, as if the first one was not potent enough? Why did she hate Larry so bitterly and show such relish at the thought of injuring him? Could she be jealous of Max's friendship for him? No. It was not in her to feel anything as strong as jealousy. He could only conclude that, hidden under her soft smooth prettiness, there lay the twisted nature of the poison-pen writer who spun out evil for evil's sake. One was utterly helpless in the face of such malice.

After a long time, he came to the conclusion that the only real solution to the whole filthy mess was Carol's death. Three people, Larry, Avery and himself, would be the better for it. He thought of the old tag about the good of the greatest number and asked himself squarely if murder was ever justifiable. He pulled himself together and told himself not to be crazy. You took what was dished out to you and if you couldn't like it, at least you swallowed it without whining. That way, Larry was safe; and Avery was young, she'd get over her feelings for him and fall in love with somebody without his appalling drawbacks. As for himself, he'd get along. He had other interests in life. Plenty of friends and work which he loved intensely. Okay. His marriage was a flop. It happened to lots of guys. Forget it.

He found suddenly that he was ravenously hungry. He went into a strange restaurant where he was unlikely to meet anyone he knew. He weighed the idea of moving to his club but decided stubbornly against it. He loved the old house and nobody was going to drive him out of it. After he had eaten, the evening stretched before him. He longed for company but knew he wasn't fit to be with anyone he knew well. His nerves and temper were still too raw. He made up his mind to avoid Larry and Avery as much as possible and to taper off his visits to them. The friendship—and the danger—would die of inanition. He had a strong urge to seek out Steve Hargrave. But Steve was too shrewd. He would see something was wrong and the time had passed when Max could confide in him. Before Sunday night it would have been possible. Now, he couldn't talk without involving Larry in actual physical jeopardy. In the end, he went back to his own house, chose a book and forced himself doggedly to read.

The next evening when he came home from the plant, and the maid, Cora, told him that Carol had gone back to Atlantic City, he drew a long breath of relief—and not merely because he was happier when she wasn't around. It gave him a breathing space, time to figure out some working arrangement by which two antagonistic people could live in the same house with a minimum of friction.

CHAPTER 13 ...

On Friday evening, Max did something that went against the grain but which he felt doggedly justified in doing: he searched Carol's bedroom from top to bottom, hunting for his letter. He hadn't much hope of finding it but he felt he couldn't leave any stone unturned. Fight fire with fire, he told himself with disgust as he rummaged through her bureau drawers. He amended this phrase acidly: fight poison with poison. After an hour's careful combing, he gave up.

He stood beside her bed, oddly shaken at having resorted to this humiliating search. He felt diminished in his own eyes at using such dirty tactics; and at the same time, bitterly disappointed that the tactics had been ineffectual. His eye fell on the silver flask which always stood on her bed table these days and he poured himself a generous drink. He needed it. The burning taste of the bourbon changed his mood. Illogically, he felt a sudden twinge of pity for Carol. The little silver flask represented her only escape from their miserable situation. He, at least, had the thought of Avery, his friends, his work. Carol had nothing. Nothing but her own corroding plots—and the little silver flask. He wondered what imaginary grievances she had against him and Larry, that she should devise such diabolic schemes against them both. Was there any way of boring through her malice and finding a trace of decency? Was she warped beyond any hope? Was she indeed altogether sane in her virulence?

With a shrug, he turned off the light and left the room. The only solution seemed to be to stay out of her way as much as possible in future, to minimize the friction by absence.

On Saturday, he played bridge at his club, afternoon and evening. His luck was terrific; his finesses went through like magic and he bid and made four slams. It was late when the evening session broke up. He went home and slept solidly through the night.

On Sunday morning, Nancy Savile called up. She was back from White Sulphur and had heard from Jerry that Carol was still away. There was no getting away from her invitation to dinner that evening.

At seven o'clock, as he was getting ready to go to Nancy's, he heard Carol come in. Again he heard her orders to the taxi-driver about her luggage, this time in reverse. He heard the man stumping upstairs with her suitcases and grumbling at her meager tip as he left. Max did not greet her or show in any way that he was aware of her presence. When he was ready, he left the house. The evening at Nancy's proved pleasant. When he returned home at twelve, his mood was lighter than he had thought possible. As he came upstairs, he saw that the light in Carol's bedroom was out.

On Monday, he had an appointment in town with the company's lawyers in reference to the purchase of some land adjacent to the plant which they needed for expansion. The appointment was for ten-thirty. Max never kept it. At five minutes to ten, the maid Cora knocked on his door and burst in, pale and frightened: "Mr. Gray—you better come—I can't wake Mrs. Gray—"

He followed her quickly to the back bedroom. Carol lay in the big bed, peaceful, beautiful—and deadly still. Max touched her hand and it was cold.

He snatched up the phone and got Dr. Liggett. In ten minutes, the old man arrived, examined Carol briefly and straightened up. His round ruddy face was pale and concerned.

"I'm afraid she is gone," he said in a shocked voice.

"But—how—?" Max stammered.

"Perhaps she knew better than I did," he said humbly. "Instinct may be wiser than cardiograms. She always said her heart was affected but I never could find— But here we have proof— My dear boy, I am deeply sorry—"

The following days were providentially busy. Max hadn't a moment to himself. There were the details of the funeral, the hordes of friends and finally the funeral itself. Over and over, he heard the subdued comments:

"Of course we all knew she had a bad heart but we didn't dream ..."

"At least, she was prepared. She told me long ago her heart ..."

"The poor girl. She's out of her misery—it's been going on for a year that I know of ..."

The funeral was large and solemn. The plant was closed for the day. In the church and at Woodlawn, Max's stony gravity passed for well-curbed grief. After the services, the Saviles, the Ryders and Larry came back to the house with Max. Jerry mixed a tray of stiff drinks and they all offered the best they could in limping comfort. They suggested that Max should go away for a trip; that he should get right back to work—nothing like work, etc., etc. And Nancy and Gigi nailed him for dinner for days to come.

When they all finally left, Max went upstairs and took a long hot bath before dinner. As he lay in the steaming tub, his tense nerves and muscles slowly relaxing, he gave a square look at the five unfortunate years of his marriage.

He asked himself where he had gone wrong, what he had done or left undone that might have contributed to the fiasco. Would their chances of happiness have been greater if they had moved out of the ponderous old house in spite of his promise to his father? Had he driven a wedge between them in his harsh disapproval in the Morgan incident? Had he been negligent during the last year when her health had seemed to fail? Shouldn't he have insisted on a checkup by a heart specialist since she had no confidence in Liggett? Were the threats against Larry and himself simply the twisted mental results of an ailing body? He admitted all these failures and regretted them sharply. But he had the honest conviction that whatever he would have done, it would not have saved their marriage. He was too level-headed to be morbid about it and too human not to feel relief that Larry was safe from her threats. For the life of him, he couldn't help looking forward. He felt deep pity for Carol's cheerless years with him but he was thirty years old and in love. He closed the door on the past and began to think of Avery.

At dinner, he found that Mrs. Evergreen had tried to show her sympathy by preparing all his favorite dishes. He did justice to them and this, he noted with wry humor, drew the disapproval of Cora, who waited on him. No word was said but as she presented and withdrew dishes, as she swished in and out of the pantry, her criticism of his appetite on the day of his wife's funeral was obvious.

After dinner, he had hardly settled in the library when the chimes sounded and Cora announced a Mr. Hagen. The name rang a faint echo in Max's mind but he couldn't quite place it. Hagen came into the room, a stocky, square-faced man with a rather pleasant smile.

"I hope you will excuse this intrusion, Mr. Gray," he said. "But I felt that I should consult you at the earliest possible moment in connection with your wife's estate."

Immediately, Max placed the echo.

"Oh, yes. You must be Benger's lawyer—my wife mentioned you—"

"I am Mrs. Gray's lawyer, too, at least to the extent of having drawn her will."

"Oh? I didn't know she'd made one."

"I—ah—suspected that was the case. She made it about a year ago. And appointed me sole executor."

Max eyed him with more attention. He liked what he saw. Hagen seemed a decent, straightforward, business-like person, if a trifle wordy.

"Well, what can I do for you?" Max asked.

"Normally, my office would have notified you and matters would have gone through the ordinary channels but as the provisions of the will are a little unusual, I felt I would like to discuss it with you informally."

"I see."

"Now, first, as is obligatory, I am submitting a copy of the will to you as an interested party before I offer it for probate."

He handed Max a blue-covered one-page document. In it, Carol Tyson Gray ("being of sound mind, etc.") left all her worldly possessions to Ilma Benger with Ralph Hagen as sole executor without bond.

Max read it through and laid it on the table. Even in death, he thought acridly, Carol had tried to take one more swipe at him.

"Well, that seems plain enough," he said quietly. "My wife was indebted to Mrs. Benger for many happy hours and this is her way of showing her appreciation. I suppose you have notified Mrs. Benger?"

"She has not yet seen the actual will. But I called her yesterday on long distance to inform her of Mrs. Gray's death and she came up from Atlantic City in time to attend the church services today. I have an appointment to see her when I leave here, but, frankly, I believe the general context of the will is no news to her. I understood that Mrs. Gray in her lifetime had informed her that she would benefit."

"Well, you might tell Mrs. Benger that if she has any fears that I intend to contest the will, she may put them out of her mind."

Hagen was obviously relieved.

"I am glad to hear it for Mrs. Benger's sake," he said with his useful smile. "Lawsuits do nobody any good but the lawyers."

"I agree. As for my wife's estate, I think you will find it consists almost wholly of her jewelry and of course her clothes, furs and so on. I happen to know that her jewel box upstairs is empty so you will find everything in her deposit box. You may tell Mrs. Benger that she is welcome to come here any time to collect and remove my wife's personal effects. If there is anything else—?"

"Well, I expect to open the safe-deposit box as soon as possible—of course in the presence of an officer from the New York State Tax Transfer office—and I wondered if you cared to be present."

Max had a moment of acute revulsion. Every ring, pendant, earring and bracelet would bring back a moment of Carol's phony passion, ending with the exaction of yet another costly ornament. He said quickly: "Thanks but I—no I don't believe so."

"In that case, I won't take up more of your time. And may I express my sincere sympathy ..."

In a few minutes, Max was alone. A few hours before, he had closed the door on the past. Now with an impatient gesture, he locked it. The five miserable years with Carol were over. He began to wonder how soon he could decently see Avery.

CHAPTER 14 . . .

Max's desk was piled high with work and he threw himself into it with zest. He found a new efficiency and admitted that for days past he had been giving only half his mind to his job. The other half had been nagged and distracted by Carol's threats. He was a little ashamed that he felt so happy and free. But he was realistic enough to avoid a maudlin hypocrisy. He told himself bluntly that he had had a long spell of tough luck. It was time the tables turned.

A week after the funeral, he received a request to come to the district attorney's office. He assumed that there was some formality, papers to sign in connection with Carol's will. He presented himself at the appointed time with no more than an impatient desire to get rid of a distasteful job.

After a certain amount of screening, he found himself in Assistant District Attorney Harold Salter's office. Salter, a dynamic and, at the same time, a bookish-looking man, with eyeglasses like portholes, introduced himself and seated Max facing both himself and the broad window behind his desk. His manner was civil but he wasted no time.

"Mr. Gray, in the matter of your wife's decease, were you entirely satisfied as to the cause of death?"

Max frowned. He said rather warmly: "I naturally accepted Dr. Liggett's word as final."

"You had no doubts in your own mind?"

"Well, I was terribly shocked and surprised. I still am. What I mean is, for the last year or so, my wife had complained a good deal and some of the time, she insisted that it was her heart. But Dr. Liggett had assured me that it was her nerves, that her heart was sound."

"And you have perfect confidence in Dr. Liggett?"

"He brought me into the world and saw me through all the usual things kids get. He's always been like a sort of second father to me. My parents thought the world of him and— Yes, I would say I have perfect confidence in him."

"I am sorry to say that this office has not."

Max gave him a long probing look. He said slowly: "This office is taking an interest in my wife's death? May I ask why?"

"A good question, Mr. Gray. And contrary to usual procedure, I am going to tell you why: your wife went in fear of her life."

"What! That's impossible!"

"In other words, you are saying your wife had no enemies."

"I am. The whole idea is fantastic."

The D.A. opened a folder on his desk and took up a paper. He held it out to Max. "Better read this, I think. It was in your wife's safe-deposit box and addressed to this office. Her executor delivered it to us."

The letter was recognizably in Carol's writing but the lines slanted crazily and the script straggled untidily across the page. It crossed Max's mind that Carol had been well fortified with bourbon when she had written it. It read:

> To the District Attorney:
> In case I should die by accident or in peculiar circumstances of any kind whatsoever, I want my death investigated by your office. In order that this request gets the attention it deserves, I enclose proof or at least reason why I am afraid that an attempt will be made on my life. It only takes a glance for you to put two and two together.
>
> Carol Gray

When Max looked up, Salter was holding another letter in his hand.

"Do you recognize this, Mr. Gray?" He did not relinquish it but Max saw his own writing and knew at once what the envelope contained. In another moment, the D.A. would connect up the telltale postmark "November 16, 9:30 P.M." and Max's unfortunate first sentence: "It's 8 o'clock and I'm alone in the house ..." with the hour that Larry was supposedly with him and the fat would be in the fire. But even as the thought went through his mind, it was followed by another: Larry didn't know what Max had written or even that there was a letter at all, and consequently couldn't have threatened her. So why should she be afraid of Larry, even granting the grotesque idea that he would ever dream of murdering her?

Max cleared his throat.

"Yes. It's my writing. I can't be sure what's in it," he stalled, thinking furiously.

"I'll read the postscript. That may refresh your memory." He took it out and Max could see the closely written pages. In a droning flat voice, Salter read: "'I advise you for your own good to give up your vicious tactics and not to fight a divorce. I can be as tough as you and I intend to be free, no matter what methods I may have to use.' Mr. Gray, you wrote that exactly one week before your wife's death?" The porthole glasses gleamed at him.

Max was stunned. With a flash of horror, he saw that the D.A. believed he had killed Carol. He was filled suddenly with a violent rage that heated him from head to foot—rage at the D.A.; rage at Carol; most of all, rage at himself because in his fear of her threats, he had behaved like a blustering fool.

"You're out of your mind!" he shouted. "Sure, I was angry—maybe I wrote things I shouldn't have—but to accuse me of a rotten, dirty murder—"

"Nobody has accused you of anything, Mr. Gray. We are simply complying with your wife's request—and looking into the matter and the manner of her death a little more closely than Dr. Liggett seems to have done before he signed the death certificate."

Suddenly Max gave a short bark of laughter. Let them investigate till hell froze over! They wouldn't discover a damned thing, because he had not killed Carol!

"Look as long and as hard as you like," he said harshly. "And don't hesitate to call on me for any help I can give!"

The D.A. was unperturbed.

"You can give us substantial help at once," he said promptly.

"Okay. Name it."

"As Mrs. Gray's husband, you can give us permission to exhume the body for autopsy."

A wave of nausea swept over him. The thing was no longer a matter of words and innuendoes, it was a ghastly, chilling horror, filled with graves and shovels and scalpels. His stomach turned over.

"And if I don't," he said through his teeth, "you'll go right ahead and do it anyway."

"Very probably."

"Go ahead! Do your damnedest! See where you get!"

"I sincerely hope we get nowhere. Meantime, may I ask you to stay in New York in case—"

"In case I can give you a tip on the poison I used!" He snatched his hat and rushed out of the office.

He was nearly a mile away before his anger cooled and he was able to think. He was ashamed of his outburst and even considered returning and apologizing to the D.A. He decided against it. He had other things to fill his mind. What did a man do in a case of this kind? He thought of going at once to the Hargraves for advice and assistance. Assistance for what? He had not been accused. Even the suggestion that he remain in town had been couched in tactful terms. And if he went to them, what could he tell them? He was not yet ready to share the truth about Larry's hit-and-run episode with anyone.

He took a sharp look at the facts: Carol had returned from Atlantic City at seven o'clock the night before her death. He himself had left the house almost immediately. As it was a Sunday, there had been no servants in the house. If anyone had rung the bell during the evening, Carol would simply have let it ring. It was one of her small fears; she had many of them, such as fear of flying, fear of boats. When he had returned around midnight, her light was out. And next morning, she was dead.

It had to be a natural death. The idea of suicide crossed his mind but he rejected it instantly. The Carol who had written that note to the D.A. was too afraid of death to be a candidate for suicide. No, the whole thing was a storm in a teacup. In view of her note, the D.A. was bound to investigate. Let him. He would find nothing, because there was nothing to find. He himself hadn't a thing to worry about. The horror subsided.

That evening, his spirits had another lift. Avery phoned. She said very little but the gist of it was potent: "When you want me, I'm here."

The words drove all other thoughts out of his mind.

CHAPTER 15 . . .

Max's next encounter with the law was less urbane. Four days after his visit to the D.A.'s office, he received an early-morning call. The visitor identified himself as a detective from Homicide and requested him bluntly to come downtown for questioning.

The next hours were a nightmare so fantastic that Max felt as if he were being bombarded by bullets. His dazed mind took in the details incredulously.

Item: The autopsy on the body of Carol Gray disclosed that death was due to a third-degree heart-block, induced by a massive dose of tincture of digitalis.

Item: The flask of bourbon whisky which stood habitually on

deceased's bed table, contained evidence of both whisky and the tincture of digitalis. The shot glass which normally stood beside it had unfortunately been removed and washed.

Item: On Saturday, November 15, eight days before the death of Carol Gray, the cleaning woman, Agnes O'Hara, heard a violent quarrel between deceased and Gray in deceased's bedroom. As deponent was using a vacuum cleaner at the time, she heard no actual words until the end of the quarrel when, the vacuum cleaner being turned off, she heard Gray say: "I ought to kill you."

Item: On Tuesday, November 18, deceased received a letter in Atlantic City from Gray containing the threat: "I intend to be free, no matter what methods I may have to use."

Item: On Wednesday, November 19, deceased returned to her home. Another violent quarrel took place in which Gray was heard by Cora Sparks, waitress, to say to deceased: "I ought to kill you! The way one kills a venomous snake!"

Item: Deceased's safe-deposit box being legally opened by Ralph Hagen, executor of deceased's will, in the presence of Officer Milton Morris of the New York State Tax Transfer Office, nothing of deceased's considerable collection of jewels was found except one diamond clip.

Item: In the medicine cabinet of the bathroom attached to Gray's bedroom, a bottle containing 43 quarter-grain digitalis tablets was found, prescribed by Dr. Archibald Liggett for Gray's father about five years before. The bottle had originally held 100 tablets.

Item: Gray, a graduate engineer of Massachusetts Institute of Technology, is known to have taken an intensive course in chemistry at the institute, presupposing knowledge of how to compound a tincture from digitalis in tablet form.

Item: The bedside flask of poisoned whisky contained the fingerprints of deceased and Gray.

Item: Dr. Archibald Liggett, long-time physician and friend of the Gray family, admitted reluctantly under questioning, that the appearance of death by heart failure could equally have resulted from a massive dose of the tincture of digitalis administered to a healthy person.

Item: The State of New York is holding Maxwell Gray on a charge of murder.

The police used no strongarm methods. There was no physical violence. There was not even the minor torture of strong lights glaring down on Max. But for seven hours, a team of detectives questioned him with the unremitting explosiveness of a machine gun. They jumped from point to point, giving him no time to adjust himself to the new subject.

There were three men on the team: Ferucci, a hatchet-faced man with dense black hair; a fat man named Reilly, who sweated copiously and whose immense belly bulged like a balloon above his belt; and Kummer, a slim gray-haired man whose soft voice pointed up the bellows of the other two. Reilly opened the proceedings: "You killed her, Gray. Give yourself a break and admit it."

"I didn't kill her."

"You threatened her twice. You were overheard."

"It wasn't a threat."

"No? 'I ought to kill you like I would a venomous snake.' What d'you call that?"

"I lost my temper—it was just an expression—people often say such things without meaning them."

"But they don't sneak up and poison her liquor afterwards."

"I didn't do that."

"Your fingerprints were on the flask. How'd they get there?"

"I took a drink out of the flask on the Friday night."

"Oh. You took a drink. You got a bar in the library and liquor in the dining room but you hadda sneak up to your wife's room—not your room, your wife's—when you needed a drink. How come?"

"I happened to be in her room."

"What were you doing there?"

"I— Is there a law against going into my wife's room?"

"Sure not. You got every right to go in there and drop poison in her liquor. Sure you have. No wonder you needed a drink."

The slim man with gray hair interposed softly: "When you took the drink out of the flask Friday night, Mr. Gray, how much liquor was in it?"

"I didn't notice."

"Was it full?"

"I don't think so."

"Was it half full?"

"I couldn't see. The flask is silver."

"Couldn't you tell by the weight? Or the angle when you poured it?"

"Well, it might have been half full."

"You're quite sure you took a drink?"

"Positive."

"You didn't just pour some of the whisky out so the tincture of digitalis wouldn't be too diluted?"

"No."

"How much of the tincture is needed for a fatal dose?"

"I don't know."

"What? A brilliant chemistry student doesn't know? You surprise me. Tell me, Mr. Gray, how do you go about making a tincture out of tablets?"

"I've forgotten. It's seven years since I studied chemistry."

"But you've got your textbooks. You could refresh your memory easily, couldn't you?"

"I could but I didn't."

Ferucci chimed in: "What'd you do with your wife's jewelry?"

"I didn't touch it."

"Did you go in her room to collect any bits that you hadn't taken out of her deposit box?"

"No."

"Why did you go in?"

"I was—looking for something."

"For what?"

"Something that belonged to me."

"What was it?"

"A paper."

Reilly roared with laughter. He said: "A paper? Now we're gettin' somewheres. We got a new fact. What was the paper?"

"Just—it had nothing to do with all this."

"What was the paper?"

"A—an invitation. I wanted to see the date—some function we had to go to—"

"Got it all down pat, haven't you? Know all the answers."

Kummer said mildly: "Then it was a letter?"

"Yes."

"It couldn't have been the letter you wrote threatening your wife with death?"

"I never threatened her."

"Didn't you write her: 'I intend to be free, no matter what methods I may have to use'?"

"I didn't mean murder."

"What did you mean?"

"I meant I'd get the divorce myself."

Reilly slapped his fat thigh and cut in: "Oh-oh, she was two-timin' you. So that's it. Come on, Gray, admit it. The law ain't too hard on a wronged husband. Any man might see red and bump off a tramp of a wife."

"You're all wrong."

"Oh? She wasn't two-timin' you? Well, maybe you was two-timin' her and your girlfriend wants marriage bells. Like that?"

"No."

"So what have we got? She was a faithful wife. You was a faithful husband. Why'd you want a divorce so bad?"

"We didn't get along. I thought we'd be happier apart."

Ferucci took a turn: "That letter you wrote. You said in it you couldn't believe she'd do what she threatened. What did she threaten?"

Max was silent.

"Take your time," Ferucci jeered. "Make it good. We like fairy tales around here."

Reilly said: "How much did you pay Liggett to sign the death certificate with no questions asked?"

"I won't even answer that. Dr. Liggett is a reputable physician."

"Yup. Maybe he is. But old. Awful. old. And servin' the almighty Gray family thirty-forty years. Maybe the old coot just couldn't believe one of the holy Grays'd commit murder. So it was easy to pull the wool over his eyes. That it?"

And on and on and on.

When at last they locked him up, he felt mentally and physically bruised. Kummer told him, civilly enough, that he could make one phone call—to his lawyer or some close friend. But Max deferred it till morning. He wanted to think, decide how much to tell, before he met Edward Hargrave.

As soon as they locked him in, he had a merciful interval of blankness. He was so dead tired that he fell into a kind of paralysis which was more stupor than sleep. He lay on the hard bunk, hardly conscious of his surroundings for three hours.

When he came to himself, his mind was clear and cool. He began to sort out the facts. He had to accept the basic truth that Carol had died of a lethal dose of digitalis. It had been introduced into the bourbon which stood on her bed table. Who had access to that? The maids, Cora and Agnes, and the cook, Mrs. Evergreen. But it was futile and frivolous to try to connect any of them with the crime. There was no motive. Beyond the servants, there had been only himself with opportunity to tamper with the flask.

When could the tincture of digitalis have been introduced? On Friday night, he had taken a drink from the flask. It had certainly not been poisoned then. On Saturday, the servants had been in the house all day and had stated that nobody had entered the house up to 7 P.M. when they all left as usual. He himself had been playing bridge afternoon and evening. So he could narrow down the time when the house was empty and unobserved to the hours between 7 P.M. and 1 A.M. when he got home from the club. But nobody could have got into the house. The locks were solid and there had been no signs of forcible entry. Anyway, it was absurd to believe that a burglar or a stray prowler could know there was a flask in Carol's bedroom or could have come armed with tincture of digitalis. And why should a casual intruder come in, poison the liquor and leave without stealing a single thing from the house? He could rule out a stranger.

On Sunday, he himself had been in the house all day. Nobody had rung the bell and only Nancy had phoned, inviting him to dinner that evening. Carol had arrived from Atlantic City a short time before he left the house. So there was the period from seven Sunday evening until midnight when he had returned, when Carol was alone in the house. If the doorbell had rung, he was morally certain that she would not have answered it. Unless ...

Unless it was someone she expected and was willing to see. The only people he could think of in that category were the Bengers. The Bengers who were also the only people who benefited financially by Carol's death. But that lawyer Hagen had said they were in Atlantic City at the time of her death and had only returned to New York when he told them of it in order to attend the funeral services.

He thought again about suicide. Could Carol's hatred of him have gone to such fantastic lengths that she had killed herself under such circumstances that he and only he would be accused of murdering her? Her note to the D.A. bore this out in a measure: she had made sure that her decease would not be glossed over as a natural death. But he repudiated the whole idea of suicide. First, she was too full of small nervous fears to steel herself to taking her own life; second, he could not bring himself to believe that any human being could be that warped. If Carol had died by violence—and he must accept that—it had not been by her own hand.

He examined the details of the police case against him. His desire for a divorce. The blustering postscript of his letter. His extravagant "I ought to kill you," overheard by the maids. He wondered ironically if they ever missed anything. His knowledge of chemistry. The old forgotten bottle of pills in his father's medicine cabinet. His fingerprints on the flask. It all sounded formidable and damning. But actually, it was flimsy and inconclusive. Because it was not true.

He considered his coming interview with Edward Hargrave. Suppose he told him of Carol's first threat involving Larry. Would it help his case? It would only hurt it. It would give him an added motive for killing her. And Hargrave was a shrewd man. He would put together the two facts that Larry had saved Max's life and that Carol's threat was against Larry, not Max, and he would have no trouble in arriving close to the truth. He would devil Max to worm out the exact situation and Max was not washing Larry's dirty linen before anybody's eyes.

Carol's second threat about the hit-and-run incident was more of the same and had the added drawback that Hargrave, as an officer of the Court, might feel it was his duty to bring the thing to the attention of the law. He would disregard the fact that these private matters were immaterial and had no bearing on the case. He would use them as a smoke screen, as a diversionary action to create a "reasonable doubt" to the jury as to Max's guilt. And Max, at this point, could not bring himself to believe that he was in great enough danger to warrant such a step. He told himself that he was not foolhardy enough to risk death in the chair in a quixotic effort to save Larry from the comparatively minor hit-and-run charge but it would never come to that. Even if he were so self-abnegating—and it would be breaking a butterfly on a wheel—Larry, as soon as he heard of it, would rush forward with the truth. No jury would believe that a man of his reputation and character would kill another human being because he feared the consequences of an inconsiderable matter like that. In the worst case, if the whole truth of the hit-and-run story came out, probably the most that would happen would be a suspended sentence for Larry and a reprimand to himself. After all, it had not even been perjury: he had not been under oath when he told his lie. As a motive for murder, it was a washout.

The important thing was that he had not murdered Carol and innocent men were not railroaded to the chair. In the long run, truth had to prevail.

He asked permission to make his phone call.

EPILOGUE

CHAPTER 16 ...

Steve Hargrave sat opposite his father, tense with worry and anticipation.

"Well?" he asked. "Does it help? Have you found anything to get your teeth into?"

"It's an excellent report, son. You evidently worked round the clock for the last week or more." He smiled faintly. "Max Gray certainly unburdened himself. You two got back on your old footing with a vengeance."

"We did. And please remember your promise, Dad. It's all strictly off the record. Max was talking to me, personally."

"Yes, yes," said Hargrave soothingly.

"Okay, then. Now the point is, does it all get us anywhere?"

"In a way, it increases our problem. Where we had one mystery before, we now have two."

"Two? What do you mean?"

"Carol herself."

"She's not much of a mystery to me. She was a conniving, gold-digging little bitch who roped Max in with a few curves and long eyelashes. After a year in Korea and eight months in hospital, he was easy meat for the first dame who staked him out."

"That doesn't quite cover it. Our first premise is that Max is innocent. So someone else is guilty. Who? Their friends, the Saviles, the Ryders and so on? I doubt it. The two Bellairs? Take the girl Avery. Excellent motive. Remove Max's wife and live happily ever after."

"I doubt that. From Max's description, she wasn't panting after marriage lines. Besides, she couldn't get into the Gray house to doctor the whisky."

"Nevertheless, we'll check on her whereabouts for Saturday night the twenty-second and Sunday night the twenty-third." Steve jotted down a note. Hargrave went on: "Then Larry Bellair, alias Dan Cupid, furthering his sister's love affair by knocking off the obstacle."

"That's out. Max made it clear that Larry knew nothing about the love affair."

"Well, could Larry have any other ax to grind?"

"I don't see what. He knew nothing about Carol's threats against him which might have been a damn good motive to knock her off. And certainly no guilty intrigue with Carol. I saw plenty of both of them the summer Larry was at East Hampton. She was barely civil to him and he was bored to death with her."

"Camouflage?"

"No. Dozens of chances to be alone with her fell right in his lap. If it was a choice between staying on shore with her or going fishing with Max and me, he always went fishing."

"Check his alibi for those dates anyway."

"Will do." Steve made another note.

"Now we come to the Bengers. An interesting setup. The wife is her heir. If Carol dies, a small fortune in jewels comes to her. Motive? Yes, if there had been jewels. But there are none. We might say we've got a third mystery—the vanished jewels. Has Mrs. Benger got them? Did she somehow manage access to the safe-deposit box and rifle it? Did Carol find out and have to be exterminated?"

"Could be. But there's a snag there. Both the Bengers were still in Atlantic City when the poison was put in the flask. They didn't come back to town until after her death. Unless—this lawyer Hagen was in cahoots."

"No. Hagen is an ethical, reputable lawyer with a good practice. He would never risk his name and his future for a cut in a small swindle."

"Then—?"

"We come back to my point: the mystery of Carol. We don't know a thing about her before she set her sights for Max on the Florida beach. I don't know what Spencer Gray was thinking of, not to investigate her a bit, the moment Max brought her home. Did she really come from this Umatta? Who was she and what was she? Was she keeping somebody back there on the proceeds of her jewelry? Did somebody have a hold over her? Was she acting under orders from this person when she refused to divorce Max? So far, we've found no obvious culprit on the present scene of her life. How about the past?"

Steve's eyes snapped with interest.

"A trip seems to be indicated," he said, grinning.

"Right. Will you go or shall we get one of Landon's boys?" Hargrave named the inquiry agency the firm used from time to time.

"I will. I've got the feel of the case. I'll know better what to look for. I can start this afternoon."

"Make it tomorrow morning. I've got a job for you here in town first."

"What's that?"

"I looked up this man Hebert in the Hotel Men's Register—the one in Florida who held out her train ticket. He's manager of the Cliveden Hotel—"

"You don't think—?"

"Let's say I just want his slant on Miss Carol Tyson, secretary."

"You think he'll remember a girl who worked for him five years ago?"

"If he does, he may add to our picture of her. If he says he doesn't, I leave it to you to judge if he's holding out on you—"

"I get it," said Steve excitedly. "He could be back of the whole setup—snaring Max in Florida—engineering the whole game and still giving the orders up to last week. Then a row between them and he had to shut her up. If that's the case, Carol would have opened the front door to him Sunday night when she was alone in the house, in spite of what Max says."

"Don't jump to conclusions, Steve. Just interview the man."

"I'll go right over—and I won't phone for an appointment. No use putting him on guard."

The Cliveden was a large respectable commercial hotel in midtown Manhattan. At the desk, Steve presented his card and without formality or delay, was conducted to the manager's office on the mezzanine floor. Steve found himself in a comfortable office, facing a big, full-blooded good-humored-looking man in the upper forties.

"Mr. Hargrave," he said with a glance at the card. "What can I do for you, sir?"

"I've come for a little information. About a former employee of yours."

"Sure. Sit down. Glad to help you." He offered a package of cigarettes and they both lit up. His blue eyes crinkled. "Well, who is it that's run afoul of the law?"

Steve smiled back.

"Nothing like that. My firm is engaged on a case and a Miss Carol Tyson figures in it. We would like a little background on her."

Hebert's nostrils flared and he stopped smiling.

"What is it?" he sneered. "The old badger game?"

"No. An action involving a will. Miss Tyson did work for you?"

"She sure did. Until she overplayed her hand. Then I threw her out so fast, you couldn't see her for dust."

"Would you tell me all about it—right from the beginning?"

"Well, it's nothing I'd like broadcast—" he began.

Steve broke in quickly: "I assure you it will be held strictly confidential. Neither your information nor your name will be used without your permission."

"Okay, then. Mind you, I don't remember every steno who ever worked here but this one I'll never forget. Even the way she got the job was out of the ordinary. Want to hear about that?"

"Please."

"Well, must be about five years ago—let's see—Arline was fourteen that summer—that's my daughter. I'm a widower, Mr. Hargrave, have been since Arline was born and I've tried to be both mother and dad to her. We did pretty good. She's always been the apple of my eye and I was some kind of a hero to her. That summer, I was driving her up to her aunt's—she had a summer home not far from Pittsburgh, and Arline was going there for the summer. She had her dog in the car, a cute little wirehair she was nuts about. Well, we're going along the Pennsy Turnpike when the dog began yapping to get out and lift a leg. I pulled off the road and Arline walked him. He must have stepped on a thorn or whatever because back he comes on three paws, squealing like a stuck pig. Arline was frantic. Something had to be done. So I drove off the highway at the first place we came to—I forget the name—some little dump—"

"Umatta?" Steve put in.

"Right! Umatta, Pennsylvania. I stopped at a gas station and asked if there was a vet in town and sure enough there was. And a very nice place, too—a white cottage with a big yard and a separate little building where the vet saw his 'patients.' While Arline and the vet went back to the 'operating room' with the dog, I waited in the cottage. A girl was typing in the same room—it was a kind of office—and she was just about the prettiest kid you want to see. Eyelashes a foot long and a little rosette of a mouth— Now, I'm no angel, you understand—no use me pretending a babe stacked like that didn't open my pores. I ambled over to her desk and began talking to her. I got an earful. She was alone in the world and had no money. Working at the vet's for peanuts. If she could only get away from the dump and try her luck in New York! I admit it. I was a pushover. Told her to come to town and I'd give her a job. Three weeks later, she showed up at the hotel. I was as good as my word and put her to work. I didn't hurry it any but it wasn't long before I took her to dinner and not much longer till we shacked up together. Now I'm not trying to whitewash myself but I was unattached, any willing gal was fair pickings and she wasn't a loser by the arrangement. She had a whole lot more than her salary from me. And that mattered a lot to her. Never knew a chick with more yens for clothes and furs and even jewelry. But I drew the line at the Tiffany stuff. My salary didn't run to that." He grinned. "This what you call background?"

"Indeed it is."

"Well, everything was okay till I took her along to Florida to a hotel men's convention. That's when she killed the goose. I don't know where she learned her tricks in a hole like Umatta, but the second night at the hotel, she hands me an ultimatum. Either I marry her or she raises a stink with Arline. Like a fool, I'd let her know what Arline meant to me and here she was, using it as a brickbat. Why, I'd as soon have married her and let her breathe the same air as Arline as jump off the Empire State. So I told her where she got off, that she was out of a job as of that minute and to do her damnedest with Arline. Privately, she had me scared because I didn't know how a kid like Arline might take a story like that. So when she hinted that she'd make a deal, I jumped at it. The upshot was, I forked over a grand and in return, she signed a memo that she was leaving my employ by mutual consent and that she had no complaints of her treatment. I must have that note somewhere in my desk to this day. I paid her in cash and she moved out of the hotel. I never saw her again. That's it, I guess."

"Why did you withhold her train ticket back to New York?"

Hebert stared in stupefaction.

"Train ticket? Where'd you get that idea?"

"She told my client you did."

"Well, it's a damned lie— Why, I flew down to Florida. She was scared of planes so I gave her the cash to buy her own train ticket. Say listen, mister, at this late day, I don't want to get mixed up with that two-timing little crook. You said—"

"I still say it, Mr. Hebert. This is strictly confidential."

"Okay, then. Not that it would matter too much. Arline's a big girl now—she was married in April—I guess she'd take a little fling like that in her stride today."

Steve rose.

"Well, thanks a lot, Mr. Hebert. You've given me a sidelight that clears up a few things."

"Glad to help. And I'll tell you this. That cookie is due for a comeuppance. She'll try her tricks on the wrong guy some day and she'll get herself bumped off."

"She already has, Mr. Hebert."

When Steve left, Hebert's astonished mouth was still open.

CHAPTER 17 . . .

After he left Hebert, Steve had time for a little research on the whereabouts of Larry and Avery Bellair on November 22 and 23. Larry was at work but Avery was at home when he arrived. He explained to her tactfully that in his efforts to help Max, he was questioning all Max's friends with both an eye to elimination and for any knowledge they might unwittingly have which might give them a lead. Avery, composed but obviously under tension on Max's account, was only too ready to cooperate.

"Saturday afternoon, I was home alone until seven when I left to have dinner with my agent. There was a nibble for my new script from a sponsor and we talked till after ten. When I got home, Larry was there. He had just come in from Long Island."

"Working on a Saturday?"

"Oh, not from the plant. He'd gone to see an old servant of Max's who was ill. Larry's like that—careless and full of himself and then all of a sudden, moved by the nicest impulses."

"That would be Morgan," Steve nodded. "The poor old girl is for it. I've been wanting to go myself and haven't had a moment, what with this horror about Max."

Avery laid an anxious hand on his sleeve.

"Is it—do you—?" She couldn't go on.

"Don't worry," he said, as cheerfully as he could. "Someone—the murderer—is trying to frame Max. But what one man can weave, another one can unravel."

She went on to tell him that on the Sunday, a classmate of Larry's was in New York for a day and the three of them went out to dinner. They took her home about eleven and Larry saw his friend back to his hotel.

"His name's Richard Gardner and he lives in Albany. If you'd like his address in the cause of 'elimination,' Larry can give it to you."

Steve smiled, convinced of her innocence. He thought her altogether straightforward and charming and felt she was one more reason to hurry with Max's freedom.

Next day, Steve enjoyed the drive to Umatta. The day was mild and sunny, more like early fall than December. With his physical disability, driving had become second nature to him and he felt as much at ease at the wheel as in a rocking chair. He reached Umatta—prototype of a thousand small towns across the country—around noon. The business street was rather shabby and unprogressive-looking, with feed stores, radio repair shops and hardware stores predominating. The one shop for women's wear displayed a dreary window full of gingham house-dresses. Steve could understand Carol's hankering to get away from Umatta.

He was pleasantly surprised at sight of the hotel. In contrast to the rest of Main Street, its clean red brick and white trim looked new and appetizing. He parked, went in and engaged a room. He had no idea how long his quest for information might take. His satisfaction with the hotel was slightly damped when he had lunch in its dining room. As he overworked his jaws on a leathery lambchop, he invited the spirit of Sherlock Holmes to help him get done fast.

From his waitress, he learned that the William Penn High School was less than a mile away. It sounded like a good starting point. Undoubtedly, Carol had gone there and her teachers might be able to furnish some information. It might even be the school where her father had allegedly taught.

But after lunch, as he started down Main Street in his car, the sight of a tall gloomy building gave him pause. Town Hall. First things first, he thought. Vital statistics. Get the date of her birth, her parents' names, maybe even the church she belonged to. He parked and went up the steps.

He put his request to the clerk. The man's inquisitive little eyes sparked with interest.

"Carrie, again?" he said. "What do you want to check? Birth or marriage?"

"Everything," Steve said in a strangled voice. Marriage!

It cost him two dollars and an hour's time. When he went out to his car again, he had the birth certificate of Caroline Emily Tyson, born April 9th, 1930, father Jasper, mother, Adeline; and a copy of the marriage license of same Caroline Emily Tyson and James Schorn, both of legal age and with no legal impediment on May 20th, 1952.

He had asked no questions of the clerk whose ferret eyes and sharp nose marked him as a snoop and a gossip. If James Schorn still lived in Umatta, an innocent inquiry at the drugstore would locate him without alerting him before their interview. Steve didn't even have to ask the druggist. The slim phonebook hanging outside the booth gave him the answer: "Schorn, J. Kls. 65 Elm Road."

He did ask the way to Elm Road and as he drove through the town and on out through a rather pleasing residential district, he wondered what "Kls" meant. Five minutes later, he had the answer to that too. He came to a white cottage set in ample grounds. On the lawn was a wooden sign:

J. SCHORN, VETERINARIAN
Kennels—Boarding
Puppies for Sale

Kennels. Arline Hebert's wirehair. So Carol had been wife as well as stenographer when Hebert first saw her.

Steve parked outside the white picket fence and limped up the path to the cottage. In answer to his ring, a tall rangy man of thirty-odd came to the door. There was a look of patience and placidity about him which animal handlers often have. Yet this was overlaid by a touch of grimness.

"Mr. James Schorn?" asked Steve.

"Yes, sir."

"May I come in?"

Schorn opened the door wider, stepped back and led the way into a pleasant room. In one corner there was a desk. The typewriter on it, Steve guessed, was the one Carol had been using when Hebert promised her a job in New York.

"Sit down," said Schorn. As Steve did so, he added: "You looking for a dog, sir? I've got some mighty taking little fellows right now."

"No. Frankly, I'm here on a—you might call it a nosy errand. I'm looking for information."

To his surprise, Schorn nodded rather cynically. "Reporter," he said without a question mark.

"Oh, no."

"Then it's not about Carrie?"

"Carrie—er— Well, yes, it is, Mr. Schorn, but if it's publicity you're worried about, I promise you there'll be none without your consent."

"Heck, it's nothing to me," Schorn said mildly. "The whole town knows the story and what the city papers print don't bother me at all."

"You've got me wrong. I'm a lawyer and Miss Tyson figures in a case of ours, so I came up to check on certain details."

"What details?"

"Well, you say the whole town knows the 'story.' What story?"

"That Carrie run out on me."

"You mean she was married to you—"

"Still is."

That stopped Steve cold. He stared at Schorn, his mouth slightly open. Schorn looked amused.

"You're like everybody else. They all clucked around saying I should get me a divorce. Heck, why should I? I'm rid of her, divorce or no divorce. If ever she tries to come back, I don't let her in is all. If that happens, time enough to get one. In the meanwhile, it's darn good protection. Girl goes to the pictures with me, she knows it is the pictures and no wedding bells to follow."

"But someday you might want to marry again yourself."

"Not me. Once is enough for a lifetime. Women are okay as a snack but for a steady diet, give me dogs."

Steve smiled dutifully at this mid-century David Harum. "How long were you married when—?"

"Over a year. Thing was, Carrie thought she was marrying a gold mine. All she wanted was to spend and go on trips and take it easy. I didn't see it that way. A wife's got earning powers same as a husband. You don't pull your weight, you don't get returns. Carrie wouldn't cook, she raised the wind every month she typed my bills and she never did give me a hand in the operating room. She was a total loss. When she lit out, it was good news."

"Did you ever hear from her after she left?"

"Never. And that's often enough."

"Perhaps she got a divorce from you."

"What with? Soon as I saw how money slipped through her fingers, I fixed it so she couldn't touch my checking account or my savings bank cash. If she had much when she left here, she had fifty-sixty dollars, if that. As I understand it, a divorce costs a sight more. Besides, that reporter fellow would have mentioned it if she had."

"What reporter was that?"

"I don't recollect his name, if ever I knew it. Came from some city paper. Said he was doing a Sunday feature on her—"

"Did he say why?"

"A kind of Cinderella story, he said. About big stage actresses who came from nothing."

"When was all this?"

"Let's see—year—year and a half ago—I can tell you exactly—it was the end of August of last year. I know because he interrupted me the day Maudie's litter arrived."

"Could you describe him?"

"Nothing much to describe. Young, I think he was and wore these dark sunglasses. I was pretty busy with Maudie and paid no mind. Does it matter?"

"Mr. Schorn, I think I owe you a story too. First I'd like to ask you if you were out of town any time last month."

"Haven't stirred out of Umatta a day in the last year."

"You can prove that?"

"Why, sure. Mrs. Cleek comes in every day to clean and cook—cheaper than a wife, at that—and she'll tell you. But what's this about 'proving'? Sounds bad."

"It is bad. Your wife is dead, Mr. Schorn. The State calls it murder. And my firm is defending the man charged with the crime. Now you see why anyone asking about her might be important."

"Well, what do you know! Carrie dead," said Schorn slowly. He might have been talking of a total stranger. "In that case, I insist you see Mrs. Cleek. And a few other people who can vouch for me."

"We can narrow it down. If you can prove you were in Umatta on November twenty-second and twenty-third, you're okay."

Schorn thought a while, then slapped his thigh.

"Cinch," he said. "Mrs. Highbird'll tell you. The twenty-second was a Saturday. I operated on her dog—Spick, she calls him—and next day, the twenty-third, she was here to take him home. Here's the snapper. She had to call for him because my car was laid up with a broken axle for three days. Chuck Semon's garage. He'll give you the dates and all."

"How about bus or train transportation? I'm only suggesting this so your alibi is foolproof."

"The stationmaster and all the bus drivers know me. Glad you mentioned it. I couldn't have gotten out of town unbeknown without I wore a mask. I'll give you all those addresses and you'll be doing me a favor if you check 'em."

"I'll do that. One more thing, Mr. Schorn. Is there anyone in Umatta who hated your wife—any enemy—?"

"Nobody." He grinned ruefully. "Carrie had nice ways with outsiders. I guess I'm the only soul in town with a real grudge against her."

"Was she friendly—chummy—with anyone either before or after her marriage?"

"No. Carrie kept herself to herself. Thought she was a little too good for Umatta. It's my guess, you'll have to look in the city for a suspect."

"Now I'll tell you something else. Your wife was never an actress. So the 'reporter' who came up here to write a feature story about her, has to be a phony. If you could try to remember any little thing about him—you can see the importance of it."

But Schorn couldn't help. He had been absorbed in Maudie and the "reporter" hadn't stayed long.

"Now I think of it, soon as I said Carrie was my wife, he made tracks. I remember wondering where he was going to get items for his Sunday feature."

Steve thanked him and left, to go back to Town Hall, remembering the inquisitive clerk's "Carrie again?" Perhaps he would be more observant. Steve found him willing enough but not too helpful.

"Yes, I remember him. What do you want to know?"

"A description. Age—build—light or dark—"

"About your height. Don't rightly remember the color of his hair. Youngish. Oh! This'll help you—he wore great big dark glasses. That's about the best I can do. It's a pretty long time ago."

"Did he have a car?"

"Could have. I didn't see it."

"Would you recognize him again if you saw him?"

"I might. I got a good memory for faces." Steve was quite sure he had.

"Mister, what's this all about?" the clerk asked, his nose pointing like a retriever's.

"Just background for a law case."

"Carrie Tyson in some trouble?"

"Some."

"Always said she'd come to grief. Didn't know when she was well-off, married to a good earner like Jim Schorn. But she was always yammering against Umatta. She was in my class at Penn High and she was forever turning up her nose at us local boys. Said she meant to get somewheres."

"She must have made plenty of enemies, always running the place down."

"Heck, no," he grinned. "She was too pretty for that."

Steve spent the rest of the day and the following morning checking on James Schorn. His alibi was solid. There was not an hour of the two crucial days when somebody couldn't vouch for him. He put out a few feelers to the hotel clerk, to Mrs. Highbird and one or two others about Carol and came to the conclusion that her murderer was not a native of Umatta.

But the trip had been fruitful. As he drove back, along the splendid Pennsylvania Turnpike, he could hardly wait to lay his findings before his father.

CHAPTER 18 ...

Steve and his father sat in the elder Hargrave's study in their apartment the same evening. The room was cheery, comfortable and a little shabby with its worn red-leather easy chairs that were truly easy.

"To me, it's open and shut," said Steve, finishing his story, his face alive with the first real hope he had had since Max's arrest. "We'll get this Umatta clerk down here to take a look at the guy and we've got him cold."

"What guy?" asked Hargrave.

"Why, Benger, of course. Who else?"

"Don't rush your fences, son."

"But, Dad—I had a good chance to dope it all out on the drive back and it all hangs together. Carol gets friendly with these people and goes along with their tippling habits. But she's not used to liquor the way they are. A couple of drinks and she opens up. Mentions Umatta and this Alec Benger is wise guy enough to see the possibilities. He takes a trip up there and finds out just what I found: that Carol's wide open for a smooth operator to put the bee on her. What comes next? His wife is down in Carol's will for the whole works. Could anything be plainer?"

"Yes, I think it could. First of all, the clerk up there calls him 'youngish.' Max says the Bengers are older than Carol."

"Only six or eight years. Mid-thirties. That's youngish."

"Then Max says Benger's a successful salesman. Makes a good living, has a nice home, even uses a sound, reputable lawyer like Hagen. Is he going to jeopardize all that, his job, his future, his freedom so that someday, in the dim, distant future his wife comes into a nice collection of jewelry?"

"You hit the nail on the head. It wasn't the dim, distant future. Put it like this. Carol does make a will in this Ilma's favor. For a while, that shuts them up. But they begin to get impatient. What are they getting out of it now? So Benger pitches a yarn to Carol about needing some cash right away—a thousand—two thousand—maybe throws out a hint that they put women in jail for bigamy— Why, it's as plain as the nose on your face. That's why Carol was so dead against a divorce. Benger throws this big scare into her—tells her if it comes to court, her whole life will be investigated and it'll all come out. So Carol trots down to her deposit box, takes out a piece of jewelry and raises cash on it. It works so well that Benger tries an encore. That's why Carol's deposit box is empty. It's a beautiful scheme. It's Carol who takes out her own stuff and sells it. All he does is accept a few big bills with nobody around when she slips 'em to him. The guy's as clean as gold. He's got no fears about his job or his freedom."

"You make quite a good case against him," said Hargrave with a faint smile.

"Here's another thing. This so-called 'reporter' doesn't go up to Umatta five years ago when Max married. If he had, it'd be understandable. Max is a fairly big shot. It'd have been news. No. It was after Carol met the Bengers that somebody thought it worthwhile to go snooping up there. It has to be Benger."

"Steve, you may be right or you may be just so anxious to find an out for Max that you're doing a bit of wishful thinking. I'm not ready to act on your theory by a long shot. We don't even know what Benger looks like. Suppose he's thin and short and doesn't fit the clerk's description?"

"We can find that out quick enough. Get one of Landon's men to go round to Benger's firm or his home and take a look."

"Does it occur to you that Jerry Savile and Tom Ryder and Larry Bellair are all 'tallish and youngish' and quite capable of buying a pair of dark glasses?"

"Dad! Those are Max's friends you're talking about."

"And the Bengers were Carol's friends."

"But people like that—"

"Don't be a snob, son. A man can have character and integrity without knowing his own grandfather."

"But, Dad! I can't understand you. Here I hand you a suspect on a platter. He fills the bill in every particular."

"I understood he was in Atlantic City on November twenty-second and twenty-third."

"Maybe. Maybe not. It's only two and a half hours from New York by bus. Maybe he even owns a car. Who'd notice if he left the Traymore in the afternoon and got back six or seven hours later? And who'd notice him on the bus especially if he used the dark-glasses dodge? Sure, he was still registered at the hotel the morning Carol was found dead, but it would've been a pipe for him to sneak into the Gray house Saturday night while Max was playing bridge with me."

"And how did he get in?"

"That's not too hard to figure. Say some afternoon when Ilma was keeping Carol occupied at gin rummy, Benger slips her housekey out of her handbag, sneaks out and gets a duplicate made and sneaks it back in again before Carol's ready to go home. He's all set."

Suddenly, as if Steve himself had unlocked a door, Hargrave's whole manner changed. His eyes narrowed with the birth of an idea. All the stern analytic traits of the defender and the keen dynamic lines of the man-hunter sprang to life in his face. There was urgency in his voice as he spoke in clipped accents: "Steve, you've done an excellent job both in Umatta and here—"

"Here?" Steve echoed, pleased. "Then you do agree it's Benger—?"

"I mean you touched off a spark that lights up my whole mind."

"How? What?" Steve was bewildered by his father's abrupt change.

"Never mind." Hargrave made an impatient gesture, brushing both Steve and the question aside, making Steve feel suddenly like a schoolboy.

"I think you might tell me," he said resentfully. "After all, we're in this together."

"You've done your share. Now I'll carry on alone."

"But why?"

"I'll tell you why: because the next step I take would be hindered, not helped, by your presence or even your knowledge—"

"Well! If you can't trust me—" Steve said, hurt.

Hargrave laid a quick hand on his shoulder and smiled.

"I don't trust you, son, but not the way you mean it. Just take my word for it that you'll be helping Max by going to your room and staying there for the next hour or so."

"Somebody's coming here?"

"I hope so. Somebody who may clear up the whole murky business—if I can get him to talk. And it's my belief that he'll talk more freely if he thinks I'm alone."

"You mean it's a suspect?"

"Everybody is a suspect to me at this stage of the game."

"I don't like it. If he is guilty, he's dangerous. He might start something—"

"I don't expect violence. This is just a—ah—fishing expedition. But if I should find I've hooked a barracuda instead of a minnow, I promise you I'll shout. Now go."

Unwillingly, Steve stumped out of the room.

As soon as he was alone, Hargrave reached for the phone book and looked up a number. He was lucky; the man he wanted answered his call. Hargrave said pleasantly: "Good evening. This is Edward Hargrave ... That's right ... Well, it doesn't look too bright at the moment ... Thank you, there is indeed. I need all the help Max's friends can give me ... Well, if you could come over, answer a few questions, clear up a few points for me ... The sooner the better, I should say ... Splendid. I'll expect you in half an hour." He gave his address and hung up.

He sat in quiet thought, wondering whether his visitor would turn out to be a barracuda or a minnow.

CHAPTER 19 ...

"Scotch or rye?" Hargrave asked, dropping ice into two glasses.

"Scotch, thanks," said Larry.

When both men were seated and had sampled their drinks, Larry said: "About Max, Mr. Hargrave, you weren't serious, were you, when you said things looked bad?"

"I was, indeed. The State has a solid case. Max threatened his wife in his letter, he was heard twice to say she ought to be killed, he had access to quantities of digitalis, he had the technical knowledge of how to make a tincture which would be undetectable in whisky, his fingerprints were on the flask and he was the only person known to be in the house besides the servants at the crucial time."

"It sounds bad but anybody who knows Max knows he's no killer."

"The jury won't know him. They will judge on the facts."

Larry grinned.

"Maybe I'm talking out of turn, but if what you say is true, then the jury system's all wrong."

"It has stood up for nearly eight centuries."

"It's still wrong. Facts aren't enough. You've got to take other things into consideration."

"For instance?" asked Hargrave.

"Character, for one. Look at Max. So straight, he can hardly bend. A real do-gooder. Always believes the best of everybody, gives 'em the benefit of the doubt. Max could no more kill a human being than I could."

"And you couldn't?"

Larry looked straight into the other man's eyes. "You're not fooling me, Mr. Hargrave. Your phone message was so innocent, it smelt to Heaven. You didn't get me here to 'clear up a few points.' You're scrabbling around for a sucker to take the rap and I look like your best bet."

"And what makes you my best bet?"

"I'm not, really. But I can see how I'd look that way to you."

"Would you expand that a bit?"

"Well, who am I? A boy without money or pull—at least, I was until I happened to do Max a service in Korea. From then on, I'm made. As soon as I graduate, Max puts me in his research lab and gives me *carte blanche*. There's a director over me but Max tells him to give me my head. Do you know what that means to a—a dedicated scientist?"

"I can guess."

"And you also guess at my gratitude to Max for the chance. Of course, you do. I can just see the way your mind works: I'm so grateful, I'd do anything for Max. He wants a divorce and can't get it. So I do the next best thing—get rid of his wife for him the hard way. Isn't that how you doped it out? And haven't you brought me here to see if I won't make some little slip that you can latch onto, so you can get Max off the hook?"

"No, Mr. Bellair. My mind didn't work that way at all. There is only one point in all that you have said that I agree with."

"And what's that?"

"You mentioned character. I agree with you heartily there. You know the old tag about making the punishment fit the crime. I believe it is far more true that we must make the murderer fit the crime."

"My point exactly," said Larry. "Max doesn't fit it."

"No. But there is a murderer. Now what must his qualifications be?"

"You tell me."

"Shall we call him X?"

"Not on my account," said Larry, amused. "Say 'you' if you want."

"I prefer X. Well, first, I am sure we agree that his moral fiber is somewhat loosely woven."

"Either that or he's a downright fanatic."

"I doubt that. X had all his wits about him. He very nearly committed the perfect murder. If it hadn't been for Carol's letter to the D.A., her death would have passed as a natural one. I read him as a man with a shrewd facile brain, morally oblique, not money-mad but not above picking up a piece of change if he can do it without jeopardizing his ultimate objective. But I also believe he is a man to whom the game means more than the candle: he likes to score against duller minds. It gives him a lift. Do you know anyone who answers that description?"

"Give or take a little, it applies to almost everyone."

"Even you, Mr. Bellair?"

"Certainly."

"Shall we—ah—try the description on you—for size, as they say?"

"Go right ahead." Larry sounded as if he were enjoying himself.

"Well, the brains we'll take for granted. Even I have heard of your brilliant mind and your glowing future. That future, by the way, could you put a name to it? Not just the vague area of science but more concretely?"

"Sure. I don't mind. The spot I'm aiming for is a partnership in Gray-Stevens with the say-so to put the accent on the solid fuel problem. I've got a thing about that. I believe it's the crux of the next war."

"It's a subject I know little about but I am sure you are a competent judge. I understand that your father was something of an automotive genius too."

Larry sat very still. He looked at Hargrave steadily. "I didn't know my father, Mr. Hargrave. Did you?"

"I only knew of him."

"How?"

"From—ah—various sources."

"If you don't tell the truth, how can you expect me to, Mr. Hargrave? Why not say right out that Max told you?"

"If you insist."

"What else did he tell you—this ornament of society—who'd be fertilizing a Korean field right now if it wasn't for me?"

"You hate him, don't you?"

"Not at all. 'Disparage' might be the word."

"Why?"

Larry laughed suddenly.

"Well, look. How can you have any respect for such a sucker? Taking candy from babies is tough compared to putting one over on Max. He's so soft, it ceases to be fun."

"It was fun in his tent when he caught you rifling his wallet?"

Larry took this without flinching.

"Yes, that took a bit of doing," he said coolly. "I had to pull out all the stops."

"Now don't paint yourself blacker than you are, please. After all, you did do a really heroic thing when you saved his life."

"That was half planning, half luck. I didn't really expect him to get into trouble that night. I only stayed behind as a gesture to get me in solid with Gray of Gray-Stevens. Of course, when it turned into real grief, I had to go through with it. Then I had it made."

"You didn't take much advantage of your fortunate position, I notice. You could have lined your pockets at Max's expense."

"Remember you said X wasn't money-mad, wouldn't jeopardize his ultimate objective? I've told you mine. I'll reach it faster if I don't dribble away Max's gratitude in handouts."

"But you figured you could safely indulge in a bit of blackmail with someone else."

"I did? With whom?"

"Carol."

"It's good we're alone, Mr. Hargrave. This is pretty libelous stuff."

"Right. Suppose we resort to X for our murderer. I'll put it hypothetically. Tell me if I'm warm. Let us assume X has a sister in California. He drives out to see her a year ago last summer. On his way back—am I reasonable in believing he took the Pennsylvania Turnpike?"

"As good a route as any," said Larry impassively.

"Yes. And on the Turnpike, he saw something. He called it 'Aladdin's lamp.' I call it a highway sign marked 'Umatta.' X's flexible brain begins to work. Why not stop over for an hour in this little town and see if there is grist for his mill in it? He does so and finds the very choicest quality of grain. He discovers that Max's so-called wife is actually Mrs. James Schorn and guilty of bigamy. That explains her fear of a divorce action because she believes that publicity will bring out the truth about her past and land her in jail. Besides, of course, putting an end to the loot she has been accumulating."

"A sitting duck for blackmail," Larry nodded.

"Now, Mr. Bellair, X is supposed to be a friend of Max's, his future depends upon Max's goodwill and now he has a chance to do Max a tremendous good turn. I confess that here my understanding of X breaks down. Can you tell me why he doesn't do the decent thing and tell Max?"

"I can give you a theory."

"Please do."

"Well, the X's of this world never do the 'decent thing.' You might call them perennial juvenile delinquents. They love a spot of fun and it tickles them to play a double game. Then you must consider the character of the blackmailee. Carol was a thoroughly bad hat. She suckered her way into a dazzling marriage and was lining her nest with a small fortune in diamonds. You'd think she might be fairly grateful, or at least smart enough to keep the marriage going with a little amiability. No. She's so stupid and plain ill-natured that the goose that lays the diamond eggs is practically at its last gasp. X isn't above teaching a lesson to bitches like that."

"So now we have X in the role of reformer," said Hargrave satirically.

Larry laughed.

"Well—he may have had a private ax. He may have wanted to give her a dose of her own medicine."

"Ah, yes. X's unfortunate letter about his light-fingered practices. Even if she didn't tell Max she had salvaged it from the wastebasket, of course she would have told X—although I can't see how she could have hoped to collect on it from an impecunious young student."

"There are people who are nasty just for the sake of nastiness. I can picture her holding it over X's head out of pure cussedness." He gave a short, cocky laugh. "I can also picture X jockeying her into a position where she was foolhardy enough to produce the letter as evidence of her power over him. A costly mistake. X would be quite callous enough to take it from her by force and destroy it before her eyes."

"Making her threat to Max a colossal bluff with nothing to back it up but the few phrases she remembered from the letter."

"Exactly my ... theory," Larry said pointedly.

"And a very sound one. It explains why she was far more careful of Max's Atlantic City letter. I understand she refused to show it to him but kept it safely in her deposit box. Once bitten, twice shy."

"So now you see how X could have a moral duty to teach her a lesson."

"To say nothing of the fact that X can use some easy money around that time for a Jaguar, for an apartment and furniture, for good brandy, even corsages for his victim—"

"Max certainly spilled his guts, didn't he?"

"Allow me a little credit for building up a case from a few hints."

"Oh? You've built up a case?"

"I think so. It goes something like this: X is sitting pretty. Carol doesn't dare tell anyone what trouble she's in or she'll be in still worse trouble. X can count on oblique handouts from Max via Carol indefinitely, and at the same time, present to Max the appearance of a disinterested, independent, unbribable young man, struggling along on his salary. What's more, he has an exquisite joke to hug to his breast. He's diddling Max to the top of his bent, a delicious state of affairs that promises to go on and on."

"You don't give X much of a motive for murdering Carol."

"Ah! But the picture changes. X has an unfortunate accident in his Jaguar which, if brought home to him, would lead to a criminal charge and a probable jail sentence— May I freshen your drink? A little stimulant at this point—"

Larry passed his glass without speaking. His nostrils flared with carefully controlled anger and shock and Hargrave saw that for the first time, he had struck a vulnerable spot. He returned Larry's glass to him, substantially darkened and waited while he took a long swallow. Then he went on in the quiet judicial tone he used so often in court:

"Carol may have been stupid but she was shrewd enough to see, at long last, a way to end the slow torture and plundering she had been enduring for a full year. In Atlantic City, she receives a letter from Max postmarked November sixteenth, nine-thirty P.M. in which he states that he is home alone. But Max, in order to protect X from the consequences of his car accident, has told the police that X was with him all evening. Now obviously, both these stories can't be true and Carol has the wit to see it. At last she can turn the tables, stop Max from divorcing her and X from blackmailing her further. A word from her, backed by the letter, can do for both Max and X. You follow?"

"It seems to me you make out a better case against Max than even the prosecution does." The shock and anger were now fully controlled and Larry's tone was again level and composed.

"Ah! But we agreed that Max isn't the killer type. That leaves only X."

"Except for the fact that Max had access to the flask of whisky and

X didn't."

"Now you have struck the very heart of the matter. X too had access to the Gray house."

"This is theory, of course? Part of your 'hypothetical case'?"

"Oh, no. A simple fact. Five years ago, during the Christmas holidays, Max's father, in order to make X feel thoroughly at home, gave him a latchkey so that he could come and go as he pleased."

Larry was still giving nothing away. He said lightly: "Congratulations, Mr. Hargrave. You've done quite a job of spadework." He set down his glass, rose and reached for his topcoat, which lay on a chair. "Well, it's been interesting talking to you. I hope I've cleared up some of the 'points' which were bothering you."

"Sit down, Mr. Bellair. Don't go. Don't even think of going," Hargrave said with quiet authority. "This isn't a scene from a stage play. I am a peace officer, as are all lawyers, with certain police powers. I am arresting you for the murder of Carol Gray." A small gun from the desk drawer appeared suddenly in his hand. "I am sorry to seem melodramatic but I am hardly a match for you physically. However, as the underworld so aptly expresses it, a loaded gun is a splendid equalizer. Please sit down with your hands over your head." With his left hand, he pulled the phone toward him.

Larry stood where he was, grinning with genuine amusement.

"Mr. Hargrave, I hate to see you make a fool of yourself," he said pleasantly.

Hargrave looked at him with slightly raised eyebrows. He laid the receiver on the desk and began to dial with his left hand.

Larry went on: "No, really. I'm not bluffing. I like you. If you complete that call, you'll be a laughingstock. You might even have a whopping libel suit against you. I'd like to save you from that."

"Kind of you, Mr. Bellair," said Hargrave, giving the dial another twirl.

"We-ell, it's not all kindness," Larry admitted. "I'm thinking of myself a bit, too. But take my advice: hang up and I'll really give you the lowdown."

Hargrave replaced the receiver. He was a keen judge of men and he recognized truth when he heard it. He heard it now in Larry's tone.

"Very well. What have you to say?"

Larry sat down, ignoring the gun which was still trained on him.

"Your accusation of murder doesn't bother me at all. If you make it, it will only backfire on you. But in the course of clearing it up, all these other minor tricks of mine will come out—my little transactions with Carol, which would horrify our upright Max, and the fact that I didn't run straight to him with the glad news that he wasn't married to Carol. My position at Gray-Stevens might well be injured. I don't want that to happen."

"I fear you can hardly avoid it."

"Oh, yes, I can."

"Mr. Bellair, Max Gray is my client and my son's friend. He is on trial for his life. I assure you I won't let you and your small peccadilloes stand in the way of clearing him."

"You will, Mr. Hargrave," said Larry with assurance.

"Perhaps you can tell me why."

"Because I—and only I—can clear Max."

"Go on."

"You see, Mr. Hargrave, I know who the murderer is."

CHAPTER 20 . . .

Hargrave laid down the gun. He raked Larry's face with a barbed stare.

"I'm listening," he said stonily.

"Oh, it's not going to be as easy as all that."

"I see. You expect to use your alleged knowledge to drive a bargain."

"You're quick, Mr. Hargrave. That's exactly right."

"Well, let's have it."

"This case of Max's. You'd like to win it."

"More than any case I ever defended. I won't pretend different."

"Yes. And I rather suspect that if your silver-tongued oratory alone gets him off, you won't be satisfied. There will still be a cloud over Max. Plenty of people will still believe that he did actually get away with murder."

"There is a certain amount of truth in what you say. I would greatly prefer to clear him without a shadow of a doubt."

"And to do that, you would have to hand the jury the real murderer."

"If I knew the real murderer, there would be no jury. No trial either. The D.A. is a sensible man. He would squash the indictment, Max would be publicly exonerated and the D.A. would proceed against the murderer."

"Yes. A pleasing state of affairs for everybody—except me.

Unfortunately, in revealing the murderer's identity, I involve myself in a rather embarrassing position. The truth about the hit-and-run incident would come out and I could be charged with manslaughter. An awkward situation, you must admit, and one which I intend to avoid."

"And how do you expect to avoid it?"

"Oh, I'll leave that to you," said Larry with a wave of his hand. "You're a smart man. You must have a dozen shots in your locker for the D.A. What do they say? 'On information received from unnamed sources.' Or I'm quite willing for you to take full credit for having deduced the truth through sheer gray matter. You should have, you know. The truth is staring you in the face. I simply stipulate that my share in the business is ruled out, that my name is never mentioned."

"In other words, I should compound a felony."

Larry grinned.

"I'm engaging your services as of now. Then you'll be covered by the 'lawyer-client' convention."

"And if I decline to act for you?"

Larry shrugged.

"If they hold me for manslaughter, they'll have to hold Max as an accessory."

"In other words, if I drag you down, Max goes with you."

"I'm afraid so. And I don't think your son, Steve, is going to like that. Max is something of an idol to him—I know that from East Hampton—and he won't thank you for pulling his idol down."

"You have a point there. In fact, I find you an extremely astute young man." Hargrave permitted himself an acrid smile. "To be perhaps unwisely frank, I'll tell you this: I deliberately excluded my son from this meeting because I knew I would have to betray Max's confidence by referring to your car accident. Steve would never have stood for that. He has an excellent brain but is, I fear, a bit too idealistic to make a really good criminal lawyer. He has still to learn the value of compromise—"

"Which you understand well, Mr. Hargrave."

"True. I realize that if I am to clear Max and bring the murderer to justice, it will cost me. I must close my eyes to your car escapade, I must conceal your blackmailing activities and I must not enlighten Max as to your cynical and rather unfriendly attitude toward him."

"That covers it completely."

"Well, I am prepared to make this compromise, but on one

condition."

"You're in a spot where you can hardly make conditions."

"No? I don't know if you realize that you handed me a good bit of ammunition. I have only to tell Max of this interview and you will be—ah—out on your ear at Gray-Stevens. Then I can inform the D.A. or the police that you are obstructing justice by withholding vital information in a murder case. The police have ways of inducing silent witnesses to speak. I'm sure you know that."

"Pretty foxy, aren't you?" Larry said with rueful amusement. "What's your condition?"

"I will give you a check for five thousand dollars which I will list on Max's bill as 'expenses.' You will resign from Gray-Stevens, saying you have an advantageous offer in Brazil or Australia—wherever you like, out of the country—any place where your sphere of influence and Max's will never coincide. You've had your last joke at Max's expense."

"You couldn't make it ten thousand?" Larry asked, taking defeat gracefully.

"I could not. I'll stretch a point by paying for your passage out of my own pocket when you let me know the destination you choose."

"You know—it's an idea," Larry said, considering. "I'm a restless type. I rather like the thought of new fields—and I've always had a sneaking idea that my father is somewhere in South America—it'd be interesting to meet him— Oh!" He caught himself up. "No, I'm afraid it's out. There's Avery to consider. South America's no good for a TV writer and to leave her here all alone—"

"Avery won't be alone. As soon as is decent, she will be Mrs. Max Gray."

"What! You're joking."

"Indeed I am not."

"And you're still set on sending Max's prospective brother-in-law away?" he asked with his most puckish grin.

"Adamant."

"Very well," he said resignedly. "Give me the check."

"Not yet. I still have to get the facts from you."

"You don't trust me?"

"Not an inch. So suppose we get on with it."

"Well, okay," he said philosophically. "But I must warn you that my story is so melodramatic and coincidental that I wouldn't believe it myself if it hadn't happened to me."

"If you will spare me the 'stranger than fiction' cliché," said Hargrave patiently, "we'll get on much faster."

"Well, it begins the Wednesday after my car accident. Carol had returned from Atlantic City and she called me up at the plant about two o'clock. She practically ordered me to quit work and drive into town to see her. I was still pretty jittery about the hit-and-run business and her tone was so different from usual—up to then, I was the one who called the tune—I wondered what gave. Anyway, I made tracks for town. I met Carol in a Third Avenue bar and she told me how that birdbrain Max had balled things up. He writes her it's eight o'clock, he's alone in the house— Well, you know all that."

"Exceedingly well. Let's have something new."

But Larry was not to be hurried.

"You know something, Mr. Hargrave, if the D.A.'s office had been on its toes, Max would never have been arrested. I would. Carol—who must have been imbibing when she wrote that note to the D.A.—said: 'It only takes a glance for you to put two and two together.' She meant a glance at the postmark, not at Max's silly postscript."

"In other words, if she went in fear of her life, it was you she was afraid of, not Max."

"Of course. That day in the bar, she told me with a smirk that my little game was over. No more jewelry forthcoming. The shoe was on the other foot now. She had only to show Max's letter to the D.A. and I'd be kaput. I did a pretty dumb thing. I wanted to throw a little scare into her so I advised her to stick to crowds after this. Hence her note to the D.A. You see?"

"Very clearly. Quite in character."

"Well, I left her with a flea in my ear. I mulled it over for a day or two and by Saturday, I came to the conclusion that I'd better make a stab at locating and recovering Max's letter if I could. I figured it ought to be in her bedroom. Well, that was okay. I still had my key to the house, as you so cleverly deduced. I knew from Max that there were no servants in the house at night and that Carol had gone back to Atlantic City. The only possible snag was Max himself if he was at home. That was easy to find out. I need only phone the house. I was at home at the time but Avery was, too, and I didn't want to answer any questions. So I said I was going for a walk, slipped a flashlight into my overcoat pocket and went out. I have a guest card to Max's club and it's only a block from where I live on Forty-eighth Street, so I strolled over there to use the phone. The first person I saw was Max himself, playing bridge with your son and a couple of other guys."

"So you knew the coast was clear."

"Well, I phoned anyway to be on the safe side. There was no answer and it didn't even cost me my dime," Larry smiled. "It was then about eight-thirty and I hotfooted it up to Max's house, let myself in and gave Carol's bedroom a good going-over. No letter. I was just about to give up and get out of there, when I heard the front door open and close softly. I snapped off my flashlight—I hadn't dared put on a light—and stood in the dark, paralyzed. You know Max's house? Those wide, dark-oak, uncarpeted stairs?"

"Quite well."

"Somebody began to climb them. Every step was distinct. I knew it wasn't Max. It was too slow. And it didn't sound like Carol either. Nobody who lives in a house would come up so stealthily. But whoever it was, I knew damn well I was in a bad spot. As the steps came nearer, I felt my way toward Carol's clothes closet and slipped inside, closing the door from inside. To my horror, the steps came nearer and right into the room. I couldn't see a thing but I could hear faint movements—small noises—one of which I later interpreted as the sound you make when you take up and set down a metal container."

"In other words, a flask." Hargrave was close to snorting.

"Yes," said Larry blandly. "Of course, at the time, it had no significance to me. Even after Carol's death, with Dr. Liggett calling it heart trouble, I didn't connect it up. It was only later— But to go back. There I stood in the dark, for what seemed an eternity. I must have lost pounds, sweating in that closet. At last, I heard the light switch click off and the steps went down the stairs again. I dared to open the closet door by that time and I heard the front door close. I had to find out who it was—"

"A possible candidate to take the place of Carol as a blackmailee?"

"Let's say merely an insatiable curiosity," Larry smiled, unruffled. "I was utterly mystified. I raced down the stairs, opened the front door an inch or two, just enough to see the person walking down the street."

"You recognized the person?" asked Hargrave, hanging on to his patience.

"Of course. Have I said enough?"

"Certainly not. I would be laughed out of court if I attempted to defend Max with a cock-and-bull story like that. Your unsupported word of footsteps and obscure metallic noises, an individual walking down a public street who might or might not be your mysterious visitor. Don't insult my intelligence, Mr. Bellair."

"Can't blame you. Sounds pretty fishy. People coming and going as if Carol's room was Grand Central. I can hardly believe it myself and it happened to me. Luckily, there's more. When the police detained Max, the bits of the puzzle fell into place. I knew he was in no real danger. I could pull his chestnuts out any time I felt like it—"

"But you let him languish in jail for more than two weeks when a word from you—"

"Look, Mr. Hargrave, why do you harp on the idea that Max is my friend and that I should break my neck to do him a service? It's the other way round. I am Max's friend. I'm the guy who saved his life at considerable cost to myself. Do you know that for two years I had to watch my step? Couldn't play tennis or dance because of the pericardial injury I did myself, lugging him into camp. Should I be grateful to him for that? Or because he gave me a job? I assure you I'm as big an asset to Gray-Stevens as it is to me. You asked me if I hated Max. I don't. But neither have I got any special feelings of affection for him. There was no question of his danger. Any time I wanted, I could clear the whole case up. But I intended to choose my own good time to do it in. In a minute, you'll understand why I had a special reason for delay—"

"I haven't the faintest interest in your special reasons and your moral issues. Would you be good enough to go on with your story?"

"Well, I figured it was only fair to give the murderer time to get beyond the arm of the law."

"Another little felony to chalk up to you?" Hargrave was white with anger.

"No. I'm innocent, for once. But okay, I'll get on with it. The day that Max was arrested, I had a talk with the murderer. I got the whole story—and a signed confession. And I didn't get it by duress either. I have it here in my pocket. I'll leave it with you. The murderer was only too anxious that the truth should come out."

"Mr. Bellair," Hargrave said, his forbearance almost at an end. "Will you come to the point? A dastardly murder has been committed—for hate or for gain—"

"Neither for hate nor gain," Larry said softly. "The murderer killed out of love. Mr. Hargrave, how dense can you get? It's open and shut. Who loved Max like a son and his parents before him? Who knew how unhappy he was with Carol? Who was in a position to get hold of digitalis and had enough knowledge of *materia medica* to compound a tincture? Who had the run of the house and probably a key to it, just as I did? Who knew directly or from someone in the household about the flask on Carol's table? You know all those things as well as I do. You should even know from your son that the poor wretch was dying of a malignant disease. Well, she made one Herculean effort to strike a blow for Max's freedom just before she died. Who could it be but—Morgan?"

Larry reached into his pocket and brought out an envelope. He took a single sheet of paper from it and laid it before Hargrave's eyes. The lines were written in a copperplate script but the perfection of the writing was marred by a wavering irregularity which, Hargrave thought, might easily be the result of illness. He read:

> To Whom It May Concern:
> I hereby swear that on Saturday evening, November 22nd, knowing that I was near death, I resolved to insure my dearly loved Maxwell Gray's happiness by ridding him of one who in my judgment was ruining his life by her wicked ways. From Mrs. Evergreen I had learned about the flask of whisky on Mrs. Gray's bed table. I had digitalis in my possession and, as a nurse, knew how to prepare a tincture. Weak though I was, I managed the trip to the house, and after ringing the bell and ascertaining that no one was in, entered the house with my own key which I still possessed. I poured the tincture into Mrs. Gray's flask and left the outcome in the hands of the Lord. I have intrusted this confession to Mr. Max's dear friend Mr. Laurence Bellair, who will deliver it into the proper hands after my death.
> Glenys Morgan

When Hargrave looked up from the letter, Larry said: "Well? Satisfied?"

"It appears to be conclusive," Hargrave said noncommittally. "It will, of course, have to be investigated, the writing checked against known samples of Morgan's writing and so on."

"Your job. Mine is done, don't you agree? I have given you your murderer with ample proof, I think. Now I know that your first step will be to free Max. Mr. Hargrave, you may not believe it of me," he said with an abashed grin, "but since you insist on my leaving the country, I'd like to be on my way at once, so as not to have to meet Max. Even I have limits of shamelessness."

"In other words, you want a check."

"Well, cash might be even better." Larry grinned. "The faster I get out of the picture, the better for everybody."

"My dear sir, you don't suppose I have five thousand in cash here in the apartment, do you?"

"Of course we have."

They both turned to see Steve standing just within the door. He limped forward into the room.

"The money from Gus Creamer is still in the safe," Steve went on. Hargrave gave his son a long, frowning stare but said nothing. Gus Creamer was an impecunious criminal whom they had once defended gratis at the request of the Court. "Father, I must apologize. I didn't know who your visitor was going to be and I was a little afraid for your safety." He smiled as he advanced to the desk and picked up the small automatic and swung it loosely in his hand. "I had forgotten you had this, so I constituted myself an unseen bodyguard. Naturally, I had to stick close, so I heard all that went on here."

"Fine, Steve," said Larry. "It saves time that the whole thing doesn't have to be rehashed for your ears." Steve turned a look of such icy contempt on him that even Larry dropped his eyes. He went on, speaking quickly, as if to appease Steve. "Look. I've got a great idea. Max has been through enough. Let's save him the shock of finding out that I—uh—didn't quite measure up to his standards. Why don't I just disappear fast for parts unknown? Then, when you explain to Max, you could tell him that I searched Carol's room for the letter to save him from a perjury charge. And that's how I came to be there and saw Morgan."

"Your solicitude is touching," Steve said witheringly. "And your 'great idea' quite in character. You should duck the consequences of your rotten actions and we should tell the necessary lies to cover you."

"I just thought it would be better for Max that way."

"Why not stay and tell Max yourself that you searched Carol's room for his sake? Your stock would go up like a rocket."

"But don't you see? He'd ask me how I knew Carol was holding the letter over him as a threat. If I'm gone, you can simply say you don't know. He may wonder about it, but at least it'll save him a painful jolt."

"Why all the sudden concern for Max's feelings, Bellair?" Steve asked in a hard tone. "Why are you in such a swivet to get out of the picture? Got something to hide? Something you must skip the country for?"

"Okay," said Larry sulkily. "If you must have it, I know Max better than you do. He's so damned self-righteous, the first thing he'll do, once he's free, is to spill the truth about the hit-and-run business and to hell where the chips fall. Well, I'm not serving any jail sentence just to ease Max's conscience. If you insist on my going, I insist that I go before I land in a cell." He turned a look of boyish appeal on them both. "I've got a thing about jails and walls and locked doors—I'm not taking any chances."

"Neither are we," Steve said dryly. "I'd feel no pain at all if you were made to pay for your filthy tricks. But my father's right. The faster you get out of Max's orbit, the better for everybody. But you don't move a step until we're dead sure this confession and your whole fantastic story are the truth. Right, Dad?"

Hargrave nodded. He still stared at his son, a look of surprised puzzlement in his eyes. This was a new Steve, even to his father.

Larry cut in quickly: "You're absolutely right. It's all there, right before your eyes. Go ahead and check." He gestured to Morgan's confession, lying on the desk. Steve picked it up and read it, not once but twice. When he finally looked up, he held it in his left hand. In his right, the small automatic was pointing straight at Larry's heart.

"Dad, phone the police," he said. "Make it Homicide East."

"You crazy?" Larry said shrilly.

"No. This thing's as phony as a three-dollar bill."

"That's a lie! Compare it to Morgan's writing—"

"Oh, the writing's a good job, damn good. It'd fool even me and I know Morgy's writing well. Ever since I was ten, she sent me Christmas and birthday cards every year as well as dozens of postcards when she was on vacation."

"Well, then?"

"Bellair, you may be an automotive wonder but like all specialists, you've got a blind side. You don't know a damn thing about locution, idiom or usage. I'm going to give you a little lesson in national language idiosyncrasy before you're marched off to jail—"

"You're out of your mind—" Larry began but Steve cut him short.

"We'll see if I am. We'll analyze this 'confession' and show you that expert forgery alone isn't enough to lay a murder on a dead woman who can't answer the charge. We'll begin with the date. Maybe you didn't know that Morgan was Welsh and educated in London. Got her nurse's degree at Barts. The 'confession' reads: 'On Saturday evening, November 22nd'— For your information, Morgan would write the date the English way—'22nd November' instead of—"

"Rubbish! She's been in America twenty-odd years."

"Would you like to see one of her postcards dated no later than last year? I believe I can oblige. However that's just one point. Here's another. No Englishwoman would ever speak of 'a flask of whisky.' She would say 'spirits,' as you should have realized. There are other boners like 'insure' for 'ensure' and 'intrusted' for 'entrusted' but here's the payoff: when I was thirteen, I lost a spelling match through Morgan's fault. She was coaching Max and me and I was a certainty to win except that she drilled me in the English way to spell 'judgment,' which, as anybody knows is 'judgement.' It lost me the spelling match and it's going to lose you your life. What kind of saps did you think Dad and I were, that we'd hand over five thousand dollars and let you skip to some part of the world where they don't have extradition, when your whole bloody guilt sticks out a mile?" The look in Hargrave's eyes was now one of undisguised admiration.

"That's a lot of hooey!" Larry shouted. "Trying to condemn a man on a few misspelled words."

"You condemned yourself out of your own mouth not half an hour ago, right in this room. I'll quote as closely as I can. You said that on Saturday night, you had to phone Max's house to make sure he wasn't home. You said something like this: 'I was at home at the time but Avery was there, too, and I didn't want to answer any questions so I went out to phone.' You also mentioned the time—eight-thirty. At eight-thirty, Avery was dining with her agent, discussing her latest TV script. When I heard that outside the door, I knew your whole cock-and-bull story was a lie from start to finish, a red herring to give you time to slip out from under before the handwriting experts pronounced the 'confession' a fake. And if all this isn't enough, there's one more point that jumps to the eye the moment one reads your 'confession.' That thrilling melodrama you unfolded to my father was full of detail—the opening and closing of the front door, the slow footsteps on the stairs, even the telling metallic noises when the flask was supposed to be handled. It takes a keen ear to hear all that. So how is it you didn't hear her ring the bell before using her key, as the 'confession' states? Dad, do what I asked, please. The number's Plaza eight-three-six-oh-five."

"Wait a minute," Larry croaked. "It's— Steve, listen—Don't dial, Mr. Hargrave—give me a minute—" Hargrave's dialing finger did not stop. He spoke briefly into the phone while Larry went on, the words pouring out like a torrent. "Okay. I know when I'm licked. You'd only have to ask Morgan's brother. He'd tell you Morgan was in no shape to leave her bed, let alone the house on November twenty-second. I saw her that evening at her home—I often went there—I liked the old girl—I happened to pick up a letter in her writing from her desk— that gave me the whole idea—she loathed Carol—I felt she wouldn't care if I used her name—she'd be dead and gone before I made it public—"

"We're waiting for the straight story, Bellair," said Steve.

"Right. I never did go to Max's house that night. It was the next night—Sunday—I phoned Carol—she'd just got in from Atlantic City and she was alone in the house. I told her I'd make a deal with her—if she'd give me Max's letter, I'd give her the record of her marriage to James Schorn. I said I'd stolen it while the clerk's back was turned, up there at Umatta. Of course I hadn't. I just wanted to get her alone. Yes, I was going to kill her unless she—God knows she was asking for it—I thought of ways—gun—strangling—but violence makes me sick. Then I thought of her tippling habits—I've got a little lab at the apartment—it's only a converted closet but I do plenty of small experiments in connection with my work—it was a cinch to cook up a strong tincture—"

"Premeditated, then." Larry ignored the comment.

"Well, Carol let me in. She could've saved her life even then if she'd played fair. All I wanted was the letter but the damned little liar stalled—said it was upstairs—I followed right on her heels—then she stalled some more, said she wouldn't bring it out till she had the marriage certificate. I flashed an official-looking paper—said I'd give it up when she produced Max's letter, so she began a bluff of scrabbling in a bureau drawer to find it. That was my chance. Her back was turned so I just whipped out my handkerchief, unscrewed the top of the flask and emptied the digitalis into it. She didn't hear or see a thing. Then she turned around and said she just remembered—she'd put it in her safe-deposit box before she left for Atlantic City. That did it. I saw I'd be under her thumb as long as she was alive. I got out of there fast and let nature take its course."

"You can tell all that to Lieutenant Brown," said Steve, tight-lipped.

"Steve—for God's sake—" Larry was white and sweating. "I—I can't take it—I'll go out of my mind—"

"Yes. I remember you once wrote Max: 'I prefer coffins to jails,'" Steve said slowly.

"Yes! Yes! I'm all washed up. I know it." His eyes shuttled from father to son, as if weighing which one to appeal to. In spite of Steve's cold antagonism, it was to him that he finally spoke: "Steve, I'm not denying I deserve the limit. But if you stick to the letter of the law, you're going to hurt innocent people. I know you think a lot of Max. Well, isn't he entitled to a little happiness after the raw deal he's had? What's going to happen to his plans and Avery's if my death in the chair stands between them? And Avery—I know you think I'm rotten to the core—but I do honestly love her—she's a swell kid—why should she suffer for my—? I'll write out a complete confession taking all the blame. I'll say I did it because I was in love with Carol and she laughed at me. Or to clear the way for Max and Avery—anything except the dirt about blackmail—"

"Your motive for the crime's your own business," Steve said stonily. "So long as you admit your guilt and clear Max."

"And if I do, you'll let me vanish before that lieutenant comes with his damned handcuffs?" There was a note of urgency in his voice. "All I ask is one little break."

Steve took paper out of the desk.

"Here. Get going. We'll see," he said gruffly, without looking at Larry.

"Thanks, Steve," Larry said with a smile.

For ten minutes, the only sound in the room was the swift whispering of the pen. At last, Larry pushed the sheet of paper across the desk to Hargrave.

"I think that should do it," he said quietly.

Hargrave read it through and was about to pass it to Steve when the bell rang. Steve laid down the gun and started for the door, then came back and retrieved the confession.

"Just to be on the safe side, I'll take this with me," he said. His eyes met Larry's and Larry nodded and smiled. Then Steve limped out of the room.

When he returned with Lieutenant Brown and Sergeant Rossi, the picture had changed. Larry was standing with the automatic pointing at his own head. He was still smiling.

"Thanks again, Steve," he said. "Just as you said, I prefer coffins to jails any day."

He pulled the trigger.

THE END

Another great 1950s mystery author for your consideration...

BERNICE CAREY

The Man Who Got Away With It / The Three Widows
978-1-944520-80-9 $19.95
"*The Man Who Got Away With It*, initially released in 1950, is a powerful psychological drama written with great literary flair, exploring lust and repression, discrimination and middle-class snobbery, and irrepressible psychopathic impulses."
—Nicholas Litchfield, *Lancashire Post*

The Body on the Sidewalk / The Reluctant Murderer
978-1-944520-94-6 $19.95
"This is a fine crime novel, arguably a classic of mid-century domestic suspense, with a pleasingly tangled (and untangled) plot... a wickedly devious suspense tale."
—Curtis Evans, *The Passing Tramp*

"...these engaging tales evoke the post-WWII era vividly."
—Wes Lukowsky, *Booklist*

"If you want to get a feel for 1950s America... essential reading."
—Kate Jackson, *Cross Examining Crime*

The Fatal Picnic / Their Nearest and Dearest
978-1-951473-34-1 $19.95
"...what makes this a strong example of the psychological crime novel is that Carey complicates notions of guilt and responsibility... all in all another great read from Carey." —Kate Jackson, *crossexamingcrime.com*

The Beautiful Stranger / The Missing Heiress
978-1-951473-79-2 $19.95
"It is, of course, primarily a murder mystery... It's also a good deal more than that."
—Anthony Boucher. Includes Carey's only short story, "He Got What He Deserved."

STARK HOUSE PRESS, 1315 H Street, Eureka, CA 95501
griffinskye3@sbcglobal.net / www.StarkHousePress.com
Available from your local bookstore, or order direct via our website.

www.ingramcontent.com/pod-product-compliance
Lightning Source LLC
LaVergne TN
LVHW011930070526
838202LV00054B/4564